TRIAL
A BUCKHEAD TALE

ETIENNE

Published by
Dreamspinner Press
382 NE 191st Street #88329
Miami, FL 33179-3899, USA
http://www.dreamspinnerpress.com/

This is a work of fiction. Names, characters, places, and incidents either are the product of the author's imagination or are used fictitiously, and any resemblance to actual persons, living or dead, business establishments, events, or locales is entirely coincidental.

Trial
Copyright © 2012 by Etienne

Cover Art by Reese Dante   http://www.reesedante.com

All rights reserved. No part of this book may be reproduced or transmitted in any form or by any means, electronic or mechanical, including photocopying, recording, or by any information storage and retrieval system without the written permission of the Publisher, except where permitted by law. To request permission and all other inquiries, contact Dreamspinner Press, 382 NE 191st Street #88329, Miami, FL 33179-3899, USA
http://www.dreamspinnerpress.com/

ISBN: 978-1-61372-363-0

Printed in the United States of America
First Edition
February 2012

eBook edition available
eBook ISBN: 978-1-61372-364-7

Praise for ETIENNE

Bodies of Work

"It had me hooked and I didn't want to put it down. The characters are so real."

—Night Owl Reviews

Drag and Drop

"Etienne is a terrific story teller and it is his skill that makes the reader continue to read. His prose is well written and his plot is literate and well thought out."

—Reviews by Amos Lassen

The Burdens of Truth

"The characters and mystery surrounding them are sure to hold the readers' attention."

—Top 2 Bottom Reviews

Birds of a Feather

"Quentin and Nate have what it takes to make a fantastic addition to the Avondale series. They are loving, considerate, and have a subtly sexy vibe that cannot be beat. The telepathic abilities they share keep things interesting, and it ramps up their adventures to a whole new level."

—Coffee Time Romance & More

The Path to Forever

"The concept of longevity as it is presented here, with all its details and consequences, is fascinating…"

—Queer Magazine Online

A word of thanks to the fans of this story, who kept asking for more long after I'd thought the idea well had run dry.

To Jim Kennedy, my valiant editor, who does his best to keep me on the straight and narrow comma path.

To my partner of sixteen years, for his support and encouragement.

1

Prologue

SHE *lay quietly, enjoying that delicious state which hovers between wakefulness and sleep, alternately drifting in and out of the latter. During the wakeful swings of the cycle, she was conscious only of occasional whispers of air as the central air-conditioning cycled on and off, stirring the dust motes hanging in the air revealed by the late-afternoon sunlight filtering through the blinds of her bedroom windows. She was, as the romance novelists are fond of saying, "basking in the afterglow." Their lovemaking had been more intense yet, at the same time, more tender than usual, perhaps because they had both known it would be the last time.*

She had been very firm about that, telling her lover that she could not continue the relationship, given her changed status. She'd expected an argument or a bitter fight. In fact, she'd marshaled a litany of reasons as to why it was for the best and had been taken somewhat aback by the quiet acceptance. The only response she had gotten to what was essentially an ultimatum on her part was a quiet "I see."

It's ironic, she thought as she dozed off again. She'd been prepared for a terrible scene—one that failed to transpire. In a way she was glad it was over, for her lover had recently become even more domineering and possessive than usual, and she was, frankly, tired of the frequent bouts of jealousy that precipitated ever more acrimonious arguments. There was another irony at work as well, in that today was Mother's Day, and it was her incipient motherhood that she had given as the reason for suspending the relationship.

She was not quite sure why she awakened again, her latest period of sleep having been deeper than the previous episodes, but as she swam up through the fuzzy layers of consciousness, she became gradually aware of a presence in the room. Coming to with a start, she recognized the leather-clad figure with the black hood.

"What are you doing here?" she said. "I thought we agreed that it was over."

The figure remained silent as it moved to the side of the bed. It was then that she saw the handcuffs and rope dangling from one of the figure's hands.

"I see we're going to be kinky this time," she mused aloud as she automatically stretched her arms and legs toward the corners of the four-poster bed, the better to allow herself to be secured to them. It was a game they had played many times before, and she allowed herself to smile in anticipation of what was surely to come, even though she knew that she should be frowning at her wishes not having been adhered to.

She was still smiling when the figure produced a duffel bag and opened it, but the smile changed to a look of bewilderment when she saw something retrieved from it that was definitely not one of their usual toys. She began to scream when she realized what was about to happen and continued screaming for a time. When the screams finally turned into a gurgle, then stopped, the black-clad figure picked up the duffel bag, restored its contents, and left, closing the bedroom door as quietly as it had been opened. For a time, the only motion in the room was that of the dust motes that had been disturbed by the closing of the door and the only sound the occasional sigh of the air-conditioning. After a while, when the cool of the evening satisfied a thermostat somewhere in the house, the air-conditioning ceased cycling, and finally even the dust motes were still.

They remained so until the next morning, when there was a knock on the door and her maid said, "Señora, I have brought your breakfast."

Receiving no answer, the maid knocked again. "Señora, are you awake? It's almost ten o'clock."

There was no response from the silent room. Eventually the door was cautiously opened as the maid backed into the room holding a tray, pushing the door ahead of her with her ample backside. She was all the way into the room before she turned around. When she saw what lay on the bed, she dropped the tray with a clatter, and for the second time in less than twenty-four hours, the room was filled with screams of terror.

2

Charles

THE late May heat, though not excessive, hit me with a blast as I entered the parking garage underneath the downtown Atlanta office building where my law firm was located. The heat did nothing to improve my mood, which had been spiraling downward for the past hour, although one would have to be intimately acquainted with me to pick up any indication of that from my demeanor.

As the scion of an old Georgia family, I'd been reared in the very best "stiff upper lip" tradition by a dowager paternal grandmother, my parents having been killed in an automobile accident when I was very young. It was an article of faith in Gran's world that well-bred people simply must not ever lose their composure—at least not in public. "If you ever have to scream, yell, or cry," she'd said to me a thousand times while I was growing up, "wait for an appropriate moment, then go into the privacy of your room and do it. Whatever you do, never allow others, particularly servants or subordinates, see you lose control."

In its own way, it had been good advice—and better training. I would most likely have phrased it "subordinates or peers," but in Gran's eyes, anyone descended from the Lewis, Marks, and Barnett families of post-Revolutionary Georgia had few equals and no superiors. I was in her debt for having thus trained me; a childhood and adolescence of rigid self-control spent displaying the proverbial poker face had benefitted me as an adult in more than one pretrial conference, as well as in quite more than a few trials.

As I retrieved my Jaguar from its reserved parking place, I reflected for the umpteenth time that I could just as easily have walked two blocks to the nearest MARTA station, ridden to the Midtown Station a couple of stops up from downtown, and then walked a few blocks to my home, which was a three-story townhouse that had been built, along with several others, on one of the cross streets running between Juniper Street and Piedmont Avenue. I lived in a midtown area that had been, during its eighty-year history, alternately grand, deteriorating, merely dilapidated, and finally, downright seedy. It was only a block or two removed from the notorious strip of topless bars and porno establishments that had flourished along Peachtree Street in the sixties and seventies.

During the seventies, the area had become something of a ghetto containing a mix of gays, blacks, and Hispanics. Then, as the strip along Peachtree was cleaned up, the inevitable process of gentrification had begun. Buildings that were too far gone were razed and replaced by highrises or, in some cases, blocks of townhouses like mine. Buildings that were still relatively solid were converted into condominiums and apartments. The area was still heavily gay, but the mix was now about half gay and half yuppie, with a few gay yuppies, sometimes known as guppies, for good measure. The majority of the blacks and Hispanics had been displaced by the workings of a free-market economy—they could no longer afford to live in the area unless they, too, were yuppies. In truth, the area was really totally yuppie, because the gays who occupied the expensive townhouses and apartments certainly fit that mold, with most of the older members of Atlanta's sizeable gay community preferring to live in and around Buckhead.

Actually, it would have taken me less time to go to and from work via the subway, but rising young (I kept telling myself, sometimes even convincingly, that thirty-two was still young) trial attorneys whose names had been appended for the past five years to the firm name of one of Atlanta's oldest and most prestigious law firms were expected to observe some conventions. Strange, I thought; Andrew—Andrew Chandler, grandson of the founder of Chandler, Todd, Woodward & Barnett, currently its senior partner and my mentor since forever, as he was an old friend of the family and Gran had turned to him regularly for advice in bringing up her orphaned grandson—hadn't batted so much as an eyelash when I'd told him in my initial interview that I was gay. He had, in fact, over the years been at least covertly supportive of gay rights and related issues. However, the old boy would have had a fit were I to ride the subway to and from the office every day. Such are the sacrifices we make for the sake of appearances.

The Todd and Woodward of the firm had, as Gran would say, gone to their respective rewards years ago, leaving only Andrew and myself representing the living among the listed names. True, we had six other partners and more than a dozen associates, but it would be years before another name would be appended to the firm's name, change being the antithesis of old-line law firms everywhere. Somewhere there was an unwritten code that allowed only one name change every decade or so.

As I pulled into the traffic heading north on Peachtree, those thoughts caused me to reflect for a moment on Andrew, who was the reason for my current annoyance bordering on anger. Andrew Chandler was tall, patrician, slim, silver-haired, in his early seventies, and possessed a razor-sharp intellect. He lived in an area of expensive old homes in Decatur with his wife of fifty-odd years, whom he referred to in the traditional southern manner as "Miss Emily." Their only son had died in Vietnam, and Andrew had long ago more or less adopted me as a surrogate for his lost heir. For my part, having Andrew serve in loco parentis had provided a sort of balance to Gran's rigidity. He and Gran were old friends, and the relationship between the two families went back decades, as indeed did that of many of the old families in Atlanta.

It was the Thursday before Memorial Day. I'd just successfully completed a grueling ten-day trial and had pretty much cleared my Friday schedule so that I could leave the office by noon and be out of the city shortly thereafter for a well-deserved (so I told myself) three-day weekend at my beach house in the Florida Panhandle. Andrew had called me into his office at four this afternoon and invited me to dinner at his club that evening to meet a prospective new client. I'd tried to persuade Andrew to have the client come to the office next week, but Andrew was adamant that the first meeting had to be both outside the office and tonight, i.e., a command performance. When pressed for details, he'd been somewhat coy, saying only that everything would be explained that evening. Hence my mood, for I could sense my weekend holiday slipping out of my grasp, and I really needed to get away. I could not, however, refuse Andrew—not so much because Andrew was my boss, but because I owed him so much. As an old friend of the family, Andrew had provided me with introductions to the right people at Harvard Law School and had further guided my career from junior associate to full partner over the course of a very short period of years. He'd been especially supportive three years ago, when Robert died.

Robert.... Merely thinking the name invoked a flood of memories. When I'd buried Robert, I'd also buried the best part of myself and very nearly all of my emotions and feelings. The few that remained were now walled up in a remote compartment of my brain, and with every year that passed, the walls grew stronger and more impregnable. I threw myself into my work with a vengeance, stretching my ten-hour days into eleven and sometimes twelve. When work as anodyne failed to ease the pain of loss, I tended to exercise myself into exhaustion and thence oblivion. Dozens of well-meaning friends had, after what they deemed a suitable period of mourning, begun to invite me to functions and dinners where I would inevitably wind up paired with their latest candidate for my perusal. Once in a while I was even tempted, albeit briefly. On those rare occasions when I felt a slight breach in my emotional defenses, I responded by adding another layer of bricks and mortar to the wall. Eventually, the invitations ceased and I achieved a sort of equilibrium with the situation.

One of the advantages of my townhouse was the presence of an attached garage, and we'd indulged in one that would accommodate three cars. As the door opened and I pulled inside, I noted the absence of my roommate Richard's Mustang convertible (a bright red GT, of course). The Mustang was part of his self-styled image as stud about town, and he was, no doubt, already at one of the after-work watering holes—most likely the Powder Magazine, a venerable old gay bar over on Juniper Street that was very popular as an after-work meeting place—looking for a companion for the evening.

Richard's love life, if one could call it that, was a succession of one-night stands. I couldn't remember any of his flings having lasted more than a fortnight, and I frequently lectured him on the inherent dangers of promiscuity in this the era of AIDS. Richard insisted that he practiced only the safest of "safe sex," and wasn't particularly worried about acquiring anything that penicillin couldn't cure. He frequently teased me about the Jaguar, saying, "As a card-carrying homosexual, you should be driving something a little more exciting." Truth be told, I would have preferred a coupe instead of a sedan, but I frequently had occasion to drive clients to meetings, and a coupe wouldn't have been practical.

The ground floor of the townhouse contained the garage, a small foyer, and a large living room that looked out into a patio and landscaped yard surrounded by a high brick wall. There was also a half bath (or powder room) for the convenience of visitors. I took the back stairs up to the second floor, which contained the eat-in kitchen, formal dining room, my study, and a large laundry room and storage area. I went into the study and put a newly acquired recording of the Goldberg Variations on the CD player, having opened a Coke (I presumed I would be drinking enough alcohol later) on my way through the kitchen. Lance, who'd evidently been down in the backyard, came in through the doggie door that led from the kitchen to the balcony overlooking the backyard. The doggie door allowed him to go out onto the balcony and down the steps to the patio area whenever he felt the need. In the small backyard he was completely protected by the eight-foot privacy wall.

Sir Lancelot of Buckhead was a three-year-old pedigreed Irish Setter. He reared up, placed his paws on my shoulders, and lapped my chin briefly in greeting. Lance was probably the only reason I was still sane. During my childhood, I'd owned an Irish Setter. By the time I went away to college he had been old and infirm, and his failing health had required that he be put down during my first break between terms. One of the very few areas where Robert and I had ever been in complete disagreement was the subject of pets, dogs in particular. He didn't like them, and they usually didn't like him. In addition, he was severely allergic to both cats and dogs, so the subject of having a pet had never been seriously raised during our years together. A few months after Robert died, Richard had brought Lance home to me—a tiny seven-week-old bundle of love covered in what was then dark fur, which turned into a rich chestnut as he matured. It had been love at first sight, and he'd become my constant companion. I'd quickly retrofitted the house to accommodate a large dog, installing the doggie door, for example. It was a rigid rule of the household that the doors leading down to the formal living room and to the garage were never left open or even ajar so that there was never any opportunity for him to slip downstairs and possibly out the door to face the dangers of busy city streets.

I decided to go upstairs and pack for the weekend—just in case this evening didn't cancel my trip. Music is and has always been my passion, and I'd indulged myself to the extent of acquiring a state-of-the-art stereo system featuring speakers in every room of the townhouse that could be turned off and on at will from a master console in the study. Had I possessed the talent for it, I would probably have made a better musician than lawyer, but alas, more than one teacher had told me what I'd already suspected—that I was meant to enjoy music but not create it at any level beyond the amateur. I did sing well enough to participate in choral activities at Harvard but hadn't indulged even that small talent for years.

Arriving finally in my bedroom, I changed into shorts, a pullover shirt, and deck shoes. Lance, who'd followed me upstairs, hopped up on my bed, selected his favorite corner, and watched me intently.

As always when I entered the walk-in closet, I was confronted with the section of clothes that had belonged to Robert and were now carefully hung, protected by plastic dry-cleaner covers. I knew I should have sent them to Goodwill a long time ago, but somehow I hadn't been able to make myself do so. I couldn't wear them even though we'd shared the same six-foot height, as the similarity ended there. I'm relatively broad-shouldered from years of working out, while Robert had been possessed of a swimmer's build and hadn't been much interested in improving upon nature.

I did my packing, then laid out the clothing I planned to wear for the evening—since I was meeting a prospective client, I settled for a pinstriped suit, white shirt, and conservative tie. Having well over an hour to kill, I decided to sweat out some of my frustration, so I donned my running shorts and shoes, which was Lance's signal to trot downstairs and find his leash. When I arrived on the second floor, he was waiting for me with his leash in his mouth, so I slipped the choke collar around his neck and led him to the door. We headed for Piedmont Park, which was only a block or so away and would be full of runners at this hour. I didn't necessarily consider that a plus, but it would be a change from my normal early-morning runs, which were almost always solitary.

As I ran, I wondered what kind of client Andrew could have lined up that required such circumspection. Since I'm a trial lawyer, it could be either a criminal case or some civil litigation, but try as I might, I couldn't come up with any ideas about the evening ahead.

About thirty minutes into my run, I began to calm down, and, more or less resigned to my fate, I headed back to the townhouse to get ready for what I expected to be the ordeal of the evening. Lance, as always, trotted easily beside me. It had taken months of training before he'd learned to repress his natural urge to surge ahead, pulling me with him.

Back at the townhouse, I paused in the laundry area long enough to strip, tossed my running gear into a waiting basket, and padded naked upstairs, while Lance headed for the kitchen and his water bowl.

Standing before the bathroom mirror, I took stock of myself—smooth body, thirty-four-inch waist, fairly broad shoulders, nicely proportioned and muscled, without even a hint of love handles around the middle, somewhat larger than average equipment (which when aroused became larger still), trimmed pubic area, shaved testicles, brown hair, handsome face, and a heart that I'd somehow managed to turn to stone. They say that lightning never strikes twice, and the metaphor most likely carries over into the interpersonal arena as well as the realm of physical phenomena. I wondered, as I sometimes tended to do, what I'd done to myself over the course of the last three years.

Ah, well, no time to indulge in self-pity, I decided and began the process of shaving.

3

Charles

AROUND seven thirty, dressed in what I knew to be my lawyerly best, I drove down Juniper Street, turned left on Ponce de Leon, and followed it east to the Greenwood Club to keep my eight o'clock appointment with Andrew and the mystery client. The Greenwood Club is even older and more prestigious, albeit less well-known outside of Atlanta, than the famous Piedmont Driving Club. It was located in a grand old Georgian home that sat serenely on a little rise overlooking Ponce de Leon, and was one of those places where you had to almost literally inherit a membership (or marry someone who had one) to belong. I believe they did accept a dozen or so new members each year, but not many could afford the reported six-figure initiation fee.

I had been there a couple of times before as a guest of Andrew and knew the food and service to be among the best in Atlanta. Their wine cellar was arguably the best in the Southeast, although fans of the famous Bern's Steak House down in Tampa might find cause to disagree with that assertion.

Surrendering the Jag to a liveried attendant, I walked through the door, which was being held open by a doorman who, despite my only having been there a couple of times, greeted me by name. The maître d', who also greeted me by name, didn't have to be told why I was there. He simply informed me that Mr. Chandler was waiting for me in one of the private rooms upstairs and would I please follow him. Such are the pleasures and perks of old money.

I'd heard about but never been inside one of the private rooms of this club. By all accounts, they were for the convenience of members and were even equipped for overnight stays—some said, with considerable envy, assignations. It was also reported that in more than a hundred years, no member of the staff had ever been known to breach the confidentiality of who met with whom in those rooms. Thus I was becoming more and more intrigued as I followed the maître d' up the stairs and down a short corridor. He stopped at a set of double doors and knocked. After a pause, Andrew opened one of the doors, said, "Thank you, Arthur," to the maître d', and ushered me in, closing the door quietly behind us.

I took in my surroundings very quickly and got the impression that I was in the living room of a small suite. Around a fireplace there was a sitting area consisting of a sofa that, flanked by a pair of wingback chairs, faced a small coffee table. Under the coffee table and extending to the fireplace there was a small but exquisite oriental rug. Beyond the sitting area was a dining table set apparently for only two. In another corner was a writing desk featuring a telephone. The entire room reeked of understated elegance.

That was as far as my quick visual survey got, because rising from the wingback chair that had its back to the door and turning to face Andrew and me was easily the most beautiful man I'd ever seen. His, I noted, was a very masculine beauty, and all the more arresting for it. He was about my height, though of somewhat slimmer build—could that be a thirty-two-inch waist?—and I guessed his age to approximate mine within a year or so. His tailored dark-blue Brooks Brothers suit exuded quality and expensive taste. His head was a mass of jet-black curls. He sported a generous smile and a pair of the most intensely blue eyes I'd ever seen—eyes so liquid and inviting that even at a distance one could get lost in them. The face was vaguely familiar, but I couldn't have said at that point why. I was, in fact, so mesmerized that I couldn't have said much about anything, at least not coherently.

One of the things I've trained myself to do well over the years—all good trial lawyers have to be able to do so—was to listen peripherally to testimony and subconsciously focus upon the drift of it while consciously thinking about something else. This training kicked in automatically just in time to keep me from appearing to have been stricken deaf and dumb on the spot. I managed to focus on Andrew's introduction of the prospective client as Philippe (Andrew pronounced it in the French manner) d'Autremont, but not much else.

I saw something in those blue eyes—recognition, perhaps, or was that wishful thinking on my part? As I returned the firm handshake, something unmistakably electric passed between the two of us, and the handshake continued well past the upper limits of normal. His voice, I managed to note, resonated like liquid gold.

Somehow I got through the pleasantries without making a fool of myself, found a seat in the wingback chair opposite him without stumbling over anything, and managed to focus on what Andrew, who'd settled on the sofa, was saying, despite the turmoil I was feeling, for I felt a crack beginning to appear in my oh so carefully constructed emotional defenses.

"—don't recognize the name?"

I realized that Andrew was addressing me, expecting a reply, so I said, "Not that I recall."

"Haven't you been following the news lately?" Andrew said.

"Andrew, you know very well that I've been in court every day for the past ten days, and when I'm immersed in a case, I block everything else out, including, and most especially the news." That was particularly true when the case itself was making the news—I didn't like to read about it while I was in the middle of it.

"Mr. d'Autremont's wife was found brutally murdered a little over two weeks ago, on Mother's Day, to be exact, in their home on West Paces Ferry Road. It's been all over the media; doesn't that ring any bells?" Andrew said.

"Now that you mention it, I may have seen a headline in the newspaper. That's probably why your face is familiar," I said to Philippe. "The photo in the paper certainly didn't do you justice. I believe I saw the headlines across the breakfast table at a morning meeting with our top investigator."

I now remembered that Richard (who was, in fact, our top investigator) had insisted on telling me all of the gory details, of which there were plenty. The victim, Lucinda Meriwether d'Autremont, had been found on a Monday morning by her maid, who had just returned to work after a weekend off. Lucinda was found naked, spread-eagled, and cuffed and tied hand and foot to the four posts of her bed. A wooden stake had literally been driven through her heart. As one might expect, the media was having a field day with the gruesome particulars.

"Well, you may need to catch up on your news," Andrew said. "There's every possibility that Mr. d'Autremont will be arrested and charged with the murder. We're here tonight because I want you to consider representing him."

"Andrew, if that's what this is all about, why not have him come to the office during the day? Why all the secrecy?"

"Because there's a very special set of circumstances surrounding this whole affair." He started to elaborate, but before he could begin, there was a discreet knock on the door and a waiter appeared, carrying a round of drinks, which Andrew had evidently ordered brought up as soon as he'd been notified of my arrival. As we settled down with our respective drinks, Andrew began to relate the "special circumstances."

"Two days after the body was discovered, I received a telephone call from an old family friend who wanted to set up a meeting with myself and Mr. d'Autremont, and we met in this very room one evening last week. All that I will say beyond that is that I am convinced of Mr. d'Autremont's innocence."

"Why?"

"Because Mr. d'Autremont wasn't in Atlanta that weekend, and I'm absolutely certain of that fact. However, you will have to agree to neither question Mr. d'Autremont concerning his whereabouts nor to attempt to trace his movements on that weekend. This is nonnegotiable."

"Again, why?"

"I have stipulated to all concerned that you are not to be told and that you will agree to neither make nor cause anyone else to make any attempt to pursue the matter."

"All concerned?"

"Mr. d'Autremont, my old family friend, and others."

He paused as if he expected some comment from me. Hearing none, he continued, "It's probably just a matter of time before Mr. d'Autremont is arrested and charged with the murder, so what we want you to do"—and he gave me his sternest look—"is to get him acquitted without using that alibi."

"And if that turns out not to be possible?" I said.

"That would be, in a word, unthinkable."

"Andrew, as one of my favorite philosophers once said—'only an unthinking mind finds anything unthinkable.'"

"I, too, am fond of Philip Wylie, I even had occasion to meet him near the end of his life, but be that as it may, it will have to suffice."

"And I'm not to know any more concerning Mr. d'Autremont's whereabouts that weekend?" I tried not to sound sarcastic.

"In my judgment, it's safer that way. You won't be tempted to try and take the easy way out."

"Andrew, you know perfectly well that I'm not in the habit of taking the easy way out of anything. Furthermore, nothing of what you've told me entirely explains the cloak and dagger routine this evening."

"The reason for the cloak and dagger routine, as you put it, is that it occurred to me that if the police don't know that you are representing Mr. d'Autremont—at least until after he's arrested—you might have a little more room to maneuver behind the scenes, so to speak. He's quite sure that he's been followed by plainclothes detectives for some time now, up to and probably including his visit here this evening. You certainly have enough contacts downtown to find out what's going on, perhaps even what's going to happen, and possibly what kind of case they're building. By now they'll probably have uncovered the rather unconventional nature of Mr. and Mrs. d'Autremont's marriage, including the fact that both he and his late wife are, as you might say, family."

Andrew prided himself on being *au courant* with the latest buzzwords and had certainly heard me use the slang term "family" on more than one occasion in reference to gays and lesbians. His logic was, as usual, impeccable, and I lacked a suitable response, so I simply sat there nursing my drink. I must add that all the while he had been discussed as though he were not even in the room, the subject of our conversation had sat there toying with his drink, taking it all in. I found myself wondering what was going on behind those blue eyes.

Andrew couldn't stand it any longer and said, "So, what do you think?"

"I think that Mr. d'Autremont and I have a great deal to talk about before I can decide what, if anything, is to be done."

"Well, then," Andrew said as he got up from the sofa, "you may talk about it over dinner. I've got to go down to the lounge where Miss Emily is waiting for me to join her for our own dinner. I've already ordered for you, and I'll tell them to begin serving as soon as I get downstairs—I think you'll enjoy the wine I selected. See me to the door, will you, my boy?"

I got up and followed him out into the corridor, closing the door behind us, and said, "Andrew, what are you playing at here? Are you auditioning for the role of Yenta?"

"Why, Charles, whatever do you mean?" he said with a look of feigned innocence. I swear his eyes had a definite twinkle in them.

"You know precisely what I mean. 1) Any first-year associate, of which we have several, could handle this in the manner you've just outlined; 2) You knew that I was looking forward to a long weekend; 3) He's damnably attractive; 4) Probably available, which brings me to 5) Are you trying to set me up?"

"Not unless you want to be, my boy," he said, patting me on the arm. "Not unless you want to be." And with a twinkle in his eye, he turned and strolled down the corridor.

The mental crack began to widen a bit as it suddenly hit me that I wanted very much to be set up with this attractive stranger—which was totally out of character for me. Even before Robert, I'd not been particularly promiscuous. In point of fact, Robert had been one of only a few people with whom I'd experienced sex on the first date, and during the time we'd been together I'd been Simon pure and Simon simple, never once looking at another man. Well, perhaps I looked—I am, after all, human—but I certainly didn't touch.

Robert and I had met during my second year at Harvard and his first at MIT. We'd struck up a conversation in the classical music section of the record department at the Harvard Cooperative Society. The Coop, as it was known (pronounced "coop" as in chicken coop), was a series of connected buildings that offered everything from clothing to office supplies to books and records, etcetera. We'd chatted for a while about favorite artists and had continued the conversation across the street at Au Bon Pain, one of a chain of pastry and coffee shops that were and are ubiquitous in the Boston area, and have since expanded to other metropolitan areas. I invited him to my apartment, and we spent not only that night together, but every night after that until his death some ten years later.

Since Robert's death, I'd simply not had the urge, even though opportunities had abounded. Richard in particular had been very much the busybody, bringing home any number of attractive studs who would have been perfectly willing to crawl into my bed. In short, I simply hadn't been up to it, no pun intended, and had more or less resigned myself to a monastic existence. That is, until now.

At the end of the term during which Robert and I had met, my roommate gracefully agreed to vacate and Robert moved in with me, turning a *de facto* situation into one that was *de jure*. As far as his family knew, he was still living in a dormitory at MIT, and he'd maintained that fiction until the end of the school year. Before the summer break, I used family contacts to find jobs in Atlanta for both of us, and he spent the summer with me in Gran's big old house in Buckhead.

Gran knew about my sexual orientation and had learned to be more comfortable with it than I would have expected, given the era in which she was reared. Early on, she'd made it clear that she would have preferred to see me married and producing great-grandchildren, but she was intelligent—and educated—enough to understand that one doesn't choose these things. She had made Robert feel as welcome in her home as any of my other friends.

That summer Robert introduced me to his parents as a new friend from Atlanta, thus paving the way for us to room together for the next year without raising any red flags at home. His parents were strict Southern Baptists and not only knew nothing of but would never have accepted the reality of his sexual orientation.

I went back into the room at the club with a sense of nervousness that I hadn't felt in years, having just realized that for the first time since Robert's death I found myself with a strong case of lust—perhaps something even stronger than lust. And for the life of me, I didn't know what to do about it—for many reasons. If he was to become a client, then I should definitely not become involved. My Seduction 101 routines (never very good, at best) were covered by more than a decade of rust. The list was endless. All of which was pointless speculation and predicated on the faint possibility that there was a mutual interest. My instincts, rusty as they were, told me that I had in fact sensed something in that electric handshake.

Carrying all of this mental baggage along with me, I sat down to get acquainted with my new client-to-be.

4

Charles

"WELL, Philippe," I said, stressing the French pronunciation (showing off?) as I settled back down, this time on the sofa, which placed me closer to and gave me a slightly different view of my prospective client, "we have so much to talk about that I hardly know where to begin. But first, let me apologize for Andrew and myself."

"Please, I'm much more comfortable with the English version of my name," he said, in that voice, which by now had begun to send chills down my spine. "Philip will do very nicely." He quickly added, "Apologize? For what?"

"For discussing you and your case as though you weren't sitting in the same room with us. It's a bad habit in which we lawyers frequently indulge, and it is, and was, rude. I assure you that no offense was meant."

"None was taken."

Before I could say anything else, there was another discreet tap on the door; then it opened and two waiters wheeled in a small cart carrying, I supposed, our dinner, or at least a portion of it. Without a word, they went to the table in the corner and quickly arranged the first course. When that task had been completed, the one in charge walked over to where we were sitting, cleared his throat, and said, or rather intoned, with the same solemnity he might have used to address a gathering of twenty people, "Dinner is served."

As we started on the soup, which appeared to be a broccoli and cheese combination—Andrew really was trying to make me susceptible; he knew that I loved anything containing broccoli—I asked Philip to tell me about himself, which, with starts and stops and occasional prompting by my questions, he did.

Philip was from a very old but somewhat impoverished Louisiana family who, during his youth, were still hanging onto a Louisiana plantation complete with a somewhat run-down antebellum mansion north of New Orleans. Lucinda, his late wife, was from a slightly less old but considerably more affluent Georgia family. As a child and young adult, she had frequently visited relatives in Louisiana who lived near the d'Autremont plantation, and they'd known each other since before adolescence. She was the only offspring of her family, and by the time she'd finished college was under intense pressure to marry and produce heirs. Neither of them, it developed, was particularly interested in marriage, oddly enough for the same reason. Philip had been interested only in boys from an early age, and while Lucinda occasionally, as they say, swung both ways, her predilection was for women.

Due to a chance meeting on Bourbon Street in New Orleans, in a setting that left little doubt—a gay bar, naturally—as to their respective sexual identities, they'd admitted the truth to each other. After that, they began to meet more often and had finally come up with a plan that would get her family off her back, so to speak. They pretended to, and actually did, date each other, dragging the process out for a couple of years before finally announcing that they were going to marry. Philip wasn't at that point, out to his family, although he'd never attempted to hide his sexuality from them, so it was easy for him to maintain his part of the charade.

Needless to say, it was a marriage of convenience. They'd occupied, as far as the rest of the world was concerned, the same residence on West Paces Ferry Road ever since their wedding several years earlier, and were in fact seen together in all of the right places and with all of the right people. Their private lives, however, were entirely separate. They had the means to and did maintain two small condos in different parts of town, which they used for the purpose of conducting those secret lives, and they had done so almost since the first year of their marriage. A very tidy arrangement, I found myself thinking.

There was much more than that, of course, and I filed all of it away for reference to be digested later. By this time, we'd worked our way through the soup, salad, sorbet, a wonderful veal dish that I recognized but couldn't immediately name, and a bottle of Mondavi-Rothschild Opus

One. I made a mental note to compliment Andrew on his choice of wines.

I needed to ask Philip some very pointed questions about the murder, but I decided to veer off on a tangent first, and over dessert and coffee got him to talking about his life. It turned out that he was a somewhat gifted writer and had published a number of novels, all of them under pseudonyms. His real talent lay, however, in the field of real estate, and he'd accumulated a great deal of income property, overseeing the management of which took considerable time, which left him little time to indulge in much else. His social life, as he put it, was confined to the occasional weekend here and there. He'd managed to have several affairs over the years, none of them of any significant duration, and there was no one in his life currently, a revelation that started another chain of thought having to do with relationships.

Robert and I had maintained the fiction that we were merely friends and school roommates until after he received his degree in architecture. Because I still had two more years of law school at the time, he decided to do some postgraduate work so that we could stay in Cambridge together. When his parents came to Cambridge for his graduation, he told them of his plans for two more years of education, without, of course, telling them the whole story. They'd been adamant that he should come home and find a job. His summer savings and part-time jobs during the school year were insufficient for his needs without their support—they knew it and attempted to use that fact as leverage to persuade him to follow their wishes. Their tactics caused him to lose his temper, whereupon he told them precisely why and with whom he intended to stay in Cambridge for two more years. That, of course, had precipitated a breach in his relationship with his parents. They'd flown home in a rage, and had neither spoken to nor written him again.

Fortunately, I had a good income from a large trust fund that had been created when my parents died, as well as a smaller amount from a trust set up by my maternal grandparents. I wasn't rich, but I had sufficient means to allow myself the luxury of not having to work during college or law school. It hadn't been quite enough to support the two of us, but that income, augmented by our summer savings, some government loans and grants—because of my private income, I didn't qualify for grants, but Robert did—and part-time jobs in Boston managed to see us both through the next two years. I finished law school and he received his master's, after which we both found jobs in Atlanta and began our respective careers.

The waiters had long since cleared the table and departed, but not before reminding us that we wouldn't be disturbed and if we needed anything we should pick up the telephone on the desk to call. By that time, we were sitting side by side on the sofa, jackets off, enjoying a fine glass of Port—W & J Graham Tawny 40 Year Old.

Just as I was about to ask my pointed questions, he surprised me by asking me about myself. I gave him the short, condensed version, starting with school—including Robert—and leading up to the present.

We'd lived together until Robert died of a brain tumor shortly after the tenth anniversary of our first meeting. Even after three years, thinking about the final months of Robert's life brought me almost to the point of melancholy. At one point, I'd very nearly sold the townhouse that we'd bought, furnished, and decorated together, because everything in it was a reminder, one way or another, of Robert. In the end, however, I decided that I couldn't part with something that we'd both worked so hard to create, and I tried to concentrate upon remembering the happy years that had preceded those final months.

I hadn't gone out with anyone since then, despite Richard's constant attempts at matchmaking. Richard, my best friend since seventh grade, had moved into the largest of the three spare bedrooms during Robert's illness in order to help with his care, and had stayed on afterward taking care of me. Richard's presence and upbeat attitude were some of the things that had kept me sane during the first months after Robert died—that, and the love and affection of Lance.

Philip was attentive during my recital and made appropriately polite and seemingly sincere responses. In fact, he gazed at me so intently and with such evident interest that I distinctly felt the foundation under my defenses begin to shift and crumble. To switch the conversation to safer ground, I decided to cut to the chase, saying, "Enough about me already. We need to talk about the murder."

"What do you want to know?"

"First, do you have any idea who might have done it?"

"None whatsoever." He paused and looked thoughtful.

"What?"

"I just thought of something that Lucinda said recently."

"What was that?"

"I need to backtrack just a moment. Did I mention that she was about six weeks pregnant?"

"No, you didn't."

"Her family was still very much on her case to produce an heir, and she got this notion that if we produced an heir it would shut them up. She had herself artificially inseminated, using me as the donor. We could have gotten her pregnant in the normal way, but neither of us derived any particular pleasure from sex with each other. Anyway, the pregnancy was confirmed, and she did mention that she was thinking about breaking off her current affair for the duration of the pregnancy, at least."

"How did the other woman feel about that?"

"I'm not sure, but I got the impression that her lover was getting somewhat possessive and that Lucinda was tired of it. You have to understand that we simply didn't talk about such things very often."

"You're suggesting that she told this person, and that got her killed?"

"I suppose it's possible."

"Did she have any other lovers?"

"Never more than one at a time, as far as I know. We jointly agreed in the beginning that we wouldn't rub each other's noses in that aspect of our lives, and kept it totally separate."

"So you never met any of them?"

"Only once, and I didn't actually meet her, merely saw her from a distance. Three or four years ago, we turned up at the same party quite unexpectedly, each of us with dates. Lucinda and I spotted each other from opposite sides of the room. I nodded to her and pointed to the door, indicating that my date and I would leave, which we did. I didn't really get a good look at the woman she was with."

"Any chance that person was the one she was still seeing?"

"I doubt it. To the best of my knowledge her affairs never lasted longer than six months or so."

"Could one of her former lovers have killed her for some reason?"

"I'm not sure. If that's what happened, it's very strange that it happened at the house on West Paces Ferry Road, because we had what I thought was a firm understanding that we would never bring any of our sexual partners there. I never did, and as far as I know, neither did she. On the other hand, she might well have brought a former lover to the house in order to keep her current lover from knowing about it. When I was being questioned by the detectives, they kept pounding away at the fact that there was no evidence of forced entry. I suppose that could be taken as an indication that she knew the killer and had let them in."

"What exactly have you told the police?"

"Well, they wanted to know where I'd been that weekend and could I prove it. I told them I'd spent the weekend out of town and refused to tell them where, but I don't think they believed me. They also asked me who I thought might have done it, and I told them that I had no idea."

"Did they say anything else to you?"

"I'm not sure. I was very upset and in shock when they first questioned me. I'd just gotten home, and it's all a blur now. As you can imagine, Lucinda and I were not in love with each other, but we'd known each other for more than twenty years and were in some ways very close, almost like brother and sister."

"What makes you think they might arrest you?"

"Just a feeling, I guess. They keep coming back and asking the same questions over and over again, and I don't think they're satisfied with the answers. I also get the impression that they aren't looking very hard in any other direction, either."

"Is there anything else you think I need to know at this point?"

"Only that I think they might have somehow discovered that I'm gay."

"What makes you think that?"

"Nothing they said overtly, just some sly innuendo in some of their questions and remarks."

"I'll be honest with you, that's not good. Our dearly beloved district attorney is a notorious homophobe, and he's so publicity-hungry that he's liable to go after you for no other reason than that of milking the situation for all the free press it's worth."

"I know, I've heard stories about him, and that's one of the reasons for my concern."

I steered the conversation back to generalities for a time so part of me could talk while the other part assimilated all that I'd just heard. He had good reason to be concerned. If District Attorney Craig Wetherbee could work a gay angle into this case, he would run with it, even if it was built on thin air. A staunch Southern Baptist of the worst hellfire and brimstone sort, Wetherbee was notorious for his homophobia. It was rumored that he had aspirations to higher office, perhaps even the governor's mansion.

I snapped back to reality, realizing that I was being asked a direct question. "I'm sorry," I said, "I was woolgathering for a minute there. What were you saying?"

"Will you help me? That is, take the case?"

"Yes, of course," I said.

He must have sensed some hesitancy in my voice, perhaps even an unspoken "but," because he articulated it for me and said, "But…?"

"Well, the firm will want a retainer of at least $50,000 against $500 per hour for my time, $200 per hour for any associates' time, and any out-of-pocket expenses for investigators, etcetera."

"No problem…." Then a sly look came over his face as he said, "And what will you want?" with a slightly mocking tone in that golden voice.

I don't know what came over me at that point, but the shifting foundations of my fortress caused the crack to yawn widely open. From a spot on the ceiling I seemed to be looking down at us on the sofa, where I saw and heard myself saying, "You."

"In what way?"

"Naked. In my arms. On that rug. Right now."

"And what else?" His blue eyes were still virtually inscrutable, but there was a definite hint of something in them.

In for a penny, in for a pound, I thought. Again, from afar, I heard myself saying, "You. In my bed. Every night."

"Not naked?"

"Well, I took that as a given and didn't want to seem redundant."

"For how long?" Still no discernible reaction.

"Until your legal problems are resolved or until we get tired of each other, whichever takes longer."

To my surprise and wonder, he stood up, said simply, "Sounds good to me," and started removing his tie. Of course, I stopped him immediately—I prefer to unwrap my own packages.

The next thirty minutes or so will be etched in my brain forever. We began to undress each other, starting with shirts and ties. His chest was as smooth as silk, and from the definition his muscles showed, I deduced that he worked out regularly. I stroked his smooth, tanned chest, moved my hand down to his extremely flat stomach, and said, "I'm glad that you're not hirsute."

"What would you do if I were?"

"Well, earlier in the evening I noticed that the bathroom is not only fully equipped but well stocked, including shaving cream and disposable razors. I guess I'd have had to try them out."

"Too bad I'm not. That sounds like fun."

I unbuckled his belt and unzipped his trousers, which immediately fell to the floor. He was wearing sexy low-rise square-cut boxer briefs, not unlike my own. I slid them down over his thighs, kneeling as I did so.

He said, "You have me at a slight disadvantage, you've still got your pants on." He proceeded to remove my disadvantage, and we embraced and kissed deeply. We sank down on the rug in front of the fireplace, and without any further conversation, it was all over with hands and mouths almost before it had begun. In point of fact, it had been so long since I'd experienced real sex—sex with oneself doesn't count—that I came as quickly as a sixteen-year-old virgin.

"Sorry to be so quick," I said, "but it's been three years."

"Not to worry, next time will be better."

"I don't see how it could be any better."

"Well, then, we'll just have to make it last longer."

And we started again. This time it did take somewhat longer, and it was, unbelievable as it may seem, better. Afterward, we lay side by side for a long while without speaking.

Finally, he said simply, "Penny."

"Well, I was just thinking of what Charles Ryder said the first time he saw Sebastian Flyte's ancestral home."

"I've both seen and read *Brideshead Revisited*, but I don't remember the line."

"Golly."

"You're surprised that I don't remember something from a series I saw several years ago?" he said.

"No. When Charles Ryder first saw Brideshead Manor House from a distance, he simply said, 'Golly.'"

"Oh yes, now I do remember. Most appropriate. Then as now."

There followed a great deal of inconsequential small talk, until finally I said, "Now that we've had some practice, let's go somewhere and try this in a real bed." Despite the fact that hours, even days, seemed to have elapsed, it was only eleven.

"My place or yours?" he said with a smile that lit up the room. With that smile I was hooked, knew it, and didn't give a damn.

"I think, given your uncertain legal status, that it had better be my place. This club has a covered entrance around back for use in weather that's too inclement for the portico out front. We can have my car brought around there, and if you were followed here, you won't be seen leaving with me—you can arrange to have your car picked up tomorrow."

He agreed, and when we were dressed and presentable, I used the phone to call down and request that my car be brought around to the rear entrance. Then he took the phone and told the appropriate person that he felt the need of a designated driver, was catching a ride with me, and would have his car picked up in the morning.

By eleven thirty we were back at my townhouse. I gave him the fifty-cent tour, and within minutes we were upstairs. We went through the ritual of undressing each other for the second time and were in bed almost in less time than it takes to tell about it. Strangely enough, I had no second thoughts about bringing this man to share the bed that Robert and I had shared for so many years.

I was hooked, all right. Head over heels, and I quite honestly didn't know what to do about it… except, of course, enjoy it while it lasted.

5

Philip

As Charles drove us to his townhouse, he fell temporarily silent and seemed to be concentrating on the late-night traffic, which in Atlanta is always heavy. In a way, I was glad of the respite from small talk, as I needed a chance to collect my wits. So much had happened this evening. For that matter, so much had happened over the past two weeks. At times it all seemed like a hazily remembered dream. Then something or other would hit me with a harsh dose of reality, and I would realize that it wasn't a dream, it was a nightmare—and very real.

One thing was very clear to me. I was or maybe soon would be entrusting my freedom, perhaps even my life, to this young lawyer, who had the saddest brown eyes I'd ever seen—except for the sad part, they were puppy-dog eyes, in spades. I also saw, although with less clarity, that I was well on the way to entrusting my heart to him as well. I had been in lust countless times over the years but couldn't remember ever having been truly in love, except perhaps for a juvenile infatuation when I was seventeen, and that was so long ago it hardly seemed to matter.

I was still lost in thought when we turned into a driveway and he reached up and touched a garage door opener that was clipped to the visor over the driver's seat. The garage door closed behind us automatically, and we got out of the car. I was touched when he took my hand, opened the garage door again, and led me around to the front entrance as the garage door closed behind us.

"There's a back way up from the garage," he said, "but I'd like to take you through the front door, at least this once."

He unlocked and then opened the front door, and we stepped into an attractively decorated foyer that opened to the living room beyond. We walked up to the kitchen on the second floor, and as soon as he opened the door, we were immediately and enthusiastically greeted by an Irish Setter. Charles commanded, "Lance, sit," and the dog settled down on his haunches and looked intently at us.

"I forgot to mention the beast," he said. "Philip, this gorgeous creature is Sir Lancelot of Buckhead." He looked at the dog and added, "Lance, this gorgeous creature is Philip."

Charles then turned to me and said, "Hold out your right hand."

I did as instructed, and Lance raised his right paw and patted my extended hand.

Charles gave me a whirlwind tour, still holding my hand, but it was all a blur. The tour ended in the master bedroom, where he turned, smiled, and said, "Coffee, tea, or me?"

"You'll do very nicely," I said, and we went to bed.

With the lights still on beside the bed, we enjoyed each other's bodies leisurely and at length, then dozed off without bothering to turn out the bedside lamps. I woke up some time later, a little disoriented because I was in a strange room. Then I spotted Lance curled up on the foot of the king-size bed and remembered where I was. I also realized that there were sounds coming from elsewhere in the house, and that those sounds were what had awakened me. I nudged Charles, who rose up, mumbled something, and rolled back over. I nudged him again. This time he seemed to wake up and said, "What is it?"

"I hear noises. I think there's somebody in the house."

"Oh, that's just Richard coming back from a night out," came the sleepy reply.

About then, a deep baritone voice called out, first from a distance, then growing louder as it grew nearer, "Hey, Charley boy, your light is still on, are you up? Wait 'til you hear who I ran into this evening, you'll never believe...." There was a pause, followed by an explosive, "Holy shit!"

I sat up and blinked just in time to see a good-looking blond of medium height and build standing in the open doorway, clearly taken aback by what he was seeing in the room. He was wearing only a rumpled pair of light-blue bikini-style briefs, which had several conspicuous dark stains across their front, and his body was covered from upper chest to legs with a thick mat of blond hair. Lance got up, walked over to the blond, and sniffed his crotch.

He leaned against the doorjamb and said, "Sooooo…." He made the word last about thirty seconds, dragging it out for several syllables. "The heart of stone has melted at last. It's about fucking time." He simultaneously and with good nature shooed Lance away.

By this time, Charles, who was wide awake and sitting up in bed as well, said, "Richard, don't you ever knock?"

"What's to knock upon, boyo, or for that matter, for? The door was open. Besides, what would I expect to see in this room for the last three years, except you jerking off?"

"Well, at least if you're going to invade my bedroom when I'm entertaining, you could wear something other than your cum-stained trick shorts."

He looked down at himself in mock horror and said, "Those aren't cum stains. Well, at least not from tonight. I'll have you know that I didn't waste any bodily fluids tonight." This was said with a slight leer, and he added, "If they bother you, I can take them off." He reached for the waistband of his shorts.

"Oh, please," Charles said, now laughing, "spare us."

Richard folded his arms across his chest at that and said, "Where are your manners, boy? Aren't you going to introduce me to the person who finally brought you back to the land of the living?"

"I'm sorry. Philip, this rude fellow is Richard Greene, my best friend since seventh grade. Richard, this is Philip d'Autremont."

Richard walked over to the bed, and I shook his proffered hand. We exchanged pleasantries, and Charles explained both my legal situation and that he would be representing me. Richard had tactfully, I thought, refrained from saying that he'd seen me all over the news, which he doubtless had.

Then Charles said, "Richard, are you still seeing that twinkie from the DA's office?"

"Well, I'm no longer seeing him in the biblical sense, but I do run into him from time to time. Actually, I saw him for about half a minute tonight at the Powder Magazine, and he made it clear that he still has a thing for me. Why?"

"I want you to find out from him, if you can, what the DA is planning to do with this murder case. I'd like to not have any surprises on this one, if at all possible."

"Will do," Richard said, and he paused before continuing, "Well, I guess I'll leave you two alone to whatever it was you were doing."

"And close the door behind you."

"Yes, Sir." He left and closed the door. I noticed as he left that his back was covered with blond hair, as well—he was truly a walking teddy bear.

Charles said, "Sorry about that. Richard is always a little larger than life, if you know what I mean, but we've been friends forever. He's also a super sleuth, and several law firms, my own included, keep his agency on a retainer and very busy."

I laughed and said, "I think you gave him a bit of a shock tonight."

"Well, as I told you, it's been a very long time. A little over three years, to be precise. Everyone I know, Richard included, has tried to fix me up, but I just wasn't ready." He smiled before adding, "Or perhaps I was just waiting for you to come along."

I really didn't know what to say to that, so I smiled back.

He yawned and said, "You know what would feel good right now?"

"I can't imagine."

"A nice hot shower—for two, of course—and then lights out for the night."

I had to admit that the activities of the evening had left me feeling more than a little bit sticky, so we went into the master bathroom, which opened directly off his bedroom. We were in the shower for a very long time, and when we were dry, he produced two robes—an old one and a new one, giving me the latter. We came out of the bathroom to find Richard, himself clad in a robe, sitting on the edge of the bed with Lance's head in his lap. Lance seemed to have taken over a spot on the corner of the bed.

Charles feigned anger and said, "You again. I thought I asked you to knock."

"I did, but there was no answer. Don't get your knickers in a twist, boyo, this is business." His tone now was as serious as the previous banter had been light.

"What do you mean?"

"I just talked to Bruce."

"Who the fuck is Bruce?"

"The twinkie in the DA's office, who else? Since I'd seen him very briefly earlier this evening and gotten definite signals, I decided to call him. I didn't even have to do any prompting to steer him around to the murder case; it seems as though it's on the tip of everybody's tongue in that office. I didn't even have to promise him my body." He managed to sound almost disappointed at this.

"Did you find out what they're planning to do?"

"Damn straight. They're going to wait until five o'clock tomorrow afternoon and then issue a warrant for Philip's arrest."

"What brought that on? Did he say?"

"Some ass-kisser in the department got wind of Philip's sexual orientation and decided to curry favor by telling Wetherbee about it, with embellishments, no doubt. As you might suppose, the very hint of a 'queer' angle to the case was like waving a red flag in front of a bull. They're going to railroad this through any way they can. Word is out that the police aren't even doing any more serious investigating—they think they've got a patsy."

"The bastards," Charles said. "A late-Friday arrest would mean no chance of an arraignment and bail hearing before Tuesday morning, what with the holiday weekend."

"Yup. Our boy Wetherbee thinks he's got a sitting faggot for a target and wants him in the cooler all weekend so they can grill him."

Charles, suddenly all business, said, "Well, then, we'll just have to beat them at their own game. Philip, is there any reason at all why you have to go home tomorrow?"

"None that I can think of, except I have no clothes. Wait a minute, I'm currently taking antibiotics for a minor infection, and I really shouldn't go more than a day without my prescription."

"Well, clothes won't be a problem. You're about the same size as Robert was, and there are lots of perfectly good clothes here that will fit you. Also, plenty of spare shaving gear and stuff. As for your prescription, I assume it's at your house."

"No, it's at my condo."

"Where's the condo?"

"Not too far from here, actually. It's off Piedmont, in the Ansley area, behind Sean & Gabe's Restaurant."

"Any problem drawing a map of how to find them and letting Richard go fetch them?"

"Not at all."

"Good, we can take care of that first thing in the morning. Meanwhile, I have a plan."

"What?"

"I don't know if I told you, but I was planning to fly down to Florida tomorrow afternoon to spend the holiday weekend at my beach place. I think instead I'll leave first thing in the morning. You'll come with me." The way he said it, it wasn't a request.

"I'm not sure I understand how that will help the situation."

"Simple. We'll spend a long weekend at the beach place and fly home early Tuesday morning just in time for you to 'discover' that there's an arrest warrant out for you. We'll then go to the police station, where you will turn yourself in and I will begin the process of getting you out on bail. You'll be in by nine and back out by two or three."

"You make it sound so simple."

"It is when you understand the system. You can even make it work for you at times. One thing, though. We'll have to plan ahead for the bail." He saw my look of bewilderment and continued, "Bail can be either in the form of a cash bond, which is recovered after the trial is over, or a bail bond that typically costs about 10 percent of the amount of the bail. In a murder case, the best we can hope for is bail in the neighborhood of half a million. You'll have to tell me whether you prefer to lay out the cash, knowing you'll get it all back, or come up with a 10 percent premium, which is nonrefundable. In either case, the funds need to be in my firm's trust account by Tuesday morning—they'll take our check, but they won't take a check from you. The choice is yours."

"No problem. I can call my broker in the morning at home. He and I have discussed liquidating some securities that weren't doing too well anyway. I can give him a sell order and have him either wire the funds to your trust account later tomorrow or even send a check over by courier."

"A wire will work just fine. We can work out the particulars in the morning," Charles said. "Richard, are you working on anything in particular at the moment?"

"Nothing I can't turn over to one of my grunts."

"Good. If your little friend is correct, you're going to have to find the killer for us with little or no help from the police. I want you on it first thing tomorrow, but for now, let's all get some sleep. We can have a council of war over breakfast."

Richard left, this time not forgetting to close the door. Charles set his alarm for six forty-five, which was barely five hours away. After we were back in bed, he turned the lights off, rolled over, and held me tight.

"Scared?"

"A little."

"No need to be, at this point."

"Easy for you to say."

"I know it's easier said than done, but don't worry. We'll get through this with flying colors."

"If we're taking a plane tomorrow, shouldn't I be making a reservation? It might not be possible to get a seat on such short notice, what with the holiday weekend and all."

"You already have a seat."

"I don't understand."

"I fly my own plane for short trips like this. You'll be in the copilot's seat." Without waiting for my response, Charles looked at Lance and pointed to the corner of the room, where I noticed what appeared to be a round doggie bed. "Lance, bed" was all Charles said, and the dog gave him a hangdog look before jumping to the floor and curling up on his own bed.

Charles

I AWOKE Friday morning in time to lie in bed for a few minutes while waiting for the alarm. My first fuzzy thought was that somehow Robert wasn't snuggled up to me in the position he usually preferred. Then I came to with a start, realizing that the snuggler wasn't Robert and that it had in fact been a long time since I'd awakened with a warm body adjacent to mine. That brought a flood of memories, and before it could invoke a flood of tears as well, I disentangled myself carefully from Philip. Then I slipped out of bed quietly so as not to wake him, padded across the room, and turned off the alarm. I opened the bedroom door so that Lance could find his way outside to take care of his own needs; then I headed for the bathroom.

Entering the bathroom, I rushed through my morning routine as quickly and quietly as possible, returning to the bedroom wearing the same old robe I'd put on the night before. Philip was beginning to show signs of waking up, so I bent over and kissed him into full awareness of where he was. "Good morning," I said. "Sleep well?"

"Um… morning. I slept well, but not nearly long enough." He yawned and stretched.

"I'm going to go put some coffee on. You'll find everything you need laid out in the bathroom. After breakfast, we can round up some suitable casual clothes for you." I gave him one more lingering kiss and went down to the front door to retrieve the paper, then went back up to the kitchen.

I started the coffee, then picked up the telephone and called the general aviation airport where I keep my plane, and told them that I would need it fueled and ready several hours earlier than planned. That detail attended to, I rounded up juice, found some frozen bagels that I could nuke, and tried to make the breakfast area presentable for a guest. A few minutes later, while standing at the sink—I was making so much noise that I didn't hear anybody enter the room—I was surprised when a pair of arms slipped around me and someone kissed me on the side of the neck.

I turned around to give my attacker a better target and said, "Mmm, you smell good."

"Not as good as that coffee does, I bet. Is it ready?"

"I think so. Why don't you pour while I go wake up Richard?"

I went upstairs, knocked on Richard's door, stuck my head in the room, and said, "Rise and shine."

He mumbled an obscenity and rolled back over, so I tried again, with the same response. I knew from long experience that it would require stronger measures, so I went to my study, turned on the receiver, set the volume at concert-hall level, turned all speakers off except those in Richard's bedroom, inserted a CD in the player, and pressed "play." Then I went back to the kitchen, where Philip was standing at the counter with a cup of coffee in his hand.

"Richard is impossible to get up in the morning, which normally doesn't matter as it's not my responsibility. Today, however, I've resorted to drastic measures." No sooner had I said that than some very loud music could be heard coming from upstairs, followed by a series of yells and curses. This cracked me up.

"Mind letting me in on the joke?" Philip said. "What did you do to him?"

"I treated him to von Suppés's Light Cavalry Overture at full concert-hall level. You know, the one with the bugles and fanfares at the beginning."

This cracked him up as well, and he said, "Please don't ever do that to me."

I bent over and kissed his cheek. "I've got a whole repertoire of much nicer ways to wake you in the morning."

I went back to the study and turned off the music before settling down to the business of preparing breakfast. We'd just sat down to our coffee, juice, and bagels when Richard came storming into the room wearing a robe, hair still wet from his shower, and said, "Goddammit, Charley, did you have to do that?"

"Well, I tried it the nice way twice, but it didn't work. You left me no choice. Anyway, you'll get over it."

"You may not, when I find a clever way to retaliate."

"Later. Right now we have plans to make, so eat your breakfast and then join us in the study."

"Yes, *mon cap-i-tan*," he said, giving a mock salute.

Philip and I finished our breakfast and went into the study, which is my favorite room in the house. For someone else, it would probably have been a family room. We—Robert and I—had redone the room with floor-to-ceiling bookshelves built into three of the walls. The fourth wall contained a built-in cabinet that concealed my computer, printer, and a couple of file cabinets. The only windows in the room were on either side of the cabinets. There was a partner's desk in front of the cabinet with a swivel chair between it and the wall, which allowed me to swing back and forth between the desk and the computer when I worked at home, which was often. The desk also held a multi-line telephone that could double as a speakerphone, and a good quality answering machine. A pair of wingback chairs flanked the desk. Across the room from the desk, in the middle of the bookcases, were the built-in cabinets that housed both the stereo system and a flat-screen television set. In addition, a small sofa and two easy chairs faced the television set.

I motioned Philip to one of the wingback chairs and said, "Help yourself to the telephone—that call to your broker probably should be the first order of business." I opened a desk drawer and found the phone book. "Do you need a directory?"

"Yes, thanks. I know his office number but not his home one. It's listed, though, as I've looked it up and called him at home before—never this early, of course."

He looked up a number, dialed, and said, "Chase? Philip. ... Yes, I know what time it is, but this is urgent. I need you to transfer half a million dollars by wire from my account to the trust account of Chandler, Todd,

Woodward & Barnett. ... Yes, that's right, the law firm. As you know, there's more than enough purchasing power in the account to cover the transfer."

He continued, "Remember that list of stocks we discussed disposing of by the end of the year to take some losses? ... The same. Sell enough of those today at market to replenish the account. Got that? ... Okay, but sell them in the order we discussed, and save the last two items on the list if possible—they might just turn around. I'm going to hand the phone to Charles Barnett of that firm, whom I've just retained. He'll explain and give you the particulars."

He handed the receiver to me and said, "This is Chase Williams of Merrill Lynch. Tell him what he needs to do about the wire."

"Hello, Mr. Williams, Charles Barnett here."

"What the hell is going on?" a gruff voice wanted to know.

"In a nutshell, we expect the DA will issue a warrant later today for Philip's arrest with regard to the death of his wife. The funds are to cover bail and other expenses."

"Jesus H. Christ!" exploded over the wire. "I've known Philip for years. He's incapable of murder."

"Tell that to Craig Wetherbee."

"That prick. He's a disgrace to this city."

"Well, he'd like to move up to being a disgrace to this state, and probably looks on this sensational case as a stepping stone. Anyway, I'm taking Philip out of town this morning; otherwise, if they arrested him this afternoon, he'd spend the entire weekend in jail. We'll be back early Tuesday, and if a warrant is indeed outstanding, he'll turn himself in. That being the case, I can probably spring him in three or four hours, and we'll need to have funds in the firm's trust account to cover a sizeable amount of bail."

"Let me get a pad and pen." There was a pause, followed by, "Okay, I'm back."

I gave him the name of the bank, the trust account number, and the telephone number of the firm, and then added, "If you have any questions later on this morning, contact Andrew Chandler at the number I just gave you. He'll handle any details until Tuesday."

"Got it. As it happens, I know old Chandler slightly. Now let me talk to Philip again, please."

I handed the phone back and tried not to eavesdrop too obviously while they spoke. When Philip had replaced the receiver, I said, "That's one down." Then I activated the speakerphone function and dialed Andrew's home number.

The phone rang a few times before a female voice answered, "Hello."

"Good morning, Emily, this is Charles. I need to speak to Andrew, please. It's quite urgent."

"Hello, Charles. Just a minute and I'll get him." Bless her heart, Emily had been a lawyer's wife long enough to know when to make small talk and when not to. We could hear her calling in the background for Andrew to pick up.

"Hello."

"Good morning, Andrew."

"Good morning, Charles. Where are you, and what can I do for you at this early hour?"

"I'm at home. Philip is with me, and the situation isn't good. He's on the speakerphone with me, by the way. We found out last night, through one of Richard's contacts, that a warrant will be issued for Philip's arrest late this afternoon, probably not until nearly five o'clock."

"I was afraid of something like that."

"Well, the situation is in hand. I'm not going to go to the office this morning. Instead, I'm going to fly down to the beach in a couple of hours and take Philip with me. We'll be back early Tuesday, and if there is a warrant, he'll surrender himself."

"Good thinking, my boy. What about bail?"

"Way ahead of you. Sometime later this morning, Chase Williams of Merrill Lynch will have funds wired to our trust account. I've advised him to contact you if there's any problem with the wire or if he needs anything. You know how to reach me at the beach, of course."

"How much?"

"Half a million."

"That should be more than enough for bail and retainer. I may give Chase a call anyway—he and I have done some business together in the past. Did you have anything scheduled this morning?"

"Nothing important enough that it can't be rescheduled. After we finish talking, I'm going to leave some instructions for Rosemary with respect to that. Speaking of instructions, I've given Richard marching orders to drop everything and work on this case. His informant says that the police have stopped looking for anybody else. Have I overlooked anything?"

"Not that I can see. Do you need anything else from me?"

"Just some advice. You might want to begin thinking about who we can ask to handle the actual defense. Mark might be a good choice."

"I expect you will do that quite well enough."

"That would be true enough, perhaps, if I weren't involved with the client."

"Of course you're involved, you're his attorney."

"No, I mean emotionally involved. It seems you played the role of Yenta entirely too well."

He gave a slight chuckle. "Really?"

"So it would seem. I'm still sorting it all out."

"I really wouldn't worry about any conflict. You're quite capable of being as detached as you need to be. Moreover, you know it, so don't go getting all humble on me now."

"If you think so. I had to lay all the cards on the table, you know how it is."

"Anything else?"

"Not at the moment. I've got a number of calls to make before we leave, so I'll let you go. I'll see you Tuesday morning." Then I remembered something "Actually, there is one more thing. We left the club last night via the back entrance in my car—in case he was being watched. His car is still there." I turned to Philip. "What would you like done with it, Philip?"

Philip said, "Can you have it sent to Morehouse Motors? It's due for servicing, and I can call them later and give appropriate instructions."

"Consider it done," Andrew said.

We said our goodbyes and hung up. Philip looked at me with a raised eyebrow. "What was that all about?"

"What was what all about?"

"The part about not wanting to represent me."

"Oh, that. Well, you see, the canon of ethics frowns upon attorneys representing spouses, lovers, sweethearts, or anyone with whom they have an involvement. An involvement is thought to impair judgment in a trial. To put it crudely, if I'm sleeping with you, I shouldn't be representing you."

"Andrew didn't seem to be particularly concerned."

"No, he didn't, did he?"

"Well, if he isn't worried about any conflict, I certainly won't be."

"Fine, but I had to lay all the cards on the table, so to speak. While I make a call, why don't you draw a diagram of your condo and where to find the prescription you need."

I handed him a yellow pad and pen. Then I punched the speakerphone again and dialed the office dictation system. A mechanical voice answered and spat out instructions I didn't really need, so I punched in a bypass code that would allow me to leave instructions that only my secretary would be able to retrieve. I dictated her marching orders for the day and hung up.

"I do love toys," I said.

"I can tell."

Richard wandered into the room just then, obviously dressed for work. "Cadet Greene reporting for instructions as ordered, Sir." He clicked his heels and saluted.

"Richard, you know as well as I do what needs to be done. First, however, you need to retrieve Philip's prescription for him."

Philip gave him the sheet with the address and diagram and then excused himself to go and retrieve his keys from the bedroom.

Richard eyed me critically and said, "Are we in love?"

"Ass over teakettle."

"I was afraid of that. Does he know? Is it reciprocal? Are the two of you going to set up housekeeping, etcetera?"

"1) He has reason to suspect; 2) I don't know; and 3) Ditto. It's much too early to tell. Besides, that's the least of my worries at the moment."

"Well, you can give me the unexpurgated version next week. I just hope you aren't setting yourself up to get hurt."

"I'm not worried. Even if it goes nowhere and is over tomorrow, it will have served a purpose in that I have, how did you put it last night? 'Returned to the land of the living.'"

"Just so you know what you're about." He started to say something else but stopped as we heard Philip coming down the hall.

"This is the key to the deadbolt and the door," Philip said, handing a brass key to Richard, "and I've written down the code for the alarm system—the pad is just inside the entrance."

I added, "Take my car, please—it's much less conspicuous—and watch out for Atlanta's finest. They may be watching."

Richard nodded, all business again, and left.

"Okay," I said. "Let's go find you some suitable weekend-at-the-beach attire."

We spent some time in my closet, discovering that he could wear my underwear, shorts, and shirts, and Robert's slacks were a perfect fit. That left shoes.

"What size shoe do you wear?"

"Ten D," he said.

"That's a half size smaller than mine, but no problem, because it happened to be Robert's size, and I gave all of his shoes to Richard."

I went to Richard's room and found a decent pair of deck shoes that would do. When I was back in the master bedroom, I said, "Where we're going, these will be more than enough. You can bring your shoes from last night in case we go out or anything."

"Will it bother you, seeing someone else wearing Robert's clothing?"

"Not if you're that someone."

There was a knock on the open door—I hadn't heard Richard return.

"Trouble in Dodge, bossman," he said, and he continued, "I spotted the proverbial unmarked sedan parked right across the street from Philip's place. I recognized one of the plainclothes guys."

"Did they spot you?"

"Not very likely. I saw them first and just drove on by." He handed Philip his keys.

"Okay," I said. "We switch to Plan B. Philip, do you know your doctor well enough that you can call his office from the airport, tell them you're out of town without your prescription, and ask them to phone one to a drugstore in Fort Walton Beach?"

"That shouldn't be a problem."

"Fine. Then we're off. Richard, I trust you'll have a short list of prime suspects by the time we get back."

"Well," Richard said, "as you know, the Hebrew children were able to make bricks without straw, but I can't conduct an investigation without information."

"I'll call the office from the car and dictate all of the particulars you need while we're on the way to the airport. Rosemary will have it transcribed for you later this morning."

Philip followed me back to the study and watched while I dialed Information and asked for the number of a CVS Pharmacy in Fort Walton Beach, which I jotted down on a memo pad. I handed the piece of paper to him, then we carried our stuff to the car, and I drove us to the airport in suburban Marietta.

7

Philip

IN THE car, traveling west toward the interstate with Lance curled up in the backseat, I watched as Charles pulled a BlackBerry out of his pocket and punched some numbers after hooking a Bluetooth set over his ear. He glanced at me and winked.

"I know," I said. "You like your toys."

"I dialed the main office number first," he said, "because there's a good possibility that my secretary will be at work by now—she prefers coming in early to staying late." He said into the phone, "Hi, Roger. You're an early bird. Has Rosemary come in yet? ... Great, I'll hold."

He turned to me and said, "We're in luck, she's already at her desk." He paused, obviously interrupted by something being said to him.

"Hi there. Glad to see you on the job so early. ... Yes, I know, the early bird and all that. Have you played back the overnight memoranda? ... Good, then I won't have to explain much to you. I'm on the way to the airport now with my client, and I have some notes to dictate for Richard when you're ready."

To me, he said, "I'm going to go over all of the particulars as we discussed them last night. Feel free to interrupt with any changes or additions. Okay?"

"Sure."

"Okay, Rosemary, here we go. To Richard Greene, etcetera, etcetera, regarding the d'Autremont case, blah blah blah. You know what blanks to fill in."

He continued at a rapid rate, repeating, as best as I could tell, virtually everything I'd told him the night before, continuing with some more detailed facts.

"Mr. and Mrs. d'Autremont resided on West Paces Ferry Road, the address is...." He looked a question at me, and I told him. "Got that? ... Good. Mrs. d'Autremont maintained a condo at...." This time, he handed me the phone, and I gave the address. Taking the phone back, he continued, "Mr. d'Autremont also maintained a condo, but you already have that address. Whatever you do, do *not* go anywhere near any of those addresses until next week, after the arraignment. There'll be plenty of time for you to gain legal access to both the residence and her condo. For now, your main objective, as I see it, is to locate Mrs. d'Autremont's lover. Without a name or description, I realize that there isn't much to go on, but it appears that we're looking for a dominating, jealous type, probably very butch, maybe even the quintessential bull dyke. You will no doubt be pub-crawling tonight, so you can combine business with pleasure. Call me at the beach house if you have any questions—we should be there by lunchtime. One more thing that I failed to mention last night or this morning: under no circumstances are you or any of your grunts to even attempt to trace Philip's movements for that weekend. This is nonnegotiable, and if you want to know why, talk to Andrew and he'll brief you."

He looked at me and said, "Anything you want to add to that?"

"Not that I can think of."

"Good. Rosemary, got all that? ... Okay, then run with it, and I'll talk to you later. Bye." He pushed a button on the BlackBerry and returned it to his pocket.

"Was she recording all that or using shorthand?"

"Shorthand, why?"

"I've never seen anyone dictate quite that rapidly."

"Well, Rosemary is special. Did you ever see *Auntie Mame*?"

"A long time ago, and more recently on cable."

"In that case, you must remember Agnes Gooch, Auntie Mame's 'sponge', to whom she dictated her memoirs. Rosemary is Agnes personified, only she comes complete with personality and looks, and while Agnes could only take dictation at 120 words per minute, Rosemary can handle 140."

We were now on I-75 North. We'd just crossed under the I-285 beltway around Atlanta and were approaching Marietta. Charles took us down a number of side roads in an area with which I was totally unfamiliar, finally bringing the car to a stop in a parking lot at a small airport. The plane turned out to be a twin-engine Cessna capable of seating six, plus pilot and copilot. Currently, Charles explained, the passenger seats were missing, as they were being reupholstered. Lance, without waiting to be told, hopped into the rear passenger compartment and allowed himself to be shut up in a traveling cage, which I later learned was called a crate. Not knowing what else to do, I simply did what I was told and sat in the copilot's seat when instructed to do so. As we taxied down the runway, I listened to him chat with the local tower and, after we were in the air, an air traffic controller located at some distant point, probably Hartsfield Airport, for all I knew. Most of the talk was in a technical jargon that made little sense to me. Charles was obviously expert at it and was totally concentrating upon the task of flying, so I distracted myself by watching the ground below. When flying, I'm endlessly fascinated by the view of earth from high in the air. Unfortunately, commercial airliners fly at such high altitudes that small details on the ground are obscured by distance. At the lower altitudes used by small planes, the ground is close enough to view in infinite detail.

"Fascinating, isn't it?"

I snapped back from the window, not quite certain what I'd heard, and said, "What?"

"The ground. It's almost hypnotic, watching it."

"For sure, especially from this height, as opposed to a commercial flight," I said, echoing my earlier musings.

"Is this your first time in a small plane?"

"Yes."

"Sorry to ignore you earlier. In about fifteen minutes I can turn the flying over to Homer, and we can talk."

"Homer?"

"The autopilot. I call it Homer."

"Because it always takes you home?"

"Good-looking and smart too," he said with a smile.

I turned to the window again, lost in thought for some time. After a while, the radio began to crackle, and Charles again started talking to a controller. I finally heard him say, "Thank you, Atlanta, over and out."

I asked him, "How long have you been flying?"

"Well, I learned to fly as a teenager and then didn't use my skills again until about five or six years ago. After Robert died, I was able to buy this plane—before that I had to rent them." He paused and looked at me thoughtfully before he continued, "Having said that, perhaps I should explain. When we bought the townhouse, we were both just starting out, and the mortgage company required term life insurance on both of us with them as beneficiary. Later, we also took out fairly substantial policies with each other as the beneficiary, so when he died, the townhouse was paid for, and I was left with sufficient funds to indulge this hobby. Understand this: I'd much rather have had him alive than have the ability to purchase this plane, but it simply didn't turn out that way. Actually, my income is more than sufficient for me to have bought this plane a long time ago, with financing, of course. It's just that I have this thing about debt and always resisted the urge."

"Well, I'm no judge, but you're obviously in your element."

"I take her up every chance I get, which is fairly often, as I also use the plane for business. It's nice to be able to take a partial tax write-off for flying clients here and there on short hops. Come to think of it, I can technically charge most of this trip as a business expense. It's also, now that I think of it, a perfect opportunity to try something that I've always wanted to do."

"What's that?"

"You'll see just as soon as I'm able to turn the flying over to Homer."

He didn't elaborate, so I turned to the window, still fascinated by the world below. After a while, the radio began to crackle again, and I heard more jargon.

"Great, now I can leave the driving to Homer," Charles said to me.

I looked over at him just in time to see him fiddling with some controls.

He looked at me, grinned, and said, "Ain't technology wonderful? Homer can fly this plane on a straighter course than I ever could."

I couldn't think of a reply.

Then he unstrapped himself from the pilot's seat, got up, and went back to the passenger area. This made me more than a little nervous, but I sat quietly and watched as he opened a compartment at the rear and produced a large quilted comforter. This he proceeded to fold over and spread out on the floor. For the first time, I noticed that the floor was carpeted, but there were gaps where the missing seats had obviously been bolted in place. Without saying anything, he sat down on the blanket and started taking his clothes off.

"What *are* you doing?" I said. This was getting bizarre.

"Something I've always wanted to do," he said with an infectious grin. "Sex in an airplane. It's time I joined the mile-high club." By this time he was totally naked, lying back propped up on his elbows and looking at me.

"You're crazy," I said. "Even with Homer, shouldn't you be in your seat?"

"No need for that. We're outside commercial traffic lanes, thousands of feet below where those boys fly. And we're being watched over by controllers—the radio will let me know if they spot anything. Besides, this plane has a radar system that will alert me if anything bigger than an eagle comes within ten miles of us." As he spoke, he lay back and used his hands to give himself an erection.

"I'm not sure about this," I said.

"Come on. Where's your sense of adventure?"

"On the ground, where yours ought to be."

"This won't take long. We have plenty of time before I have to report to the controllers in the Pensacola area. Come on, indulge me."

Needless to say, I indulged him. It was hard to resist an attractive, well-muscled, naked body that was already primed for my attention—especially in light of how I realized I was beginning to feel about this man. In my defense, I will add that I didn't allow the "adventure" to be dragged out too long. We were dressed and back in our respective seats twenty minutes later, and sat quietly for a while.

"Wasn't that great?" he said finally.

"Well, it was certainly different." I wasn't going to encourage him.

"Come on, you can do better than that."

"Fishing for compliments, are we?"

"Shamelessly."

"Well, as a one-time experience, it was interesting, but I was too nervous to fully appreciate it."

Any further comment he might have had was cut off by the radio, and for the next few minutes he was busy receiving instructions and, shortly thereafter, permission to land. We landed at a small airport near Fort Walton Beach and picked up the rental car he'd reserved. Evidently Lance was familiar with the drill, because he followed Charles obediently to the rental counter, and when Charles opened the door of the rental car, the dog took over the backseat as his own.

The city of Fort Walton Beach appeared to mostly consist of, as far as I could tell, one continuous strip of businesses, motels, and restaurants. We finally turned off the strip, crossed the Intracoastal Waterway, and headed east on a road that paralleled the beach. At first we passed a seemingly endless strip of beachside motels, but the motels finally gave way to an area of beach homes and cottages of all shapes and sizes. Eventually, we turned off the road, went up a short asphalt drive, and stopped at a fair-sized three-story structure, the first floor of which, Charles explained, consisted of a two-car garage, storage, and utility areas. I could see that the second floor had decks cantilevered from three sides, and the house was covered with cedar siding, which had been allowed to weather naturally.

Charles led me up to the second floor, which was revealed to be one open living and dining area separated by an island from the kitchen. There were four barstools at the island. Sliding glass doors opened to the deck on three sides of the living area, and the kitchen was across the back of the house. An exposed flight of stairs led to the bedrooms, of which I learned there were four, the two largest having private baths, the other two sharing a common bath. In addition, there was a small shower room off the kitchen that opened onto stairs leading down to ground level and the beach.

The house had a musty smell, for which Charles apologized. Lance appeared to regard this house as his territory and bounded off on his own pursuits—but not before Charles had located, rinsed out, and filled a water bowl for him. "I forgot to call the caretaker and tell him to come over and open the house," he said, obviously annoyed with himself at this omission.

"That's all right," I said. "It'll air out in a hurry."

"Right you are. Make yourself at home."

Charles

I STARTED around the room, opening some of the patio doors so that the sea breeze could air things out; then I went to the phone on the counter and dialed the office, punching in Rosemary's direct number. When she picked up, I let her know that all was well at the beach and determined that there were no messages from Richard. I wasn't particularly interested in any other items at the moment. Turning to Philip, who'd walked over to stand beside me, I said, "You probably just have time to call your doctor before he closes up shop for lunch."

"Right," he said, going to the telephone. He dialed a number, spoke to a nurse, told her he was out of town sans pills, and extracted a promise to have the prescription called to a pharmacy here in Fort Walton Beach.

The rest of the day somehow evaporated out from under us. I found two pairs of Speedos in a dresser drawer, and we tried the Gulf, which was rather cold for late May. Lance, true to his genes, was at home in the water and loved to play in it. Philip and I lay in the sun for a while, took a long, leisurely walk on the beach, then cleaned up and dressed in shorts, T-shirts, and deck shoes. The only problem was getting a long-haired dog clean after a romp in the sand and salt water. I checked the larder and made a shopping list, and we headed to a shopping center to stock up on supplies, stopping by the pharmacy on the way to pick up Philip's prescription. While he was at the prescription counter, I purchased a supply of Trojans and a tube of K-Y—after three years of abstinence, I was thinking "sex" again.

It was late afternoon when we returned, just in time to grill some steaks on the deck and watch the sunset while we consumed them. Philip helped me clean up the kitchen afterward, and it all seemed very cozy, domestic, and extremely comfortable. He shooed me back out to the deck while he finished in the kitchen and appeared on deck a few minutes later with a drink in each hand. He handed me mine and said, "You look lost in thought."

It wasn't really a question, but an answer seemed necessary, so I said, "I was just thinking that I've never brought anybody to this house before. Robert and I came here, and his sister Lydia frequently joined us, occasionally with a date in tow, but that's all. Richard has never even been here."

"That seems strange, considering how long you two have known each other."

"I don't know why he never came here, I guess we never got around to issuing an invitation. Also, in the beginning, Richard was very uncomfortable around Robert and me. I suppose Robert and I thought of it as 'our' place and were somewhat loath to share it. Lydia was a special case."

"Does she come here still?"

"Oh yes. Robert and I owned it as joint tenants with right of survivorship, but after he died, I deeded his half-interest over to Lydia, and she and I divide the holidays. I get Memorial Day, she gets the Fourth of July, and we sometimes draw straws for Labor Day. Other times, my secretary keeps a calendar, and if I want to plan a trip down here, I sign up for a time slot. When Lydia wants to come, she calls Rosemary and has her pencil in the dates. It's been a satisfactory arrangement, and we have yet to select the same dates. Even if we did, there's ample room here for several people without crowding."

"Are you sensing the presence of ghosts?"

"Not really." He was still standing beside the chaise lounge with a drink in his hand. I pulled him down to sit beside me. "Understand this, please. There are no ghosts, at least not any with which you'll ever have to compete, but there are lots of memories, all of them good ones. There have been times when I've had trouble dealing with them, but those times are coming less frequently. I expect that with a little help from you, I'll be able to deal with anything." Having said that, I sat up beside him and kissed him thoroughly.

After I released him, he stifled a yawn and said, "Sorry, but I'm bushed."

"Me too. What say we lock up and climb the well-worn stairs?"

"Sounds good to me."

I locked up and turned out the lights, leaving only a small night-light in the kitchen. We went upstairs, and I said, "Do you think we need the A/C turned on?"

"Not unless you want it on. The sea breeze is great."

We made love again and eventually fell asleep fitted together like two spoons.

Waking up Saturday turned out to be an instant replay of Friday morning, except it took place two hours or so later. This time I allowed myself to remember what it was like to wake up with someone. I lay there, savoring it, and let the tears flow quietly for a few minutes. Soon, Philip started to stir and eventually woke up. He'd been sleeping with his arms wrapped around me from behind. He stretched his head around from behind me and kissed my cheek. He must have noticed that it was damp, for he unwrapped one arm and touched my cheek with his fingers.

"What's this? Have you been crying?"

"I'm sorry. I woke up and started thinking about how very long it had been since I woke up with someone. The same thing very nearly happened yesterday morning, but I got out of bed before it could start." I turned over on my side to face him. He started to say something, but I put a finger to his lips. "Let me finish. It's very strange. At first I was sad... remembering. Then I was happy because you're here to wake up with now. That seemed to make me misty-eyed as well. You're bringing out all sorts of feelings in me, many of them ones that I never really expected to feel again. I really don't know what's gotten into me. I *never* lose my composure—I was brought up believing it simply was not done, at least not in front of anyone. It's only happened once before since I was a child, and that was the day before Robert's funeral."

"Surely you must have to let go once in a while."

"Yes, but I have my own way of dealing with it."

"How?"

"I take a long shower and shed whatever tears are necessary while the water runs over me—I've no idea what a Freudian would make of that. As for this morning, as I said, you're bringing things out in me that have been long suppressed."

"I'm sorry."

"Please don't be. I sense that you are very good for me, and look forward to more of the same."

"Well, I expect you'll tire of me eventually."

"Don't count on it. Speaking of showers, it's time to get up and face the day."

9

Philip

IN THE bathroom, we got into the large stall shower together and began to soap each other's bodies. Charles turned me so my back was to him and said, "Did I ever tell you that you have the best ass I've ever seen?"

"Not that I recall."

"Well, you certainly do."

We moved from the bathroom to the bed, where we spent a pleasant hour. Neither of us seemed to have much to say at that point, our bodies having said it all, and neither of us seemed to be willing to admit that we couldn't stay in bed any longer.

I finally broke the silence, asking, "Didn't you tell me that you run regularly?"

"I probably did, and I certainly do. As a matter of fact, I run early every morning, weather permitting, and when it doesn't permit, I try to make it up in the evening."

"Great, because so do I. Do you suppose you could find us some suitable shorts?"

He thought a minute and said, "I usually bring that sort of thing with me, but I think this time I forgot. However, there ought to be some around here somewhere. If not, the Speedos will certainly do—we lack the proper shoes, though."

"Can't we run barefoot on the beach? We ought to be able to log a few miles."

He could see that I was serious, so he said, "I'm certainly game." He got up, rummaged around in the closet, and managed to produce suitable running shorts for both of us.

After we were outside, I said, "Do you have any particular route that you use when you're here?"

"Well," he said, "it's about five miles down to where the strip of motels begins. We could run down and walk back."

"It's ten o'clock now, so that will get us back here in time for lunch."

"Which we ought to enjoy, since we skipped breakfast."

"Is that a complaint?"

"No, just a passing comment. I'll certainly take a morning in bed with you in lieu of breakfast anytime." With that, we were off, Lance bounding ahead of us.

Charles and I ran at a steady but not tiring pace, about ten minutes to the mile, I guessed. We ran in silence, each lost in our own thoughts, until we reached the first of the motels, turned, and started back. A few minutes after the turn, I said, "My feet are telling me that it's time to stop and walk. I'm not used to this kind of uneven surface, not to mention running barefoot."

"Mine too," he said.

"How far do you usually run?"

"I try to get in six or eight miles, and once in a while I bump it up to ten. It really depends on how early I get up and how I feel on any given day. How about you?"

"Six miles is about my usual limit, although I've never really pushed myself to see how much more I could achieve."

We lapsed into small talk for the rest of our walk back to the house. When we got there, we went up a side stairway to the little shower room. By this time we were pretty much cooled down from our run. After we'd washed the sand and salt out of Lance's fur, we dried him off and let him into the kitchen. Then we got a little playful in the shower while washing the sand off each other. So much so, in fact, that we dried off, threw our towels over our shoulders, and stepped naked into the kitchen. We were both on the way to becoming fully tumescent. We walked hand in hand around the counter and into the living area. Before we reached the stairs, we came face to face with a man and a woman sitting on the sofa. Lance had his head in the woman's lap, and she was petting him. The woman appeared to be in her late twenties, had red hair, and was quite pretty; her companion, whom I judged to be a little older than she, was not unattractive. They both stood when they saw us. I dropped Charles's hand as though it were scalding hot, grabbed the towel from my shoulder, and frantically wrapped it around my waist. He didn't even break his stride but walked straight over to the woman and gave her a long hug and a brief kiss.

"Lydia," he said, "what a pleasant surprise. It is so good to see you—it's been much too long."

She laughed and said, "Well, it's always good to see you too, although I certainly didn't expect to see quite so much of you. In fact, I really didn't expect to see you at all—I thought you weren't coming down this weekend."

Charles, not in the least nonplussed at having been reminded of his nudity, his semi-erection mercifully having subsided, wrapped his towel around himself and seemed not to have heard her last remark. "Well, we've just been on a run down the beach, walked back, and were heading upstairs to dress. Lydia, I want you to meet my friend Philip d'Autremont." He looked at me and said, "Philip, this is Lydia, Robert's sister."

We shook hands, and she finally remembered her companion, who seemed to be trying to make himself invisible. "Charles and Philip, this is Harry Bronson," she said, completing the introductions.

Charles took charge of the situation. Looking at Lydia, he said, "We have a great deal to catch up on, but first Philip and I should go up and get dressed. I trust you and Harry haven't had lunch."

"No, we just got in from Tallahassee," she said.

"Good, then I'll impose on you. How about going into the kitchen and getting creative? We went shopping yesterday afternoon, so there's plenty of everything." Without waiting for her reply, he took my hand and led me upstairs—which was probably a good idea, because my feet seemed to have become rooted to the floor.

When we were back in the bedroom, he said, "Come on in the

bathroom and talk to me while I shave. You look as though you're in shock."

"No kidding. I'm not used to parading in front of a pair of total strangers of either sex while sporting what amounts to a half erection, although it didn't seem to bother you particularly."

"Lydia has seen me naked before. She frequently joined Robert and me down here with a date, and the four of us would invariably skinny-dip in the Gulf. It's no big deal."

I didn't have an answer for that. By this time I was perched on the bathroom counter and he was busy shaving—something we hadn't done after our earlier shower. "It's too bad she got mixed up about the weekend," I said, quickly adding, "but it won't bother me if she and her boyfriend want to share the house with us until Tuesday."

"He's not her boyfriend, and she certainly didn't get mixed up about the dates."

"Why do you say that?"

He put the razor down and started counting his fingers, beginning with the little one. "1) He's not her type; 2) Lydia never forgot anything in her life; 3) Least of all our respective schedules concerning use of this house; and 4) Harry is as queer as a three-dollar bill."

"Are you sure?" It all sounded strange to me.

He finished shaving, washed the dregs of lather from his face, and resumed the count. "5) In case you didn't notice anything else about him, you must have noticed that he was practically salivating at the sight of our naked bodies."

"I was too busy covering up my own naked body to pay much attention."

"Well, I noticed the signals loud and clear, which leads me to conclude that, 6) It would seem that Lydia has decided that it's her turn to play Yenta. My guess is that Harry is a sacrificial lamb enticed down here to seduce me." He pulled me off the counter and kissed me. "They're forty-eight hours too late, so Harry will have to learn to live with disappointment—not that he would have been successful."

"How can you be sure of that?"

"Better men than he have tried and failed. You can't imagine the number and variety of eligible studs that well-meaning friends have thrown at me over the past three years. None of them had what it took."

"And what, pray tell, was that?"

"Your eyes."

"Is that all?" I was fishing for more and not ashamed to let it be known.

"No, but I don't want you getting all smug on me." He grazed my cheek with his lips. "Now, get rid of that stubble and let's go down and visit."

I quickly completed my ablutions and returned to the bedroom to find him already dressed in shorts and a polo shirt. Taking a cue from Charles, I dressed similarly, and we descended the stairs as we had ascended them—hand in hand.

We found Harry sitting at one of the barstools, chatting across the counter with Lydia, who appeared to be nearly finished with her assigned task of laying out lunch. The counter already held a platter of cold cuts, cheese, and other condiments very prettily arranged, as well as a large bowl filled with potato chips. An opened loaf of multi-grain bread was beside the platter, and Lance was sitting next to the counter in a begging pose, waiting for a handout.

Charles walked around the counter and gave Lydia another hug and kiss. "It really is good to see you, even if we had to fly down here to do it."

"Well, you know what my schedule is like in Atlanta—it's probably as bad as yours, perhaps even worse."

He gave her an easy grin. "Maybe our respective secretaries should pencil some visits into our calendars."

She gave him a somewhat stern look. "I've called you any number of times in the last six months, but you never seem to be at home."

"I'm sorry about that," he answered, giving her a mock hangdog look. "I'm nearly always home these days, but I've been such a moody bitch lately that I simply haven't answered the telephone very often."

The stern look dissolved into one of concern, and she said, "Charles, you really must get out of your shell. You can't keep up this self-imposed exile from life forever."

He looked pointedly at me and said, "That's very good advice, and it has already been taken. I rejoined the world Thursday evening."

She saw the look he gave me, and her expression became temporarily unreadable. Then she said, "It's about time." Before he could say anything else, she looked at her handiwork on the counter and announced, "Lunch, I think, is ready. Where shall we take it?"

He thought about it for half a second and said, "It's so nice outside, why don't we move the table out onto the deck? Philip, can you give me a hand?"

I followed him to a corner of the living area and helped him move a small table out to the deck. Harry, unbidden, started bringing the matching chairs out as well. Lydia brought up the rear, her arms laden with the tray of food, bowl of chips, and another tray containing bread, small plates, and utensils. I was sent back in to round up glasses, ice, and beverages, and in short order we were all busy assembling sandwiches.

Conversation over lunch was mostly trivial. Charles and Lydia obviously had a lot to catch up on, but they managed rather deftly to involve both Harry and myself in the conversation. I learned during lunch that Lydia was a clinical psychologist, and one of her specialties was working with abused children. Her parents lived in Tallahassee, and she'd spent the previous day and night visiting them. Harry, it seemed, also resided in Tallahassee and had known Lydia for some time, although in what capacity was left unsaid. Now that I was over the shock of them catching us naked, my gaydar had started working again, and I recognized Harry as family.

Lydia apologized for having "forgotten" that Charles was going to be at the beach this weekend.

He made no reference to the conclusions that he'd already drawn concerning her presence and simply said, "Now that you're here, there's no reason for you not to stay. Philip and I are in my usual bedroom. The rest of upstairs is up for grabs." They accepted as gracefully as possible, under the circumstances.

Lydia asked about our plans for dinner. Charles replied that we'd purchased steaks the day before, were planning to grill them this evening, and he and I could run to the market for a couple more.

She would have none of that and said, "Nonsense. Harry and I can run down to the store and take care of that. I need to pick up a couple of things anyhow." We had, by this time, cleared the table and carried the remains of lunch back into the kitchen. A few minutes later, they were in her car and on their way to the store.

Charles walked over to the stool I was sitting on, kissed me thoroughly, and said, "Want to go upstairs and pick up where we left off earlier in the shower, big boy?"

"That's the best offer I've had all day," I said, and this time I took him by the hand and led the way upstairs. We spent a leisurely half hour in bed and had just gotten dressed and walked back downstairs when we heard Lydia's car pull up.

10

Philip

THE four of us spent a pleasant afternoon on the beach, alternately swimming and lying in the sun. By seven, Charles had set up a grill on the deck and was overseeing the steaks. Lydia had bought baking potatoes, which had been in the oven for some time, and she'd taken charge in the kitchen. Harry and I tried to make ourselves useful but finally wound up in deck chairs making small talk with Charles while he tended the grill.

By the time we were at the table attacking the steaks, we'd all managed to consume two or three drinks apiece and were beginning to feel them. That, coming after an afternoon of sun and surf and generally getting acquainted, had dissolved the tension that had been almost palpable before and during lunch. All of which might account for Charles looking at me and saying, "Did I tell you that Lydia was an absolute Rock of Gibraltar for me after Robert died?"

"Not that I can recall."

"Well, by way of background, their parents are dyed-in-the-wool Southern Baptists and literally cut off all contact with Robert after he came out to them. By the time he died, they'd neither seen him nor attempted to establish any form of contact with him for six or seven years. Lydia, of course, saw the both of us two or three times a week." He paused for a moment.

"The morning after Robert died, I asked her to notify their parents at least as a courtesy, which was something that neither she nor Robert had wanted to happen. He'd known for some time that his tumor was terminal, and we'd talked about his wishes at length. He was adamant that since they'd cut him off in life, they didn't deserve any consideration afterward, and she tended to more or less agree. My grandmother raised me to do the right thing always, so I talked Lydia into notifying them." He stopped for another minute, apparently lost in recollection.

Finally, he continued, "She brought them by the townhouse late in the afternoon the day before the funeral. Gran had unexpectedly dropped by about a half hour earlier and was still there, and it was a very awkward moment for all of us. They weren't there very long before Mr. Brannon made it clear that he and his wife intended to, as he put it, 'take their boy home for burial in the family plot'. Somehow I summoned up the courage to tell him that they would do no such thing. Mr. Brannon informed me that they were his parents, blood kin, if you will, and since I was a total stranger I had no say in the matter."

This time Charles paused for a very long time, so I decided to prompt him, saying, "What did you say to that?"

This got him started again, and he said, "I told him that they were very wrong. Robert and I had executed mutual wills, including powers of attorney and other legal documents giving each other the absolute right to act if something should happen to one of us. We had by then lost a great many friends to AIDS and at least twice had seen families of deceased friends barge onto the scene and take charge, totally and legally excluding the lover of the deceased from any say in either the funeral arrangements or the disposition of effects. One of them had even been barred from attending the funeral services. I believe I said something like 'Robert really didn't want you to be here, considering your treatment of him over these last years, and Lydia was also reluctant to call you, but I insisted that you should, as a matter of common courtesy, be told. Understand, however, that you are here on sufferance, and I will not allow you to interfere. The funeral and burial will take place according to Robert's wishes, and I'm well equipped to go to court to see to it that those wishes are adhered to. Period.'"

"That must have been quite a scene," I said before he could continue. "What happened then?"

"Well, Mr. Brannon seemed to think I was bluffing, and I suspect he thought that he could bulldoze his way past any of my objections, saying they would be glad to settle things in court. When he ran out of steam for a moment, I reminded him of the publicity that any legal action would produce, pointing out that the papers in his hometown would have a field day. I further reminded him that any legal proceedings would be a matter of public record, and there would be absolutely no way to prevent all of their friends from knowing about their fight with a gay man in Atlanta over their deceased son's body. I don't think he believed me, and he made a comment to the effect that publicity could cut both ways. I told him that was fine with me, because everyone in my law firm had both known and liked Robert, and all of them would be at the funeral the next day."

"I'll bet that stopped him cold."

"Not quite. He started to make noises again, and that's when Gran entered the fray, so to speak. Then, as now, she cut quite an imposing figure. Robert used to refer to her privately as 'the dowager duchess of Buckhead'. She got our attention by rapping her cane loudly on the hardwood floor and said something like 'Be quiet, you silly little man.' I don't think Lydia's father had ever been spoken to in quite that manner, but he was smart enough to know when he was both outranked and outclassed. Gran made quite an impromptu speech, reminding Mr. and Mrs. Brannon that Robert had lived in her home for several summers and that in later years she'd been a frequent visitor in our home. The gist of her remarks was that in her many years of living, she had never observed two people more suited to each other than Robert and me.

"Mrs. Brannon then asked Gran point-blank if she wouldn't have preferred that I had married and had children. Her answer caught them both off guard, I think, for she said that she would have much preferred me married and producing great-grandchildren. Furthermore, she said that she knew that both Robert and I would have preferred that kind of life as well. Then she reminded them that though she was old and from a different generation, she was also extremely well educated and well-informed enough to know that these things are not matters of individual choice. She even reminded them that experts now agree that sexual identity is established well before the onset of puberty. As I said, it wasn't an answer that they'd expected.

"Gran subsided for a moment, and before anything else could be said, Lydia jumped in. She said to her parents, 'You have no idea what Robert's life was like, and I think it is time that you found out.' She asked me to find a video that she had taken two summers before down here at the beach. There was only one video to which she could have been referring, so I went to the study and found the copy she'd made for Robert and me. I brought it to her, and she asked me to play it for them. We all went upstairs to my study and watched the video." He stopped again.

"What was on the video?" I said.

He'd lapsed into silence, so Lydia replied. "About thirty minutes of Charles, Robert, and me at the beach. I'd just gotten a new camcorder and was trying it out down here one weekend. I managed to catch a number of candid shots of the two of them at odd moments, both separately and together. I'd brought a date that weekend, and he took a number of shots of the three of us. Even the most hardened cynic would have known, seeing them together on that video, just what they meant to each other, but the final scene was the clincher. It was a close-up of Robert asleep on one of the chaise lounges. Somehow, I managed to get Charles in the shot as he slipped up behind Robert, bent down, and kissed him on the forehead. That caused Robert to wake up and look around to see what had disturbed his sleep. When he saw Charles, who'd knelt down beside the lounge, he smiled at him with a look of absolute serenity and happiness. The last shot shows both of them lost in each other, and I froze the screen on that final image. By that time, Mama was crying, both Charles and I were on the brink, and Daddy looked very embarrassed.

"I was also angry as hell and said, 'Mama, you saw that video. It should be perfectly obvious to you that Robert was happy with this man, happier than any human being has any right to expect to be. You and Daddy lost Robert years ago by your own choice, although you could have made up for that at any time, had you chosen to do so. Now you've lost your son permanently, and if you make trouble at this late date, you'll lose a daughter as well.' Mama wanted to know what I meant by that. I told her that I would never speak to either of them again if they tried in any way to prevent Charles from carrying out Robert's last wishes. She looked at Daddy, who had once again started to make angry noises, and said, 'Sidney, shut up. She's right. Even you must have seen that he was happy. She also means what she says, I can see that too.' Then she looked at Charles and said simply, 'Thank you for asking us to come, we're grateful, and there will be no trouble.' Somehow we got through that evening, although things were a little tense when we went to the funeral home to receive visitors. The casket was closed, and Charles was adamant that it remain so. Viewing the remains is a strong tradition in the deep South, but I've always found it barbaric. Robert had shared that view, as did Charles, and that was that as far as I was concerned. They were very quiet at the funeral mass the next day, which was held at St. Philip's Cathedral. Neither of them had ever, to my knowledge, been to an Episcopal service of any kind and were a little uneasy in those surroundings. They were quite taken aback when I went to the altar rail with Charles to receive communion, as I'd never told them that I had converted.

"They went with us to Mrs. Barnett's home after the services, and I could see that Mama was grappling with her inner conflicts. Both she and Daddy were a bit overwhelmed at the surroundings—I don't know if you've seen her home, but it's in Buckhead and positively reeks of both class and old money—and were smart enough to know when they were out of their solid middle-class element, so to speak. Later that day, I drove them back to Tallahassee, and Mama only asked me for one thing—she wanted a photo made from the last scene on the videotape."

Lydia paused before continuing, "There's an epilogue to the story, as well. A few months later, Mama withdrew from the Baptist church and started attending a little Episcopal church near where they live. She's really quite bitter about her upbringing and blames the Baptists for her having missed out on any part of the last seven years of her son's life."

I don't know what possessed me to do it, but I said, "That must have been some videotape. I'd certainly like to see it sometime."

She smiled. "You can see it right now, if you like. I was feeling kind of blue last spring and needed to be reminded of happier times, so I brought a copy of it down here over the Easter holiday and watched it myself for the first time since the funeral. It's upstairs in my bedroom." She looked at Charles. "Do you mind?"

"No," he said, slowly, "I don't think so."

He sounded reluctant, so I said, "Are you sure?"

"Yes, it's all right. I haven't looked at my copy of that video since the funeral; perhaps it's time."

Charles, Harry, and I cleared the remains of dinner and put things away while Lydia went to her room and retrieved the video. When we were finished, we went to the living area and sat down, Charles and I side by side on the sofa, the two of them in opposite chairs. The only light in the room was coming from the kitchen, the sun having long since gone down, and we didn't turn on any more lights. Lydia took the video over to where the television and DVD player were, inserted it in the latter, and turned both devices on.

It was a typical home video. Shots of Robert on the beach, Charles on the beach, Robert and Charles on the beach, etcetera, pretty much as Lydia had described it. I hadn't yet seen a picture of Robert other than a studio portrait in Charles's study, so I was interested to see that he was my physical type, but with brown hair. He obviously wasn't into running or weightlifting, for he wasn't particularly well developed in the muscle department, although he certainly filled his Speedos impressively. I immediately dismissed that thought, and wondered if I was feeling smug because I had a better build than my predecessor. I'd put my arm around Charles when the video started, and he'd snuggled up against me, intent on the video and his thoughts. The final scene was indeed a long lingering shot of Robert asleep on a chaise lounge on the deck. The camera panned back for a moment to focus on Charles, who was walking up behind the chaise lounge with a finger to his lips in a gesture for silence. He bent over Robert and kissed him on the forehead. Robert stirred, and Charles kissed him again. Robert woke up, stretched his arms, and looked around. When he saw that it was Charles kneeling beside him, his face lit up with an expression that I will never forget. Lydia's description of that look was absolutely on target, perhaps even a little understated. My concentration on the television screen was broken by Charles stirring to life beside me.

"Excuse me," he said, and he went hurriedly out to the deck.

Harry broke the spell, saying, "Jesus. No living creature has ever looked at me like that, except maybe my dog. My mother would be a distant second." Having said that, he excused himself and went upstairs, presumably to the bathroom.

I ignored him, looked at Lydia, and said, "Will Charles be all right?"

"He will if you go out there and give him a hug," she said. I started to get up, but she stopped me with a gesture and added, "Charles is the most controlled person I've ever known. To my knowledge, he's never been able to allow his grief to properly vent itself. As far as I know, that episode with my parents was the only time that he ever even came close to losing his composure over Robert's death. Maybe you can help him with that, as he's obviously in love with you and if I'm any judge, it's mutual."

"You're very observant."

"It's my profession," she said with a smile. "Besides, I've known him for over ten years, and he looks at you the same way he used to look at my brother. On the other hand, I don't know you at all, but it's plain to see that the feelings are mutual, so go out there and tell him how you feel. Just be warned that he's been wound up tight for three years and when the dam bursts, there's likely to be a flood."

I took her advice, got up, and walked out to the deck. Charles was sitting upright on one of the chaise lounges, straddling it like a horse. I walked over and sat down on it facing him, straddling his legs, and said, "Are you all right?"

"No, but I will be," he said, tears flowing freely but quietly.

I put my arms around him. "If there's anything I can do, you have only to ask. I know it's only been a couple of days, but there is no doubt in my mind."

"What are you trying to say?" he said.

"Only that I love you."

"That's okay, I love you too. You may not have guessed it, but I fell in love with you the minute I saw you."

"I sort of figured that out, especially after your conversation with Andrew the other morning."

He was still trying to control the silent tears. Finally, he said, "Take me upstairs, please, I need to get in the shower."

We got up, I put my arm around his shoulders, and we walked back into the house, up the stairs, and to the bedroom without a word to Lydia or Harry, who had come back downstairs. They politely pretended not to notice us. As soon as we were in the bedroom with the door closed, Charles threw his clothes off, went into the bathroom, and turned the shower on. While he waited for the water to get hot, he came back to the open door and said, "Join me." It was neither a request nor a command, more like a plea born of desperation.

I undressed, turned the covers down on the bed, and went into the bathroom. The shower was a built-in tiled affair as wide as a bathtub, with sliding doors, and there was a tiled bench at one end of it. I stepped inside and found Charles standing under the water, still crying silently. I pulled him to me and held him while the crying changed to great racking sobs. He held onto me so tightly that it was, at times, difficult to breathe. It went on for a very long time, finally subsiding about the same time that the hot water began to become exhausted. I managed somehow to get him to sit down on the bench. Then I turned off the water, which was getting cooler by the second. He sat there helplessly while I toweled myself dry, then dried as much of him as I could reach. I pulled him to his feet and finished the task, and he allowed himself to be led to the bed.

We lay in bed a long time, face to face, with our arms around each other. Finally, he said, "I'm sorry."

"For what?"

"Subjecting you to that."

"It was something that you obviously needed to get out of your system," I said. "Who better to help you through it than someone who loves you?"

"You're right, of course. I know that at an intellectual level. Understanding and dealing with it at an emotional level, however, is another matter." He squeezed me. "I really thought that I'd never be able to feel anything for anyone again." He smiled and said, "I still don't know where I found the guts to make that silly bargain with you Thursday night."

"Yes, you do," I said. "You even alluded to it earlier."

"Oh yes," he said, remembering. "I found it in your eyes, didn't I?"

We talked about nothing for a while, and he finally dozed off, eventually showing all signs of being in a deep sleep. I was more or less still wired from the experiences of the evening, so I carefully untangled myself from him and the bedclothes and got up. I found a robe, put it on, and slipped downstairs. As it was, by then, well past midnight, I'd expected to be alone. When I walked into the kitchen area, I surprised, and was surprised by, Lydia, who was sitting at the counter with a cup of tea.

I spoke first. "Sorry to startle you. I didn't think anyone would still be up."

"I couldn't sleep, so I came down for a cup of tea," she said. "Please, join me."

"I was thinking in terms of a nightcap, but tea sounds even better," I said, and I walked over to the cabinet where I knew the cups and saucers to be stored and retrieved one of each. I went back around the counter and sat down beside her.

She poured me a cup from the pot she'd made and said, "Is everything under control?"

"I think so. To borrow your metaphor, the dam burst... big-time, and I think he achieved some sort of emotional catharsis." I remembered her profession and quickly added, "Although from your professional point of view, that's probably a very imprecise way of putting it."

She smiled. "Actually, that says it very well." She thought a moment and then continued, "He's been building up to something like this for three years. I'm just glad he didn't have to go through it by himself."

"You were right about him being in love with me. I only hope he can come to feel half as much for me as he clearly felt for your brother."

"If you're worthy of it, he'll do more than that," she said. "Charles has never done anything halfway in his entire life."

"If you don't mind talking about it, tell me about the two of them."

She said that she didn't mind and spent more than an hour describing what she knew of how they met and what she'd later observed of their relationship and life together. Finally she realized that we were both yawning and said, "I think it's time we both went to bed."

Stifling a yawn, I said, "It has been an exhausting day, hasn't it?"

She agreed with me, then did something very strange. When we were at the foot of the stairs, she turned, gave me a hug, and said, "I think you're going to be very good for him."

"Thank you," I said. "I certainly hope so."

She continued, "In a way, I'm glad I got my weekends mixed up."

I couldn't resist an opening like that. "Charles says that you did no such thing."

"Whatever do you mean?" she said, affecting an air of innocence.

"When we went upstairs this morning after encountering you and Harry, I told him that it wouldn't bother me if you and your boyfriend stayed the whole weekend."

"What did he say?"

I demonstrated for her. "He said, '1) Harry was not her boyfriend, he's not her type; 2) Lydia never forgets anything, least of all weekends; 3) Harry is obviously queer; 4) Lydia is surely playing Yenta; and 5) She's two days late and the wrong man short.' That's the short version."

She laughed. "I can just picture it. That counting routine is his most frequent mannerism. Of course, he's absolutely right: I'm guilty on all counts."

We said goodnight and walked up the stairs without another word. I took off my robe and slipped into bed carefully so as not to disturb Charles, but I needn't have worried. He was dead to the world, lying on his side facing out, and barely stirred as I snuggled up behind him, wrapped one arm around him, and closed my eyes. I think I went to sleep almost instantly, which is most unusual for me.

When I began to wake up, I was in the same position on my side, but when I became fully awake, I realized that he'd turned over to face me and was wide awake, so I said, "How long have you been awake?"

"I don't know. I woke up, rolled over, and have been lying here, watching you sleep."

"You should have wakened me."

"Why? You were sleeping soundly and obviously needed it. It was nice to lie here and watch over you." He paused, then continued, "I also want to thank you for last night."

"It really isn't necessary, but you're welcome."

"Oh, yes, it was," he said, "and so is this." With that, he started kissing me, at first innocently and then with increasing passion. This time, however, there was less urgency in our lovemaking.

11

Charles

AFTER Philip and I finally got out of bed, I suggested a morning run along the beach. It was about nine o'clock when we went downstairs, and there was no sign of either Lydia or Harry, so we repeated our run and walk of the day before. We lingered in the shower room only long enough to rinse the sand from our feet and Lance's fur. When we emerged into the kitchen, we found Lydia and Harry sitting at the counter, drinking coffee. This time, we had our towels tied modestly around our waists.

"Excuse us," I said, adding, "I think we've played this scene already."

Lydia laughed at that and said, "You two run on upstairs and get dressed, and I'll round up some breakfast. I was waiting for you to get back before I started it."

We went upstairs and showered, shaved, and dressed in shorts and knit shirts. By the time we returned to the kitchen, all the makings of breakfast were laid out on the counter. Philip and I washed the dishes and cleaned up the kitchen after breakfast, while Lydia and Harry sat at the counter drinking coffee, the four of us carrying on an intermittent conversation about nothing in particular. When all the dishes were put away, including the cups she and Harry had been using, Lydia looked at me and said, "I think it's time Harry and I went back to Tallahassee."

"Must you?" I said. I meant it too.

She looked at me with a strange expression and said, "I think we must." Then she walked over and whispered in my ear, "You know damn well that Harry and I are here under false pretenses. Besides, I think you and Philip need to be alone. It'll do you both a world of good."

I really couldn't argue with her logic, and within the hour they'd gathered their respective belongings and were in her car. As we stood in the yard watching them drive away, I said, "Alone at last."

Philip smiled and held out his hand. I took it, and we went back up the stairs to the living area. We spent the rest of Sunday and all of Monday doing as little as possible except for our morning runs along the beach, which had become a ritual. We also continued the process of getting better acquainted, embarking over the course of a day and a half on a voyage of discovery. Monday evening we decided to go into town and dine at one of the better restaurants. When we got back to the house, I decided it was time to broach the subject that I knew must be foremost in both our minds. I had, until then, pointedly refrained from mentioning the murder, and so had Philip.

"Much as I hate to break the spell," I said, "I guess I'd better call Richard and see what's been happening in Atlanta."

Philip looked at me and said quietly, "I know."

I went to the telephone and managed to catch Richard at home. He told me that the warrant had been issued late on Friday, as expected. His investigation was under way, but it was early days at this point and he had little to report. He started to quiz me about the weekend, but I told him that he'd have to wait until we returned before his curiosity could be satisfied. I told Philip what I'd found out; then I dialed Andrew's number.

He answered the phone on the second ring, and I said, "Hello, Andrew, this is your protégé calling." The protégé bit was an old joke between us.

"Charles, I'm so glad to hear from you. Is everything all right down there? Richard has kept me posted on things here in Atlanta."

"Everything is just fine down here, and we've had a wonderful weekend."

"You certainly do sound more like your old self," he said.

"I suppose I must. It's been quite a weekend, in more ways than one. To make a long story short, you'll be glad to know that I think I've finally laid Robert to rest."

"It was high time you did so," he said. "Perhaps you'll tell me about it sometime, if you feel like it."

"Most likely. Anyway, we'll be in the office around eight o'clock tomorrow morning for a brief conference before we go to the police station and set things in motion."

"I'll see you then. Give my regards to Philip."

"I will. By the way, I forgot to ask Richard if there had been anything new in the papers about the murder or, for that matter, the issuance of a warrant."

"No. There's been absolutely no mention of new developments in the case in any of the media, as far as I can tell. My guess is that they're waiting to make the arrest, then they'll make the most of it with the press."

"I expect you're right." I said goodbye and hung up the telephone before turning to Philip and continuing, "Andrew sends you his regards."

Philip didn't reply. He was clearly thinking about something else. Finally he looked at me and asked, "What exactly will happen tomorrow? At the police station, I mean."

I described the process of booking, fingerprinting, etcetera. "It'll be pretty much cut and dried. If they ask you any questions, you'll simply refuse to answer without your attorney present. Meanwhile, I'll be arranging to have you arraigned at the one o'clock court session, which is held daily for that purpose. Basically, we'll appear, the charges will be read, and I'll enter a plea of not guilty. The prosecutor will ask for an exorbitant amount of bail, and I'll argue that it be reduced. In the end, the judge will rule on a sufficient amount of bail to satisfy the court, and they'll take you back to a holding cell while I go and post the bail. As soon as the paperwork has been completed, you'll be free to go."

"Then what?"

"We get to work preparing a defense. You and I will have a series of conferences with Richard concerning the investigation that's under way. We'll also spend a lot of time with one of my associates, a young man named Mark Tatum. He'll be assisting me with the preparation for the trial, as well as the trial itself."

"When do you think the trial will be?"

"From what I know of the court's current case load, it could be as late as the first of the year. On the other hand, if Wetherbee plans to make a show of the trial, it might be as early as the week after Labor Day. We'll just have to wait and see, but my guess is he'll try to delay until spring if he can get away with it—he expects to win and it will look good just before the primaries. During the interim, you can get back to your normal daily routine."

He thought for a moment, and then a sly smile spread across his face as he said, "And what about my nightly routine?"

That caused me to smile, as well. "As far as I'm concerned, your dance card is full every evening." Before he could respond, I quickly added, "Unless, of course, you have better things to do."

"None worth mentioning or, for that matter, worth doing."

"Concerning logistics, I'll be more than happy to have you stay with me for the duration. If you need your own space, I can certainly understand, but it's already difficult for me to contemplate not having you around all of the time."

"Well, then, I guess you've got yourself another roommate. Besides, I haven't forgotten our agreement."

We made an early night of it and were at the airport by four the next morning and in the air ten minutes later. Aided by a tailwind for most of the flight back, we arrived in Marietta just in time to beat the rush-hour traffic, and we were back at the townhouse with plenty of time to dress for our meeting with Andrew. I'd left instructions for Richard to take Philip's suit and dress shirt to a one-hour cleaner on Friday so there would be no need to go by Philip's condo—it would have been too risky, anyway. Thus prepared, we arrived at my office around a quarter to eight and knocked on Andrew's door a few minutes later.

Andrew was clearly astonished at my appearance and said, "I don't know what happened to you this weekend, but it's obviously done wonders. You sounded like your old self last night, and you look even better this morning."

"That's surprising, considering that we were in the air a little after four this morning. However, you're right, it was a wonderful weekend."

Small talk out of the way, I got down to the case at hand and outlined again for Andrew my intentions for the morning and afternoon. Then Philip and I excused ourselves and went into my office, and I said,

"You might want to leave all of your belongings locked up here. They'll make you empty your pockets at the police station, and signing for and verifying the contents later will slow things down this afternoon when I spring you."

"Okay, I'm in your hands," he said, and he emptied his pockets of wallet, keys, etcetera.

I locked them in my desk drawer, then called Rosemary in and gave her a few instructions, and we were ready. When Rosemary left, I closed the door and turned to Philip, who was standing beside me. I hugged him quickly and kissed him. Then I said, "I won't be able to do that where we're going. However, I promise that I'll get you back out just as fast as humanly possible."

"I know."

We walked a few blocks to the police station, went up the steps, and waited in line to see the desk sergeant. When it was our turn, I gave the sergeant my card and said, "This is Mr. Philip d'Autremont, my client. It's our understanding that there is a warrant out for his arrest, and we're here so that he can surrender."

The sergeant, obviously recognizing Philip's name, picked up his telephone and spoke to a higher authority. Then he said, "Wait just a minute, please, and someone will be right out."

We were in luck—the detective who came to fetch us was one that I knew at least casually, and more importantly, one for whom I had a great deal of respect. He could have, had he chosen to do so, placed Philip in handcuffs on the spot. Instead, he permitted us to follow him back to his small cubicle, where I explained that I would like for Philip to be booked as quickly as possible, as I wanted his case included in the afternoon arraignments. He saw no problem with my request and initiated the paperwork, and in what seemed like no time, Philip was led away from me.

I spent some time visiting the appropriate functionaries in the jail and courthouse in order to set the wheels in motion to have Philip's arraignment that afternoon, and satisfied that I'd done all that was humanly possible, I went back to the office to catch up on work and to wait.

Andrew called me around eleven and suggested that I join him for lunch, which I was happy to do, as it would get my mind off the waiting process. I walked down the hall to his office, then we walked to a nearby restaurant, where it was possible to find a quiet table if one arrived early enough. I ordered a salad and nothing else, and he selected a soup and salad.

After we ordered, I gave him a bare-bones outline of the weekend, pausing only while the waiter placed our food in front of us. He was perceptive enough to fill in the blanks and didn't ask too many questions.

After I finished, he said, "When was the last time you talked to Caroline?" He and Gran were old friends.

"Not since last week. I'd planned to call her before I left for Florida, but as you know, things got a little out of hand. Why?"

"She called me Saturday, voicing some concern. I told her a little of what was going on, and she made me promise to remind you to call her when you got back. She's been worried about you for a long time, as have we all. I think perhaps it would be good if you and Philip dropped by to see her this evening, if at all possible. She will immediately see, as would anyone who knows you, that you're well out of your doldrums."

I promised to call her as soon as we got back to the office, and said that a visit would be nice, if Philip felt up to it after the ordeal of the day. Our conversation then turned to the murder case, and I again outlined my game plan to Andrew, using him as a sounding board, as I often did. As usual, he made a few minor suggestions.

We arrived back at the office in time for me to place a couple of telephone calls, one of them to Gran.

"Hi," I said on hearing the familiar voice at the other end of the line. "This is your long-lost heir."

"Oh, Charles"—she, not believing in nicknames, had never once called me Charley—"I have been so worried about you. I even called Andrew and asked him about you."

"I know, he just told me about it over lunch." Before she could reply, I added, "Are you free this evening?"

"Aren't I always, these days?" she said with a chuckle.

"Well, then, I might come over with a friend for you to meet."

"Might?"

"Well, he just surrendered to the police, and I have got to go and get him out of jail in a few minutes. If he isn't too exhausted from the ordeal, we may drop in later."

To her credit, she didn't probe, no doubt having learned enough from Andrew to guess what was going on. We said goodbye, and I began to gather the items I would need for Philip's arraignment.

I arrived in the courtroom a few minutes before one and found it packed. *Three-day weekends have a definite impact on the courts*, I reflected. I went up to the clerk, who was already in her seat, and obtained a list of the cases on the docket. It was a lengthy one, and I was thankful that I'd been able to pull a few strings that morning, because Philip's name was fifth on the list. I found a seat in the section reserved for attorneys just in time to watch the first dozen defendants, Philip among them, being led into the courtroom. He sat about two rows in front of and a little to the right of where I was sitting. He turned around to look for me, and I gave him a smile of encouragement, studying him as closely as I could from where I was sitting. He looked pale and not a little bewildered, but his face brightened at my smile.

Finally, his case was called, and I went down to take my place beside him. "Charles Barnett of Chandler, Todd, Woodward & Barnett, representing the defendant," I said.

The charge—murder one—was read, and I entered a plea of not guilty. The prosecutor, one of the deputy district attorneys, asked that bail be set in the amount of $1 million.

I responded, "Your Honor, we feel that is extremely excessive. The defendant has been a resident of this city for at least a decade, has property here and many ties to the community. Furthermore, he voluntarily surrendered to the authorities the minute he returned from the long weekend and learned that a warrant for his arrest had been issued."

The DDA and I wrangled back and forth for a bit, and the judge finally set bail in the sum of $250,000. There followed further haggling with the DDA as to the date for the trial. I'd expected that the DA wouldn't be in hurry to set a trial date, but I was wrong; the date we finally arrived at was the first Monday after New Year's.

Finally it was over, and the next case was called. I leaned over and whispered to Philip, "What did I tell you—in by nine, out by two."

Before he could reply, he was led away and out of the room. I walked down the hallway and made the necessary arrangements and was finally ushered into a small conference room containing two chairs on opposite sides of a table, where Philip was eventually brought to join me while we waited for word that he was free to go. I motioned him to the other chair and said, "Might as well have a seat. It'll be a few minutes before the paperwork is finished."

He sat down but didn't say anything, so I said, "Was it as bad as you feared?"

"No, not too bad. I got the impression that the word was out to handle me with care. You must have had something to do with that." He added, "Have you ever been locked up in jail?"

"No, I haven't, but I have a feeling for what it must be like. Lord knows enough clients have described it to me over the years."

"Well, I don't know what they told you, but it's very disconcerting."

I decided to distract him a bit and said, "Did they feed you?"

"There were some sandwiches and Cokes available, but I wasn't hungry."

"Are you up to a meeting with Mark and me after we get out of here?"

"Once I get out of here, I'm sure I'll be up to almost anything."

"Good. We'll make it as short as possible. We're both tired from the early flight, and I prescribe an early evening."

I'd seen this reaction to jail before and kept him talking about anything and everything—except, of course, the situation at hand. Finally there was the rattle of a key in the door, and one of the policemen stuck his head in the door and said, "Okay, counselor, you can take your client out of here."

I thanked him and ushered Philip out the door, down the stairs, and to the main entrance of the court complex. I should have had enough sense to slip out the back door, because there were several reporters hanging around, including at least one television news team, obviously waiting for Philip to appear. I spotted the reporters, but not in time, and whispered to Philip, "Oh shit, somebody's been spreading the word. I should have expected this."

"What should I say to them?"

"You should say 'no comment' and refer them to your attorney."

He followed my advice, politely deferring any comment to his attorney. They then pounced on me with a dozen questions at once. I'd been through this before and said, "You folks know that I can't talk about the case. My client has entered a plea of not guilty, and we intend to set about proving him so."

They saw that they weren't going to receive any tidbits from us, and we got past them and down the steps. When we were away from the area, I said, "I'm sorry about that. If I'd gathered my wits properly about me, I'd have seen it coming and we could have slipped out the back way."

"It's all right. I went through a lot of that for the first few days after the body was discovered."

It was nearly three when we got back to my office, so I postponed the conference with Mark until first thing the next morning. I retrieved Philip's belongings from my desk, and we went down to my car. I prescribed a short nap for both of us before we did anything else, and drove us home, where we went straight to bed. We slept for an hour or so, took a shower—together, of course—shaved, and dressed in slacks and plaid shirts. "How hungry are you?" I said.

"I don't know, a little, I guess."

"Well, I only had a small salad for lunch, so I have an advantage over you in that department. However, if you're up to it, there's someone I would like very much for you to meet. We'll make it a quick visit, and then I thought you might enjoy a truly happy place for an early dinner."

He asked me what I meant, and when I told him, he said, "Sure, that's one of my favorite spots."

"Great, but first, you have to meet Gran. Andrew said she called him Saturday because she was worried about me, and he filled her in on where I was and why. I promise it'll be a quick visit this time."

"Sounds like I'm being inspected. Will I pass, do you think?"

"Actually, I'm the one being inspected. Andrew says that I look like 'my old self', and he thought she ought to see that for herself. She'll understand instinctively that you're responsible for the change in me, and consequently it wouldn't matter if you were hunchbacked and had warts."

"I don't know what to say to that."

"Then, don't say anything, just go with the flow." We were on Peachtree, up near St. Philip's Cathedral, by that time. Gran lived in a grand old house on one of the side streets off West Paces Ferry Road, but it was more easily reached by turning down one of the side streets near the cathedral for a few blocks and then turning north on her street.

I pulled into the circular drive in front of the house, and we walked up to the front door and rang the bell.

Goodman, her butler/handyman, came to the door. "Master Charles, this is a surprise. Why didn't you let yourself in?"

"I just wanted to make you feel useful, Goodman."

He laughed at that—it was an old joke with us—and I said, "Goodman, this is my friend Philip d'Autremont. Philip, this is Mr. Goodman, who has served Gran for many years."

"Any friend of Master Charles's is welcome in this house," Goodman responded. "Mrs. Barnett is in the front parlor."

"Thank you, Goodman. I know the way."

12

Philip

CHARLES took my hand and led me through a large and very grand foyer, which was typical in large old houses of the period, then through an archway and into a parlor, which, though quite large, managed to convey an air of intimacy. His grandmother, who had been sitting in a rocking chair beside a small table, closed the book she'd been reading after marking her place, set it carefully on the table, and rose with the aid of a cane when we entered the room. She was tall for a woman of her generation, slim, very elegant, and every bit the patrician I'd been led to expect. Charles led me halfway across the room before he let go of my hand and walked over to embrace the old lady.

"Hi, Gran," he said. "I'm sorry I forgot to call you before I left town on Friday, but my departure was much earlier than originally planned. I trust Andrew told you why."

"He did," she said in a firm and commanding voice that contradicted her apparent age. She stepped back from him for a minute and continued softly, "My dear boy, you look wonderfully relaxed. I haven't seen you look that way in a very long time."

There was a pause while she gave me a penetrating look. "And you, I suspect, are the reason for this improvement."

Charles reached out, grabbed my hand, and pulled me over to where they were standing. "Gran, may I present Philip d'Autremont. Philip, this is my grandmother."

"How do you do, Mrs. Barnett," I said.

"Much better, now that I have seen this young man looking like himself again," she said. She sat back down in the rocking chair and indicated that we should sit on the sofa across from her.

"Gran, we can't stay but a few minutes. We were up at four o'clock this morning, neither of us has had much to eat all day, and we're frankly exhausted. I just wanted to say hello and introduce you to Philip before we go out for an early dinner. Perhaps this weekend we can have a real visit."

If she was surprised to learn that we weren't going to linger, she chose not to comment, saying only, "Of course, I understand. I'm so very glad you took the time to come by, as I've been concerned." She shifted her gaze from Charles to me and continued, "Charles probably doesn't know it, but he and I were distantly related to your late wife."

Charles was stunned at this and said, "Really? I certainly don't remember you mentioning her."

"Charles, think about her maiden name. You cannot be descended from the Marks, Barnett, and Lewis families without being related to the Meriwethers somewhere along the line. You're related to all three families, whereas I come from the Marks and Lewis side." With that she was off and running about family connections for a good fifteen minutes. She finally began to wind down, saying, "I'll have to look it up to be certain, but I think you and Lucinda were probably third cousins twice removed."

Charles laughed at that and said, "I'll take your word for it. And now, we really have to be going. Tomorrow is going to be another very long day."

"Run along, then," she said. "I will expect the two of you for dinner Sunday, however, and bring Richard with you, if you like."

He promised that we'd be there, and we made our departure. When we were a few blocks down Peachtree, he glanced at me and said, "What *is* it about old Southern ladies and genealogy?"

"I know what you mean. You should have heard my grandmother on the same topic. Your grandmother certainly was surprised at your appearance."

"Good old Gran, she doesn't miss much," he said. "As far as she's concerned, I can assure you that you're already part of the family."

We finally arrived in the lower Midtown area, and he pulled into the parking lot behind Annie's Bistro, which was our destination. He turned the car over to the parking attendant, and we walked around to the entrance. Annie's Bistro has been an Atlanta favorite since it opened in the early seventies. Situated in an 1890s building that had originally housed a drugstore, it retained the original tin ceiling and tile floor. The dining room wasn't large but was always bustling and was indeed one of the happiest places in Atlanta. Since it was a weeknight, we didn't have to wait very long for a table.

I knew the maître d' slightly from many previous visits and discovered that Charles knew him similarly. On the way to our table, we each spotted one or two acquaintances, though none that we'd known in common prior to that evening. I commented on this when we were finally seated at our table, saying, "Funny, we seem to have traveled in totally different subsets of the same circles."

"Greater Atlanta has a population of over four million, of which considerably more than 10 percent would statistically be gay. Add to that the fact that it has been sort of a gay mecca for decades, and I would guess the percentage to be much higher than ten. I certainly don't know more than a tiny fraction of that number, so I guess it's not too strange that we never met before, and I'm sure that we didn't."

Changing the subject, I said, "Do you think it'll be safe for us to stop by my condo on the way home? I really do need to gather some clothes and things."

"No problem. There's no reason for anybody to be watching and/or following you now."

We ate leisurely and well, consuming a bottle of a very good Sauvignon Blanc in the process, and were on the way to my condo about an hour after we'd been seated. Charles didn't ask for directions until we were well up Piedmont Avenue, but when we neared the Ansley area, he glanced at me and said, "From here on you'll have to navigate."

I directed him down the appropriate side street, which led to the street my condo was located on, and, once there, to my parking space. The empty parking space reminded me of something, and I said, "I forgot to call the dealer about my car Friday."

"You can take care of that in the morning. Meantime, if you have errands to run tomorrow, you can use my car. I'm not likely to need it during the day, and if I did, it wouldn't matter. I can always use Andrew's car during working hours."

"Thanks, I appreciate that. I'm on the second floor." I led the way upstairs and ushered him into the condo, then said, "Make yourself at home. It won't take me more than a couple of minutes to round up a few things."

He ambled around, looking the place over, while I gathered enough clothes and personal items to last for several days. After a time, he tracked me down in the bedroom and said, "Do you spend much time here?"

"Not really. Weekends, mostly, when I'm not out of town. Why?"

"Well, the place looks very comfortable, and it looks occupied, but it doesn't really look 'lived in', if you know what I mean."

I laughed at that and said, "You're too shrewd, counselor. No, it isn't really 'lived in', as you put it. I spend time here mostly working in the little den you saw, and I spend time at the house on West Paces Ferry, but neither of them could truly be called 'home'. That's been a fact of my life for quite some time, and one that occasionally bothers me, but I simply haven't known quite what to do about it. I do have a retreat up in the mountains of North Carolina where I truly feel 'at home', but I don't get to spend very much time there, either. At times, I feel almost like some sort of latter-day nomad."

Charles looked thoughtful and said, "Well, maybe after the trial and everything, we can do something about that."

He didn't elaborate, and I chose not to press the matter. I assumed him to be alluding to some sort of arrangement for living together, and was quite content to take things one day at a time for the near term.

I finished packing, and he helped me carry things down to the car. It was just a short hop down Piedmont to his townhouse, but we had to turn off Piedmont at the point where it became a one-way in the wrong direction, cross over to Juniper, and then down to his street. As he pulled into the garage, he said, "I see the super sleuth is home."

"The car suits his personality, or at least what I've seen of it," I said.

"You're on the mark there. I'm glad he's home, as I really didn't want to wait until tomorrow to get a rundown from him on the investigation."

We carried my stuff upstairs, and Charles created more than enough space in the closet. He also made room in the bathroom for my gear. Richard hadn't turned up to greet us, so Charles went looking for him while I wandered around the house. Things had happened so rapidly on Thursday evening and Friday morning that I really hadn't taken a good look at his home, and I spent some time admiring it, starting at the ground floor.

The living room was painted in neutral tones, its parquet floors covered in places by small oriental rugs. There were a number of very good prints on the walls, and the furniture had obviously been expensive. It was a very warm and comfortable room, bordering on what is sometimes referred to as understated elegance. Large colonial-style windows looked out onto a small patio and backyard that was enclosed and made private by a high brick wall.

Upstairs, the same effect had been created in the dining room, which overlooked the garden below, its view being somewhat restricted by a deck running across the back of the house at the second-story level. I wandered from there into the kitchen and found Charles lounging against a counter talking to Richard, who was at the breakfast table, which I noted had a view through sliding patio doors of the deck and backyard below. Richard was in the process of finishing what appeared to be a late supper, while Lance was sitting at attention beside the table, waiting for handouts.

When Charles saw me enter the room, he said, "Richard has a bit of news for us but refuses to talk until he's finished stuffing his face. Come into the study with me, we can wait for him there."

I followed him as requested. When we were seated on a sofa, I said, "I've been admiring your house. There was really no time Thursday or Friday to take it in. You and Robert must have done the decorating because it looks much too comfortable to have been the product of a decorator."

"Thank you. Actually, it was mostly Robert. As an architect, he had an eye for how things should look." He opened one of the desk drawers and rummaged for a minute, turning back to me with a key in his hand. He said, "You'll need this. Tomorrow morning, I'll show you how to arm and disarm the security system."

I added the key to my key case. "Thanks." Suddenly I realized how tired I was and said, "How much longer do you think Richard will be?"

"Not long, why?"

"Because I'm sinking rapidly. You must be exhausted as well."

"Too true, and I'd suggest bed right now were it not for the hints he dropped earlier. Here he comes now."

Richard came over to the desk, followed closely by Lance. Richard took one of the wingback chairs, seemingly determined to make conversation about anything but the case, while Lance curled up at Charles's feet. Charles let him ramble for a bit before finally cutting him off, saying, "Richard, you're looking at two extremely exhausted men. We were up before four this morning, and it's been a *very long* day, so cut to the chase and give us a condensed version of your report, please."

"Okay. To make a long story short, I made some progress. As you know, Philip wasn't able to safely go by his house or condo and retrieve a photo of his wife, so I went down to the newspaper office and managed to obtain a fairly good photograph, one that had appeared in the society pages last year. I spent Friday, Saturday, and Sunday evenings doing some serious pub-crawling. I bought a lot of drinks for a lot of people, but since I was working and needed to be sober, I mostly drank Sprite or tonic water. Early Sunday evening, in a dyke bar down on Peachtree, I found a bartender who thought she recognized the deceased. Better still, she dimly remembered seeing the deceased with another woman once or twice. That's not much to go on, but it gets better. Alice, the bartender I spoke with, only works there on a part-time basis. The regular bartender, who is almost certain to be even more helpful, is on vacation and isn't expected to return to work until next week."

"Well done, Richard," Charles said. "That's more than anyone could hope for on such short notice."

"I'm impressed" was all that I could think to add to the conversation.

"You'll be even more impressed when you see my bill," Richard said with a grin.

Charles stifled a yawn and said, "On that note, I'm ready to call it a night. Tomorrow morning we can have a formal conference with Mark at the office, and then maybe Philip can arrange for you to gain access to the murder scene, as well as his wife's condo." He looked at me with a question mark.

"I can escort him to both places tomorrow, and he can poke about as much as he likes." I was yawning too.

Charles got up and walked around the desk to my chair. He held out a hand. "Coming?"

I took his hand, let him pull me to my feet, and said, "Right behind you."

We started toward the door, saying goodnight as we left the room. Without waiting for a response, we went upstairs and were undressed and in bed in a matter of minutes. Charles pulled me to him and said, "I set the alarm for six, so we'll have time for a run in the morning—that is, if you want to."

"Sure. I missed not having a run on the beach this morning. It'll be good to get back into a regular routine."

Charles started kissing me and doing things to my body, and said, after a few minutes, "How tired are you, really?"

"Well, the spirit is weak, but the flesh is obviously willing."

All Charles said in response was "Lance, bed," and Lance obediently jumped to the floor and curled up on his own bed, giving us a look of reproach. Lance, ever the optimist, always began the night by curling up between our legs at the foot of the bed, and he was always ordered to his own bed sooner or later. He'd done the same thing at the beach house. Afterward, I fell asleep immediately, and I suspect Charles did too.

When the alarm went off the next morning, I awakened to find myself both refreshed and relaxed. Charles got up and turned off the alarm, then went to the closet. After coming back to the bed with running shorts and shoes in hand for both of us, he sat down on the bed, leaned over and gave me a brief kiss, and said, "Still feel like that run?" It was a rhetorical question. He was already pulling on his shorts.

"You bet. Let me go splash some water on my face." I got up and went into the bathroom. When I came back into the bedroom, he had his running shoes already laced up and was sitting quietly in a chair in the corner, waiting. Lance was sitting beside him, leash in mouth. I quickly pulled on my shorts and running shoes and in a couple of minutes stood and walked over to him. "Lead on," I said.

He hooked Lance's leash onto his collar and then led me to the kitchen and down the back stairs to the garage. He opened the garage door and, once we were clear of it, produced an opener from the fanny pack he was wearing and said, "It's more bulky than carrying a key ring but avoids tracking through the living room. Ready?"

"After you."

We ran over to Piedmont and up to the entrance to the park. There were a few runners out at this hour, as well as several people walking their dogs. Surprisingly, Lance seemed to take no notice of the other dogs and appeared to be quite content to trot along beside Charles and me. Charles led us in a wide circle through part of the park, and we arrived back at the same entrance some time later. While we were waiting for the traffic light to change, I asked him how far we'd run.

"By the time we get home, about six miles."

The light changed before I could say anything else—I've never been able to carry on much of a conversation while running—and we headed down Piedmont. When we were back at his house, we retraced our steps as far as the kitchen, where Charles removed Lance's leash before detouring into the laundry room and removing his shorts, shoes, and socks. He dumped the shorts and socks into a laundry basket, picked up his shoes, and, naked, turned toward the door.

Reading my mind, he answered my unasked question. "Richard won't be up and about for another thirty minutes or so, and even if he was, it wouldn't matter—we're quite casual around here. Besides," he said, grinning, "neither of us has got anything he hasn't seen plenty of."

I followed his example, and we went upstairs and shared the bathroom, shaving side by side at the double vanity, then showering together. The process of washing each other's backs led, as always, to more interesting things, and I said, "This is getting to be a habit."

"Well, we all need a few more good habits."

We went down to the kitchen. This time he wore his newer robe, and I wore the one I'd brought with me the previous evening. We were seated at the breakfast table having coffee, juice, and toast and sharing the morning paper when Richard came in wearing a pair of exercise shorts and nothing else. He obviously hadn't yet showered; his face was covered with blond stubble, and the word "bedraggled" came quickly to mind. Charles's mouth was full of toast, so I said cheerfully, "Good morning."

"The words 'good' and 'morning' are mutually exclusive, as far as I'm concerned," Richard said.

"Maybe you'd feel differently about that if you had gotten up with us and gone for a run through the park," I said.

"Oh God, not another one," he said, groaning. "I can't stand it."

"Another one what?"

"Early-morning exercise puke. Living with one of them was bad enough. I don't know if I can take it in stereo."

"What's wrong with exercise?" I said. "You obviously indulge in a good deal of it yourself, judging by the shape you're in."

"Nothing wrong with exercise," he said. "Exercise is okay. Exercise can even be wonderful. Early mornings, however, are not." Before I could say anything else, he added, "And don't give me that bullshit about the early bird and the worm. If the worm had stayed in bed, he'd have been better off."

Charles finally joined the conversation and said, "Don't pay any attention to the grouch. I've known him for nearly twenty years, man and boy, and he's always been like this first thing in the morning. One learns never to expect civility from Richard before at least ten o'clock."

Richard went to the coffeemaker on the counter, and poured himself a cup before taking a seat at the table with us. We finished breakfast and the paper in silence until Charles looked at the kitchen clock and said, "If we're going to be at the office by nine, we'd better go up and get dressed."

13

Philip

FIFTEEN minutes later, we were on the way downtown. When we pulled up to the entrance to the parking garage underneath his office building, Charles opened the glove compartment, retrieved the card that activated the barrier across the entrance, showed me how to use it, and explained that I would need to use it to exit the garage. Charles parked in his reserved space; then he replaced the entry card in the glove compartment and extracted a set of keys attached to a clicker, and handed them to me. "Here's a spare set of keys that I keep in the glove compartment. They come in handy when I leave the car to be serviced. If you happen to pass near a locksmith today, stop and get a set made for yourself, as well as a copy of the key I gave you to the house."

"Thanks. I know a place in Buckhead where I can have them made after I take Richard to the house."

Then we took the elevator up to his office, where he suggested that I settle down in a side chair near his desk to wait for the meeting to start. While he read his accumulated messages, I took a good look at his office. The visit yesterday had been so hurried, and I'd been in such an unsettled state, that I really hadn't noticed many details. It was a large office on the corner of the building, containing, in addition to his desk, a small conference table in one corner and a sofa and seating arrangement in the corner opposite. His desk, which was a large mahogany affair, was placed so that the outside corner of the building was right behind him, and the two windows allowed light over both his shoulders. The shape of the wall space behind his chair didn't allow for a conventional credenza; instead there was a built-in cabinet, which appeared to house and partially hide a large flat-screen monitor. The wall behind the conference table was covered with floor-to-ceiling bookshelves, which were overflowing with legal volumes.

After a time, there was a knock on the door, and a young man in his twenties entered the room. Charles introduced me to the new arrival, who turned out to be Mark Tatum, the associate who'd be assisting with the preparation of my defense. We moved to the conference table and chatted amiably for a few minutes. Finally, there was another knock on the door and Richard came in, followed by Charles's secretary. I'd noted the previous day that, as he'd said, she was as attractive as she was efficient.

When we were all settled around the table, Charles looked at me and said, "What we're about to do is second nature to us, and we sometimes take it for granted that laymen understand the process, even if they don't. Please feel free to interrupt and ask for explanations and/or clarifications at any time."

I nodded my understanding, and he went on, "What we're going to do this morning is lay out a preliminary plan of action for your defense. This plan may or may not evolve into the final one—that will depend upon how the prosecution proceeds."

He looked at Richard and said, "Speaking of the prosecution, is your contact in the district attorney's office aware of your relationship with me? And more important, will that prevent him from talking to you about the case?"

Richard said, "Yes to the first question. Probably no to the second. Considering who he works for, he has to be circumspect and very closeted. We certainly won't be able to meet openly, but I can create some opportunities to find out from him what's going on."

"Well, create whatever opportunities you can. My feeling is that it'll be very helpful to have an inside track for this particular case." Charles gave him a look that clearly conveyed that Richard should use sex in exchange for information.

He continued, "During the process of discovery, we may be able to learn the thrust of their case. Philip, do you understand what we mean by discovery?"

"I think so. Basically, isn't it a process of show and tell for each side of the case?"

"Just so. However, the presumption of innocence on your part will place the onus on them to prove your guilt, and the current rules require that they show and tell all, but we're allowed to hold things back. At the very least, they'll have to prove that you had motive and opportunity. We all know that they can't place you at the scene of the crime, and since they can't prove you were at the scene, they'll most likely concentrate on developing a motive. What they'll come up with is anybody's guess at this point. That's where Richard's friend may be helpful, for the sooner we know what their case is predicated upon, the sooner we can develop an appropriate response."

"For the record," Charles said—Rosemary was busily making notes, and I noted that she also had a small mini-cassette recorder on the table—"the facts of the case are as follows." He recited a précis of my life, Lucinda's life, and our relationship pretty much as Andrew had described it the previous Thursday evening. "Our job is to obtain a verdict of 'not guilty', period. The matter of an alibi is off-limits now and forever. Richard, please give us a rundown of your findings to date."

Richard recited the long version of his weekend. Actually, there really wasn't much more to this than the bare facts he'd told Charles and me the previous evening. "For a working hypothesis," Richard added, "try this on for size. Mrs. d'Autremont is getting a little tired of her current lover, for whatever reason. She's also several weeks pregnant, so she decides to reveal her pregnancy and use it as an excuse to break off the relationship, either temporarily or permanently. Her lover kills her in a fit of rage."

"Not bad for a theory built mostly on thin air," Charles said. "Have you got anything at all to support it?"

"Not really, except that the bartender I interviewed described the deceased's friend as very butch and probably mean."

"Well, perhaps the other bartender will be more helpful when she gets back from her vacation. Meanwhile, you can begin the customary investigation of the scene, etcetera. As soon as we're finished here, Philip will get you into both his home and his wife's condo. Comments or questions, anyone?"

Mark had a couple of questions, but nobody else said anything.

"Good," Charles said. "One last thing. It's very clear, given what we've already learned from our source, that the police aren't actively pursuing their investigation. As far as they're concerned, they've got their man, so it'll be up to us to do their job for them."

Rosemary and Mark excused themselves, then Charles wrote something on a business card, handed it to me, and said, "The first number is my private line here at the office, and the second number is my cell phone. Call me if you think of and/or need anything. Would you like to meet somewhere for lunch, if you have time?"

"Sure, when and where?"

"Well, if you can get back here by about one, we can walk to any of several places. I won't make any commitments in case you can't make it."

"Don't worry," I said, "I'll make it."

Richard said, "What about me?"

"What about you?" Charles said.

"Am I invited to lunch?"

"Only if you have something useful to report. Now go out and flirt with Rosemary for a minute while I talk to my client."

"Yassa, Massa," Richard said and retreated to the outer office, closing the door behind him.

Charles looked at me and said, "The wheels of justice are turning."

"So it would seem."

He moved to stand very close to me and said, "If you can't make it for lunch, I'll understand. Disappointed, of course, but understanding." He leaned over and kissed me. "Now go escort the boy wonder to the scene of the crime, and don't let him give you a hard time."

"Yassa, Massa," I said, mimicking Richard, and I walked out the door before he could come up with a rejoinder.

Richard was sitting in a chair beside Rosemary's desk, and from their casual manner and chatter, it was obvious that they were old friends. Their conversation wound down as I approached, so I said, "I'm ready whenever you are, Richard."

"Then let's go," he said, tossing a casual "Bye, babe" to Rosemary.

As we walked to the elevators, I thought about logistics and said, "Shall we take one car or two?"

"Why don't you drive us there? That'll give us a chance to talk. I'll have one of my grunts meet us there to help me snoop, and he can bring me back here for my car."

When we were in the car, I gave him the address on West Paces Ferry Road, as he requested. He took a cell phone from a holster hanging from his belt and called his helper. Replacing the telephone, he said, "Isn't technology wonderful?"

"I've noticed that Charles likes his toys. Apparently, you do too."

"They have their uses. Speaking of Charles, you've certainly had an effect on him. I've watched him slowly turning into some sort of zombie over the last three years. The process seems to have reversed itself over the weekend. Clearly, he's in love with you." Adopting a slightly lighter tone, he added, "I just hope your intentions are, as they say, honorable."

"He is, they are, and for the record, it's mutual. We sorted all that out over the weekend."

"He hasn't told me about it yet, but it must have been *some* weekend."

"It was. In a nutshell, Lydia turned up at the beach house Saturday morning with an alleged boyfriend in tow. I say alleged because Charles saw right through it—she was playing matchmaker. They stayed until Sunday afternoon. Saturday evening after dinner, Charles told us about his encounter with Robert's parents the day before the funeral. We wound up watching a video that Lydia had shown to her parents on that occasion. Watching that video served as a catalyst, triggering something in Charles that allowed all the grief he'd been holding back to come flooding out."

"I know the video you mean, and I'm not surprised that it produced a reaction. But right there in front of everybody? That doesn't sound like him at all."

"No. He excused himself and went outside. I followed him and managed to get him upstairs before it happened."

"In the shower, I'll wager."

"You know about that?"

"He and I have few secrets after all these years."

"You're right on target. He went to the shower, asking me to join him there. After it was over, I managed to get us both dried off and into bed."

"I guess I owe you an apology."

"For what?"

"My tacky remark about honorable intentions."

"No problem," I said, and I changed the subject. "I'm surprised that you and Charles were never an item."

"There was a time, when we were teenagers, that I would have liked that, but I've been covered with this bear rug since I was fifteen, and Charles has this thing about hair."

"So he told me." I suspected that there had been more to it than that, but I chose not to pry.

While we talked, he'd produced a notebook, and he said, "I need to ask a few questions, if you don't mind?"

"Fire away."

He did just that for the next several minutes, winding up just as I turned off the street and down the driveway of the house on West Paces Ferry Road. *Strange*, I thought, *I've always thought of this place as "the house on West Paces Ferry Road," but never as home.* It was merely a place where Lucinda and I had ostensibly set up housekeeping and had lived ever since our marriage. In reality, it was little more than an enormously expensive prop. One of many props that were part of the drama we'd enacted over the years for the benefit of society and our respective families. All that effort just for the sake of appearances. *What a waste*, I thought. I pulled into the covered entrance at the side of the house, and we got out and walked to the door. I rang the bell, then unlocked the door, explaining, "The bell was so that the servants won't be surprised. They're probably in a state of panic already, as I haven't contacted them since last week."

"How many are there?"

"A married couple. He doubles as butler and gardener, and she serves as cook and housekeeper. They live in a garage apartment at the back of the property."

"Which one of them found the body?"

"Neither, actually. It was a part-time maid."

"Will she be here?"

"No. There wasn't anything for her to do after Lucinda's death, so I let her go. I'll get her address for you." Before I could say anything else, I heard footsteps coming from the back of the house, and Martha Starling appeared.

"Oh, Mr. Philip, where have you been? We've been so worried about you. We heard that you were arrested."

I smiled at her patter and said, "Slow down, Martha. All in good time. Where's Henry?"

"He's out back."

"Why don't you go find him and bring him to the library? Then I'll tell you both what's been happening. This is Richard Greene, a private investigator I've hired to look into Lucinda's murder."

She said hello to Richard and then escaped to find her husband. When she was out of earshot, I said, "Poor thing, I guess they've both been kind of adrift for the past week. I hated not to contact them, but Charles said it wasn't a good idea."

"Can we take a look at the murder scene while we wait?"

"Of course." I led him upstairs to Lucinda's bedroom and said, "This is where they found the body. I can't tell you much more than that because the body had already been removed by the time I got here. The room has obviously been thoroughly cleaned since then, so I don't know what you expect to find."

"Probably nothing, but you never know."

"Well, I'll leave you to it." I went to the door, adding, "By the way, what's the name of your associate—I'll tell Henry and Martha to expect him and show him right up."

"Alex Markham."

I repeated the name, then went down to the library to calm the ruffled feathers of Henry and Martha. I told them that I'd been out of town and that my attorney had thought it unwise to tell anyone, including them, where I was. They were understandably worried about their future and wanted to know what I planned to do with the house. I reassured them as best I could, explaining that they were provided for in Lucinda's will and would receive a generous lump sum and a small pension. As for the house, I told them it would probably be sold, but not until after my trial sometime next year. I asked them to stay on and take care of it just as they'd always done, hinting that I hoped it might be possible to find a buyer for the house who'd want to retain their services. I could see that I'd said the right words, as they were obviously pleased at the prospect of staying where they were. Before we could discuss anything further, we were interrupted by the doorbell.

"That will probably be a man named Alex Markham, who's here to assist Mr. Greene with the investigation," I said. "They'll want to ask you both some questions. Also, you'll be getting a call from Charles Barnett, my attorney, or one of his associates, as they'll have some questions as well."

Henry excused himself to answer the door, and I went to the small den that had served as a sort of household office, to locate the keys to Lucinda's condo. I found them and went back upstairs to the bedroom, where Richard introduced me to his helper, a short, heavyset man in his early forties who could have passed for the stereotype of a tired and jaded PI.

I handed Richard the keys and said, "You already have the address of her condo. I don't know whether the police have been there or not."

"Thanks. We'll go there from here."

"Do you need me to go with you?"

"Not this time. Maybe later."

"Good. Right now I've got a number of errands to run. You can reach me at the townhouse or leave word with Charles. I'll be seeing him for lunch."

14

Charles

AFTER Philip left, I went back to my desk and started organizing the accumulated messages in order of what I deemed to be their importance. When I'd finished that chore, I buzzed Rosemary and said, "Shall we have a go at it?"

"I'll be right in."

She came in and took her usual seat. Before I could begin, she looked closely at me and said, "I don't know what you did over the holiday weekend, but it certainly agreed with you. You look like your old self again."

"Lord, if one more person says that to me...."

"But it's true. I don't think you realize just how tired and drawn you'd begun to look. Everyone in the office has remarked about it at one time or another."

Before she could continue, I cut her off and said, "Okay, so I've had a rest cure. Right now, I need to play catch-up." I handed her the stack of messages. "Let's start returning these right now, in that order. The d'Autremont trial is set for the first Monday after New Year's. Are there any conflicts?"

"Too far off to be a problem, or at least nothing that I can't move up or back. Will two weeks be enough to set aside for the trial?"

"Probably, but keep the third week flexible, just in case."

"Anything else?"

"Not at the moment. Oh, yes. Pencil in lunch at one o'clock with Mr. d'Autremont, and make us a reservation at the Peachtree Grille. He'll call and confirm sometime later this morning."

She looked thoughtful and started to say something, then evidently changed her mind.

I decided to pry and said, "What were you going to say?"

"I just figured out why you look so rested and so much more yourself. He's responsible for that, isn't he?"

"You're too smart for your own good sometimes. Now get going on those calls."

She left, and shortly I was caught up in the routine of soothing clients, most of whom were in one sort of trouble or another, many of whom needed—or thought they needed, which from the client's perspective amounts to the same thing—desperately to see me. These I referred back to Rosemary for the purpose of scheduling appointments. I'd completely lost track of the time when, between calls, my private line rang.

"Hello."

"Hi. Are we still on for lunch?" Philip said.

I suddenly became aware of the time and was surprised to find that it was nearly noon. "Absolutely. I had Rosemary make reservations at the Peachtree Grille for one. If you can be here a little before that, we can walk over there."

"Sure."

"What have you been up to?"

"Well, I left Richard and his helper at the house, and I've been running errands. I stopped by and emptied my post office box earlier, and I'm at my condo now, going through a week's accumulation of mail."

"I've been doing the same thing with a backlog of urgent messages from clients whose hands need holding, metaphorically speaking."

"You can hold this client's hands anytime, metaphorically or otherwise."

"You're on. There's another call coming in, so I'll let you go. See you shortly."

I picked up the other call and was immediately caught up in someone else's problems. The calls finally ceased around a quarter to one, and Rosemary came in, followed by Philip. Without preamble, she said, "Boss, your dance card is nearly full every morning next week. I tried to keep the afternoons open, as usual."

"Good, the billable hours need to be shored up a bit. I'll be back from lunch by two thirty. You can take off if you want to and turn the phone over to reception."

"Thanks," she said, and she left, closing the door quietly behind her.

I got up from the desk, went around to Philip, and held both his hands. "This is nicer than the metaphorical kind," I said, and I pulled him to me.

"Absolutely." It was all he could get out before I covered his mouth briefly with my own. When I released him, he said, "Aren't you afraid someone will walk in on us?"

"Not at all. Everyone, including Andrew, knocks first—it's office protocol around here. Ready for lunch?"

"Yes."

"Then let's go."

We went downstairs and walked three blocks to the Peachtree Grille. Some people liked it very much, and some did not. I belonged to the former group and had always been pleased with both the food and the service. We were quickly seated at a small table in a corner, which suited me. I ordered soup and a house salad, and Philip selected a blackened chicken salad. After the waiter had departed, I said, "How are you holding up?"

"I'm okay. Yesterday morning seems more like a bad dream than it does something that actually happened."

"Good. Over time, the memory will fade almost completely away. At least that's what other clients have told me often enough."

"By the way, my car is ready. They had sense enough to perform the scheduled maintenance without waiting for me to call, so I'm going to go pick it up after lunch."

"Need a ride over there?"

"If you have time."

"I'll make time."

Lunch arrived, along with Richard, who gave the waiter an order without waiting for a menu.

"You didn't wait for me," he said.

"We didn't know for sure that you were coming."

"You said I was invited if I had something useful to report."

"Do you?"

"Possibly." By this time, he'd borrowed a chair from another table and pulled it up to ours. "I'd like Philip to go back to his wife's condo with me. There are some things there that just don't quite fit, and I'd like to know if they belonged to his wife, or perhaps to someone else."

"I'm not sure I can be of any help, but I'll try," Philip said.

"I won't ask you what you think you've found," I said, "because I know you won't tell me until you're ready."

"It'll keep."

"You can do one other thing."

"What's that?"

"Give Philip a lift to pick up his car. You can also stop by the house on the way and get him one of the spare garage door openers."

Philip and I continued to eat, and the three of us talked off and on while waiting for Richard's food to arrive. By the time it arrived, we were finished, and I asked Richard where he'd parked. "At your building, why?"

"Then we'll go on back to the office, and you can catch up with us when you're finished here."

"Okay, fine. Just run off and leave me by myself."

"You'll get over it. Besides, I saw you eyeing that busboy when you thought nobody was looking."

"He did have nice buns, didn't he?"

"I really wouldn't know. Busboys and their buns are more your style than mine."

We left him there, presumably plotting a possible conquest. I paid the check and got a receipt, and we walked back to the office. Coming out of the elevator, we ran into Andrew, who was on his way out of the office, and he stopped and visited with us for a minute before he excused himself to go meet a client.

Back in my office, we visited until Richard came in and took Philip off with him. Rosemary came back from lunch a few minutes later, and we began the afternoon, which was pretty much a carbon copy of the morning. When I've been tied up in a trial for a week or two, there's always a backlog of sometimes-urgent needs among the clientele. The long weekend following the end of the trial had added to that backlog.

About four o'clock, Philip called to ask, "What time will you be home?"

"About five thirty, why?"

"Just wondering."

I chose not to pry, and we hung up. Rosemary came in a little later to inform me that my mornings were fully booked for the next two weeks from nine 'til twelve every day, so I said, "In that case, tomorrow you'll have to start making afternoon appointments."

I signed the correspondence that she'd brought me, and when she'd taken it away, I started to finish dealing with the accumulation of mail. This took me up until five fifteen, and I decided to call it a day. I was home in my garage twenty minutes later and noted Philip's car was there. I had not, despite my interest in cars in general, asked him what he drove, although from his mention of Morehouse Motors, I knew it had to be a BMW or a Mercedes. It was, in fact, a BMW coupe—a very expensive piece of machinery.

I went up the stairs, becoming gradually aware as I neared the kitchen door that the Shostakovich Fifth Symphony was coming through the sound system at concert-hall level, which was fine with me. I quietly opened the kitchen door at the head of the stairs and looked in. I could smell something in the oven, and Philip was standing at the sink, his back to me, apparently peeling potatoes. Lance, as always when there was food being prepared, was lying on the floor watching Philip hopefully. The level of the music, combined with the running water, prevented both Philip and Lance from hearing me. I almost spoke; then I noticed that Philip was wearing an apron, and obviously nothing else, as his bare ass was fully exposed. That gave me an inspiration, so I closed the door quietly and slipped upstairs, quickly undressed and hung my clothes in the closet, then slipped downstairs in a state of total nakedness. I tiptoed up behind Philip and put my arms around him, pressing my crotch into his backside. He was startled but recovered quickly. "Am I being attacked?" he said as he reached around behind him and grabbed my erection.

"You bet," I said, turning him around to face me. "I like your outfit, but weren't you afraid that Richard might come in and be driven wild with desire?"

"No. He told me that he's going to be very late, and even if he had surprised me and been stricken with lust, he would've had to live with disappointment."

I kissed him and said, "Does the chef have time for an appetizer upstairs?"

"Absolutely." He turned the water off and placed the pan of potatoes on a burner. Turning the burner on low, he said, "Last one in bed has to do the dishes." He dashed upstairs, with me right behind him.

He beat me to the bed, and I said, "That's not fair—you had a head start."

"This will have to be a quickie," he said. "If I don't get back down to the kitchen in about ten minutes, dinner may be ruined."

I was beyond conversation by that time, and we took care of each other's needs and were dressed and back in the kitchen in less than fifteen minutes. This time Philip wore a pair of cutoffs and a T-shirt under his apron. I dressed similarly, sans apron, and asked if I could help with dinner.

"You can round up the ingredients for a salad," he said.

"I don't think we have any lettuce."

"Yes, we do. I took inventory earlier and went to the grocery store."

I opened the refrigerator, quickly surveyed its contents, and said, "My God, there hasn't been this much food on hand around here since forever ago."

"I noticed that the cupboard was pretty bare. You and Richard don't cook much, do you?"

"I used to but seem to have fallen out of the habit."

"We'll just have to get you back in that habit."

I tossed a salad and set the breakfast table for two. Then I sat down at the table for a minute, thinking that it seemed so cozy and domestic. This, of course, brought back memories of Robert, and I must have been quiet for a long time, because Philip said, "You have a faraway look about you."

"I was just thinking how nice this was, and of course that started a chain of memories of earlier days."

"Are you all right?"

I got up, walked over to where he was mashing the potatoes, and gave him a hug from behind. "Never better."

"Good. Now, go sit back down while I finish this."

Soon, we were enjoying the food, which turned out to be a meatloaf with mashed potatoes and steamed broccoli. The salad, along with tall glasses of iced tea, completed the meal.

"This is really good," I said.

"Well, I'm a bit rusty at cooking, so I decided to keep it simple. Later, when I learn more about your culinary likes and dislikes, I'll be a little more creative."

Richard came in as we were finishing. "Something smells good," he said. "Is there any left?"

"More than enough, I think," Philip said, and he got up and fixed a plate for Richard.

I suddenly remembered their visit to the deceased's condo and said, "Richard, what did you find out this afternoon?"

"You always ask me these questions when I'm eating. Let me finish and I'll fill you in."

Philip and I cleaned up the kitchen together, despite his having won the race upstairs. As we carried our glasses toward the study, I said, "Richard, you can rinse off your dishes, load them in the dishwasher, and push the button."

His mouth being full, he merely nodded his assent, and Philip and I went into the study and made ourselves comfortable on the sofa. As I sat down, I noticed what appeared to be a couple of boxes of CDs on my desk and said, "Planning to do some computer work?"

"Yes, if you don't mind my using your machine."

"Not at all." I had an inspiration and continued, "If there are too many distractions down here, we could fix you up a complete office upstairs in one of the spare bedrooms. I sometimes retreat up there myself when Richard has visitors."

"Sounds better all the time. I do have a great deal of research material and wouldn't want to create too much clutter down here. I may have told you that all of my contact with the publisher is handled through a law firm in Boston. It's a bit awkward, writing under a pseudonym, but I prefer it that way, and without the arrangement with the Boston law firm, my anonymity would be totally lost. Anyhow, to make a long story short, I received a message from Boston today reminding me that Lindsey, that's my publisher's name, is getting nervous about a deadline to which I'd committed. I have about ten days of very hard work ahead of me which I could do over at my condo, but I'd much prefer to be here around you."

"Come on upstairs, then, and let's have a look at that room."

He followed me upstairs, where the third bedroom was outfitted as a guest room and the fourth bedroom was mostly vacant. Although it was the smallest of the four bedrooms, it was still a good-sized room, about twelve by fifteen feet. Currently it contained only a small desk in one corner, complete with telephone, computer, and printer. In another corner were a few boxes of stuff waiting to be thrown away or stored, although I couldn't remember which. "You can take over the entire room, if you like. As I said, I use it only when Richard has company, and that isn't very often. There's a jack on the wall beside the desk where you can plug in a cat-5 computer cable and get high-speed broadband."

"This will do very nicely," he said. "You've saved me once again. Thank you."

"I assure you, the pleasure is all mine."

We went back downstairs, where Richard was waiting for us, stretched out in a recliner. Philip and I settled back on the sofa, and I looked at Richard expectantly. "Well?"

"We may have had a little luck today. It appears that the police haven't been through the deceased's condo. Alex and I went over it with a fine-tooth comb. In one of the closets, we found some clothing that stuck out like a sore thumb."

"How so?"

"As you know, I'm not particularly style conscious, but even I could see that it had been selected by someone with different taste than was evident in the rest of the clothing. Looking more closely, we determined that it was of a different size, as well. When Philip got there, he seemed fairly certain that none of it belonged to his wife."

"Can it be identified?"

"That's the best part: there were some cleaners' tags on a couple of the garments. It may take a while, but we should be able to identify the cleaners and perhaps even the customer."

"Anything else?"

"Nothing to write home about. A few odds and ends here and there that also clearly didn't belong with the rest of the furnishings, but nothing that could be traceable."

"Fingerprints?"

"Many, but it'll take a while to sort them out."

"Once again, you appear to be earning your exorbitant fees."

"Thank you, thank you, one and all," he said with a grin, and I could tell that he was pleased.

"Doesn't one of your grunts, as you call them, drive a van?"

"Yes, why?"

"Philip is going to turn the vacant bedroom into a small office so that he can work here at home instead of at his condo. Some muscle power and a suitable vehicle are called for."

"No problem. We can get together tomorrow morning and have it done before noon."

"Have you talked to your friend Bruce yet?"

"No. He wasn't at the Powder Magazine earlier, so I'm going to call him after a while."

"What exactly is his job with the DA's office?"

"I believe he's in charge of the computer system and the clerical functions."

"My God. Do you realize what that means? He would have access to any and all documents relating to everything they do."

"Slow down, boyo, you're almost salivating."

"Think about the implications. If he could be persuaded to do a bit of snooping, we might be one step ahead of them all the way through this case. What would it take to elicit his help, do you think?"

"I'm not sure. He might do it for the sake of gay rights. He might even do it for my body."

"Well, by all means, make the sacrifice. I take it he's attractive?"

"Oh yes, cute, and eminently fuckable. But—"

"But nothing," I said, interrupting him. "This is business."

"You don't understand. I stopped seeing him, in the biblical sense, because he wants to settle down, pick out china patterns, and set up housekeeping. You know I'm not into that."

"You could certainly string him along a bit for a good cause. Where else could you get paid your daily rate for getting laid?"

"When you put it like that, it almost sounds attractive."

"Better yet, why don't you invite him over here for dinner, and we can give him the hard sell?"

"He might not want to be seen entering these premises."

"True, although in a car after dark, you could drive directly into the garage and close the doors before he gets out."

"You win. I'll talk to him and see what happens."

With that, we stopped talking shop, and eventually the conversation dwindled to a halt. Philip and I went upstairs, crawled in bed, and watched television for a while. We quickly became bored with the tube but managed to find something interesting to do to each other before we drifted off to sleep.

15

Philip

THURSDAY morning I was awake long before the alarm was scheduled to go off. Charles had somehow managed to wrap himself around me in such a way that I didn't want to move for fear of waking him, so I lay there for a while, thinking about events and speculating a little on what lay ahead for both of us. A few minutes before the alarm sounded, he stirred and woke up. When he realized how tangled our arms and legs were, he extricated himself and said, "It's a wonder I didn't cut off your circulation."

"I don't think there was any damage done, and everything seems to be functioning."

We got up and, without further conversation, dressed for our morning run and covered our usual six miles. On returning to the townhouse, we dropped our clothes in the laundry room as before and went up to shave and shower.

In the shower, Philip said, "How many pairs of running shorts do you have, anyhow?"

"Enough to last until I do the weekly laundry."

"Which explains why you can toss your gear in a laundry basket every day."

"Absolutely."

We were in the kitchen finishing up our coffee when Richard came in looking, if possible, even more bedraggled than he had the day before.

Charles couldn't resist saying, "Good morning, sunshine," which elicited a surly "Up yours" in response.

I got up and poured Richard a cup of coffee before another exchange could take place, and Charles excused himself to go up and dress for work. I poured myself a second cup and carried it upstairs to the bedroom, where Charles was struggling with the knot in his tie. Setting my coffee cup on the dresser, I reached over, turned him sideways away from the mirror, and said, "Let me do that."

"Thanks," he said as I finished the job for him. He slipped his hands inside my robe and around my waist. "I wish I could stay home today."

"What would you do if you could?"

"Play with you," he said in between kisses.

"Sounds like fun, but it'll have to keep until tonight. Besides, we have a nice lazy weekend ahead of us."

"I suppose so," he said with a sigh. "I guess I'd better run along before this gets out of hand."

I retrieved my coffee, followed him downstairs as far as the kitchen, and sat down across the table from Richard, who seemed to be pulling himself together and said, "Whoever decreed that days should begin with mornings was a sadist."

It was obviously a rhetorical statement, and I chose not to encourage him. When he saw that I wasn't going to take the bait, he changed the subject, saying, "How much stuff did you say you need to bring over here?"

"Not much, just a desk, computer, printer, and a couple of filing cabinets."

He finished his coffee and promised to have two of his people at my condo around ten o'clock, describing both of them for me before he went upstairs to clean up. I lingered over a third cup of coffee, then spent some time emptying the dishwasher. Then I cleaned up the kitchen and took a more thorough inventory of the groceries and supplies on hand, making a list of the things I'd overlooked yesterday. I turned to go upstairs and dress and found Richard dressed for work, standing at the foot of the stairs, watching me.

"You're very domestic," he said.

"When I have to be."

"You and Charley are beginning to look like the real thing," he said in what I now knew to be his serious mode.

"So it would seem. It hasn't quite been a week since we met, but already I find it hard to contemplate not being with him."

"Have you contemplated it?"

"Perhaps that was an unfortunate choice of words, more a figure of speech than a conscious thought. Let me start over. I've never been truly in love before, but I can certainly recognize it for what it is, and as far as I'm concerned, it's forever, or until he gets tired of me."

"Clearly, he feels the same way."

"Have the two of you talked about it?"

"Not really, but I know Charley. He doesn't do anything less than thoroughly. It's all or nothing with that boy."

"She said that too."

"She who?"

"Lydia."

"She's one sharp gal."

"I noticed." I sensed that he was leading up to something with this line of questioning, and I turned out to be correct.

"Would you and Charley be more comfortable if I made other living arrangements?"

"The subject hasn't come up, and I see no reason why it should. Besides, he doesn't need any more disruption in his life."

"That was a cagey answer, worthy even of a lawyer."

"It wasn't meant to be." I had a faint thought and chose to express it. "I realize that I've sort of invaded the living arrangements around here, and I certainly hope my presence isn't resented."

"It would be, if I thought you were bad for Charley, but since the opposite is clearly the case, it's not a problem. I'm happy to see him come back to life. You can't imagine what it's been like, watching your best friend in all the world turning into a zombie over a period of three years and not being able to do anything about it."

A lightbulb suddenly went on in my mind, and I said, "You're in love with him, aren't you?"

"I've loved him since high school, but he doesn't know it—and he's never to know it, understood?" His tone brooked no argument.

"I thought I detected something in what you said yesterday in the car. It's really none of my business, but isn't it hard for you to be around him when he's with someone else?"

"Not anymore," he said. He was quiet for a moment, then continued, wistfully, "When he first brought Robert home to Atlanta, I was devastated—so much so that I could hardly bear to be around them. I guess the torch was still burning brightly then, and I'd fooled myself into thinking that there was still hope for the two of us. After that first summer, I finally realized that it wasn't meant to be, so I began to deal with it. The next summer was easier, and the following one easier still. By the time they'd finished school and moved back to Atlanta permanently, the pain was gone, and I could relax and be glad that he was happy. By then, it wasn't really that difficult, because anyone with half a brain could see that they were right for each other."

Not knowing what else to say, I said simply, "I'm sorry."

"Don't be. It was all a long time ago, and I've never told a living soul. Robert didn't even know how it was with me."

"Thank you for sharing that with me, and you may be sure that your secret is safe with me. And let's have no more talk about moving out, either, okay?"

"Okay," he said, totally surprising me by giving me a hug. Then he left without another word.

I went upstairs and dressed quickly, having noted that I hadn't much time if I wanted to visit my broker before I went to the condo to wait for Richard's helpers. My brief meeting with Chase revealed that I hadn't done too badly in dumping the stock necessary to cover the wire transfer he'd made last Friday. We discussed my investment strategy for the end of the current quarter and the beginning of the next, and I was on my way back uptown with plenty of time to run my errands. I stopped by the post office and picked up my mail, then by a U-Haul outlet and purchased a number of cardboard cartons, along with tape to secure them, arriving at the condo with ample time to pack the items I wanted moved.

Richard's men were half an hour late, and by the time they arrived I'd changed into jeans and T-shirt and had literally stripped the condo of all personal items and packed them, including the groceries and household cleaning supplies from the kitchen and bathrooms. There really wasn't that much to pack, and it occurred to me that I could very quickly rent the place furnished for an outrageous sum, considering its location. When the men saw the stuff I'd lined up to be moved, they tactfully refrained from mentioning that the quantity of material seriously exceeded their expectations, although I did detect a raised eyebrow. However, it didn't take the three of us very long to load the van, after which they followed me back to the townhouse.

It took slightly longer to unload, because all except the two boxes of kitchen stuff had to be carried up to the third floor. I sent them on their way after giving them each a can of Coke and a fifty-dollar bill. They tried to protest the tip, saying that it wasn't necessary. I told them that if they wouldn't tell Richard, neither would I, and we let it drop. They'd just left when the telephone rang.

I answered, thinking it would probably be Charles wanting to plan lunch. Instead, it was Rosemary calling to explain that Andrew had dragged Charles off to a meeting, which was expected to continue through and beyond lunch. In a way, I was glad not to have to clean up, as I had a lot of work to do, and by one thirty I'd done most of it. The kitchen and bathroom supplies were stowed away, eliminating many of the things on the shopping list I'd made, and I'd organized one corner of the spare room into an efficient work area for myself. The closet in the bedroom took a little longer but was finally arranged to my satisfaction.

Before showering and changing from my work clothes, I took a couple of the now-empty boxes and went back to my condo. In less than fifteen minutes I'd gathered up the few things that I'd overlooked earlier, including the telephones. On the way back to the townhouse, I dropped the condo keys off with the rental agents who handled my various properties, instructing them to have the place cleaned and the furnishings inventoried with an eye to having it rented as soon as a satisfactory tenant could be located. Arriving back at the townhouse, I found suitable places to store the rest of the stuff from the apartment and then disassembled all of the empty boxes and stowed them carefully away.

After I'd showered and changed, I went downstairs, called the telephone company, and arranged to have the telephone disconnected at the apartment and a new number set up at this address. They made an appointment for the following Monday morning to do the installation, and I went back upstairs to survey my handiwork.

As I entered the room, the telephone rang; it was Charles calling to apologize about lunch, and I assured him that it hadn't been a problem and that I'd been very busy. He wanted to know what I'd been up to, but I told him he'd have to wait and see.

"Sounds like you've been cooking again."

"Not this time, I've been too busy to start."

"Well, hold off for a while. I'd like to go swim some laps before dinner this evening. It helps me work out the kinks of the day. Want to join me?"

"That would be great. When and where?"

"I'll be home by six, and we can go over to the Y together. I can get you a guest pass."

"No need for that. I'm already a member."

This caused him to again express surprise that we hadn't heretofore run into each other. After we said goodbye, I decided to finish what I'd started that morning, so I went downstairs, retrieved my now-shortened shopping list, and went to Publix. Within an hour, I was back and had everything put away to my satisfaction. Realizing that I was suddenly very tired, I went upstairs, undressed, and crawled in bed for a nap. Lance, who'd been following me around the house all day, curled up beside me.

I woke to Charles kissing me and saying, "Wake up, sleeping beauty."

I realized then that he'd undressed and was in bed with me, so I said, "What about our swim?"

"Later. They're open 'til nine and this is much more urgent."

He was right: it was much more urgent.

By six thirty, we were up and dressed in shorts and knit shirts and on the way to the Y, spending about fifteen minutes in the steam room before we headed for the pool. There was one lane not in use, so we shared it, swimming at a steady pace until we'd each completed a mile of laps. Afterward, we decided to stop by Rick's, one of a chain of restaurants in town. The one we stopped at was in fact next door to Annie's Bistro. We consumed large chef's salads, offsetting the healthiness of the salad by sharing a truly wicked dessert. Over dinner, I told him what I'd been up to during the day, concluding by saying that I hoped he didn't mind my having a telephone installed.

He seemed hurt at the thought and said, "Why should I mind?"

"I don't know. I just didn't want to give the impression that I'm taking over your house."

"I don't see it that way, babe, but to put it in those terms, you're free to take over anything I have that you want or need, and if I don't have it, I'll certainly try to get it for you."

"While we're on the subject, I should pay you something toward rent and utilities." He gave me a hurt look again, so I said, "I've never sponged off anybody in my life, and I certainly don't intend to start at this late date. If I'm going to be living there, it's only right that I contribute. Richard doesn't live there for free, does he?"

"No, he gives me a hundred bucks or so each month for utilities, and every so often we sit down and figure out what his share of the grocery bill amounts to."

"Then I should contribute at least that much for my share of the utilities and a like amount toward upkeep and maintenance." This very nearly precipitated our first argument, so I finally backed down from my position and agreed to a flat hundred per month. This I did in order to keep the peace, resolving in my own mind to make up the difference by buying the major portion of the groceries.

When we got home—it was beginning to feel like home—we went directly upstairs to freshen up, stopping by the laundry room to air out our gym bags and hang our Speedos over the laundry tub to dry. Charles walked into the closet and came back a moment later.

"I need to make some more room in there for your stuff."

"It's all right the way it is. I managed to put everything away."

"No, it's too crowded, and I know why. I'm going to take all of Robert's clothes down to the laundry room. Tomorrow, they can go to Goodwill."

Before I could say anything, he went back into the closet and quickly emerged with an armload of clothes, which he spread out on the bed. He immediately went back for more, and soon a second pile joined the first, and he said, "If you see anything you can make use of, help yourself," before he went back for yet another load.

Although I wasn't terribly enthusiastic about the idea, there were some very expensive things displayed on the bed, a few of which were very much to my taste. Knowing that he'd be hurt if I refused the offer, I selected just under a dozen items that I knew I would make some use of and carried them back into the closet, saying, "These will do very nicely."

He seemed pleased at that, and I surmised that he probably understood all too well the reasoning behind my having taken him up on the offer. We carried all of the remaining garments down to the laundry room, carefully stacking them in one corner. "I should have done this a long time ago," he said. "It was wrong of me to hang onto things like that."

"Would you like me to take them to Goodwill in the morning?"

"Would you? It would be appreciated."

"Of course," I replied. I quickly changed topics. "Now, let me show you what I've done to your house."

"Our house," he corrected me as I led him up to the spare room cum office.

He seemed pleased and was obviously impressed with the way I'd organized the office space. He looked at the boxes of stuff that he had left in one corner and said, "Let me show you what we can do with these."

He picked up two of the boxes, and I followed with the other two. He led me down to one corner of the garage and opened a door to which I hadn't paid any previous attention. It led down to a large partially finished basement under the garage. We carried the boxes to one corner, which was already in use as a storage area.

"Anything you don't have an immediate need for but don't want to throw out, you can bring down here."

"Thanks, I will."

"Sometimes it's a little too convenient, and I find myself saving stuff that really should be thrown away. I guess I must have some squirrel blood in my veins."

I looked around the basement, which was mostly unused. There was a bench press and some weights in one corner. Noticing my look, Charles said, "That's Richard's workout gear. I'd always planned to build a real exercise room down here, up to and including a small sauna, but somehow never got around to it."

"There's certainly plenty of room."

He didn't answer and turned off the lights, and we went back up to the spare room, where he said, "With all this, I don't imagine you actually got any work done today."

"No, I barely had time to begin organizing things a bit. Tomorrow I'll finish the organizing, and Monday morning I'll begin working on my current project."

"Will you have any trouble meeting your deadline?"

"None whatever. Once I get started, the creative juices usually start flowing, and things progress very rapidly."

During this bit of conversation, we'd walked back down to the kitchen, where I fixed each of us a drink, which we carried into the study. We sat on the sofa, and he asked me about my current project, which I told him was a novel set in eighteenth-century New Orleans—the third in a series featuring the same family. He wanted to know what the previous two titles had been, and I told him.

"Those were yours?" He was incredulous.

"I'm afraid so."

"Don't be so modest. I read both of them even before they made the best-sellers list. Although they were clearly aimed at a female audience, I found them terrific. Can I read this one now?"

"Please don't ask. I'm superstitious about anybody reading my stuff before it's finished."

"Then I'll reserve a copy at the Battle Bookstore."

"You don't have to wait quite that long. As soon as I get the galleys back from the publisher, you can help me proofread them."

"When will that be?"

"With luck, by the first of November. Speaking of the Battle Bookstore, want to run over there? I haven't browsed for a while."

"You're on."

We took my car over to Peachtree Street and up to the Peachtree Battle Shopping Center, where my favorite bookstore is located. The Battle Bookstore had been a staple in this little strip center for years. They'd recently opened a much larger outlet in Buckhead in a humongous building that had begun life as a car dealership, but I preferred the original store. They stocked tens of thousands of titles and had a small coffee shop on the mezzanine known as the "Cup and Chaucer." We were both recognized by name by one or more of the store personnel, and it was my turn to comment on the fact.

"How can we both be so well known in so many of the same places without ever having run into each other?"

"Beats me."

As usual, I came away several dollars lighter than I entered, as did Charles, although our selections didn't fall within the same genres. My selections were in the area of historical fiction and science fiction, while his ran to mysteries, popular fiction, and a small volume of poetry.

When we got back home, we carried our purchases up to the study and discovered Richard on the sofa talking to another young man.

Richard's guest was in his midtwenties, of medium height, with a face that was attractive in a square-jawed sort of way. He also had dark-brown eyes and an abundance of curly black hair. They stood when we came into the room, and I noticed that the friend had a very nice body. Richard then introduced us to Bruce Larson. As he did, his descriptive words from the previous evening echoed in my mind—"cute and eminently fuckable." *An apt description*, I thought.

After we were all seated, Richard explained that Bruce was more than willing to help us if he could, which seemed to be Charles's cue to take charge of the conversation. He started by asking a few basic questions about Bruce's job and how he felt about it. It developed that he loved the job, liked the people he supervised, and was well liked by them. He had little respect, however, for Wetherbee, but as he had virtually no contact with the man, it wasn't a problem. He administered two local-area networks of personal computers, the file-servers for both being located in his office.

Charles then asked him, "Aren't you worried about consequences if they find out you're gay?"

"Not really. I'm civil service, which protects me from discrimination. There isn't a whole lot they can do as long as I behave myself."

"Well, helping us, even in a small way, with this case certainly falls somewhat outside the parameters of 'behaving yourself'."

"I know, but I hate the way they're handling this case, and if I can help, I will." He stopped and looked thoughtful before continuing, "I've always been closeted, and this case gives me a chance to strike back."

"Thanks. Philip and I will appreciate anything you can do for him."

"What, exactly, do you want me to do?"

"I think it will be a case of 'forewarned is forearmed', so basically, if you see any documents or hear any scuttlebutt as to the direction the case is taking, you can pass the information along verbally to Richard."

"I can do better than that with the documents."

"How?"

"I walk into and out of the department every day with DVDs or thumb drives in my pockets, and nobody takes any notice—it's part of my job. I even do a lot of housekeeping-type work in the computer systems from home after hours, so it'll be easy to snoop. If I find anything really important, I can bring you the whole document."

Charles could barely contain his elation at this offer, and we both thanked Bruce in advance for anything he might do. We excused ourselves at that point and left them in the study. We undressed, got in bed, and once again attempted to watch TV for a while. As before, the tube was boring, so we found more interesting things to do, and having done them, we decided that a thing worth doing was worth doing again. In the midst of our second round, there was a knock on the door—which we only then realized had been left open.

We stopped what we were doing and sat up in bed. Charles looked crossly at Richard and said, "How long have you been standing there?"

"I'll never tell, but don't you guys know that it won't wear out?"

Charles ignored his jibe. "Is there a reason for this intrusion?"

"Yes, to talk about Bruce tonight while I'm alert and not tomorrow at the crack of doom, when you usually try to pick my brain."

Charles quickly got down to cases and said, "He'll certainly be a godsend, especially if they try to spring any surprises on us."

"He's extremely eager to help."

"Did you have to promise him your body?"

"Not explicitly, but it was sort of understood that there would be strings. Fortunately, he's smart enough to realize that he can't afford to be seen with me in public for the duration of this case. The resulting circumspection will minimize my sacrifice."

"From where I sit it doesn't look like much of a sacrifice."

"Except for the setting-up-housekeeping part that I told you about, it isn't. That boy has an ass that just won't quit." This was delivered thoughtfully. Then his mood changed, and he looked pointedly at the two of us. "Well, you two carry on with what you were doing, I'm going to bed." He turned on his heel and left.

We decided to call it a night and were both asleep very quickly.

Charles

PHILIP and I awakened at the same time on Friday morning, just before the alarm went off. With little more than a good-morning kiss, we quickly dressed and commenced our morning run, this already having become a part of our daily ritual. Before I knew it, we'd returned, bathed, had breakfast, and I was on the way downtown.

I had an early session scheduled with Andrew, following which there was to be a staff meeting—a sometimes-boring but always-necessary biweekly event. Andrew and I discussed several pending cases, including Philip's. I wasn't quite certain what Andrew's reaction would be to our inside source in the DA's office, but he seemed to think it was a case of poetic justice.

The staff meeting managed, as it usually did, to kill most of the morning, which was remarkable in light of our concerns over billable hours.

After the meeting, I tried to reach Philip to set up a lunch date, but there was no answer at home, so I worked through lunch and launched into my afternoon with a bit of a head start. Five o'clock came soon enough, and I was on my way home a few minutes later. Philip's car was in the garage, and he was in bed, sound asleep, as he had been the day before. Lance was curled up on the bed, snuggled up next to him. Quietly undressing, I studied his face in repose, amazed both at the quality his beauty took when his face was relaxed and the fact that such beauty had been surrendered to me. I slipped under the covers with him and snuggled up close, which of course, caused him to wake up.

"Hi," he said sleepily.

"Hi, yourself."

As usual with us, one thing led to another. Afterward, as we dressed to go and swim some laps, I asked him about his day.

"It was busy enough. Yesterday, as you know, I cleaned out my condo and turned it over to the rental agent. Today I cleaned out Lucinda's condo and turned it over to the same agent. Well, actually, I didn't do it by myself. I went by and gathered up all of the truly personal stuff, then sent Henry and Martha over to pack up everything else and clean up the condo. While they were doing that, I removed all of my personal belongings from the house on West Paces Ferry Road. That may have been a bit cowardly of me, but I felt if they saw me making a point of moving out, they'd become unduly worried concerning their futures. I also took Robert's clothing by Goodwill, as promised. Oh, and I had a conference with Randolph Forney, my tax attorney."

"A very busy day."

"No, that was just the morning. I spent the afternoon upstairs getting my work area truly organized."

"No wonder you were asleep when I got home."

"Well, if I can count on being awakened in the same way every afternoon, I'll make a habit of it."

"We could make it a standing appointment. Shall I have Rosemary pencil in 'sex with Philip' for five forty-five daily?"

"Sounds interesting, but perhaps just a trifle too regimented."

While we talked, our hands had been busy, and suddenly we found more important things to do than carry on a conversation. Afterward, we went to the Y and swam some laps; then we returned home and made a joint effort of the preparation of dinner. We cleaned up the kitchen and went into the study, and I loaded the CD changer with three discs. Philip sat down on the couch, and I lay down on it with my head in his lap, in which position Richard found us sometime later, when he came in.

"That's so charming and domestic I could just puke," Richard said.

"Richard, just because you lack a basic nesting instinct is no reason to belittle those of us who do possess one."

"Yeah, yeah, yeah." He'd heard it all before.

"What are you doing tomorrow?"

"Going up to Lake Lanier with some of the guys."

"Well, don't forget to be back in time for dinner at Gran's."

"No problem. What are you guys up to tomorrow?"

"As little as possible."

"That doesn't sound very exciting."

"It is when you make your own excitement."

"Yeah, yeah, yeah, here we go again."

"Richard, if you must interrupt Kiri Te Kanawa in midwarble, at least interrupt with something important."

He let my remark pass and sat in silence for a while before excusing himself to go up to his room and watch TV. Philip said, "Do you think Richard will ever settle down with someone?"

"Actually, he probably would have settled down with me many years ago, had I been interested."

Philip surprised me, saying, "I didn't know that you knew about that."

"What do you know about it?"

"I guessed, and during a heart-to-heart talk the other morning, he confirmed my suspicions. He has no idea that you know how he feels."

"I love Richard dearly as my oldest and best friend, but I've never had so much as a flicker of sexual interest in him. I was aware that he was still carrying a torch when I met Robert, and it took him a long time to be comfortable with our relationship. In the end, however, he seemed to get over it and be happy for me. What exactly did he say to you?"

"Basically what you just told me. He said he only wants to see you happy and was glad that I appeared to be able to accomplish that goal. My guess, however, is that at some level he still wishes that things could have been different between the two of you. I suspect, therefore, that he'll require some time to be comfortable with us."

"That must have been quite a conversation."

"More or less."

"What else did he say?"

"Not much. He did offer to move out, if three was in danger of becoming a crowd."

"Interesting. What did you say to that?"

"Basically, that it wasn't a problem and that in any case you didn't need any more disruptions in your life right now."

"Good. And is it?"

"Is it what?"

"A problem?"

"No. I like Richard, and it's not a problem now, nor will it be in the future."

Shortly after that, I turned off all of the speakers in the house except the ones in the master bedroom. Then I set the stereo system to play for two hours before turning itself off. We went upstairs and lay propped up in bed, each of us reading one of the books we'd purchased the night before. Around midnight, we came to stopping places in our respective books, turned out the lights, and snuggled up to each other for a while. As usual with us, it didn't stop with mere snuggling.

The next morning, we slept until nearly eight and then went for a run in the park. There were a great many runners out at that hour, it being a Saturday, and I even spotted a few faces to which I could attach names. After we'd gotten home, showered, and shaved, we went down to breakfast and were surprised to find Richard not only up and dressed but evidently awake, alert, and ready for anything. I couldn't resist ragging him a bit, saying, "You're certainly bright-eyed and bushy-tailed, considering the ungodly hour."

"I can be, if I'm sufficiently motivated," he said, with an enigmatic look about him.

"Are you going to explain that, or must we pry it out of you?"

"Simple. The guys I'm going up to the lake with are Jerry and Roger, a couple whom I met last summer. We're going to stay with a friend of theirs named Martin, at his lake house. I'm their hostess gift to Martin, so to speak."

"It's not like you to get so wound up over a blind date."

"Too right. However, it isn't truly a blind date. I have seen pictures of our host, and I think he'll do nicely for an evening or two."

Philip had brought us juice, and I pulled him down in my lap as I spoke. "Whatever it takes to get you through the night," I said, adding, "fortunately, I don't have to drive sixty or seventy miles to find it."

He chose to let that remark pass, gulped down the last of his coffee, and excused himself to go up and pack an overnight bag. Philip moved over to his chair, and we finished our breakfast and the paper. While we were cleaning up the kitchen, the doorbell rang.

Richard yelled down the stairs, "I'll get it, it's probably for me."

A minute later, he passed through the kitchen on his way down to the door. I called after him, "Don't forget Gran's tomorrow night."

"I'll be there," he said, and he was gone.

I said, "Alone at last."

We loafed around the house for a while, then got in my car and drove over to an area along Virginia Avenue, north of Ponce de Leon, that had in the not-too-distant past turned into an area of antique shops and restaurants. We spent an hour or so browsing through the various shops, then went back home, where we left the car. Then we walked over to the MARTA station and took the subway to Lenox Square. At Lenox, we had lunch at one of the mall restaurants before walking around the mall. In Neiman Marcus, I spotted a tie that I liked, but it was priced considerably higher than my usual self-imposed limit for ties. While we were in another department of the store, Philip excused himself, he said, to find a rest room. When he returned, he took a package from under his arm and handed it to me.

"From me, to you."

It contained the tie, and I said, "Thank you. That was sweet of you."

"I just wanted to give you something."

Later, across the street at Phipps Plaza, I noticed that he tried on a sweater in Saks, clearly unable to decide whether he wanted it or not. I managed to surreptitiously purchase it without him seeing me do so. Instead of carrying it with me, I arranged to have it delivered to him at the house the following Monday.

We were home by four and went immediately up to take a nap before deciding what to do about dinner. When we'd gotten up and dressed, I asked Philip if he had any preferences for dinner.

"I was thinking about taking us to Sean & Gabe's," he said, "if that's to your liking."

"Very much to my liking."

"Good, I'll make us a reservation for later."

"That might be a problem on such short notice."

"Not to worry, I have connections," he said, grinning, and he went to the telephone.

So it was that at seven fifteen we arrived at Sean & Gabe's on Piedmont, which has been an Atlanta favorite since at least the early seventies. The cuisine is Northern Italian, and always prepared to perfection. Robert and I had eaten there often but without having gotten to know the staff very well. When we walked in the door, Philip was greeted effusively by the hostess and in no time we were in the main dining room, which featured red walls covered with paintings, the effect stopping just short of being garish. I ordered veal piccata and Philip selected the veal marsala. We were lingering over dessert and coffee when some people I knew were shown to the next table.

It was a couple that Robert and I had known fairly well for a number of years. I'd more or less lost touch with them in the last year or two, as I had with so many other people. They were clearly delighted to see me "finally out and about" and, more to the point, "with someone." I introduced them to Philip, and they promised to call us soon and set up a dinner date.

On the way back home, we were content and quiet.

I broke the silence, saying, "I'd sort of like to go to church in the morning. You're more than welcome to come along, but I'll certainly understand if you don't want to." I already knew that his family had been Catholic originally but for the last century or more had been Episcopal.

"I'd like that. Where were you planning to go?"

"Well, my membership has always been at St. Philip's Cathedral, but they're so low church these days that I really don't like going there. For the last few years, I've mostly gone to St. Martin in the Fields."

"Where is it located?"

"Northeast, out beyond the Lenox area."

"Sounds fine to me."

We got home, changed into more comfortable clothes, and settled down in the study to read for a while. I put a disc of Satie piano pieces on the stereo, and when it had finished, I replaced it with Kiri singing Puccini arias. Shortly before eleven, we went up to bed and were settled down in time to watch the late news and weather.

Sunday morning, we got up around eight, ran, had breakfast, then dressed and went to church. On the way back down Peachtree, I suddenly thought of Patty's Place, a restaurant occupying part of the ground floor of a relatively new high-rise building at the corner of Peachtree and West Paces Ferry Road. I hadn't been there for a while, but it was a favorite.

"If it weren't for dinner at Gran's this evening, I'd suggest brunch at Patty's Place right now," I said.

"There's always next Sunday."

"You've got a date."

We decided to drive on down Peachtree to a Rick's outlet for a light lunch, after which we returned to the townhouse. As we were removing our Sunday best, Philip said, "Feel like taking a nap?"

"Would that be a nap nap, or a euphemism nap?"

"How about the latter, followed by the former?"

As I was then down to my underwear, I didn't bother to reply, I just removed my remaining garment, walked over to the bed, and held the covers back. He quickly slipped under them, and I joined him. After we made love, we dozed off, being awakened by a knock on the open door.

Richard said, "Hey, have you guys forgotten Gran's dinner?"

I rubbed my eyes, trying to wake up. "What time is it?"

"After five."

"Shit."

"Exactly," he said, and he disappeared.

I bent over Philip, who still looked groggy, and said, "We've got to get ourselves in gear. She expects us promptly at six for drinks."

We got up and took a quick shower, together, as usual, but without our normal horseplay, and were freshly shaved and dressed by five thirty. A few minutes later, the three of us were in my car and on our way.

17

Philip

AS CHARLES pulled up to his grandmother's house, I felt a twinge of apprehension over the evening that was now at hand. This would be no quickie in and out visit, and I knew that I would once again be very much on display and under scrutiny.

Goodman answered the door and ushered the three of us into the library, where Mrs. Barnett was waiting. The room was indeed a library—the only wall space not covered by built-in shelves filled with books contained a tremendous fireplace with a beautifully carved mantel. There was a painting of a man in late middle age hanging over the mantel, and I presumed him to be Charles's grandfather. Placed directly in front of the hearth was a coffee table, and at either side of the table were matching sofas, upon one of which Mrs. Barnett was sitting. She stood expectantly as we entered, and Richard walked up, said, "Hi, Gran," and kissed her cheek.

Charles followed on Richard's heels, also greeting her with a "Hi, Gran" and a kiss on the cheek.

I was right behind Charles and, acting partly on instinct and partly on impulse, echoed their greetings with a very lightly delivered "Hi, Gran" and a kiss on the cheek.

She was caught off guard by this but quickly recovered, giving me an intense look quickly followed by a genuine smile. "I'm glad you could join us, Philip" was all she said, but I could see that I had made a gesture of intimacy and acceptance that had touched her deeply.

Looking past Mrs. Barnett, I could see that both Charles and Richard had turned to stone on the spot, their expressions clearly indicating that they were prepared for some sort of explosion precipitated by my brashness. Charles gave a little start when his grandmother turned to him, smiling, and said, "Charles, where are your manners? I presume you know what everyone would like to drink." She motioned Richard to the sofa beside her and me to the one opposite, while Charles went to a sideboard that I'd overlooked in my first brief survey of the room, and mixed each of us a drink.

We spent an enjoyable hour visiting, during which Mrs. Barnett reminisced at length—for my benefit, I suspected—about Charles and Richard as boys and young men. It became apparent from her anecdotes that Richard had spent more time in her home growing up than he'd spent with his own family. From time to time she managed to skillfully draw me into the conversation with questions about Louisiana and my family. I realized finally that without having made an inquisition of the process, she'd managed to gather more information about my history than one would have thought possible. Just in time to prevent us from having a third round of drinks, Goodman appeared in the doorway and announced that dinner was served.

The dining room was in the grand tradition, with a large cut-glass chandelier and heavy mahogany furniture. The table at which we were seated, even with all of its leaves removed, could have seated eight in relative comfort. Dinner consisted of lentil soup followed by a salad, then by rock cornish game hen, wild rice, broccoli, and southern spoon bread. The latter dish, literally a yellow cornmeal soufflé, was one that I hadn't tasted since my high school days, when my mother had still been alive, and I proceeded to tell our hostess just that.

"My compliments to the cook," I said. "I haven't tasted spoon bread since I was in high school. My mother used to prepare it, and it was a family favorite."

"I'm so glad you liked it," she said.

"I wonder if Mrs. Goodman could be persuaded to part with the recipe?"

"I don't see why not, but don't you have your mother's recipes?"

"Sadly, no. She died long before I became interested in cooking, and I have no idea what happened to her recipes."

Gran promised to see what she could do about prying the recipe from Mrs. Goodman, and the conversation turned to other topics. When we were back in the library having coffee, she asked Charles about the murder case in general and the investigation in particular.

"There's not a great deal to tell at the moment," he said. "Richard is waiting for a potentially important witness to return to town next week, and until we see where her testimony leads us, there isn't much to do. Fortunately, we have many months in which to complete our preparations."

Seeing that she wasn't going to learn anything there, she switched the conversation to the political arena. She was remarkably well-informed on current events and seemed to have strongly held opinions on almost any topic one could name.

The conversation grew lively at times, when one of us would dare to disagree with her. She made it clear that if we couldn't support a position, we shouldn't hold it, and cross-questioned us mercilessly when our views contradicted what she deemed they should be.

Around ten thirty, we said goodbye and prepared to go, all three of us giving her a kiss as we left the room. When we were in the car and on the way, Charles looked at me.

"Jesus, Philip," he said, "you showed brass balls when we first got there. I nearly wet my pants when you said 'Hi, Gran.' Whatever made you do it?"

"It just seemed like the right thing to say and do."

"Obviously it worked, but it surely gave me a scare."

"Your grandmother is a remarkably well-informed woman. She could have been a politician's wife or perhaps even a politician herself."

"So she could have. If she were thirty years younger, I suspect she might even try it. In reality, she was a federal judge's wife, but he was appointed not elected."

After we got home, Richard announced his intention to settle down with a late movie, and we went up to bed.

The next morning, we resumed what had become our weekday routine—up at six, go for a run in the park, shower and shave, then coffee, juice, and toast. Charles excused himself to go up and dress for work a full minute before Richard arrived in the kitchen looking, if possible, even more ragged than usual.

I looked closely at his eyes, said, "How many late movies did you watch last night?" and got him some coffee.

"Two, I think," he said, holding up three fingers.

I laughed at that. "Well, Mother always said 'when you play, you have to pay.'"

"Well, I'm paying, and I didn't even get to play."

"Can I get you some juice or toast?"

"Sure."

I put some bread in the toaster and brought him a glass of juice. "I haven't asked you about the case in a couple of days. What day is that bartender due back in town?"

"Wednesday."

"Have you had any luck with those laundry tags?"

"Not yet, but there are a lot of cleaners in this city. It takes time to cover them all, and we still might not find anything. For all we know, she could have lived over in Conyers, or for that matter, in any of dozens of surrounding towns."

"You're telling me not to get my hopes up."

"Yep. On the other hand, if that bartender can give us a name or will cooperate with a sketch artist to produce an image, or both, then my guys will have something more concrete with which to work."

He finally went upstairs to get ready for work, and I cleaned up the kitchen and went up to get dressed as well. I settled for shorts, polo shirt, and deck shoes, went down and selected about five hours of music, then placed the discs in the CD carousel and went upstairs to sit down in my new "office" to see if I could get the creative juices flowing. After a quick read of the last several chapters and a look at my notes, I was able to pick up the thread of my new book where I'd left it two weeks before and, in fact, became totally oblivious to the passage of time. So much so that when the doorbell rang, I looked at my watch and was surprised to see that it was ten o'clock. I nearly tripped over Lance when I got up to go to the door—I'd been so deep in concentration that I hadn't noticed him curled up next to my chair.

The visitor turned out to be the telephone installation man. I showed him the multi-line phone in Charles's study, telling him that my line should be on the third button, then took him upstairs and indicated where the telephone jack should be by my desk. Being a typical union employee, he grumbled a bit at the trouble this would take, but he brightened when I told him that the house was already pre-wired with enough cable pairs to accommodate several more telephone lines—all he had to do was tap into the correct pair. The job was a great deal easier than he'd feared, and he was gone forty-five minutes later. I sat back down at my computer and placed my first call.

"Chandler, Todd, Woodward & Barnett," a female voice said.

"Charles Barnett, please."

"One moment, I'll connect you."

"Mr. Barnett's office," a voice I recognized as Rosemary's said.

"This is Philip d'Autremont calling."

"Oh, Mr. d'Autremont, I'm sorry, but Mr. Barnett is in a meeting. Do you have his private number?"

"That's all right, I could have used his private number but chose not to. I just wanted to give him my new private number."

"I'll be happy to pass it along."

I gave her the number, and we said goodbye. I repeated the process with my broker and my tax attorney, then placed a call to the law firm in Boston that acted as a go-between between myself and my publishers and gave the information to them. I was deeply engrossed in my manuscript when my new telephone rang for the first time.

"Hello."

"Hi, am I interrupting anything?" Charles said.

"Not really, I'm just trying to figure out a novel way for the hero to entice the heroine into his bed for the first time."

"Well, you could simply have him say 'wanta fuck?' and see what happens."

I laughed and said, "Not in what passed for high society in eighteenth-century New Orleans."

"I suppose they said '*Voulez-vous coucher avec moi ce soir?*' instead."

"Not quite. It was a little more subtle than that in those days."

It was his turn to laugh. "I don't want to drag you away from your muse, but would you like to do lunch?"

"Certainly, when and where?"

"One o'clock, at the Prince William."

"It's a date. I'll be the one with a red hibiscus behind my ear."

This elicited another laugh. "I felt sure you'd be familiar with that restaurant."

"Oh yes, very much so." Then I thought about my attire. "I'm not exactly dressed up—shorts and polo shirt—should I put on my semiformal gown in case someone sees us?"

"You can come naked, as far as I'm concerned. Seriously, you must be aware that it's a casual place, and I'm more than happy to see you no matter what you're wearing—or not wearing, as the case may be. If anybody sees us, they'll conclude that you're some trick that I'm trying to pick up."

Before I could respond in kind, our conversation was interrupted by the doorbell, and I said, "I've got to go answer that. See you at one."

"Okay, bye."

I went downstairs, opened the front door, and found a deliveryman from Saks with a package in his hand. "Package for Philip d'Autremont," he said.

"That's me, but I'm not expecting any package."

"Well, you got one anyway, just sign here," he said, holding out a clipboard, handing me a pen, and pointing to a blank line on the form.

I thanked him, took the package, went back inside, and carried it up to my desk. I opened it curiously and was pleasantly surprised to find the sweater that I'd almost bought on Saturday. That prompted me to dial Charles's private number.

"Charles Barnett."

"Hi. The doorbell was Saks delivering. Thank you very much for the sweater. You shouldn't have, but thank you anyway."

"Of course I should have. You clearly wanted it but just couldn't quite convince yourself. So I decided to surprise you."

"And so you did."

We said goodbye, and I carried the sweater into the bedroom and hung it in the closet. I went down and made some iced tea and, armed with a glass of it, returned to my computer. Before I started working again, I took a small alarm clock out of the desk drawer and set it for twelve thirty, knowing that I lose all track of time when I'm creating.

The alarm took me by surprise, as it always does when I'm concentrating on my writing, and I made a quick backup copy of my work on a thumb drive—I'd once learned the hard way about computers and hard-disk failures—then shut things down and went to clean myself up. As it wasn't a particularly hot day, I chose to walk to the restaurant, which was on a side street between Juniper and Peachtree only a few blocks from the townhouse. The Prince William was in fact adjacent to the Powder Magazine and was operated by the same people. It has been a favorite lunch spot for years, frequented by a fairly mixed clientele, some gay, some straight. Arriving ahead of Charles, I took a seat at the bar and ordered a Coke. I was sipping it slowly and not paying much attention to other customers in the room when the bartender came back to me.

"Excuse me," he said. "Guy over there wants to buy you a drink." He pointed at a not unattractive thirtysomething man on the other side of the horseshoe-shaped bar.

I smiled at that and said, "Tell him thank you, but I'm meeting a very special someone in just a few minutes."

As the bartender walked away, Charles came up to me. "Hi, been waiting long?"

"Just long enough for someone to try to pick me up," I said, and I told him about the drink offer.

I left some money on the bar to cover my drink, and we went to wait for a table, winding up at a small table in the bar area because they were busy. We ordered Caesar salads, which arrived promptly, and a pleasant hour later we were making our way out of the restaurant.

"I didn't see your car out back. Where are you parked?" Charles said.

"Actually, I walked over here."

"Want a ride back?"

"Sure."

Minutes later, we were in front of the townhouse, and he said, "I've got a meeting in a few minutes, so I have to run."

"That's okay, I've got a horny hero still waiting to get laid."

I leaned across the console, gave him a kiss, and got out of the car. He drove off, and I went back up to see if I could get my story line moving again. This time, before I settled down, I set the alarm for four o'clock, and before it alarm interrupted me, I'd managed to write quite a few pages. I left the computer up and running and went down to the kitchen to see about dinner, selecting and preparing some simple things that would be 80 percent done by the time Charles came home but that would survive being put on hold while we went to the Y and swam—and could be finished after our return.

Having set dinner in motion, I went back up to my computer and spent some time reviewing the day's work and making a few changes and corrections here and there, and was in the process of doing another backup when Charles came home. He came into the room with a smile on his face, but I thought I detected an underlying trace of disappointment. "I was hoping to find you naked in bed," he said. Which explained the look.

"That can be arranged, if you don't mind disturbing his highness," I said, pointing at Lance, who was again curled up as close to my chair as he could get.

He leaned over, kissed me, and said, "He'll get over it. When?"

"Just as soon as I turn this thing off. While I'm doing that, why don't you go down and turn off the burners on the range."

"Consider it done."

After he was out of the room, I finished my backup, turned things off, and went to the bedroom, arriving at the same time as Charles, who went quickly into the closet to remove and hang his clothes. I simply placed mine on a chair, knowing that I'd be wearing them to the Y later.

We fell on the bed and into each other's arms with a hunger that surprised me. Charles and I had discovered that neither of us liked labels such as "top" or "bottom," and we were both extremely versatile. Our lovemaking had become a mix of oral and anal, and we were pretty evenly matched in terms of who did what and to whom.

This time, without even talking about it, we automatically assumed a classic sixty-nine position and very nearly had simultaneous orgasms in no time, after which we cuddled face to face on the bed. He broke the silence, saying, "Sometimes we're so in synch that it's really spooky."

"I know. I've never been so in tune with someone else, sexually speaking. It's truly amazing."

Later, when we'd dressed and were on the way to swim, he asked about dinner.

"I just put together a few things that can be quickly finished when we get back," I said.

"You're pretty amazing, you know that?"

"It takes one to know one."

We spent some time soaking up steam, swam a little over a mile, and then returned home, where I immediately busied myself with dinner, which consisted of a steamed vegetable platter for each of us containing a baked potato, broccoli, and carrots. With the addition of a small salad, it made an adequate supper, particularly in view of the heavy meal we'd eaten the night before.

I'd noticed that Charles had brought a briefcase home every evening, but I hadn't seen him open it. I thought I knew the reason why, so I broached the subject. "Did you bring some work home from the office?"

"Yes, but I can leave it unlooked at."

"No need to do so on my account. I really need to put forth some extra effort if I'm going to meet my deadline, and even if I didn't have work to do, I think we're beyond the point of having to entertain each other twenty-four hours a day."

He looked relieved at that but said nothing. We cleaned up the kitchen together, leaving a plate of food for Richard that he could nuke later, if he so chose, and went upstairs to work. As I was booting my computer, he said, "Will music bother you while you work?"

"Of course not, I've had it on most of the day."

"Any requests?"

"No. Look at the five discs in the machine and guess my mood from them."

He went downstairs to select some music and was back in a few minutes, preceded by sounds of Bach from the speakers. We worked separately, and in silence, until nearly ten o'clock, interrupted only by Richard, who stuck his head in the door to make a tacky comment about "long hair" music. He shut up when I told him there was food waiting for him, and excused himself to go eat it. Charles and I were in bed by eleven and asleep a half hour later.

The rest of the week passed in much the same manner, the only sour note of the next four days being that the elusive bartender hadn't returned and was now not expected until Saturday. I got so much work done that by Friday afternoon I was able to call my publisher and schedule a meeting for a week from Saturday. He agreed to the meeting, so I had to make a call to set it up. As a precaution against my identity becoming public, we never met in the New York offices of the publishing house, instead using the offices of my Boston lawyers for our infrequent meetings.

I called Boston and talked to William Lane, one of my two lawyers. A Saturday conference was set up, and I arranged to have dinner with William and his partner on Friday evening. I told him I'd probably be bringing a friend; then I called the Taj in Boston to book a room for two nights and my travel agent to handle the airline reservations.

When Charles got home, I said to him, "Can you get away from the office by noon next Friday?"

"If I have to, why?"

"Because we have a plane to catch."

"Excuse me?"

"I have a conference in Boston with my publisher a week from tomorrow, and we have a dinner date with my Boston attorneys a week from this evening. We also have reservations at the Taj and with Delta."

Without a word, Charles picked up the telephone, dialed his office dictation system, and left a note for Rosemary to clear his calendar for next Friday from eleven o'clock on. "Any more surprises?"

"Not really. Well, maybe one. This place could stand some cleaning."

"I know, and that's my least favorite task."

"Well, as it happens, I know a couple of gay guys who do a superb job of housecleaning at a reasonable cost, and I'd like to engage them on a weekly basis. They call themselves The Merry Pop-Ins. It'll be my contribution to the maintenance of this household."

He agreed and, to my relief, made only a token argument about my paying for it, which made me feel much more comfortable with our arrangements.

We went to the Y as usual and, afterward, to Rick's for a light supper. When we'd finished our supper, we decided to go back to the bookstore, where we killed nearly an hour browsing. On the way home, we stopped at a sidewalk café for coffee and dessert, lingering over both for some time.

"Tell me about your Boston lawyers," he said.

"There's not too much to tell. The firm is Cabot Lodge Lane. The two principals are William Cabot Lane and Henry Lodge Lane. They're a couple and live in a townhouse on Beacon Hill. As you might expect from their middle names, they're descended from two of Boston's best-known first families. For that matter, the Lane family has as much claim to prominence in that city as do the Cabots and Lodges. I think you'll like them."

"What kind of practice do they have?"

"That part is kind of strange. The two of them handle the affairs of a number of Boston's moneyed families, charging them outrageous fees. They use those fees to subsidize a number of associates who provide legal services for the working poor, that is, those folks who make a little too much money to qualify for legal aid but can't afford to hire lawyers. They both have considerable incomes from trust funds set up years ago, so money isn't of paramount importance."

"Do you go to Boston often?"

"Two or three times a year."

"Done much sightseeing there?"

"Very little, actually, why?"

"As you know, I spent seven years in Cambridge, during which time I explored Boston extensively. Maybe we'll have time for me to play tour guide for you."

"I'd like that."

"One thing, though."

"What's that?"

"There might be one or two ghosts hanging around Boston, considering who I shared it with. Robert and I used to go back there once or twice a year ourselves."

"If we encounter any ghosts, we'll just have to exorcize them."

He had no reply for that, so we finished our coffee, went home, and settled down to read for a while. I was nearing the end of a chapter when he, apparently having reached a stopping place in his book, began to get playful. I made him wait until I finished three or four pages before we went upstairs to bed.

Saturday was almost a mirror image of the previous Saturday, except that we went back to Annie's Bistro for dinner. We arrived home early, as we were hoping that Richard would be waiting with some news of the elusive bartender when we got home, but he hadn't yet returned by the time we were ready to retire.

Sunday morning, Richard's bed appeared not to have been slept in. Charles said this was not unusual, given Richard's lifestyle, so we went on with our planned schedule. After church, we went to Patty's Place and had a wonderful brunch, returning home about two thirty. There was still no sign of Richard, so we crawled in bed for a nap. Around four o'clock, we dressed and went downstairs, where Richard was sound asleep on the sofa in the study. Charles immediately woke him up.

18

Charles

WHEN I saw Richard lying there asleep while we'd been kept in suspense, I became more than a little annoyed and said rather loudly, "Where have you been? We waited and wondered last night, but you never showed up."

Richard roused himself slowly and said finally, "For your information, I was on the job last night."

"All night long?"

"Well, not quite all night, but most of it."

"Can you take it from the beginning? Please?"

"Okay, okay. Don't get your boxers in a bunch. I went back to the dyke bar last night, and the missing bartender was back on the job. Her name, by the way, is Lily Sanders. I showed her the picture Philip gave me when we were at the house on West Paces Ferry Road, and she immediately recognized the deceased. More to the point, she clearly remembers having seen the deceased in that bar on the Saturday before the killing, and she was with a real bull dyke, one that Lily remembered seeing her with before on a number of occasions."

"Did she give you a name?"

"Don't rush me, I'll get to it. All she knows the woman by is Ruby. No last name. Lily promised to make some time available for my sketch artist on Monday morning—for a fee, of course."

"Of course. Well, that's something. It does not, however, explain why we haven't heard from you."

"On the job, boy. On the job."

"Continue."

"After my chat with Lily, I went over to the Powder Magazine, where I ran into Bruce. He invited me over to his place, and he had some interesting tidbits for me."

"Such as?"

"Well, for one, you caught Wetherbee completely off guard when you got Philip in and out of the jail so quickly. In a word, his people missed out on an opportunity to grill Philip, and Wetherbee was royally pissed."

"Good. What else?"

"It seems that the working hypothesis of their case, at the moment, is that Philip was living off of his wife, it being widely believed that he doesn't work for a living. And that her pregnancy, which was revealed by the autopsy, was a threat to him—clearly they can't picture a faggot as being responsible for fathering a child—in that he doubtless feared that she was going to leave him for the father of her child."

"Wetherbee and company have overactive imaginations, and we can blow that hypothesis out of the water quickly enough. Anything else?"

"Nope."

"None of which explains your present condition."

"Oh, that. I had to spend the night with Bruce. The information I just gave you was extracted slowly over the course of the evening, late night, and early morning. That boy is absolutely insatiable, and I'm bushed. I only got home a little while ago and decided to take a nap while I waited for the two of you to wake up."

"Before you collapse again, can you call in and dictate a complete report?"

"I already did that before my nap." He changed the subject and said, "Are you guys hungry?"

"Speaking for myself, not particularly. We had brunch at Patty's Place."

Philip echoed my sentiments, adding, "A small salad might be nice, but later."

"Why?" I asked Richard.

"Because I'm ravenous, and I thought you guys might like to join me."

"Why don't you call Bruce? I bet he'd join you in a heartbeat."

"True, but then he'd want me to fuck him again, and human flesh can only take so much."

"Richard! Have you finally gotten the over-thirty syndrome? I can remember a time not too long ago when you used to brag about the number of orgasms of which you were capable in a twenty-four-hour period."

"Me, over the hill?" he said indignantly. "Never. I probably had too much medicine last night, most of which will be on my expense account."

"Well, I appreciate your nobility and sense of self-sacrifice, and I'm sure that Philip appreciates it also."

Philip agreed with that sentiment. We left Richard on the sofa and went to the kitchen for some iced tea. When we carried it out onto the deck, Philip looked around and said, "I haven't spent any time out here before. It's really pleasant."

"Yes, it is, isn't it. The northern exposure, combined with the privacy screens at each end, makes it comfortable on all but the hottest summer evenings."

"Are you encouraged by Richard's findings?"

"Yes and no. The information as to the nature of their case is very encouraging. You and I both know that we can burst their bubble very quickly, although I'll have to put Randolph Forney on the stand to do it."

"I'm sure he'll be glad to testify."

"As a tax attorney and financial consultant, he may be reluctant to discuss privileged matters. We'll have to draft a very carefully worded authorization from you indicating which areas he can talk about and which areas should remain under the seal of privilege."

"Fine. You said 'yes and no', if that was the yes part, what about the no?"

"I was referring to the other woman. It's a long shot. If she's the killer, she may well be hundreds of miles away by now. Richard and his people will scour Atlanta once they get that sketch. If she can't be found in Atlanta, we'll have to consider hiring one of the big national agencies such as Wackenhut or Pinkerton to look for her in other cities, and that will be really expensive."

"I don't care what it costs if it will help."

"That's just it, there are no guarantees that they'll find anything, and they'll expect to be paid for their effort."

"I still don't care. We'll simply have to make the attempt."

"Excuse me just a minute, I just thought of something I want to ask Richard."

I went back to the study. Richard was still prone on the sofa, but not asleep. "You told me you had a fingerprint team go through the deceased's apartment, right?"

"Ah, you were listening at the time."

"Very funny. Did they find anything?"

"I don't know yet. They lifted several sets of prints, and we sent them off to a lab for analysis, along with the deceased's prints for comparison."

"When will you know?"

"Week to ten days."

When I returned to the deck, Philip raised an eyebrow.

"I asked Richard about fingerprints found in Lucinda's apartment," I said.

"And?"

"He doesn't have a report back from the lab yet."

"What can they learn from a report?"

"Well, if there are any prints that don't belong to the deceased, we can send them through our usual channels and see if they have any record of them."

"Sounds good."

"Just another long shot."

We finished our tea and decided to go out for a salad. First, we went back to the study, where Richard was as I'd left him. "Since you've been such a good boy, we're going to reward you. We're going down to Rick's for a salad. Come along with us, and we'll treat you to as much food as you can handle."

He sat up at the mention of food and said, "I hope you've got plenty of money or plastic."

The three of us went upstairs to clean up and were back in the kitchen some time later. I went to the stairs leading down to the living room, and Richard stopped me, saying, "That's not the way to the garage."

"It is such a nice evening, we thought we'd take the subway."

"But that's three or four blocks away."

"And three blocks at the other end, don't forget that."

"Exactly."

"Come on, the walk will do you good."

We left the house and started walking to the closest MARTA station. Richard grumbled the whole way, not stopping until we arrived at Rick's, where his face brightened at the prospect of food. Philip and I each had a small salad, and Richard managed to consume a salad, an entrée, and an enormous dessert. Over the meal, we talked about the missing Ruby and the slim chance that there might be a useful fingerprint among those found in the apartment. Richard talked at length, mostly with his mouth full, explaining details as to how an investigation was conducted that I took for granted but were probably foreign to Philip. When we were back home, Richard went straight up to bed, and Philip and I settled down side by side on the sofa.

I got up and selected two discs, one containing the Mozart *Requiem* and another that offered both the Fauré and Duruflé *Requiem*s. I turned the stereo on, then sat back down, put my arm around Philip, and said, "Hey, I just remembered something I forgot to ask you. Did your hero get laid?"

"Well and truly."

"Can you tell me how?"

"He and the heroine went riding in the woods, got caught in a drenching rain, and had to take shelter in an abandoned woodsman's hut. Naturally they had to take their outer clothing off and dry it near a fire. After that, one thing led to another."

"Sounds like a winner."

"I don't know, I have the feeling that it's probably been done that way before, and I wanted something unique."

He rested his head on my shoulder, and we sat for a long time listening to the music. When the Mozart ended and the Fauré began, he became more attentive to the music.

"That's beautiful," he said. "What is it?"

"Gabriel Fauré's *Requiem*."

"I don't think I've ever heard anything quite so sublimely beautiful."

"Then you're obviously not familiar with Berlioz's *L'enfance du Christ*."

"No, I'm not. You seem to be something of an expert on choral music."

"I don't know if I'm an expert, but I have an extensive collection of choral works. During my years at Harvard, I never missed a performance of the Handel and Haydn Society."

We talked about music for a while, having already determined that our tastes were very similar in some areas, and Philip was even more impressed with the Duruflé. When it was over, we went up to bed.

Monday morning came all too soon, and we settled quickly into our ritual of an early-morning run and an early-evening swim. That evening, Richard came home with a copy of the artist's sketch of the elusive Ruby. Philip and I had the same reaction, which I voiced, saying, "That is one mean-looking woman."

PHILIP cooked dinner every evening and had the cleaning service in on Mondays. The house hadn't looked so good in a long time. I got caught up in the daily round of appointments, mostly with clients whose legal problems were minuscule compared to the trial that Philip was facing. Contrary to popular belief, trial lawyers do not spend even half of their time in court. Most of the work involves maneuvering behind the scenes, and many of the civil matters get settled before coming to trial.

Thursday night before we went to bed, I packed my battered old Samsonite cases, remarking to Philip, who was placing garments into a matched set of Louis Vuitton luggage, "Do you think the Taj will allow me to check in with these beat-up old suitcases?"

"The Taj used to be the Ritz-Carlton, and I can assure you that the staff of a hotel of that caliber will take no notice. They're quite accustomed to dealing with the eccentric rich."

"Good. I certainly don't want to embarrass you."

"I don't think you could ever do that to me."

Friday, I left work at eleven thirty and was home just in time for Richard to drive us to the airport. We arrived at the security gate about forty-five minutes in advance of our one fifteen flight, which is about as close as I like to cut it. I've always made it a point to be at least an hour early when I fly commercial and as a result have never been bumped from a flight.

Philip had booked first-class seats, and after we were in the air and had been served drinks, he said, "How long has it been since you've been back to Boston?"

"It was the fall before Robert died. We went up in October for a visit, then rented a car and drove through New England to see the foliage."

"I'd like to do that sometime. I try to get to my place in North Carolina in mid-October for the leaves, but I've always heard that New England is much more spectacular."

"Having seen both, I'd have to agree. Maybe we can arrange for you to see them this fall."

"Thanks, I'd like that very much."

The double-strength drinks served in first class took their toll, and we both dozed off, not waking up until the call to fasten seat belts in preparation for landing came over the speakers. The landing was very smooth, and for once at Logan International Airport we didn't have to wait on the tarmac before the jet could be towed up to a gate. When we were settled in the backseat of a taxi, our luggage stowed away in the trunk, Philip told the driver where we were going, and we settled back for the ride into Boston. When we emerged from the Sumner Tunnel in Boston's North End, I watched our progress carefully. I knew from the lane we were in that, as I'd expected he might, the driver was clearly planning to take us through the heart of the city for a more expensive ride, so I leaned forward and directed him.

"I think you'll find that at this time of day you'd do better to head toward the river and down Charles Street, which will bring us to Beacon Street just a couple of blocks from the hotel."

He muttered something but changed lanes and headed in the

direction I'd indicated.

"He was going to play us for suckers," I said to Philip.

"I'm glad you're along. I wouldn't have known the difference, and I hate being ripped off like that."

We arrived at the Taj without incident and were eventually shown to a large room overlooking the Public Garden. Philip joined me at the window, where I was looking down at the gardens. "It's beautiful, isn't it?" he said.

"Oh, yes. Did you know that the Boston Common was the first public park in the country?"

"No, I didn't."

I gave him a rundown of the history of the Common, winding up by asking him, "What time are William and Henry expecting us?"

"They live on Brimmer Street, just a few blocks from here, and are going to come by and pick us up at seven, which"—he looked at his watch—"gives us time to rest before we dress for dinner." His blue eyes had that look in them.

"You mean this kind of rest?" I said as I gathered him in my arms.

He was unable to answer because my mouth was fastened to his. We spent some time thoroughly rumpling one of the two beds and left a six thirty wake-up call before dozing off for a while. By a quarter to seven, we were freshly showered, shaved, and suited. The latter, Philip said, was a precaution, because he didn't know where they were taking us for dinner but presumed that it would be dressy. We went down to the bar to have a drink while we waited.

We'd just finished our drinks when two very attractive men, obviously our hosts-to-be, approached our table. While they greeted Philip, I studied them carefully. They were both of medium height, about five-ten, I guessed, and both looked extremely fit and athletic, which was not difficult to determine as they wore suits that had clearly been tailored to fit them to perfection. I guessed they were about four years younger than me.

Philip made the introductions, and I shook their hands in turn. "Will you join us in a drink?" I said.

"No, thanks," William said. "We have reservations at a restaurant in the North End, and we've allowed just enough time to get there."

"What restaurant?" Philip said.

"One of our favorites. You'll be pleased, I think," Henry said.

We followed the lawyers out onto the sidewalk on Arlington Street, where William said, "We walked down from the house and thought we'd take the subway to dinner. Boston is a terrible place for cars."

They led us down Arlington Street to the familiar T sign that announced the Arlington Street stop of the venerable old Green Line subway. Along the way, William kept up a running commentary concerning Boston, the Common, and historic this and that. We were walking behind the two Lanes, and Philip leaned over and whispered in my ear, "Shouldn't you let him know that you've familiar with Boston?"

I whispered back, "He's obviously done this before and enjoys it. Just play along."

We descended into the subway station just in time to catch an inbound train. The trains on the Green Line are actually double trolley cars powered by an overhead catenary. The other subway lines utilize conventional subway cars powered by a third rail.

There was standing room only in the crowded car, so William was unable to continue his commentary. When we emerged at the Haymarket Station, he picked up the thread of his discourse, pointing out places of interest along with some background information on each. We walked past the Quincy Market and Faneuil Hall, and when we turned up North Street in the direction of Paul Revere's house, I suddenly realized with a terrible certainty where we were headed. Paul Revere's house started William off on a new thread, and as we rounded a small bend in the street, he looked straight ahead and confirmed my suspicions (fears), saying, "That's where we're going." He pointed at Mamma Leone's Restaurant, which is located at the head of what is known as North Square.

He continued talking about the restaurant and its food until we reached the steps leading up to its entrance. I paid no attention to what he was saying after that, as I was suddenly overwhelmed with a flood of memories.

13

Philip

CHARLES'S expression was a little odd as the four of us climbed the steps leading to the entrance of the restaurant, and we were barely inside when I began to understand why. The maître d', a good-looking young man who was a poster boy for the quintessential Italian, saw Charles and literally sprang from behind his little podium and trotted quickly forward to greet us instead of waiting for us to come to him.

"Charles," he said, ignoring the rest of us while giving Charles a hug and a kiss on both cheeks European style, "it's been too long since we've seen you. Wait right here while I run and get Mama and Papa." Before Charles could reply, the young man literally ran to the back of the reception area and disappeared from view for a minute or two. Then he returned, followed by an older Italian couple, who in a matter of minutes were all over Charles with hugs and kisses. The woman, who was short and heavy with an enormous bosom, rushed forward with outstretched arms, saying what sounded like "Sharleeee," followed by a stream of Italian. The man, an older and heavier version of his son, greeted Charles somewhat less noisily but no less demonstratively.

Their greetings were in rapid Italian, and to my surprise, Charles responded in kind. After a few minutes of this, they seemed to run down for a couple of seconds—perhaps they needed to catch their breath. It was then that they noticed the rest of us for the first time, after which there was more Italian, and I managed to catch a reference to "Roberto," obviously a question as to his whereabouts, because I heard the word *morte* quite clearly when Charles said it. This prompted another stream of Italian, followed by more hugs and kisses. Both the man and the woman were obviously upset at the news, and there were tears running down the woman's cheeks while her husband merely looked uncertain as to how to act. I looked closely at Charles and saw that he, too, had tears in his eyes.

William and Henry looked at me with puzzled expressions, so I took a stab at explaining and said, "I'm not sure what's happening here, but I can guess. Charles met his first lover, Robert, when he was a sophomore at Harvard and Robert a freshman at MIT. They lived together in Cambridge until Charles finished law school, then in Atlanta until Robert died three years ago—this was obviously one of the places they frequented. He told me last week that there might be a few ghosts waiting for him in Boston—he hasn't been back since the last time he and Robert were here."

Henry summed the situation up for both of them, saying, "Oops."

The Italian conversation had ground to a halt by this time, and Charles introduced me to Luigi and Maria aka "Mama" Leone, the owners, and their son Tony, the maître d'. Luigi repeated my name, exaggerating the pronunciation, and said, "This is a French name, yes?"

Charles laughed and said, "Perhaps originally, but his family has lived in Louisiana for about three hundred years."

This prompted a short round of Italian. When it finally subsided, I said, "What was that all about?"

"Well," Charles said, "Luigi has no love lost for the French, and that places a cloud of suspicion over you that even three hundred years in this country doesn't quite remove. However, he's going to overlook your tainted ancestry due to the exalted company you're currently keeping." At this, he grinned.

"Thanks a lot, I think."

The owners were obviously fairly well acquainted with William and Henry, and Tony finally led us to a table in a very nicely appointed dining room, where Charles and I were placed on a banquette along the wall and William and Henry were seated opposite. Tony left us after handing us menus, and when the four of us were alone, Charles said, "In case you're wondering, Robert and I discovered this place the first month we were together. We used to save our money and come here almost every Friday or Saturday. After he came out to his parents and they cut him off, we both worked here every weekend for two years. The Leones became very much our family in Boston."

Henry asked, "When was the last time the two of you were here?"

"The year before Robert died—about four years ago."

William added, "Maybe we made a mistake bringing you here."

"No, it's all right. I have only happy memories of this place. Before I met Philip, it would have been decidedly not all right, because I was carrying around a ton of grief which I hadn't been able to release. Thanks to him, I've finally begun to deal with the past." As he said this, he slipped his hand under the table, found one of mine, and squeezed it.

William said, "Why didn't you tell me you knew Boston? I wouldn't have gone through that dog and pony show had I known."

Charles gave him a devastating smile—well, it was devastating to me, anyway—and said, "You were so good at it, and seemed to be enjoying it so much, I didn't have the heart to stop you."

This both pleased and mollified William, and before he could answer, Luigi came up to the table. Seeing the menus in our hands, he said, "Give me those menus, they are for the tourists. Tonight you dine *con la tua famiglia.*" He then snatched the menus from our hands without waiting for our consent.

As soon as he was out of sight, I said, "What did he just say?"

"'Tonight you dine *con la tua famiglia,*' literally 'you dine with your family.'"

"I didn't know you spoke Italian."

"I've always had an affinity for languages, and I became interested in Italian because I love opera, so I took a couple of years of it in college. Luigi and Mama helped me get rid of my American accent."

"Do you speak any other languages?"

"Oh, one or two," he said in idiomatic French.

This time I was able to reply in the same language.

He laughed and said, "Very good, except for the atrocious Creole accent."

"I do not have an accent," I said somewhat testily.

"Have you ever used your French in Paris?"

"No."

"If ever you do, you'll find out what I mean about the accent."

Over the next hour and a half, we were served an incredibly delicious meal. First there were sautéed mushroom caps stuffed with cheese, then a wonderful cup of minestrone, followed by an excellent salad. The entrée was osso buco—veal shank with rice and a sauce—which was new to me but evidently well-known to Charles and to both of the Lanes. With the soup and salad we were served a bottle of pinot grigio, also new to me, which was a wonderful Italian white dry wine. The veal was accompanied by a very fine bottle of Tignanello, and I made a mental note of both of the labels. By the time our dessert arrived—a classic tiramisu—with the espresso, we were already stuffed.

Over dinner, under William's gentle questioning with an occasional prompt from Henry, Charles talked about his years in Cambridge with Robert. Both William and Henry had gone to Harvard, entering the law school a year after Charles graduated. Henry, ever less tactful than William, wanted to know how Robert had died, and I guessed that AIDS was on his mind.

Charles must have had the same thought, for he said, "Not from what one might expect, considering all that has happened in our circles over the last several years. Robert and I hadn't been very promiscuous before we met, but just to be sure, we had ourselves tested, and we both came up negative.

"To answer your question, Robert began to have severe headaches and did little for them except take more and more Tylenol. Finally I talked him into seeking treatment—he hated going to the doctor. They eventually found a brain tumor, which was by then judged to be inoperable. It was also of a type that wasn't known to respond well to either chemotherapy or radiation, and Robert opted to forego both rather than endure the side effects for naught.

"He chose instead to take increasingly stronger pain medication until he reached a point at which even they weren't terribly effective. We'd discussed that eventuality, and he was determined not to go to a hospital to die, as he put it, 'with tubes sticking out of every opening in my body'. To make a long story short, he began hoarding pain pills, and when he decided that he couldn't take the pain any longer, he took a massive dose of the pills. He did it with my reluctant blessing, and I held his hand until it was over."

William asked him, somewhat tactlessly I thought, if he'd been worried about being charged as an accessory to suicide. Charles took no offense and said, "The issue never came up. Robert had also discussed his intentions with his doctor, who had both the grace and the good sense not to make an issue of it. There was no autopsy, and his death certificate doesn't mention suicide."

We were spared from having to comment further on this by the arrival of our host and hostess. All four of us were effusive in complimenting them on both the food and the service. They finally took their leave, but not before they elicited a promise from Charles that he would never again stay away so long, and "Mama" promised to "light a candle and say a novena for Roberto."

When they were out of earshot, Charles smiled and said, "Don't even think about asking for a check—they'll be mortally offended. Luigi meant what he said about this being a family occasion."

"Shouldn't we at least leave something for the waiters?" I said, as only the entrée had been served by our host. The rest of the service had been provided by the staff.

"Yes, I think that would be very appropriate," he said.

The Lanes and I discussed and settled upon a suitable gratuity and left it on the table. We were in the reception area saying goodnight to Tony when "Mama" came up and said something in Italian to Charles. He replied in kind, and she embraced him and kissed him on both cheeks. After we were outside, I asked him what she'd said, but he just smiled and pretended not to have heard me. I let the matter drop, making a mental note to ask him again when we were alone.

We retraced our steps as far as the Quincy Market and Faneuil Hall complex, where we walked around the area and watched the people for a while before going to a different subway station. After emerging from the Arlington Street Station, we walked back to the hotel, where Charles invited our hosts to the bar for a nightcap. The four of us were quickly seated at a table in the lounge, and after drinks were served, we sat in silence for a minute.

Then Henry said, "After your meeting with your publisher tomorrow morning, Philip, we've discovered a building we think you ought to see."

"A building?" I said.

"Yes," he said, "a former factory building, vacant for years, and one that's in the right place to be converted into lofts or flats, either for sale or as rental units. The price is right, and we think it's just the sort of project you enjoy taking on."

"Where's it located?"

This time William answered. "Near the North End, where we were tonight, in an area that's ripe for gentrification."

"Okay, set up an appointment with the listing broker, and we'll look it over."

The Lanes engaged Charles in conversation about Harvard and professors they'd all known, finally departing around eleven, and we went up to our room.

As we were getting ready for bed, I said, "Well, what did you think of them?"

"I liked them both very much. How did you meet them?"

"Through Lindsey, my publisher. We were trying to work out some way to meet occasionally without my having to appear in his office. He has family in Boston, so he visits here frequently. I think some member of his family made the referral."

"You go to great lengths to maintain your anonymity."

"It's vital. Occasionally, I do some serious work, but what brings in the money are the steamy historical romances. We decided, in the beginning, that a gay male would never be accepted as an author writing in that genre, so I write under a female name, and my publisher is extremely careful about keeping the secret."

"Evidently, it works."

"Oh, yes. There's even a female employee of the publishing house whose picture appears on the dust jacket of every one of my books."

We got into bed and were almost immediately engaged in some very pleasant activities. Before we drifted off, I remembered the mental note I'd made earlier and said, "What did Mama Leone say to you as we left the restaurant this evening?"

"Oh, something to the effect that I had good taste in men, and she was happy for me."

Saturday morning, we got up at seven and went for a run. When we returned to the hotel, we bathed and dressed, then went down for a light breakfast. Afterward, I retrieved my briefcase from our room and we walked to the offices of Cabot Lodge Lane, which occupied the first floor of a brownstone on Beacon Street. The office was, of course, closed for the weekend, so we had to knock. William met us at the door and ushered us into the conference room, where Lindsey Woolverton was waiting. William left us, and I introduced Lindsey to Charles.

We got down to business and discussed schedules and deadlines as well as some ideas he had for the cover. It took us about an hour, during which time Charles sat listening with a thoughtful expression on his face. After Lindsey left, I asked Charles what he'd been thinking, and he replied that he hadn't seen the business side of me before and was impressed.

I thanked him for the compliment, about which time William returned with the Realtor in tow, whom he proceeded to introduce as Stanley Copeland. The Realtor had a car parked down the street, and William ushered us out, locking up as we left.

"Where's Henry?" I said.

"He had to go hold the hand of one of our dowager clients," he said.

We rode in relative silence to the North End and were soon parking in front of what had clearly been a small factory or warehouse at one time. It appeared to have a height of about ten stories, and Stanley launched into a spiel about the building and the area as he unlocked the door. I paid little attention to what he was saying, being more interested in the structure itself. It was quite run-down but seemed to be structurally solid, and by the time we'd finished the fifty-cent tour, I'd made a tentative decision.

The asking price was $2 million, which I considered to be much too high, so I asked Stanley if he thought the owners would accept an offer that was about 25 percent lower and more closely in line with reality. He said he'd try but didn't sound too sure of their probable response.

We returned to William's office and went back to the conference room. Stanley produced a standard real estate contract and began to fill it out. I directed him to list the purchaser as Philip d'Autremont or nominee. He handed the document to me, and I looked it over, adding a few provisions concerning building codes, zoning, and other matters that I knew from experience were essential to a viable project.

Then I handed the contract to Charles and said, "Run your legal-beagle eyes over this, and tell me what you think."

"You know that my specialty is civil and criminal law, not real estate law," he said, but he took the proffered document and studied it at length, suggesting two or three things that I hadn't thought to stipulate. I asked him to add the appropriate clauses, which he did; then I signed the document and handed it to Stanley along with a check for a binder, giving him my number in Atlanta in the process.

After Stanley left, I said to William, "You did well. If the owners accept anywhere near the amount I offered, this will be a real moneymaker. Do you want a finder's fee?"

William looked peeved at the thought and said, "Of course not. Henry and I are happy to have been of assistance."

"At the very least, you can earn a legal fee by preparing some documents related to this transaction."

"Certainly, what would you like done?"

"Set up a Nevada corporation, let's call it 'B & D Properties, LLC', with myself as president and Charles as vice-president. One of you can be the resident agent for Massachusetts. You can send the papers to Charles's law firm when they're ready for execution." I looked at Charles as I said this and saw his raised eyebrows, but he remained silent.

"It'll be taken care of next week."

"By way of additional thanks, let me take all of us out to dinner this evening."

"Agreed. When and where?"

Charles spoke up. "Be at the hotel by seven. I believe we can think of something that will please you."

As we walked back to the hotel, I said, "Sorry about springing 'B & D Properties' on you like that, but it suddenly occurred to me that it's time I got you into the real estate world."

"I'm not sure that I have enough ready cash for a project of that size," he said.

"Of course you do. All that's needed at the moment is a portion of the purchase price. The rest will be financed with the property as equity.

And if you don't have enough ready cash, I'll lend you the difference."

He looked slightly offended and said, "I don't want any handouts."

"I'll charge you two points above prime, which is about what any bank would charge you right now, which hardly constitutes a handout."

He knew when to give up, so he said, "Sure, why not? With your track record in real estate, how can I lose?"

I tried a lighter tack and said, "Stick with me, kid, and you'll be filthy rich in no time."

He smiled at that and said, "Actually, when Gran dies, I really will be filthy rich; right now I'm merely comfortable."

When we were back in our room, he found a telephone directory and made some reservations for eight o'clock. When I asked him where, he said, "Wait and see. Now, let's get some more comfortable clothes on, it's time for me to play tour guide."

Which he did. We took the Green Line out to the Boston Museum of Fine Arts and spent a couple of hours there before we walked over to the Isabella Stewart Gardner Museum, which was located in a building built in the style of a Venetian renaissance palace. Fenway Court, as it was called, was built by Mrs. Gardner to house her collection, which included sculpture, textiles, furniture, ceramics, metalwork, and, of course, paintings. She was a turn of the twentieth century Boston socialite and rather eccentric. When her mansion on Beacon Street was demolished, she demanded that the City of Boston never issue that particular street number to any other structure—and they complied, or so the story goes. Under the terms of her will, the museum trustees were forbidden to ever change any aspect of the museum or its contents, so it remained in a sort of time warp and was all the more impressive for it.

After leaving the museum, we took the Green Line back to a station at the opposite end of the Common from where we'd boarded it, and Charles led me to the downtown shopping district, where he pointed out the former site of what he said had arguably been the most famous bargain basement in the country, Filene's Basement.

Filene's, I learned, was a chain of New England department stores, and the downtown Boston store had once possessed a gigantic bargain basement. It was now part of a different chain, and the famous bargain basement only existed as a small chain of separate stores.

We returned to the hotel with about an hour to spare, a portion of which we spent in bed. Diversions notwithstanding, we were freshly groomed and downstairs in the bar well before William and Henry arrived. As before, their arrival coincided with our having just finished our drinks, and as before, they declined an offer for another round.

Henry was curious and asked, "Where are we going tonight?"

Charles said, "How do you feel about Ristorante Toscano on Charles Street?"

"Terrific, we haven't been there in ages," Henry said.

William said, "I agree."

20

Charles

WE WALKED down Arlington Street and turned right on Beacon Street, then left on Charles Street a couple of blocks later. During our walk, William once again assumed the role of tour guide, filling Philip in with facts and anecdotes as we walked past each point of interest. Evidently, he assumed that I was conversant with the data he was offering, and for the most part, I was.

When we'd been seated at the restaurant, handed menus, and had placed our drink orders, Henry wanted to hear about our day.

Philip said, "Well, after our meeting with the Realtor, Charles took me on a little guided tour."

"What did you see?" Henry said.

"Let me think. The Fine Arts Museum, where I saw more pornographic Greek vases than I knew existed, the somebody Gardner Museum, and lastly, the department store where Charles told me Filene's Basement used to be. After that, we ran out of time."

"You covered a lot of ground in one afternoon," William said, smiling at but otherwise ignoring Philip's reference to the Greek vases.

"I tried to pack as much as possible into a limited time frame," I said.

Henry asked me, "What are your plans for tomorrow?"

"After church, I thought I'd take Philip out to Harvard, find a place to have lunch, and then show him the Coop. We'll have just enough time to do that and catch our seven o'clock flight."

Henry said, "Where are you going to church?"

"As far as I'm concerned, in Boston there's only one place to go—Church of the Advent."

"We're communicants there," William said. "It's across and two doors down the street from our home."

"In that case, I expect we'll see you there."

Our conversation was interrupted by the arrival of the waiter, who was ready to take our orders. When we'd ordered, I selected a bottle of wine that I thought would suit our various entrées. Then the conversation turned to the real estate venture that we were about to begin.

During a lull, I asked Philip a question that had been on my mind all afternoon, "How were you able to make up your mind so quickly about that building?"

"Truthfully, I don't know. All I know is that I can look at a project and somehow determine almost immediately if it will succeed. Something, perhaps a sixth sense, tells me that it will either be a go or a no go, and I act accordingly. So far, that instinct has never failed me."

Henry said, "We've seen him do it before on a couple of projects."

Since our arrival, they'd carefully avoided the topic of Philip's arrest and pending trial, but William finally broke the ice and asked about it. We discussed the case fully, and they seemed to agree that we were on the right track. That discussion led them up to the subject of how Philip and I had met. I looked a question mark at Philip, who nodded his assent, and then I told them the story, omitting nothing.

William said, "Goodness, that's like something right out of a fairy tale!" It dawned on him suddenly that his words had a double meaning, so he added, "No pun intended."

I laughed at that, saying, "The evening did have a sort of dreamlike quality to it. Looking back, it all seems like a fantasy come true."

Henry raised his glass and said, "Here's to fairy tales and happy endings."

We drank to that. Then William said, "Have the two of you made any long-range plans?"

I again looked at Philip, whose face this time was impassive, before I said, "Right now, we're just focused on getting Philip acquitted. After that, I expect we'll ride off together into the sunset or something like that."

It was Philip's turn, and he said, "Seriously, we haven't talked about a future—there are simply too many uncertainties in the present. Clearly, we have something special going for us, and if we can survive the present problem, I expect we can survive anything."

I added, "I'd say that we're in it for the long haul. I spent the last three years wondering if I would ever be able to share my life again. Now I find myself wondering how I ever managed without this guy."

Philip slipped a hand under the table and found mine, which was response enough for me. After that exchange, the four of us spent the rest of our time in the restaurant discussing anything and everything. I think we were all sorry to see the evening end, but end it finally did with the arrival of coffee and Port, followed by the check. Philip paid for the dinner, using plastic so he'd have an adequate receipt, saying, "This will be the first entertainment expense for B & D Properties."

During the walk back to the hotel, we once again began discussing the real estate project. We tossed around several possibilities for developing the building, ranging from creating a small number of large lofts to developing a larger number of flats. Lofts, it seemed, were becoming popular in Boston, but flats would probably be more profitable in the long run. In the end, Philip said it would depend upon what the structural engineers and the architects recommended.

We had a nightcap in the hotel bar, and finally the Lanes left for their townhouse, but not before extracting two promises from us. First, that we'd stay with them the next time we came to Boston, and second, that we make it soon. We went up to our room and, somewhat contentedly, to bed.

Sunday morning, we were up and running by eight, which got us back to the hotel in time to linger over the paper and breakfast. Around ten thirty, we walked up Arlington to Beacon, and then one block east to Brimmer Street. At the corner of Brimmer and Beacon was the bar that had inspired the *Cheers* television series. I'd once known its former name but couldn't remember what it was. It was a couple of blocks up Brimmer to the venerable old Church of the Advent, which, in the midst of all the modern self-inflicted horrors the Episcopal Church has undergone, had managed to remain unabashedly high church, bordering on Anglo-

Catholic. We arrived well before William and Henry, who eventually joined us in the pew. After they arrived, a man and woman came and sat down in the pew in front of us, she being led by a seeing-eye dog, a beautiful Golden Retriever.

She motioned him under her pew, and shortly afterward, I looked down and saw the golden face resting on the kneeler in front of me. I wanted to reach down and pet the dog, but somewhere I'd read that you weren't supposed to do that, although I couldn't remember why. The poor dog became a little confused during the service; it was so attentive to its mistress that every time she stood up as called for in the service, the dog thought that it was time to go and started to get up. I was amazed that when she got up to go to the altar rail to take communion, she motioned the dog back, and it stayed meekly under her pew while her husband (boyfriend?) led her up the steps.

After the service was over, William and Henry walked with us as far as Beacon Street, and we said our goodbyes at the corner by the *Cheers* bar. Philip and I returned to the hotel, where we changed into more casual attire. We'd already arranged for a late checkout, and we packed everything except the clothes that we needed for the flight. We caught the Green Line downtown and changed to the Red Line for the trip to Harvard Square, arriving there in a relatively short time. We had a pleasant lunch in one of the student hangouts in the area, then went into the Coop, eventually winding up in the record department.

"This is where Robert and I first met."

"Does it bother you, coming here?"

"Not anymore."

We browsed for a while, then went down to the bookstore, which occupied more than one level. We ambled through both levels of the bookstore and made a couple of purchases; then we went back to the square, after which we wandered around Harvard Yard looking at the old buildings. Almost before we knew it, it was time to board the Red Line back to Boston.

On the subway, I said, "We'll definitely have to come back here for about a week sometime. Then I can really show you Boston and Cambridge."

"Good, and maybe we can go to Cape Cod. I've always wanted to see P-town. Have you ever been there?"

P-town, slang for Provincetown, was a gay mecca at the tip of Cape Cod. During the summer, there was a regular ferry service from Boston out to P-town, and gays from all over went there in search of sun and sex. "Well, I've never been there on the make, so to speak, but Robert and I went there two or three times."

"I've no idea whether or not I would find it interesting," he said. "It's just one of those places that I've heard so much about and would like to see for myself."

"I think we can take care of that one of these days."

We arrived back at the hotel around four, quickly changed clothes for the trip home, and checked out. This time, I didn't have to keep the cab driver on course. We went through the express check-in at the Delta counter, and I took a minute to telephone Richard and remind him of our arrival time. While we were in the waiting area, I said, "I just thought of something."

"What?"

"We didn't have time for a nap this afternoon."

"Not to worry, we'll make up for it tonight."

While we waited, Philip spent some time with his PDA, recording the details and expenses of the trip. He reminded me that we could deduct the cost of the trip as a travel expense related to the investment we were about to make.

The return flight was smooth and uneventful, and Richard was waiting for us, looking as tired and drawn as he had the previous Sunday.

"Don't tell me, let me guess," I said. "You spent the night with Bruce again, yes?"

"Does it show that badly?"

"Only to those of us who know you intimately."

"It was another wild night."

"Are the two of you getting serious?"

"Of course not!" he said, perhaps a little too defensively.

A famous line occurred to me at that point, the one about protesting too much, but I changed the subject, asking, "Any luck locating the missing Ruby?"

"Yes and no. My people have found a number of individuals who recognized the sketch, but nobody admits to having seen her since the weekend of the murder. Eventually, we ought to find someone who can help us. As you know, very often it's simply a matter of legwork."

We walked to the luggage area, discussing the implications of his news while waiting for our bags. Richard led us to the car, and we were soon home.

As we went up the stairs to the kitchen, I asked Richard if there had been any more revelations from Bruce concerning the case.

"None so far."

"Well," I said, with what I hoped was a lewd grin, "keep pumping him."

"Very funny, very funny."

Philip and I left him in the kitchen and went upstairs to unpack. Lance followed us and hopped up on the bed, so I sat down on it and spent a few minutes rubbing all his favorite places. He especially liked to have the bridge of his nose rubbed, and he leaned into it as I did so.

"What are your plans for tomorrow?" I asked Philip.

"Well, as you know, I made some rash promises concerning the manuscript, so I'll try to fulfill them. I also need to call Randolph and get him started setting up books for the new venture. By the way, do you have a tax man?"

"My affairs have never been complicated enough to require someone at that level of expertise, so I usually take care of my own stuff. Why?"

"If you're going to get involved with this and future projects, you'll doubtless need someone's help. I'd like to introduce you to Randolph with that in mind. You'll also need to meet him at some point to discuss his testimony, won't you?"

"Okay. Why don't you have him call Rosemary and find a time when the three of us can get together?"

"Will do, as soon as I see him."

"Also, I need to know the timing and mechanics of my investment in the project."

"No need for that until the Articles of Incorporation are filed and we can open a bank account, or better yet, an investment account for the corporation. We can contribute equally at that point, and the corporation can reimburse us for expenses already incurred, such as the trip to Boston and the binder that I gave the Realtor."

"Do you have any idea as to how much our total investment will be?"

"Hard to say at this point, but probably something in the neighborhood of a quarter of a million."

"Each?"

"No, that would be a combined figure."

"I'm surprised that it can be accomplished for so little."

"Basically, there are two ways to approach one of these projects. If it's a relatively small project, I prefer to use my own capital and bypass the banks—it saves a lot of time and a lot of closing costs, not to mention a great deal of interest. On a project of this size, however, it's more practical to use borrowed money to the extent possible."

"Why?"

"One, because interest rates are at record lows, and two, because I'd have to sell some stock to raise that amount of money, which I really don't want to do even with the preferential tax treatment for capital gains."

We were both tired and, having finished unpacking, were soon in bed.

Monday morning, the daily routine began. Shortly before lunch, Rosemary buzzed me and said, "Mr. d'Autremont is on the line."

I punched the appropriate button and said, "Hi, where are you?"

"At Randolph's office. He can confer with us tomorrow at two. Rosemary says that you have that slot free."

"Fine. My office or his?"

"Since you'll be discussing my case, we'll come there, if that's all right."

"Sure. Lunch?"

"Rain check, okay?"

"No problem. See you tonight. Love you."

"Me too, bye."

I got back to work, somewhat surprised at myself. Even with Robert, I'd seldom ended telephone conversations with endearments. This was really getting serious.

When I got home that evening, Philip was hard at work at his computer. I knew, however, from the odors I'd detected when passing through the kitchen, that he'd found time to cook. We went to the Y and swam, then came back home and ate. After supper, he went back to his computer, and I carried my briefcase up to the spare room and settled down for an evening of work. We were in bed by eleven thirty.

Tuesday, Rosemary and I had to work straight through the lunch hour. About one o'clock, we sent out for sandwiches and iced tea, and had only just finished them when Philip and his tax attorney arrived. Randolph Forney turned out to be a dapper little man approaching, as nearly as I could tell, his late fifties. He was impeccably dressed and wore a pair of half glasses, over which he peered when he wasn't looking through them for the purpose of reading. We spent about an hour at the conference table discussing his probable testimony, with Rosemary taking notes. When we'd finished with our discussion of the case, Rosemary left, and we changed topics.

I said, "Philip seems to think that you can be of assistance in my personal affairs, and as you know, we're undertaking a joint project."

"Well, without knowing anything about your situation, it's somewhat hard to say."

"That had occurred to me, so I've rounded up most of what I think you might need." I handed him a list of my investments, together with the most recent statement from my broker, and copies of my last three federal and state income tax returns. I also gave him the most recent reports from the two trust funds from which I was still receiving income. He perused the documents at length for twenty minutes or so, finally looking at me over the top of his glasses.

"Your investment strategy seems to be both sound and thorough, if somewhat conservative. However, I think you've been too generous in your tax returns."

"What do you mean?"

"I need to run the numbers through my computer, but at a glance, I would say you've overpaid considerably in a couple of areas. May I take these documents with me?"

"Certainly, they're copies I made for your use. Anything else?"

"Yes. Is there any particular reason why you've never taken control of the principal in these two trusts?"

"Not really. I've had the right to do so since I was twenty-five but have never really needed the money, so I've been content to merely use the income."

"Please don't misunderstand what I am about to say, but these are very conservative vehicles. If you were to withdraw some or all of the principal, you could easily double your current return."

"Wouldn't there be some tax consequences from such a withdrawal?"

"If you do it over a period of time, the consequences can be minimized, and the gains will more than offset the taxes."

"Lay out a program and present it to me, and I'll think it over."

We discussed his fees, which seemed reasonable considering his reputation and knowledge. I'd made some discreet inquiries as to his ability and reputation despite Philip's enthusiastic endorsement, although I hadn't told Philip that I'd done so.

Philip lingered in my office after Randolph gave me his business card and departed. "Well?" he said.

"I'm impressed, especially if he can amend those returns and get me some money back, not to mention the potential increase from the trusts."

"Great." He gave me a kiss. "I've got to get back to my computer."

"Okay, see you tonight."

That night as we went to bed, he asked me about the Fourth of July weekend, which was getting close. "The Fourth is on Saturday. Will your office be closed on Monday for the holiday?"

"Yes, why?"

"How about a long weekend in the mountains?"

"Sure. How long a weekend?"

"Starting Friday afternoon, if you can get away, otherwise Friday evening after work."

"Actually, I'm scheduled to participate in the Peachtree Road Race on the Fourth, but if we can leave right after the race, no problem."

"I'd forgotten about the Peachtree—it's something that I've never attempted. I'll cheer you on, though."

"You're perfectly free to run with me as a bandit."

"A what?"

"An unofficial entrant; we call them bandits."

"I'll think about it."

The days rushed by, and before I knew it, the month of June had very nearly evaporated. Richard, Mark, and I had been having weekly meetings to discuss the progress being made in the murder investigation, which unfortunately was very little. Ruby had yet to be located, the laundry tags hadn't been identified, and the fingerprint lab seemed to have lost or misplaced the raw material that had been sent to them. All in all, the lack of progress was very discouraging, although I tried not to let Philip see my disappointment with the results.

Two weeks to the day after our first meeting, Randolph presented me with a plan for gradually dissolving my two trusts and investing the principal somewhat more aggressively. In addition, he'd amended my last two tax returns with some fancy footwork, resulting in sizable refunds for both years. If I followed his advice with the trusts, it appeared that I would nearly double my investment income with no significant increase in risk. That same day, the incorporation documents arrived from Boston, as did an offer of acceptance from the owners of the building. I gave the incorporation papers my blessing, and Philip and I executed them and returned them to the Lanes for filing. We also set up a corporate cash management account to handle the funds of the new entity, and I managed to raise my share of the initial capital required without having to borrow from Philip. He was a little annoyed at the owner's ready acceptance of his offer and said, "If they jumped at my offer, they probably would have accepted an even lower one."

"It was still a good buy, wasn't it?"

"Yes, but obviously it could have been a better one."

"What now?"

"I have to get busy and arrange for both an architect and an engineering firm to look over the property. As you may recall, if either of them fails to give the project their blessing, I have the right to cancel the contract."

"Do you have anyone in mind?"

"No. I wasn't too happy with the way my last Boston project was handled, so I need to look at the options."

"How much time will you have to spend in Boston?"

"Very little, actually. In fact, probably none at all until the end of November, provided I can make one quick trip there between now and then. Would it be a problem if we took a long Labor Day weekend in Boston to handle things? We could go up on Thursday evening and come back on Monday."

"I don't think that will be a problem."

"Good, then it's settled."

We spent a few minutes Friday evening packing for the trip to the mountains. Saturday, we were up at six so that we could take the subway to the Lenox area—site of the race's starting line—along with several thousand other runners and spectators. The Peachtree Road Race has been an Atlanta institution for over twenty years. It's a 10K event, starting at Lenox Square and continuing down Peachtree to 14th Street and then into Piedmont Park. It has grown so in popularity over the years that the Atlanta Track Club, organizer of the event, limits participation to 60,000 runners.

The course runs a leisurely three miles, mostly downhill, and then turns uphill for two miles, this section having become known as "cardiac hill" due to the number of fatalities that have occurred on it over the years. From that point, the course is up and down to the finish line. Running nearly 6.3 miles on a July morning in Atlanta is not for the novice, nor is it for the unfit. Temperature and humidity can and do take a toll—despite the spots along the route where hydrants are opened and a spray of water is directed across the course at the participants. The water feels wonderful as you pass through it—until you realize that a soaking wet T-shirt weighs significantly more than a dry one.

It remains, however, a great event, and the camaraderie is fantastic.

The race sponsors have gotten the problem of managing that many participants down to a science over the years. Participants are directed to areas behind the start line by the number. That is, your assigned number dictates your starting point. Last year, I'd been in the 40,000 series of numbers. In front of each such group, there are two or three officials carrying pole-mounted placards that say "stop" on one side and "walk" on the other. When the race begins, these officials literally walk the group to the starting line stopping and starting as needed until finally, at the starting line, the group is allowed to run free, the prior groups being sufficiently out of the way. Last year, by the time I crossed the starting line, the official clock had been running for nineteen minutes and seventeen seconds.

This year, I was in a slightly lower number group and was able to cross the starting line a mere twelve minutes into the race. Although it's frowned upon, Philip, who lacked an official entry number, ran with me—bandits are expected to run at the extreme back of the pack. Participants aren't automatically entitled to a T-shirt when they reach the finish line, as is the custom in most races—you have to finish the race within a certain time frame. We finished just under fifty minutes after we crossed the starting line, which wasn't a bad time for me, considering the events of the past weeks.

It was just a short walk from Piedmont Park and the finish line back to the house for a quick shower, and we were soon on our way out of town in Philip's car, having decided to patronize the drive-through window at the first McDonald's we came to on I-85 for a quick lunch.

21

Charles

PHILIP'S BMW, unlike my Jaguar, was designed for maneuvering and speed, and he obviously enjoyed exploiting its capabilities. He turned on the radar detector, and we flew up I-85 at a rapid pace. In less than two hours, we'd covered the 120 or so miles to Greenville, South Carolina, and turned onto a secondary road for a trip across the mountains to our destination in North Carolina.

I'd assumed—hoped?—that the two-lane highway through the mountains would slow him down, and it did, but only slightly, as he was seemingly intent upon defying gravity, flying up steep grades and around hairpin turns. We spent nearly half an hour in silence as he concentrated on upshifting, downshifting, and generally keeping the car under some semblance of control. Finally, on a brief level stretch, he glanced over to where I was clearly hanging on for dear life.

"Isn't this great?" he said.

"What this is, is payback, isn't it?"

"Whatever do you mean?"

"I scared the shit out of you flying on autopilot while we joined the mile-high club, and you're extracting your pound of flesh in revenge."

"Would I do that to you? Besides, where's your sense of adventure?"

I ignored this reprise of my words from Memorial Day weekend and closed my eyes as we ascended yet another series of turns, opening them only as we began to go downhill. None too soon for me, we were in a broad valley, and the road straightened out until we reached the town of Brevard. Beyond that small city, we climbed to the top of yet another mountain, then down through more switchbacks, finally turning off on a side road that began to climb up through a long, narrow valley that was for the most part heavily wooded, although I could see one or two houses perched up on the sides of the surrounding mountains.

Philip slowed the car as we neared the upper end of the valley, and I could see a tall stone structure in the shape of a tower on the side of the mountain at the head of the valley, jutting straight out of one edge of a newly mown field. On the other side of this tower was a series of small waterfalls cascading down the mountainside, disappearing eventually under a stone bridge over which the road continued. The tower made me think of a medieval keep.

He slowed and came to a halt about a few hundred yards from the structure and said, "This is it."

"What?"

"That tower just ahead."

"What about it?"

"It's my mountain hideaway."

He started slowly up the hill toward a driveway protected by a gate, which I hadn't noticed at first glance. As we drew closer, I inspected the building more carefully. I couldn't, at first, judge how tall it was, but later learned that it rose about sixty feet from ground level. It appeared to be rectangular, but I had no feel for its dimensions from my present point of view. Most notable was the fact that there appeared to be no openings in the two walls that were currently visible. Somewhat below the roofline, I could see a metal construction of some sort, which appeared to be folded up against both visible walls. If these features of the building had been located at ground level, they might have been taken for drawbridges in the up position.

We were now at the driveway, and I noted that the gate was operated by a keypad, which Philip accessed by unlocking a small control box set in a post beside the driveway, and touching some numbers on a ten-key pad inside the control box. The gravel drive led around through the field on the right side of the building, which I now saw was a carbon copy of the two sides of the building I'd already seen, and around to the back, where it approached an embankment and made two very sharp ninety-degree turns, ending at a heavy roll-down metal door of the type sometimes used to shield shop windows at night in large cities. This door was the only discernable break in the otherwise featureless rear stone wall of the building.

Philip stopped the car, got out, unlocked the door, and then rolled it up. A light came on inside what appeared to be a sizeable garage, and he returned to the car to drive it inside. We got out of the car, and he closed the exterior door before unlocking a steel door that was set deeply into one of the interior walls.

Philip said, "We can explore the rest of the place later, but first I want to show you the top floor."

He turned on lights in the stairway and led me up several flights of steps, and we arrived in a darkened but evidently very large room. When he turned on some lights, I discovered that we were in what must be a great room at the top of the building. It had an extremely high beamed ceiling of rough-hewn timbers, which must have been at least twenty feet above us, and was paneled with a type of wood that I couldn't identify.

As with my beach house, three of the walls consisted of sliding glass doors. The resemblance ended there, though, as these doors didn't admit any light and appeared to be covered with some sort of planking on the exterior. In addition, the wall we were facing, and which I took to be the front of the building, was dominated by an immense stone fireplace that was flanked by the glass doors.

Philip walked over to a small control panel set into the wall and flipped a couple of switches. Somewhere above us, electric motors began to whine, and the planks covering the glass doors began to drop away. I now saw that my perception from the road below of drawbridges wasn't too far off the mark, because in less than five minutes, daylight was pouring in through all of the glass doors, and I could see that the planks that had covered them were, in fact, decks that were now lowered into position on three sides of the room. I noticed that above the glass doors were large windows that rose four or five feet above the doors but stopped short of the ceiling beams.

We walked over to the side of the room that overlooked the waterfalls below, and out onto the deck. The view was spectacular.

"Well, what do you think?" he said.

"I'm speechless."

"It does take your breath away at first, doesn't it?"

"It's magnificent." I looked down at the waterfalls, which had a mesmerizing effect.

We walked back into the great room, and I continued my visual inspection of its interior. The rear third of the room featured an exposed loft under one end of which were tucked a small kitchen and dining area. The area around the fireplace contained comfortable seating, and in one corner of the room I saw a stack of chairs and chaise lounges, obviously meant for the decks. Philip led me up an open stairway at one side of the room, and I discovered that the loft contained a king-size bed in one large open space, beyond which were a bathroom and a closet. From the loft, we could look out through the large windows and see nothing but the surrounding mountains.

We were standing side by side, and he leaned over, kissed me, and said, "I've never brought another person up here."

"Never?"

"Never. This has been my retreat for many years. There's a local couple who watch the place for me and keep it clean and for that reason must have access. Other than the two of them, nobody else has been here."

"Thank you for sharing it with me."

"Let's go down and get our bags. There's a great deal to see around here."

We descended to the car and retrieved our gear. On the way back up the stairs, I noticed a doorway at each of the three levels below the great room, a detail that I'd missed on the trip up. Philip saw my curious glances and told me that there were a few surprises in the place. When we'd stowed our belongings in the sleeping loft, he looked at me.

"How about a swim?"

"Where?"

"There's a nice deep pool in the stream above the waterfall, and although it's getting late in the day, the air will still be warm enough."

"We didn't bring suits, did we?"

"Not necessary. The pool is on my property and totally secluded. We can skinny-dip."

We changed into khaki hiking shorts and T-shirts and put on tennis shoes. Philip produced a backpack and stuffed two towels into it, and we were off. He led me up the mountain and behind the keep, which was how I thought of it, following a narrow path through the dense woods. When we emerged from the woods, I saw that we were on the edge of the stream just above the waterfalls—the sounds from which were quite audible.

It was a beautiful spot. The stream ran down over a series of smoothly rounded boulders into a level area, where it formed a wide and quiet pool for perhaps fifty yards before it cascaded over still more boulders and rocks and continued down the mountainside. Looking more closely, I saw that many of the rocks at the lower end of the pool had been placed there in order to partially obstruct the stream and make the pool deeper.

"How deep is it?"

"Probably not more than five feet in the middle."

"How cold is it?"

"You really don't want to know," he said as he pulled off his clothes and ran into the pool. He quickly submerged in the middle of the stream and came back up gasping for air. "What are you waiting for?"

"My sense of adventure to return," I said, and I began to undress, piling my clothes beside Philip's. I walked gingerly into the ice-cold water and stood at calf depth for a minute.

"Come on. You can't do it gradually. It's all or nothing—you just have to take that first plunge." With that, he used his hands to send great splashes of frigid water in my direction. This, of course, had the desired effect, and I jumped in and went after him.

He was right. After the shock of jumping in and ducking under the water, I quickly adjusted to the temperature. We splashed around for a while, indulging in horseplay like a couple of kids. I discovered that the middle of the pool was both deep enough and long enough to allow us to swim some laps, which we did, but without keeping count. Finally, the water began to chill us through, so we retrieved the towels and dried ourselves. Philip spread the towels side by side on a large flat boulder located in the middle of the stream above the pool. The boulder was dry and more importantly, warm from the sun. We lay down to let the sun soak in, first on our stomachs and then on our backs. We lay there in silence, listening to the sounds of the stream, for some time.

"You know," he said, "there's something that I've always wanted to do in this spot."

"What's that?"

"This," he said, and he rolled over on top of me. "I've always wanted to make love with someone special here beside this stream."

"Well, I've done it in the open air in broad daylight on the deck of my beach house, but that was on a nice soft pile of cushions, and this rock is hard."

"That's okay," he said. "I've got something equally hard to take your mind off any discomfort from the rock."

He was right, of course.

When we'd dressed and returned to the keep, Philip went to the kitchen and made a brief shopping list. There were plenty of staples on hand, he explained, but we needed some fresh vegetables and other perishables. We drove down the valley to a point at which it tapered to a narrow pass at the lower end. The road emerged from the pass into a larger and seemingly more inhabited valley, and we stopped at a small general store. It was operated by a mountain couple of late middle age who seemed well acquainted with Philip. After he introduced me to them, we selected and purchased the necessary supplies and were soon back at the keep.

When we were reclining in chaise lounges on one of the decks with drinks in our hands, I said, "You call this your hideaway, but I think of it as 'The Keep'."

"I like that. It's a very fitting description."

"Have we an itinerary for the weekend?"

"Not really. We can lounge around here all weekend, or we can do some of the tourist-type things in the area."

"Such as?"

"Well, there's the Biltmore House in Asheville, the Blue Ridge Parkway, Gatlinburg for shopping, and the play *Unto These Hills* in Cherokee."

"As it happens, I've done most of those things at one time or another, and they're certainly worth doing again, particularly with you. Why don't we play it by ear for this trip?"

"Sure."

"I do have one suggestion, however."

"What?"

"Church at St. Mary's in Asheville, which is a lovely little Anglo-Catholic parish, followed by brunch at the Grove Park Inn."

"Sounds good. I've heard of the Grove Park Inn but never been there."

"Then you're in for a treat, as they have the best Sunday brunch that I've ever seen."

We made a joint project of making a salad and grilling some steaks for dinner, most of which was done on the deck, Philip having rolled a small cart outside to serve as a preparation area. Before we went up to the sleeping loft, he closed the glass doors, explaining that there was a better method for fresh air at night. We went up to the sleeping area, and he walked over to the wall and opened a double set of awning-type windows that I'd failed to note earlier. These admitted both fresh air and the sounds of the waterfalls below, the latter of which lulled us to sleep almost as soon as we were in bed, but not before we had satisfied other needs.

22

Philip

EARLY Sunday morning, when I awoke, Charles was still sleeping soundly, and I lay there thinking about the previous afternoon. For years I had wanted to bring someone to this place but had never before let anyone get close enough to me for that. I was pleased that he wasn't particularly interested in spending the weekend in tourist-type activities; there would be plenty of time for such on future trips, of which I hoped there would be many. I ruminated for a while and must have dozed off, waking up again only when I felt him roll over and push against me.

"Awake?" he said.

"Yes, although I woke up earlier and dozed off again."

"Good," he said as he started doing things with his hands. After we'd taken care of those needs, we dressed in running gear and jogged down the valley.

"I presume you have some landmarks indicating how far we've gone?" he said.

"Definitely. When we reach the pass at the lower end of the valley, it's just about two and a half miles. Coming back, it'll seem more like five, since it's all uphill."

We ran in silence after that, enjoying the fresh air, the distant sounds of the stream somewhere below us, and the sounds of birds. There was only an occasional vehicle on the road to disturb the tranquility of nature. When we'd returned to but hadn't entered the keep—he'd gotten me to thinking of it in those terms—we were panting. "The return trip seemed more like ten," he said.

"That's okay, it's good for you. Even better, we can go up to the pool and cool off a bit before we go upstairs for a hot shower."

"Are you some sort of masochist?"

"No, just a nature lover," I said, and not waiting for him to consent, I trotted up the mountainside. He followed and this time was in the water ahead of me.

We splashed around a bit, then, lacking towels, pulled on our shoes and shorts and ran back down the trail, letting the air dry us off a bit. Before we'd had time to become totally chilled from the experience, we arrived at the door and went up to the bathroom, where we shaved quickly and then got into the shower, letting the hot water soak us thoroughly. As usual, one thing led to another, and we wound up back in bed for a time. We were, however, dressed and on the way to Asheville with plenty of time to spare.

As we approached the city from the west on I-40, I told Charles he'd have to navigate, which he did, directing me along an expressway to the exit that gave access to Charlotte Street. St. Mary's turned out to be a small gothic church in red brick. Charles explained that it had been unabashedly Anglo-Catholic for decades but had managed to operate within the Episcopal Diocese without any problems. The service was very formal and reminiscent of Roman Catholic services that I'd occasionally attended with friends when I was a child.

After church, Charles guided me up the street that ran from St. Mary's to the Grove Park Inn.

This was an immense old stone building that had been built by a patent medicine millionaire named Dr. Grove, who'd settled in Asheville at the turn of the twentieth century. The center portion of the structure was made of rounded stones that had obviously been taken from streams and rivers, and was flanked by two wings of newer construction. I'd heard of it, of course, but had never been there. In fact, I'd spent most of my time in the mountains relaxing and/or working in my retreat and had never spent any significant time elsewhere in the area. As it turned out, Charles had vacationed in the area regularly.

We were directed down a corridor off the main lobby and arrived in one of the newer wings. The dining area was a glassed-in terrace offering a wonderful view of the mountains beyond and a bird's-eye view of the golf course below. We hadn't climbed any stairs, but the site sloped sharply down from the main entrance, and the dining area was at least forty feet above the ground below. In two large rooms adjacent to the terrace, the most incredible variety of food that I'd ever seen at a Sunday brunch was on display and waiting for us. We ordered a bottle of wine and spent a pleasant two hours sampling the various offerings. As we drove out of Asheville, Charles said, "We'll have to run ten miles tomorrow to make up for all that food."

"Too right."

We were back in the valley by four and went straight to bed. Later, we relaxed on the deck and tried to do as little as possible.

Monday morning began as Sunday had, except that after a swim and hot shower, we spent some time on the deck with coffee, juice, and toast, enjoying the view and each other's company.

"Somehow, I never get tired of this place," I said.

"I can understand why. The sound of water over rocks is even more soothing than the sound of the surf."

We spent most of the rest of the day driving around the mountains and along a portion of the Blue Ridge Parkway, eventually stopping for lunch at a small restaurant in Maggie Valley. We were back at the keep by midafternoon, with plenty of time for a swim. Afterward, as we were sunning ourselves on the rocks, Charles was the one to be playful. Later, as we were dressing, he said, "I've heard of love on the rocks but never thought of it quite like this."

That evening I gave him a quick tour of most of the rest of the building. Adjacent to the garage, the ground floor housed a small shop area equipped for woodworking and other activities, whereas the second floor was entirely given over to storage. The third floor consisted of a well-equipped office area, an equally well-stocked library, and a file room that contained all of my old tax records, manuscripts, and other papers.

When we returned to the great room, I said, "I've always planned to move here on a permanent basis when I retire."

"This would appear to be an ideal place for that purpose."

The exertions of the day had left us both very hungry, so we grilled some chicken breasts and prepared steamed vegetables. Afterward, we cleaned up the remains of our meal and tidied up the premises. Charles packed our gear and loaded the car; then I secured the building.

The trip back to Atlanta was a little more leisurely than the trip up to the mountains had been, and I don't know whether I slowed down for Charles's benefit or because I was relaxed. We traveled in relative silence until we were again on I-85.

Charles said, "I've been thinking."

"What about?"

"Your mountain hideout and certain things about it."

"What about it?"

"You're one of them, aren't you?"

I guessed what he meant, but I said, "One of whom?"

"For want of a better word, a survivalist. One of those people who believe that our society is going to collapse on itself one day and therefore have prepared sanctuaries for themselves in remote areas."

"What leads you to that conclusion?"

"1) The keep is in a very strategic location; 2) The only door is situated such that it can't be easily breached, that is, the pair of ninety-degree turns would make it impossible, for instance, to ram it with a vehicle at any significant speed; 3) The walls appeared to be at least a foot thick, perhaps more; 4) There were enough tools and things in that workshop to repair almost anything; 5) There was enough food in the storeroom to last one or two people for a very long time; and 6) I just ran out of specific clues."

I was silent for a moment before replying, "As usual, counselor, you're too perceptive, and you're absolutely correct on all counts. The walls are actually two feet thick; the contents of the storage room will feed two people for about five years, provided they supplement the staples with game and can grow some vegetables from the seeds also in storage. And there are some other things that I didn't have time to show you on this trip."

"Such as?"

"A diesel generator for power with a large fuel supply, and a small arsenal. As a backup to the diesel generator, I have plans to one day tap the stream above the waterfall for hydroelectric power. Also, there's a bolt hole leading to a natural cave, which in turn provides a way to escape if necessary."

"You really believe that society will collapse?"

"It's one of several possibilities. I prefer the word implode, as it's more descriptive of what could possibly happen. Most of the inner-city areas in this country are already little more than battle zones. The politicians don't have the balls to even talk about what needs to be done to correct the situation, let alone do it. And the ones that do suggest realistic solutions for urban ills are for, the most part, crucified by the media. Yes, I think there is a possibility that the violence will get out of hand and spread to the suburbs and perhaps beyond. One best-selling author recently described parts of our nation's capitol as resembling a 'third-world shit hole'."

"You may be right. I've never really dwelt on it."

"Unfortunately, I have. The other residents of that valley are all similarly prepared in one way or another, and we have a sort of mutual-defense pact, including plans to block the highway at both ends of the valley should our worst fears be realized. Even if it never comes to that, the site is a perfect place for eventual retirement."

"Well, the secret is safe with me."

"If I didn't trust you, I'd never have taken you up there."

He seemed lost in thought, so I concentrated on the traffic, which was becoming increasingly heavy as we approached Atlanta. We arrived home well before ten and carried our bags up to the bedroom, with Lance bounding up the stairs ahead of us. When we went down to the study, Richard was on the sofa talking to Bruce, and we visited with them for a while before excusing ourselves to make an early night of it.

23

Charles

ON TUESDAY, Philip and I resumed our regular schedule, interrupting it early Thursday morning when I drove Philip to the airport so he could catch a flight to Boston for two days of conferences with architects and engineers. Meanwhile, I was preoccupied with a pending trial, which had become a media sensation. A thirty-five-year-old businessman stood accused of forcing a fifteen-year-old boy to perform oral sex on him, or as the lawyers say, *intercourse per os*. The man was a pillar of the community and had a live-in girlfriend and absolutely no prior history of any sexual misadventures. The trial was to have begun the previous week, but I'd asked for and been granted a continuance of one week, so it was to resume this morning. In fact, I went straight from the airport to the office and then to court. Jury selection went quickly during the morning, and by midafternoon the prosecution had the kid on the stand, sticking doggedly to his story that my client, Rodney Bates, had, in the course of doing volunteer work at a local charity for underprivileged kids, forced the kid to fellate him after having failed to obtain the same service with a bribe.

By four o'clock, I knew that I wasn't getting anywhere in my attempts to shake the kid's story, so I requested and was granted a recess until the next morning. In the course of my conversations with the defendant in preparing his defense, I discovered that he was also an avid swimmer and belonged to the City Club of Buckhead. That afternoon, as we were walking back to my office from the courthouse, we were both feeling the stress, and he suggested that we go swim some laps and then take some steam to sweat out our frustrations at his club while we talked about the case. Since Philip was out of town, I readily agreed.

I stopped by the house to retrieve my gear and met Rodney at his club a few minutes later. It's not considered polite to pay undue attention to bodies in locker rooms, and I wasn't interested in him, anyway, so I took no notice as he suited up, being involved in doing the same thing myself. Nor did I pay attention to his body after we left the pool and wrapped towels around our waists to head for the steam room, which was unoccupied, so we were able to talk about the case. In all the weeks of preparation, we'd failed to come up with a working hypothesis as to what would have motivated the kid to lie.

We left the steam room, went to the shower area, and hung our towels on hooks by the door. As we stepped under adjacent showerheads, I thought I noticed something out of place about Rodney, so I took a closer look. Then I found my gaze riveted to his pubic area, which, of course, he noticed. Before he could ask me why I was staring at him—in fact, he probably already knew—I said, "You didn't tell me about that."

"I didn't think it was relevant."

"Not only is it relevant, it may well be the means by which we'll win this case. We need to get dressed and get back to my office, pronto." Which we did, and I spent an extremely busy evening at the office and was back there at the crack of dawn getting things in order. The trial resumed at nine thirty, and the kid was led back to the stand. His name was Joe Woods, and he was a typical street punk, which was why he'd been a regular at the youth facility. I reminded him that he was still under oath, and he affirmed his understanding of same.

"Now, Joe," I said, "you say that Mr. Bates forced you to fellate him."

"Yes, Sir, he did."

"Did he take his clothes off?"

"No, Sir, but he unbuttoned his shirt and dropped his pants and shorts down to his knees, I guess."

"You guess? Did he or didn't he?"

"Yes, Sir, he dropped his pants and shorts to his knees."

"Was the room well lighted?"

"Yes, Sir—it was after hours and nobody was around, but the lights were on, and we were alone."

"Was he wearing boxers or briefs?"

"What?"

"What kind of underwear was he wearing—boxer shorts or briefs?"

"I dunno, boxers, I guess."

"The court isn't interested in your guesses. Which was it?"

"Boxers."

"So, you got a good look at most of Mr. Bates's body—at least from the neck down."

"Yes, Sir, I guess so."

"More guesses, but let's move on. Tell us about his body."

"I don't understand."

"Describe his body—what did you see?" He didn't answer, so I continued, "For example, did you see his bare chest?"

"Yes, Sir."

"Was it hairy?"

"What?"

"Was his chest very hairy, slightly hairy, or did he have no hair on his chest at all?"

"I dunno, about average, I guess."

"Thank you. Now Joe, I want you to describe Mr. Bates's penis for the jury."

"I don't know what you mean."

"Well, was it long, short, or average? Fat, thin? Circumcised, uncircumcised? What?"

This elicited an objection from the prosecution. "Your Honor, this boy would certainly have no frame of reference by which to judge such things."

To which I shot back, "The witness is a high school student… when he chooses to attend classes… and has surely been in enough locker rooms by now to have a fair idea of such things. Not to mention the fact that he's probably seen more than one X-rated movie."

TRIAL ❖ 183

After some more sparring, the objection was overruled. His Honor said, "Answer the question, son."

Joe, looking a bit bewildered, replied, "I dunno, about average, I guess."

"What about his pubic hair?"

"I don't understand."

"His pubic hair. Did he have a lot of it, not very much, average, what?"

Chauncey Daniels, the prosecutor, was on his feet "Your Honor—"

I cut him off. "The witness, by his own testimony, had his face buried in my client's crotch in a lighted room—he cannot help but have noticed such a detail."

Chauncey wasn't through. "Your Honor, I fail to see the relevance."

I fired back, "Your Honor, my client's reputation has already been damaged, perhaps irretrievably, by these accusations, and his very freedom is threatened. I assure the court that this line of questioning will ultimately become very relevant."

"Objection overruled."

"All right, Joe, please answer the question."

The boy once again hesitated, then said, "I dunno, about average, I guess."

"You're very certain about that?"

"Yes, Sir." He'd recovered some of his cockiness by this time.

"I expect you might even have gotten some caught in your teeth."

"Maybe."

"Your Honor, is this really necessary?" the prosecutor said.

I cut him off and addressed the court. "Your Honor, I respectfully request an immediate conference in your chambers with yourself and Mr. Daniels, the prosecutor."

"For what purpose?"

"If the court pleases, I would like to keep that privileged at the moment."

"All right, Mr. Barnett, I trust you have your reasons. Court stands in recess for fifteen minutes."

The bailiff said, "All rise," and Chauncey and I followed the judge back to his Chambers.

When we were settled down around his desk, Judge Brown looked at me. "Mr. Barnett, I hope you have a good reason for this."

"I do, Your Honor. I also have a request before we begin."

"And that would be?"

"Simply that what I am about to reveal to you will not be made public, and if I'm successful in what I am about to do, that it be kept off the record."

"That's a large order."

"Yes, Sir. However, Mr. Bates has suffered enough public embarrassment and doesn't need more publicity. What I'm about to reveal will create even more of a media circus than we already have."

"All right, Mr. Barnett, I will agree to your request—with the reservation that you had better be damn convincing. What is it that you wish to reveal?"

"Simply this, Your Honor: young Joe could not possibly have performed fellatio upon Mr. Bates. Could not, in fact, have even seen him naked. If he had, he would have known that Mr. Bates doesn't have any hair on his chest, and more importantly, he doesn't have any pubic hair."

"Say what?" This from Chauncey Daniels.

"I had no idea myself until he invited me to swim laps with him in the City Club of Buckhead pool after court yesterday. I noticed something unusual about him in the shower room and asked him about it. It seems that he and his girlfriend are nudists. Moreover, they belong to a subset of the nudist community who keep their bodies free of hair from the neck down. They call themselves 'smoothies'. My client and his girlfriend have, as have some of their fellow 'smoothies', taken the additional step of having laser hair removal treatments. My client has not had any pubic hair for at least ten years, and for the past six years, due to the laser treatments, his body has been incapable of growing pubic hair. I have paperwork from the laser clinic in support of this."

"Indeed!" the judge said.

"Yes, Sir. In addition, I have here a sworn affidavit from his girlfriend, as well as sworn affidavits from six members of the City Club of Buckhead, all of them to the effect that nobody has seen Mr. Bates with other than a hairless pubic area for several years. Apparently he took a lot of kidding when he was first noticed in the locker room, but the members got over it in due course."

I handed him a set of the affidavits that I'd spent most of the last evening rounding up. He looked at them and passed them to Chauncey, who quickly scanned them and handed them back to me.

"If necessary, Mr. Bates is prepared to come into these chambers and drop his pants to prove what I've just said."

"That certainly puts everything in a new light," the judge said.

"Yes, Sir. Clearly the boy is lying, although we have no idea why. Perhaps Mr. Bates has an enemy of whom he isn't aware. I really don't know. On the other hand, I think his innocence is clear, and I don't see any need for the media to get hold of this. I can see the headlines now—'Pubic-Hair Defense Wins Trial.'"

Chauncey Daniels, who'd remained quiet during this exchange, added, "They'd have a field day with it."

Judge Brown asked, "What do you propose we do, Mr. Barnett?"

"With your permission, I'd like to get the kid in here and see if we can get the truth out of him, up to and including who put him up to this. In which event, the case can be dismissed and the pubic-hair matter needn't even appear on the record."

The judge said, "Mr. Daniels?"

"Fine by me—this case has left a bad enough taste in my mouth already. I didn't want to take it on in the first place, but the boy was absolutely unshakeable with his story. I'd like nothing better than to lay it to rest."

The judge touched an intercom button on his desk. "Sergeant Jones, please escort the young man on the witness stand into my chambers."

Moments later, the door opened and the boy entered, followed by the bailiff.

"Sergeant Jones, please pull a chair over here between Mr. Barnett and Mr. Daniels for the young man to sit in."

When a slightly worried-looking Joe was seated, the judge took the initiative. Putting on an extremely stern face, he said, "Joe, Mr. Barnett has just proved conclusively to both Mr. Daniels and myself, that it is not possible for you to have seen Mr. Bates naked, let alone performed the act you describe. What do you say about that?"

The kid started stammering. "But he did, I mean, I did do it to him."

"No, son, you did not. Mr. Barnett knows it, Mr. Daniels knows it, and I know it. Now who put you up to this?"

"I don't know what you mean."

"Yes, you do. You didn't simply wake up one day and decide to make a false accusation out of the blue. Somebody must have talked you into it—or perhaps paid you to do it."

There was a long silence.

"Well, son? We're waiting."

In a voice that was almost a whisper, the kid said, "What'll happen to me if I tell you?"

"That's hard to say until you tell us your story. Maybe, if you help us catch whoever is responsible for putting you up to this, I'll be inclined to be lenient."

"Okay. I guess so."

"Good. Mr. Barnett, would you like to do the honors?"

"Yes, Your Honor." I turned to Joe. "Joe."

"Yes, Sir."

"Did you perform oral sex on Mr. Bates?"

"No, Sir."

"Has Mr. Bates ever done or said anything to you that would indicate that he was interested in young boys?"

"No, Sir."

"Then why did you do it?"

"Somebody gave me a lot of money."

"Who?"

"A man. He said he wanted to get even with Mr. Bates. Something about a business deal that he lost out on—I dunno all the details."

"Can you identify the man?"

"Yes, Sir."

"Well?"

"His name is Wallace Moseley. I think he has a business out on Ponce de Leon near some property that Mr. Bates owns. Something like that."

"What kind of business?"

"Used car lot, or something to do with cars."

"How much money did he give you?"

"A lot—two or three hundred dollars. Something like that. He said it would be a piece of cake."

"Did he, indeed!"

"Yes, Sir."

I said, "Thank you, Joe," and I turned to the judge. "Your Honor?"

"Well, Mr. Barnett, it seems to be your show, what do you suggest?"

"I would like for us to take Joe back out to the witness stand and have him repeat the answers he just gave us. In that way, justice can be served—and the matters that were disclosed earlier need never come out."

"Mr. Daniels?"

"That's fine with me, Your Honor."

"All right, then. Young man," the judge said, "we're going to take you back to the courtroom, Mr. Barnett is going to ask you the same questions he just asked you, and you are going to tell the truth in public."

"And then what will happen to me?"

"Well, son, if you help us apprehend and convict the man who put you up to this, you'll probably be let off with probation. But I'll expect you to walk the straight and narrow from now on."

"Yes, Sir."

At which point we returned to the courtroom, and I asked the relevant questions. When Joe had finished answering them, I asked that the case be dismissed, and without objection from Chauncey, the judge dismissed the case. Rodney and I fought our way past the crowd of reporters, answered some of their questions, and quickly walked back to my office. He was so grateful it was embarrassing. It turned out that Rodney had been successful in blocking a zoning variance that had been sought by Moseley, and Moseley was apparently out for blood—he'd stood to profit enormously had his zoning change gone through. All in all, a good day at court, and I got home in time to change clothes before I headed out to pick up Philip at the airport.

24

Philip

WHEN I passed through the security area of the airport that evening, Charles was waiting for me. As I had only a carry-on bag, we were quickly on our way to the car. He was grinning like the proverbial Cheshire Cat, which prompted me to say, "You look like the cat that just ate the canary."

"I'm just glad to see you."

"Perhaps, but there's more to it than that, I think."

"Too true. Tell you about it in the car." In the car, he said, "This is the longest we've been separated."

"I know."

"It felt really strange to come home to my lonely bedroom, never mind that for the three years prior to our meeting I'd done precisely that on a daily basis."

"Well, I'm back now. I shouldn't have to go to Boston again before our Labor Day trip."

"How was your trip?"

"Very encouraging. Preliminary reports are that we can have a winner with either of several scenarios."

"Can you elaborate?"

"Sure," I said. "The first alternative is to create several large lofts on each floor, lofts being something of a novelty in Boston right now. Second, we could cut the building up into condominium flats. Third, we could do the same, but with smaller rental units."

"Are you leaning in any particular direction?"

"We'll have to talk about it—it should be a joint decision."

"I'm content to defer to your superior experience in such matters. However, one thought has occurred to me," he said.

"What?"

"If we go the condominium route, one of the most common complaints from condominium owners is the fact that monthly maintenance fees for the common areas seem to have a way of escalating out of control."

"I know."

"We could consider making the ground floor into a series of retail spaces for lease. They could be part of the common areas owned by the condominium association and might one day generate enough income that the monthly maintenance fees could be greatly reduced, or perhaps even eliminated. I wonder if anyone has ever tried that?"

"I've no idea, but it wouldn't surprise me. The sales price per unit would have to be higher, but the advantages more than compensate, so I'll certainly look into it. What made you come up with that idea, anyway?"

"I know the area fairly well, both from my time in Boston and from subsequent visits, and got to thinking. If gentrification is going to take place, the residents have to have a place to shop. The Quincy Market area is just down the street, of course, but except for the vegetable stalls, it's mostly for tourists, and the shops in the North End are a little too far away for heavy shopping."

"Sounds good. Now, tell me what you were grinning about at the gate."

"Just thinking about a case I won today," he said.

Our discussion of the pubic-hair defense carried us all the way home, where we went straight to bed. I was worn out from the trip, and I could see that Charles was tired too. Well... not too tired.

A couple of days later, Charles came home from work a bit earlier than usual and surprised me in the bathroom, where I was standing naked in front of the mirror with one hand across my crotch.

"Hi," he said. "What *are* you up to?"

"Oh, I was just wondering what I would look like with no pubic hair."

"Oh, goody," he said, "that sounds kind of kinky. Let's get some clippers and find out."

"Well... I will if you will."

"Deal."

He practically tore his clothes off and hung them in the closet. Then he produced a set of electric clippers and said, "Hop up and sit on the counter so I can have better access."

I did as he asked, and he began to trim all of my pubic area down to a nub. Having finished, he handed me the clippers and eased up onto the counter himself. I proceeded to trim him just as he'd done me. By this time we were both hard as rocks. Then Charles took a can of shaving gel and a razor and set them on the counter. Wetting a washcloth with warm water, he proceeded to moisten my entire crotch, after which he spread the shaving gel and started to work. In short order, I was bald as a newborn.

"Bend over," he said.

"Why?"

"Got to shave your butt as well."

"Okay," I said, and I complied with his request.

When he had finished shaving me, he handed me the washcloth and other supplies. "Your turn."

I repeated the process, doing to him as he'd done me. When I was through, he turned on the shower and we used it to thoroughly rinse ourselves. We left the shower, dried each other off, and stood side by side in front of the mirror.

"Wow," I said.

"Wow, indeed."

We were both still rock hard. Freed of the distraction of pubic hair, our erections looked amazing. Charles took me by the hand, led me to the bedroom, and pulled me down on the bed.

"That was just about the sexiest thing I've ever done," he said.

"Too right. I had no idea it would be such a sensual experience."

We turned it into a different kind of sensual experience for a while, until eventually we stopped and came up for air, lying back side by side on the pillows.

"Does it get any better than this?" he wondered aloud.

"I can't imagine how."

THE days began to truly fly by, with little or no progress having been made on the investigation. I could sense Charles's growing frustration at the lack of progress and tried to hide my own disappointment from him as best I could. I finished the final draft of my manuscript and sent it on its way to Boston, where William or Henry would see it safely to New York. Having finished that project, I began to focus my attention upon the building in Boston, finally deciding that Charles's idea was absolutely perfect for both the building and the location. The architects in Boston agreed, and the Lanes said that obtaining the necessary zoning variances shouldn't be a problem. I took the final estimates and projections to Randolph, and he gave them his blessing a couple of days later. I decided that all systems were go, and having received a commitment from my usual bankers for financing both the purchase price and the renovations, I scheduled the closing for the Friday before Labor Day.

Charles came home from work that Thursday, surprising me in the midst of packing for both of us, and said, "I really appreciate this, babe. It's been a jungle of a day."

"Want to talk about it?"

"Not much to tell, really. Anytime I plan to take off for even a day, I have to pay a certain price in extra work for a day or two before I leave."

"I'm sorry."

"No need to be, it's simply part of the job. By the way, as far as your case goes, I'm as ready for trial as I'll ever be, absent the elusive Ruby."

"What do you suppose has become of her?"

"Evidently, she's gone to ground somewhere. Richard and his people have found a long list of people who recognize the sketch, many of whom can even identify her by name. None of them, however, have been able to tell us her last name, her address, or her occupation. Even the Wackenhut and Pinkerton organizations have come up empty-handed in other cities."

He'd undressed and changed into shorts and a T-shirt as he talked, and I said, "It sounds as if she's found someone to shelter her somewhere, or as you put it, she's 'gone to ground'."

"I'm afraid so. Sorry."

"Don't be, it's not your fault. Besides, anything can happen between now and January. Take a look at your suitcase, will you, and tell me if I've forgotten anything."

He examined the contents briefly and said, "Looks okay to me. Do you mind if we take time to go get some steam and swim a few laps? I've got to get the kinks out."

I didn't mind at all, and an hour and a half later we were back home, having stopped by a drive-through to pick up our supper. Richard wasn't due to take us to the airport until nine, which gave us ample time for a romantic interlude, and we were waiting in the study when Richard arrived to perform his chauffeur duty. When we were on the interstate, Richard spoke up, saying, "I don't want to get your hopes up, guys, but we may have our first positive lead on our missing witness."

"Details, please," Charles said.

"As you know, none of our numerous witnesses claim to have seen her after the weekend of the murder."

"We know."

"Late this afternoon, one of my grunts talked to somebody who just might have seen her a week or two after the murder. I'm really short on particulars at the moment, but I've got three people working on it. Perhaps by the time you two get back from Beantown, there'll be more to tell."

"That's the first encouraging thing we've heard in two months," Charles said. "Keep on it."

"You betcha."

I decided to switch topics and said, "How are you and Bruce getting along these days?" I knew they'd been seeing a great deal of each other.

"Hard to say. He's getting awfully possessive."

"You don't seem to mind too much," Charles said.

"I don't know. It must be the over-thirty syndrome at work."

Richard pulled up in a vacant spot directly in front of the door leading to the Delta ticket counter, and we checked in and hurried to the gate area to wait. Hurry up and wait seems to be a recurring theme in flying. Both of us were equipped with books, and we sat quietly reading until our flight was called. On the plane, as we settled back with drinks, Charles said, "I wish we hadn't flown first class this trip."

"Why?"

"Because the seats are too far apart. If we were in the economy section, we could turn out the lights and I could casually slump over with my head on your shoulder pretending to be asleep, and no one would think anything of it."

"I hadn't thought of that."

Soon enough, we both dropped off, once again not waking until preparations for landing were well under way. We were met at Logan Airport by William, who greeted us warmly.

"Where's Henry?" I said.

"Circling in the car, waiting for my call."

Charles made an apology for the hour, saying, "We really should have gone to a hotel. It's most uncivil of us to drag you guys out at this hour."

"Nonsense," William said. "We'd have been insulted if you hadn't chosen to stay with us. Besides, we can all sleep late tomorrow if we like—the closing isn't until eleven, and Henry and I have no pressing appointments."

While we waited for our luggage, we made tentative plans for a morning run, Charles having discovered that our hosts were avid runners. When our bags arrived on the carousel, William called Henry, and by the time we got to the curb, a Jaguar sedan was waiting for us with Henry at the wheel. Traffic at that hour was extremely light, and we were on Charles Street in short order and at their door a few minutes later after the usual roundabout trip, Brimmer Street being one-way toward Beacon Street.

William got out of the car with us, and as soon as we'd collected our bags from the trunk, Henry drove down the street to the Brimmer Street Garage, where the car would be put away for the night. Their townhouse was about twenty-five feet wide and three stories tall. William unlocked the front door, then hurried to disarm the alarm system before leading us up to a guest suite located on the second floor. As I'd stayed with them before and was therefore familiar with the layout, he said good night and left us without taking the time to show us around our quarters.

I showed Charles quickly around our suite of rooms, which consisted of a small sitting alcove off of a large bedroom dominated by a four-poster bed, and a very modern bathroom. He took out a travel alarm and set it for seven; then we undressed for bed and were quickly sound asleep.

The alarm sounded much too soon, but we got up and shaved, then put on our running gear and went downstairs. Our hosts, similarly attired, were waiting for us with coffee in a small breakfast nook on the first floor. Since they'd very nearly finished their coffee, we declined a cup before we ran. Henry had determined the night before that we usually ran five or six miles, and asked if Charles had a particular route in mind.

"No. You guys lead, and we'll follow wherever you take us."

They led us down Brimmer to Beacon Street, where we turned right and ran a block or so to a side street. Turning right again soon led us to a pedestrian bridge over an expressway. Coming down off the bridge, we ran through a park that paralleled the Charles River. We continued through the park until the Lanes determined that we had gone far enough, at which point they made a U-turn, and we retraced our steps back to Brimmer Street and their house.

Upstairs in the shower, Charles said, "Those guys set a fast pace, considering that their legs are shorter than ours."

"They're also three or four years younger than we are."

"There is that."

Groomed and dressed for the closing, we met our hosts downstairs for a light breakfast and by ten thirty were walking to their office, briefcases in hand. The closing came off without a hitch, which was no surprise given that all the fine points had been agreed to in advance. B & D Properties, LLC was now the owner of one slightly run-down former factory building. After the other parties to the closing had departed, we had a brief meeting with our hosts, who wanted to know our plans for the weekend.

"This afternoon we have meetings with the architect and a couple of contractors, and tomorrow Charles is going to show me the Freedom Trail. I've never seen Cape Cod or P-town, and we'd talked about going to an early service Sunday morning, then renting a car and making the drive."

Charles said, "Not knowing what your schedules were like, we've kept the evenings free, and would be more than happy to have you join us tomorrow or Sunday, or both." Before they could reply, he added, "As far as evenings go, I think Philip would get a kick out of Durgin Park."

We decided not to firm up our dinner plans until after our hosts were home from their office, and Charles and I agreed to be back from our meetings no later than six. Henry gave us a key to the front door of their house along with the code to disarm the security system, and we went to our various meetings. We were waiting for the Lanes in their living room when they arrived home a little after five. William immediately asked, "How did your meetings go?"

"With the architect, just fine. With the contractors, less so. We weren't impressed with either of them, although they came highly recommended, and we've been sitting here trying to come up with a game plan."

"And have you?"

"We have some ideas, but nothing definite. I was hoping that the two of you might have some recommendations."

Henry said, "We just might. Why don't we talk about it over dinner?"

They wanted to take us to a French restaurant on Newbury Street, and we agreed to be dressed and ready by seven, which gave us time to relax in our room for a while. We went upstairs and lay down for a half hour or so, but never really got to sleep. At the appointed time, we were back downstairs, suited up and ready to go. The walk to the restaurant required about ten minutes, during which time William again assumed the role of tour guide. At the restaurant, our conversation was confined to generalities until we'd been served drinks and had placed our orders.

Finally, Henry returned to the subject of contractors by saying, "What exactly did you not like about the contractors to whom you spoke?"

"Costs and attitude. The tentative costs we discussed seem way out of line, even given the fact that contractors up here are saddled with union contracts. As for attitude, they both seemed to give the impression that they'd be doing us a favor—which does not compute, given the general slump in construction in this area."

William asked, "What alternative ideas have you come up with?"

"Nothing concrete, other than having a reliable contractor from Atlanta take on the job."

"That would be a non-union outfit, I suppose?"

"Certainly."

"That might pose a few problems in this area. The unions have a stranglehold on the trades, and you have no idea how many delaying tactics they could impose on you."

"We thought that might be the case, hence our dilemma."

"We might know someone who can help you," Henry said. "He usually handles much larger jobs, but with the slump in construction, he's begun to get into smaller projects, particularly renovations."

"Do you suppose we might see him tomorrow afternoon?"

"It's possible. He's a client of ours and owes us a favor or two. While you're doing the Freedom Trail tomorrow morning, we'll see what we can set up. If he isn't available Saturday afternoon, he might see you Sunday, although that might preclude your trip to P-town."

"I can live with that. There'll be plenty of future opportunities to go to Cape Cod."

Charles, who had been listening quietly until now, asked, "Have you told them about the idea I came up with?"

"Yes, but only briefly. Why don't you run it by them in more detail?"

He explained at length his concept of shops on the ground floor, which would be owned by the condominium association as a possible means of keeping monthly maintenance costs to a minimum. They were immediately receptive to the idea, adding that as far as they were aware, it would be a first for the area.

This conversation had occupied us through the soup and salad. Our entrées arrived, and we ate in relative silence for a while. Charles and our hosts agreed that I should be taken to Durgin Park for dinner on Saturday night, telling me only that it was an experience I would never forget. Leaving the restaurant, we strolled back to the townhouse, where we changed into more casual attire and joined our hosts in their study for a nightcap. They declined an invitation to join us for an early-morning run, as they wanted to sleep late. Charles gave them his cell phone number, saying that he'd carry it with us on the Freedom Trail in the morning, in case they needed to reach us concerning the contractor. We were in bed asleep well before midnight.

Saturday morning, we were running around the Common by six, and by eight we were at the information kiosk on Tremont Street near one of the corners of the Common, ready to begin our walk. The Freedom Trail consists of a painted line on the sidewalk or, in some places, a double row of bricks set into the sidewalk. It led us across the Common to the State House, then back to Tremont Street and to the Granary Burial Ground, where many famous figures from the Revolutionary era were buried. The Trail continues past several historic sites, including the Meeting House where the Boston Tea Party was planned, as well as Faneuil Hall and the Quincy Market, before it crossed into the North End, where it passed Paul Revere's house, the oldest house in the city. We walked right by the restaurant where we'd dined on our previous trip and then to the Old North Church with its quaint enclosed pews, finally crossing the Charles River.

From the bridge, we could see the USS *Constitution* docked at the Charlestown Navy Yard, and a few minutes later we were waiting in line for a tour of that famous ship. After touring the ship, we lingered in the small maritime museum next door, then followed the trail to its terminus at Bunker Hill. There we climbed the steps up to the Bunker Hill Monument (all 294 of them), enjoyed the view, and climbed back down again. As we sat down on a bench to rest for a minute, Charles said, "We can walk a few blocks and catch the subway back, or we can retrace our steps across the bridge and walk by our new property and then to a subway stop nearby."

"By all means, let's go take another look at our building."

We followed the Freedom Trail back, eventually crossing the Charles River, where we left the trail to go look over our building. From the building, we walked around the neighborhood, becoming more and more convinced that we were right on target with our plans. As we approached the building again, Charles's cell phone rang. It was William calling to let us know that the contractor would see us at three at the new building. We had a key with us and agreed to meet him there. As it was already one and we hadn't had lunch, Charles suggested that we walk over to Faneuil Hall and try one of the food stalls. It was only a few blocks away, and we spent some time deciding among the various offerings, finally electing to try a combination platter from a vendor that specialized in Greek cuisine, which turned out to be a delicious choice.

By three o'clock, we were back at the building waiting for the contractor, whose name was Austin Danforth. Austin, it developed, was a fortysomething bundle of energy and enthusiasm, and we liked him immediately. Perhaps more importantly, we felt immediately comfortable with him. The three of us made a thorough inspection of the premises, and Austin appeared to like both what he saw and our ideas for the ultimate direction the renovations should take. I looked a question mark at Charles and, seeing his nod of approval, asked Austin to contact the architect for the preliminary sketches and provide us with an estimate as to time and possible costs as soon as he could. He agreed, then went on to another appointment, leaving us at the building. We secured the building and went directly to the nearest subway station for the ride back across town.

William and Henry were waiting for us in their study, clearly eager to learn what we thought of Austin. They seemed pleased when we informed them of our decision, and the four of us toasted the success of the project.

After we'd consumed a couple of drinks, we went up for a short nap before dinner. By seven thirty, we were at Faneuil Hall waiting in line for a table at Durgin Park, which I learned was a well-known Boston eatery famous for very good food and extremely casual service. After a wait of nearly thirty minutes, we were led upstairs and seated at one of a row of long tables, each of which was designed to accommodate about a dozen guests. We were handed menus as we sat, and shortly a waiter came around and tossed a bundle of silverware on the table in front of each person seated.

This, it turned out, was part of the "casual" service, which at times extended to a brusqueness that stopped just short of rudeness on the part of the wait staff. Both the beef and seafood entrees were well prepared, and the portions were more than generous.

An hour or so later, we were walking around the Faneuil Hall area, complaining in a good-natured way about how much we'd eaten. Over dinner we tried to persuade the Lanes to come with us on our excursion to Cape Cod, but they declined on the grounds that four would be a crowd for this, our first trip there together.

Sunday morning, we were up early for a run around the Common before we attended an eight o'clock church service. After church, we went back to the house to change into clothes more appropriate for our drive. Then we walked over to Copley Place, where we'd reserved a rental car. The drive out to Cape Cod was all that I had hoped it would be, although the scenery didn't begin to live up to my preconceived notions until just before we reached the point at which the road curved sharply north and aimed toward the tip of the cape.

Provincetown was thronged with people, predominantly male and mostly young to middle aged. We found a parking spot, but not without some difficulty, and spent two or three hours exploring the area and inspecting the numerous small shops. For lunch, we tried a seaside restaurant, where the view of Cape Cod Bay proved superior to both the food and the service. By four, we were in the car and on our way back to Boston.

We spent a quiet Sunday evening at home with our hosts, and Monday morning we all slept late, finally going out for a run around ten o'clock. Later, we walked down Newbury Street and had lunch at an outdoor café. We'd kept the rental car so that we could turn it in at the airport and spare our hosts the trouble of driving us there, and by five o'clock, we were at the appropriate departure gate, waiting for our flight to be called.

Richard was waiting for us in Atlanta, and we both noticed that he appeared to be exhausted. Charles couldn't resist asking, "Bruce still wearing you out?"

"I wish it was that simple," Richard replied wearily. "Actually, I've been on the trail of Ruby almost all weekend."

"Any luck?"

"Not yet. We get the impression that she's right there but always just a hair beyond our grasp."

"What are the chances of success in the near future?"

"Hard to say. I don't want to get your hopes up; on the other hand, I don't want to paint too gloomy a picture, either."

We didn't press the matter and rode in silence the rest of the way home. As soon as we were home, we went straight to bed. Travel was always exhausting.

25

Charles

THE rest of September went by in a rush. Philip and I settled down into a routine of domesticity that we both found very comfortable—he kept himself busy and occupied by working on a new book and keeping tabs on the progress of the Boston project, while I settled back into my regular routine of work and more work. There was nothing else I could do in terms of preparation for the trial—it all depended upon Richard locally and other agencies on the national scene, all of whom were searching frantically for our missing dyke.

We took a few days off in early October to spend a long weekend in Boston and New England, ostensibly to check out the building project, but really to see the leaves. Later in October, we went to Philip's mountain retreat to enjoy the North Carolina foliage, which was usually at its peak during the third week of October, depending upon rainfall and weather.

In mid-November, an opportunity arose for me to go to Pittsburgh on business, and I asked Philip to go with me—for the company and to keep his mind off what was on the horizon. I had clients based in that city and had been there on a number of occasions over the years, so I looked forward to showing the city to Philip.

We arrived at the Pittsburgh airport on a Tuesday evening, picked up a rental car, and drove to the Omni William Penn in the heart of downtown Pittsburgh. The William Penn is a grand old hotel and features an elegant lobby, wonderful dining room, unusually large rooms for an older hotel in a major city, and impeccable service. We had a late supper in the dining room, then went straight to bed.

Wednesday morning, we were up early and ran down through downtown to the point at which the Allegheny and Monongahela Rivers joined to form the Ohio, and then back to the hotel by a roundabout route. I left Philip to his own devices for the rest of the day while I met with my clients.

That evening, we had dinner at the Wooden Angel, a restaurant located some forty miles north of Pittsburgh in the city of Beaver. The Wooden Angel has been a fixture in the area since the late sixties and is reportedly the only restaurant in the country to have won a major award from *Wine Spectator* magazine for a wine list consisting exclusively of American wines. The food and wine were superb, as was the service.

Thursday morning, we visited the Carnegie Museum and the Cathedral of Learning, which is basically a college situated in a skyscraper. After lunch, we visited the Frick Museum, a small museum on the grounds of the home of the industrialist of the same name. We also toured the elegant old Frick mansion, and that evening we walked across the Smithfield Street Bridge to Station Square, a shopping and restaurant complex housed in a former Pittsburgh & Lake Erie Railroad Terminal. Then we took the incline up to the top of Mt. Washington to enjoy the view of downtown Pittsburgh at night from several hundred feet up. We had a light supper at one of the restaurants on the side of Mt. Washington, and enjoyed both our food and the view of the city at night.

Friday morning I had one more session with my clients. After lunch, Philip and I explored an area along Penn Avenue known as the Strip, which offered many small shops and restaurants. That night, we went to a performance of the Pittsburgh Pops at Heinz Hall, a grandly restored 1920s movie palace that is now the home of the Pittsburgh Symphony. After the symphony, we went across the street to an Italian restaurant and had a wonderful dinner.

Saturday, we drove out into the country to see Fallingwater, the famous house designed by Frank Lloyd Wright for the founder of the local Kaufmann's department store chain. That night found us back on top of Mt. Washington for dinner at LeMont, an elegant restaurant that had won many awards over its fifty-year history. We were seated side by side on a banquette, looking across our table through floor-to-ceiling plate glass at the city of Pittsburgh at night. The point of view was rather like that of a low-flying airplane, and it was a special, romantic setting that had an effect upon both of us. When we got back to the hotel, Philip used the bathroom first, emerging after only a few minutes. I used the facilities and found him facedown on the bed with his naked buns enticing me.

"God, I do love your ass," I said, quickly shedding my clothes. Later, we kissed deeply for a long time.

Philip said, "Do you think we'll ever get tired of doing this?"

"God, I hope not. That was awesome."

"Yes, it was, wasn't it?"

"In spades. Now we need a nightcap and a shower," I said as I picked up the phone to call room service. I ordered two glasses of Port, then led Philip to the bathroom, where we took a shower together. We'd left the bathroom door open to listen for the waiter, and I heard a knock on the door just as I was drying my hair with a towel.

I called out, "Just a minute" and wrapped the towel around my waist before going to the door to admit the room-service waiter.

The waiter, whose nametag identified him as José, carried the tray into the room and set it on a table in the corner. As he handed me the bill to sign, I caught him perusing my body. Then Philip emerged from the bathroom, also wearing only a towel. José was just short of salivating when Philip came over, stood beside me, and placed an arm around my waist. His eyes kept darting back and forth between Philip and myself.

"Look, but don't touch," I said.

"Sorry, Sir, but you guys are so hot," José said.

"We're also very much unavailable," Philip said.

I signed the check, added a generous tip, then said, "But if we were into threesomes, you'd be a prime candidate." Before he could respond, I opened the door for him.

After I closed and locked the door, Philip and I burst out laughing and he said, "Did you see his pants? He was sprouting wood."

"I guess we should be flattered, but as I told him, 'Look, but don't touch.'"

We took our glasses of Port, placed a stack of pillows against the headboard of the bed, and snuggled up against each other while we sipped the Port. Shortly thereafter we were both deeply asleep.

Sunday morning, we were up at dawn for a quick run, then attended an eight o'clock service at Trinity Episcopal Cathedral, which was located only a block or so from the hotel. The service was over just in time for us to check out of the hotel and drive back to the airport for our flight home. All in all, a very relaxing trip, which did us both a world of good, given that the trial date was only a couple of months away and there was still no progress.

26

Philip

BY THE second week of December, Charles and I began to feel the need for distraction and/or diversion, both of us being painfully aware that the trial was only a little more than two weeks away. He arrived home from work a little earlier than usual one afternoon while I was still at my desk. He came into the study and wrapped his arms around me from behind.

"Be careful you don't step on his highness's tail," I said. "Every time I roll this chair from one side to the other, I fear the worst, but so far we've managed to avoid disaster."

"Got it covered. Dogs want nothing more than to be as close to their humans as they can possibly get, and he seems to regard you as just as much his human as I am."

"We have bonded, haven't we, boy?"

Lance looked up at us from his spot under my chair—he knew he was being talked about.

"You know, the next two weeks are going to be extremely difficult because of the trial date looming ever closer. I think we need another diversion."

"You must be reading my mind—I was just thinking the same thing."

"Great minds follow the same path, do they not?"

"Knowing you, you wouldn't have brought this up unless you already had the genesis of an idea."

"Guilty as charged. One of my favorite things to do at Christmas used to be to go to New York."

"That sounds like a good idea. What would the itinerary be?"

"Christmas Eve Mass at Smokey Mary's, Christmas brunch somewhere special, a performance at the Met if any interesting opera is on stage, etcetera."

"Smokey Mary's?" I parroted.

"The Episcopal Church of St. Mary The Virgin on 47th Street, called Smokey Mary's because they use a *lot* of incense."

"Oh, I see, but I sense a 'but' somewhere in all of the above."

"But it's way too late to get reservations for brunch anywhere decent. That has to be done in early September, and the same might be true for decent seats at the Met."

"So?"

"How about a three-day weekend in the Big Apple and a big Christmas celebration here at home?"

"I just had a thought. What does your grandmother do for Christmas?"

"Not a lot in recent years, but just a few years ago, she would have a large dinner party the week before Christmas for family and friends."

"Well, to tell the truth, I'm more or less traveled out at the moment. New York sounds great, but perhaps later. Why don't we persuade your grandmother to host a Christmas dinner? I can help prepare some of the food, and you could handle the wines."

Charles gave it a moment's thought and said, "You're on. Let's do it."

Charles called his grandmother the next day and set things in motion. As it turned out, she was delighted to be entertaining again.

The week wound down and Saturday arrived. We showered together and then stood side by side at the double sinks, shaving. Shaving, I might add, everything, as we had come to really love the "smooth" look. We usually made a quick job of shaving ourselves, but every few days we would get playful and give each other a thorough shave, just as we'd done the first time. It was wonderful and sensual and always left us aching for release, but this evening there was no time for play, as we were going out to dinner.

Two hours later, after a terrific meal at one of Atlanta's newest restaurants, we arrived home.

"Thanks for a great evening," I said.

"My pleasure, babe. Ready to climb the well-worn stairs?"

It was a totally rhetorical question, and I was naked and in bed before he was halfway up the stairs.

On the Saturday before Christmas, we dined with Charles's grandmother, who, despite the somewhat short notice, had somehow managed to round up several other dinner guests. There were a total of twelve people at the dinner table, and the conversation was lively and spirited. I even managed to completely forget about the looming trial date for a few hours. We went to midnight Mass Christmas Eve, and Christmas morning found us again at Mrs. Barnett's home, where we sat beside an enormous tree in the library and exchanged gifts.

27

Charles

MONDAY began with a cold front passing through the area, followed by a drenching early-morning rain that served to both dampen our spirits and prevent us from running. This, in turn, caused me to arrive at the office in something less than the best of moods, which was not the best of ways to begin the final week of preparation for a major trial. Somehow I got through the day without losing my cool, and by six, Philip and I were running in the park, after which we went to the Y and swam some laps. We retired early to the spare room, which we'd begun calling the study, the former study downstairs having acquired the new title of library.

He was working on a new novel, principally as a distraction from the period of waiting for the trial to begin, and settled down at his computer. I'd brought home a bulging briefcase and busied myself with working my way through its contents. As usual, I had placed several hours' worth of music on the stereo system. We worked steadily and without interruption until nearly eleven, when Richard came in. The door was open, and I don't think either of us were aware of his presence until he said, "Knock, Knock."

I looked up from my desk and said, "Hi, what's up?"

"News from Bruce," he said. "First, Wetherbee himself is going to try the case."

"That's hardly surprising, but good to know for sure. What else?"

"Second, I've managed to acquire every name and address on the list of prospective jurors."

"Great, that gives you five days, counting the weekend, to check them out. Anything else?"

"Geez, Charley, isn't that enough?"

"Well, to quote from the gospel according to Richard, one can't get enough."

"That was said in an entirely different context."

"But applicable nonetheless. If you want me to say 'well done', then 'well done'. Now, go to bed and get some rest. You're going to be extra busy tomorrow and for the rest of the week."

After Richard left the room, Philip said, "What's so important about the jury list?"

"In this case, it could be vital. I'll only be allowed to dismiss so many jurors summarily, that is to say, without a specific cause. If I know a little something concerning the background of each juror before I question him or her, I may be able to ask questions that will elicit answers which will allow me to dismiss for cause. Considering the way Wetherbee is going to present this case, it's vital that we have no certified homophobes on the panel. Background data will help me in weeding out the Baptists and fundamentalists, for example, without wasting my other options."

"I see, I think."

I stood up, stretched, walked over to his desk, and began to massage his shoulders. "Are we anywhere near a stopping place?"

"Actually, we are," he said. "Why?"

"Oh, I was just wondering if I could entice you to bed."

Within ten minutes we were in bed, and half an hour later we were asleep.

Tuesday morning, we were able to resume our habitual morning run, which allowed me to arrive at work in a better frame of mind. The rest of that day was uneventful, as was the rest of the week, the working portion of which ended at noon on Thursday, it being New Year's Eve. We went out to dinner that evening and came home in plenty of time to relax in the library before toasting the New Year with champagne. We spent a relaxing three-day weekend and were in bed early Sunday evening, having gone for a run through the park before bedtime in hopes that physical exhaustion would ensure soundness of sleep despite a certain amount of nervous anticipation concerning the events of the next morning.

Monday, we rose at our usual hour, ran, and then breakfasted. Philip rode with me to the office and waited there while I took care of a few odds and ends. Andrew came in around eight thirty to wish us luck, and shortly thereafter Mark, Philip, and I walked over to the courthouse. We took our places in the front of the courtroom, with Philip sitting between Mark and myself at the defense table. Mark and I had just finished arranging our documents when Craig Wetherbee came in with Tom Shields, an assistant district attorney, or ADA, who was to help him with the prosecution. There was no time to exchange pleasantries with the opposition, as was sometimes the case, because the bailiff entered the room, demanded that "All rise," and we were under way.

The process of jury selection lasted until Wednesday afternoon around four o'clock. Richard and his team had done their work well, and I managed to eliminate all of the prospective jurors whom I thought might be remotely prejudiced against homosexuals without exhausting all of my rights to dismiss jurors without cause. During the process of questioning the panel, I clashed repeatedly with Wetherbee, who objected vehemently every time my questions strayed into or near the area of religion. As expected, the judge granted a recess until the next morning due to the lateness of the hour, and we walked back to the office, where we had a brief conference before calling it a day. Mark and I were as pleased with the jury as we were with the degree of Wetherbee's apparent displeasure, and I explained our reasoning to Philip, who seemed to understand.

Philip and I arrived at home a little after five, where we changed into casual attire, having decided to go directly out to eat after our swim. We had a light supper at Rick's, after which we visited our favorite bookstore and browsed for a while before returning home. Once we were home, we went up to the study and spent an hour or so at our respective desks, then changed into running gear for a short run around the park. This had the desired effect, and afterward we went straight from the shower to bed.

Thursday produced no real surprises. Wetherbee's opening statement boiled down to one or two items: that Philip, who had no visible means of support, was dependent upon his wife's income; that her pregnancy (he managed to imply, without coming out and saying so, that Philip was obviously not the father) represented a threat to his financial security, and, fearing that he was about to lose his gravy train, he'd killed her. How they intended to prove this was beyond me.

Knowing in advance that this was the gist of their argument, I'd prepared an extremely brief opening statement to the effect that we would prove to everyone's satisfaction that their case was based upon total fantasy. I concluded my remarks and sat down, whereupon Wetherbee called his first witness, and we were off.

The first two witnesses were the officers who had appeared at the scene in response to the call from Martha Starling. I found little fault with their testimony and chose not to cross-examine them. The next witness was the former maid, Maria Santos, who'd discovered the body, and when my turn came, I had a few questions for her.

"Miss Santos, were you present at the house when Mr. d'Autremont returned home that morning?"

"Yes, Sir."

"Did he seem upset at the discovery of his wife's death?"

"Objection," Wetherbee said. "The witness is not a qualified psychologist."

"She is a human being, Your Honor, and capable of recognizing human reactions," I said.

"Overruled," the judge said. "The witness may answer the question."

In her slightly accented English, Maria Santos continued, "Yes, Sir, he seemed to be very upset."

"Thank you, Miss Santos. I just have one or two other questions, and then you may go."

"Thank you, Sir," she said.

"Miss Santos, who paid your wages?"

"Mrs. d'Autremont."

"Are you sure about that?"

"Of course, she handed me a check every week."

"She handed you a check, but do you know if it was her money that she paid you with?"

This prompted an objection and some arguing between Wetherbee and me, and finally we had to approach the bench. Wetherbee jumped right in, saying, "Your Honor, this is totally irrelevant and has nothing to do with the murder."

"On the contrary," I said, "it has everything to do with the prosecution's case, which seems to be predicated upon the fact that the defendant is some sort of gigolo who was afraid of losing his meal ticket."

The judge overruled Wetherbee, who went back to his seat. I walked over to the defense table, picked up two canceled checks, and turned to face the witness. "Miss Santos, I'll ask you again, do you know that the deceased paid you with her own money?"

"Like I said, she handed me a check."

"One of these?" I asked, and I handed her the two canceled checks.

"Yes, Sir."

"Would you read, for the court, what name is printed in the upper left-hand corner of these checks?"

"d'Autremont Household Account," she read, continuing with the address and telephone number that were also printed there.

"And whose signature is on these checks?"

She squinted at the signatures, then frowned and said, "I can't read them."

"Let me help you," I said. "Both checks are signed, as in fact were all of your paychecks, by Randolph Forney, who is a certified public accountant and a tax attorney, and who handles the financial affairs of Mr. d'Autremont and his late wife."

"Oh." She seemed surprised.

I took the checks from her, handed them to the bailiff, and said, "Defense enters these two checks as Exhibits A and B for the defense."

I turned back to her and said, "Now, Miss Santos, if I asked you once again who paid you for your services, how would you answer?"

"Well, the mistress handed me a check, but I guess I don't know where the money came from."

"Thank you, Miss Santos," I said, and I went to my seat before I addressed the judge. "No more questions, Your Honor."

Wetherbee then called, in turn, both Martha and Henry Starling. After he'd finished with each of them, I asked them basically the same questions I had the maid, eliciting the same surprised responses from both of them when they were confronted with their paychecks. My questions about Philip's reaction upon his arrival at the scene drew the same response from them and the same objections from Wetherbee.

All of this took us up to eleven o'clock, at which time the judge ordered a recess for lunch. We walked to a nearby restaurant for a light lunch, over which Philip asked how we were doing. "Well," I said, "we planted a seed of doubt this morning concerning money and where it came from. There's not much more we can do with that until our turn comes and we put Randolph Forney on the stand. His testimony will blow their theory out of the water."

Mark said, "It's good, however, to be able to get the jury to think about the matter now. Then, when Mr. Forney testifies, it won't be such a novel idea to the jury."

"The judge is female," Philip said. "Is that good for us or not?"

"This particular judge has a reputation for fairness," I said, "and that's good."

When the trial resumed after lunch, Wetherbee called the pathologist who'd performed the autopsy. He described in some detail the nature of the wounds and the cause of death, and when he was asked if there were any other findings, he added that the deceased was about six weeks pregnant.

Wetherbee returned to the fatal wound. "It would have taken a strong man to drive a stake through the body with such force, wouldn't it?" he said.

"Objection." It was my turn to protest. "Mr. Wetherbee is leading the witness."

"Sustained," the judge said.

Wetherbee took a different approach, asking the doctor, "In your opinion, how much force would have been required to push a wooden stake through the deceased's body and into her heart?"

"A considerable amount," he said.

"More than a woman could muster," Wetherbee said.

"I should think so."

When it was my turn, I focused on the strength issue and said, "Doctor, you described the murder weapon as a wooden stake about two feet long, pointed at one end and flat at the other, is that correct?"

"Yes, Sir."

"Anyone of average strength, even perhaps a female, could have used a hammer to drive that stake into the deceased, could they not?"

Wetherbee cut off any reply, saying, "Objection. No evidence has been introduced concerning any hammer."

I looked at him and said, "Surely the prosecutor is familiar with popular culture?"

This stopped him cold, and he said, "What?"

"In the movies, a wooden stake is always driven through a vampire's heart using a hammer or wooden mallet. Everybody knows that. The similarity is so obvious that even the prosecution should have thought of it."

That caught him slightly off guard, but he renewed his objection, which was ultimately sustained. I turned back to the pathologist and said, "Rephrasing my question, Doctor, are the wounds consistent with the wooden stake having been pounded into the deceased using some unknown instrument, perhaps even a hammer, to provide the force?"

"They are not inconsistent with that scenario," he said.

"Doctor, in plain English, doesn't 'not inconsistent' mean the same thing as 'consistent'?" I made two words out of it so it came out "con-sistent."

"Yes, Sir."

"Doctor, did you actually examine the stake in question?"

"Of course I did, and it had the victim's blood on the sharp end."

"What about the other end?"

"Excuse me?"

"Did you examine the opposite end for evidence that it might have been pounded upon as a means of forcing it into the body of the deceased?"

"No, Sir."

"Why didn't you do that? I thought that would have been part of your job."

"All I was asked to do was confirm that it had in fact been the murder weapon."

"Thank you, Doctor, I have no further questions."

The next witness called was Sergeant Harold Kellerman, the detective in charge of the investigation. Kellerman was in his late forties, considerably overweight, and judging from his face, clearly an extremely heavy drinker. Later, when I was up close, questioning him, the odor about him told me that he smoked to excess, as well. In short, he was a stereotypical career police detective. Wetherbee led Sergeant Kellerman through his report detail by painstaking detail, finally turning him over to me for cross-examination.

"Sergeant Kellerman," I said, holding a copy of his report in my hand, "according to your report, there were no fingerprints found in the murder room other than those of the deceased, the defendant, the maid, and the housekeeper."

"That is correct."

"All of whom one would expect to have been in the bedroom of the deceased at one time or another, correct?"

He gave a faint smirk and said, "Well, we have reason to believe that the defendant wasn't a regular visitor to his wife's bedroom."

"Do you?"

"Come on, counselor, everybody knows that they didn't sleep together."

"Sergeant, if by 'sleep together' you refer to conjugal relations, I must remind you that 'everybody' does not know anything of the kind. Moreover, there has been no testimony introduced to that effect."

"Well, they certainly had separate bedrooms."

"So did my great-grandparents," I said, "but they somehow managed to produce five children." This produced a titter from the audience and a bang of the judge's gavel.

When quiet was restored, I continued, "Sergeant Kellerman, how many sets of my client's fingerprints were found at the scene?"

"One very faint print was located on an item on the deceased's dressing table."

"Just one?"

"Yes, Sir."

"Located on"—I studied the report briefly for emphasis, although I knew the answer—"a bottle of perfume. Is that correct?"

"Yes, Sir."

"Which, according to the housekeeper, my client had given to his wife Christmas before last, is that also correct?"

"Yes, Sir."

"How, then, can you conclude that my client was ever in that room, given that the only object bearing his fingerprints had been a gift to his wife Christmas before last and given that it is your theory that he did not know his wife in the biblical sense?"

This drew a violent objection, which was finally overruled.

"We feel that he wiped the room clean of prints."

"If that's the case, Sergeant, how do you explain all those other prints you found?"

"What other prints?" he said, just a shade nervously, which got me thinking.

"Those of the deceased and the servants."

"Well, he must have missed a few."

I paused for such a long time, lost in my train of thought, that the judge had to prompt me to continue. "I'm sorry, Your Honor," I said.

"Sergeant Kellerman, this is a remarkably lucid document," I said, holding up his report. "May I ask how it was prepared?"

"I don't understand?"

"Did you write it out on a yellow pad and then type it, or did you dictate it to a secretary?"

"Oh. I have a computer on my desk and use word processing software to prepare my reports. I'm a poor speller, so the program helps me a great deal."

Suddenly, I wanted very much to see the sergeant's computer, but all I said was, "I'm impressed. I didn't know that the police department was so automated."

"Oh, yes, we even transmit reports electronically to the prosecutor's office."

"Do you, indeed! Well, the taxpayers' money seems to be being used efficiently, for once."

Wetherbee couldn't stand it any longer and said, "Is this drivel leading somewhere, or can we get on with it?"

I looked at him with a smile. "No, I think I'm finished with this witness... for now. However, I reserve the right to recall him later." I went back to the defense table and leaned across Philip so I could whisper to Mark, "Go call Rosemary. Tell her to find Richard wherever he is. I want him waiting for us at the office immediately. I'm going to try to get an early recess, and I want him there stat, no matter where he is or what he's doing." He gave me a puzzled look but got up and left the room to make the call.

Philip gave me a puzzled look as well, so I quickly wrote on a yellow pad, *Brain wave. Wait and see,* and showed it to him before I focused on the next witness, who was yet another police detective who'd conducted some routine portion of the investigation.

I questioned this detective briefly and without result, as I did the next two similar witnesses, by which time it was three thirty. The next witness on the list, a woman, was an unknown in that Philip had no idea who she was or what she might have to say. During discovery, I'd learned only that she was crucial to the prosecution's case. Before Wetherbee could call the witness, I stood up and said, "Your Honor."

"Yes, Mr. Barnett?"

"May we approach the bench?"

"You may."

When Wetherbee and I were in front of the judge, she looked at me.

"Your Honor, the prosecution has indicated that its next witness is a crucial one. I don't know how long Mr. Wetherbee intends to question her, but I expect my cross-examination to be lengthy, and I would prefer that it take place on the same day as his questioning of her, rather than the next morning."

She took the bait and said, "Yes, I see your point, Mr. Barnett. You are suggesting an early recess."

"If it pleases the court."

"It does."

Wetherbee, caught off balance, had nothing to say, and we went back to our respective seats. As soon as we were seated, the judge ordered a recess until nine o'clock the next morning.

I hurried Mark and Philip out of the courtroom and back to the office. They obviously wanted to know what I was up to, but I didn't give them a chance to ask questions. Richard was waiting in my office, also with a puzzled look about him. I directed the three of them to the conference table.

When we were seated, I explained, saying, "Mark, did you notice Kellerman's reaction when I asked him about other fingerprints at the scene?"

"Well, he looked a tad nervous," Mark said somewhat thoughtfully.

"He looked a damn sight more than a tad nervous. He looked to me like a kid who'd been caught with his fingers in the cookie jar."

Mark said, "Aren't you reading too much into too little?"

"No, I don't think so. Anyway, I want to get my hands on the sergeant's computer, or at least the hard drive from it."

"How are you going to do that, and what good will it do?" Richard said.

I said, "You and I will discuss the how later. As for the what, the good sergeant uses word processing software to prepare his reports. He even transmits them electronically to the prosecutor's office. Many people who use word processing will prepare several drafts of a document, sometimes keeping the old versions on hand for various reasons. In point of fact, some of the better software even allows this to happen automatically. There might be one or more older versions of that report still stored on his hard drive. I would like very much to compare them to the final version."

"What if they've been erased?" Richard said.

"Richard, you really should gain some technical expertise," I said. "Your computer illiteracy is showing."

"Can't you just give me a straight answer without the abuse?"

"Surely you know that a competent technician can recover data from a hard drive—even data which has been erased?"

"Yeah," Richard said, "now that you mention it, I do know that."

"For that matter, even if the data has been overwritten, it's possible, with the right equipment, to extract data that has been 'erased' and overwritten."

"So what?" Richard said. "It's still in Kellerman's office in the police department."

"Yes, but I know somebody who might just have legitimate access, and we're going to go see him."

Mark asked, "What do you expect to find?"

"Gentlemen, I can barely permit myself to think about what we might find or not find, but we must try, because I have a hunch that it will be crucial."

28

Philip

MARK left the room looking slightly concerned, so I said, "Charles, I don't think Mark approves."

"His youthful idealism is having a conflict with reality. He thinks we're going to do something quasi-illegal or quasi-unethical."

"Are we?"

"Not really," he said. Then he got up from the conference table and went to his desk, where he looked up a number and dialed. The phone at the other end couldn't have rung more than twice before Charles said into the receiver, "Hello, Sam. Charles Barnett here, how are you? ... Yes, that's right, Tommy's lawyer. ... Yes, it is, and I'm fine, how's he doing? ... Good. Listen, I called because I finally need that favor you owe me, remember? ... Great, I'd like to come over there with a couple of friends and talk to you about it, okay? ... Fine. We'll see you in thirty minutes."

He hung up and came back to where Richard and I were still sitting. "Richard," he said, "do you remember the Tommy Silverman case?"

Richard thought a minute and said, "Kid who got in with a bad crowd, right? Something to do with drugs?"

"Exactly. They were going to throw the book at him until we proved that he'd been set up by his so-called friends. Tommy Silverman is something of a hacker and a rough-hewn computer genius. His father, Sam Silverman, has a small computer business out on Ponce de Leon and, does a great deal of service work. More importantly, included among his customers is the police department. Need I say more?"

Charles drove us to a small business district near the old Sears store on Ponce de Leon, an area which has seen better days. Sam Silverman, a lively little man with a badly receding hairline, greeted Charles warmly and remembered that Richard had helped with his son's problems as well. Charles explained what we were after, and Sam thought about it for a minute and said, "No problem. My guys are in and out of the department all the time, and we routinely swap out whole computers for maintenance. We take a new machine in, transfer the contents of the old machine's hard drive, and then bring the old machine back to the shop for maintenance. It'll take no more time than a normal preventive maintenance routine. Once we have the old machine in the shop, Tommy can dig into the hard drive at his leisure."

"What about password-protected documents?"

"You've got to be kidding. Passwords are a piece of cake."

"Great, Sam. Just tell him not to take too long. The trial will probably be over by this time next week, after which it'll be too late."

"Not to worry," the little man said with a smile.

"Thank you, Sam. You can contact Mr. Greene when you have something to report, and he'll handle things from there."

"It's my pleasure, I assure you."

On the drive back to the office, Charles evidently had one other thought, one that had occurred to me also, and he said, "Richard, this might be where Bruce can help us. If Kellerman transmitted earlier versions of his report electronically to the DA's computer system, the documents might be accessible to your friend."

Richard groaned and said, "I don't know if I have enough energy for that tonight."

"Force yourself, my boy, force yourself."

Richard reluctantly agreed to do just that. Then we dropped him off at the parking garage and went home.

I kept silent until we were changing clothes in preparation for a trip to the Y, and then I said, "Just what do you expect to find in that computer?"

"I'm afraid to tell you. It might raise false hopes."

"Raise them, please."

"All right. Based on Kellerman's reaction to my question about other fingerprints, I suspect they may have found something. Perhaps even something that's being suppressed after having been mentioned in an early draft of his report. If I'm right, and we can prove it, we can blow this case out of the water and Wetherbee with it."

"Wow, you do think big."

"It's only a faint possibility, but I get paid to think big."

"Well, my love, I'll trust your instincts any day, and you certainly do earn those big bucks."

We sealed that with a kiss and then went to swim. We stopped for some Chinese takeout on the way home, and after we ate, we went up to the new study and worked for a couple of hours. We were still somewhat wired and decided that an evening run was in order. This, as usual, relaxed us enough that we were in bed asleep well before eleven.

FRIDAY morning, the first witness was Anne Toliver, a very severe-looking fortyish bottle blonde dressed in an expensively tailored suit, her bleached hair pulled back in a bun. Charles wrote on his pad, *Ever seen her?* I shook my head to indicate that I hadn't.

Mrs. Toliver, a widow, testified that she and Lucinda had been friends for some time. The last time she'd seen Lucinda had been over lunch about two weeks before the murder. Under Wetherbee's questioning, she went on to say that Lucinda had been excited about something and made much of the fact that she was going to make some unspecified changes in her life. Wetherbee asked the witness what she thought the deceased was referring to, but Charles objected before she could answer.

The prosecutor then brought up the gay issue for the first time, asking, "Mrs. Toliver, did the deceased ever discuss with you her feelings about her husband's homosexuality?"

Charles was on his feet before the witness could answer, objecting on the grounds of relevance. I was afraid, for a moment, that he and Wetherbee were going to come to blows, so heated was the ensuing exchange. At last it died down, and the judge asked Charles if he had anything else to add before she ruled on his objection.

"Only this, Your Honor: defense will stipulate that Mr. and Mrs. d'Autremont entered into a marriage of convenience and were husband and wife in name only. In actuality, they'd agreed to and did, in fact, lead almost totally separate lives, up to and including same-sex relationships on both sides."

Her Honor chose to sustain Charles's objection. Wetherbee then changed direction and asked about Lucinda's romantic involvements.

"I know she was seeing somebody at the time," the witness said.

"Did she tell you his name?" asked Wetherbee.

Charles jumped in. "Objection. Hearsay."

The judge agreed. "Sustained."

Wetherbee tried again. "Mrs. Toliver, were you aware of the identity of the deceased's lover?"

"No, Sir, I was not."

Wetherbee finally turned the witness over to Charles, who jumped in with both feet. "Mrs. Toliver, were you aware of the sex of the deceased's current lover?"

"No, I was not, but I thought it might be a man."

"Had the deceased, to your knowledge, ever taken a male lover?"

"No, but I suspected it might be different this time."

"You suspected, but you did not know?"

"Yes."

"The deceased did, to your knowledge, have female lovers from time to time."

"Yes, that is true."

"Were you ever one of them?"

"No," came the somewhat wistful answer.

Charles must have picked up on this, because he said, "But you would like to have been, wouldn't you?"

Wetherbee said, "Objection."

Charles replied, "Withdrawn."

Before he could ask another question, she answered the question anyway. "There was a time when I might have done."

"But you became friends instead."

"Yes."

"The deceased gave you no clue as to what it was that she was excited about?"

"None whatever."

"Describe her excitement, if you can."

"I'm not certain I know what you mean."

"Was she excited in a happy way, i.e., about good news; in an unhappy way; how, exactly?"

She thought a minute. "I think she was both happy and sad at the same time."

"She mentioned changes in her life that she was planning."

"Yes."

"But she didn't say about what."

"That is correct."

"Could she have been planning to dump her current lover?"

"Objection, calls for speculation," Wetherbee said.

"Withdrawn."

"I thought she was planning to dump her husband," she said smugly.

Charles said, "Your Honor, I ask that the witness's remarks be stricken from the record."

"I agree," the judge said. "The jury will disregard the last remarks of the witness."

Charles changed tactics and said, "Did you know that she was pregnant?"

"Not until I read it in the papers."

Charles looked at her and said, "You know what I think? I think you told this preposterous story to the prosecutor because you were jealous.

You'd been hoping that she would dump her husband because you wanted to take his place. Isn't that true, Mrs. Toliver?"

Wetherbee objected, Charles withdrew the remark, and the witness sat there, clearly shaken at his having struck so close to home. Charles, obviously deciding to quit while he was ahead, said, "No further questions," turned, and sat down at the table.

The rest of the day was taken up by several witnesses who seemingly had little to add, including two men with whom I'd once upon a time had brief relationships, and to whose testimony Charles objected vehemently and successfully. Around four o'clock, the prosecution rested their case.

By four thirty, Charles, Mark, and I were at the conference table in Charles's office, where the two of them conducted a postmortem of sorts over the week's events. The consensus was that the week had been a draw, with neither side scoring any significant gains over the other. They discussed briefly the plan of attack for Monday, and we headed for home.

CHARLES and I spent Saturday doing as little as possible. We drove out Roswell Road, stopping to browse in a couple of bookstores, then drove over to one of the malls out on the I-285 loop around Atlanta. On the way back into town, we stopped by Lenox Square to take in a movie, and were back home reading in bed by ten thirty. An hour or so later, we'd put our books aside and had just finished enjoying each other when we heard a door slam downstairs, followed by the sounds of Richard coming home. The bedroom door was open, and there was enough light coming from one of the bedside lamps to reveal a hand reaching around through the opening to knock on the door, and Richard said, "Can you guys stop whatever it is you're doing for a minute?"

Charles said, "Come on in, Richard."

The owner of the hand appeared in the open doorway and said, "I just have a quick update from Bruce."

"Yes?"

"He hasn't found anything in the current files but will start going through some of his old backup tapes on Monday."

"Good."

"Maybe. He seems to think that it's a long shot at best, and I tend to agree. I think your friend Sam is our best bet."

"Any word from him?"

"Not yet." He excused himself, presumably to go to bed, and Charles reached over and turned out the light before he snuggled back up against me. We drifted off to sleep without discussing Richard's news or lack thereof.

Sunday morning, we were up early for a run, followed by a light breakfast. We decided to attend a different church where Charles wasn't known, the trial having attracted a great deal of publicity, none of it welcome. After church, we picked up Charles's grandmother and took her with us to brunch at Patty's Place. She was obviously pleased at the invitation and was shrewd enough not to talk about the trial. Evidently she was intent on taking our minds off things, and entertained us with stories about the 'old days' in Atlanta.

I had a sudden inspiration and asked her if she'd ever thought about writing a book.

"A book about what?" she said.

"About the things you've been talking about with such wit and detail for the last hour and a half. A book about what it was like to live in Atlanta just before and after World War II, for example."

Obviously flattered, she said, "I wouldn't know where to begin."

"It's easy," I said. "Let me bring a tape recorder over two or three times a week and spend an hour recording the sorts of things you've just been talking about. The more you talk, the more you'll remember. I'll have the tapes transcribed; then we can edit the material. It could either be the genesis of a novel or perhaps merely a book of reminiscences."

Before she could answer, Charles jumped in, "Gran, I think that's the best idea I've ever heard. I've heard you talk about these things all my life. There aren't very many people around who remember those days as vividly as you, and it's time somebody wrote it all down for posterity."

She made a few more protests but finally warmed to the idea. I couldn't commit to any sessions during the day until after the trial, so I agreed to bring her a small dictation device Monday evening for her to try on her own in the interim. We stopped by her house afterward just long enough to walk up to the front door with her, where she gave each of us a warm hug and a kiss on the cheek.

As soon as we were alone in the car, Charles said, "You sure do have a way with old ladies."

"She did seem pleased with the idea, didn't she?"

"Pleased hardly describes it. I haven't seen her so excited about anything in years."

"Good. It'll not only be an interesting project but probably a gold mine of ideas for future projects."

"Who will you get to transcribe the tapes?"

"There are secretarial services who do that, why?"

"Rosemary does some of that sort of thing on the side."

"There you go, problem solved."

We arrived back at the townhouse and went straight up to bed, but not straight to sleep, other more pressing needs having arisen before we could nap. Later, we went downstairs, where we spent the rest of the day reading and listening to music. Around seven, we went for a run through the park, and after we'd showered, I made a salad for dinner. We were in bed by ten and asleep before eleven.

29

Charles

MONDAY morning when the trial resumed, I called Randolph Forney as the first witness for the defense. After he was sworn in and had been seated, I began by saying, "Mr. Forney, you are a tax attorney as well as a certified public accountant, is that correct?"

"Yes, Sir. I handle financial affairs and tax matters for a number of clients, and have done so for nearly thirty years."

"The defendant is a client of yours, as was his late wife, is that correct?"

"You are correct. Mrs. d'Autremont's family have been clients of mine for twenty years, and I took care of the affairs of the deceased from the time she became old enough to have need of my services. After her marriage to Mr. d'Autremont, I began to handle his affairs as well. That was some ten years ago."

"Mr. Forney, the prosecution seems to think that Mr. d'Autremont was, for want of a better phrase, living off of his wife's money."

"Well, the prosecution can think what they like, but nothing could be further from the truth."

"Describe for the court, if you will, the financial condition of both Mr. and Mrs. d'Autremont at the time of their marriage."

He took a small notebook from his breast pocket and consulted it before peering at me across the top of his glasses and saying, "At the time of their marriage, Lucinda d'Autremont had an income from a trust fund established by her late grandparents of approximately $50,000 per year. She had almost no net worth, that is to say, she had few assets other than some jewelry and an automobile. That same year, Mr. d'Autremont had an income of approximately $100,000, and his net worth was in excess of $1 million."

"And what would the same statistics be for last year?"

He consulted his notes again and said, "For the year just ended, Mrs. d'Autremont had an income of around $100,000 and a net worth of $5 million. For that same period, Mr. d'Autremont had an income of $1 million, and his net worth was almost $10 million."

"We'll get to the sources of their respective wealth in just a minute. First, please tell the court a little about their domestic financial arrangements."

"It was really quite simple. The house on West Paces Ferry Road was given to her by her parents one year after her marriage. Mr. and Mrs. d'Autremont established a household account, out of which I pay all of the bills relative to the running of their home. In the beginning, Mr. and Mrs. d'Autremont contributed equally to that account. Later, Mr. d'Autremont began to contribute all of the funds so that his wife's income could be invested on her behalf."

"Invested how?"

"When they married, Mrs. d'Autremont had no income other than from her trust fund. The income was hers for life, but the principal was to pass to her children, should she have any. I discovered, during the first three years of their marriage, that Mr. d'Autremont possesses an uncanny ability to choose real estate and other investments that will do well over time. After he started paying all of their expenses, I was able to invest most of her income in some of the same projects in which he was investing. Were it not for that, Mrs. d'Autremont would have died owning little more than the house and her jewelry."

"Thank you. Now, can you be more specific about the details of their income for last year? The prosecution has characterized Mr. d'Autremont as having no visible means of support; perhaps you can educate them."

"Certainly," he said, and he looked at his notes again. "Mr. and Mrs. d'Autremont filed a joint income tax return for last year, as they did every year, even though they owned no joint assets. Her income consisted of

$60,000 from her trust fund and $40,000 from various investments. His income consisted of $200,000 in rental income as well as interest and dividends from various investments, $300,000 in capital gains, and $500,000 in royalties."

"Royalties?"

"Mr. d'Autremont is a prolific writer and publishes one or two books a year."

"Books the court might recognize or be otherwise familiar with?"

"I really don't know, although it's possible. I do know that he writes under a number of pseudonyms, but I know neither the titles of any of the books nor the names under which he writes them."

"How are the payments handled?"

"His publisher remits funds to a Boston law firm, who in turn pass them along directly to my office. They arrive quarterly, along with a statement indicating that the payments are for this or that project. The projects are identified by code names known only to the publisher and Mr. d'Autremont."

"That seems to be a great deal of trouble."

"Not if one values one's privacy. I gather that Mr. d'Autremont's identity is one of the three or four best-kept secrets in the publishing world."

"You are a great respecter of privacy, are you not?"

"Mr. Barnett, a number of people have, over the past thirty years, paid me a great deal of money to handle their affairs with utmost discretion. A discretion that has never once been violated. You have no idea how much it pains me to have to talk about a client's affairs in open court, even if I am doing so with his permission."

"Thank you, Mr. Forney," I said, turning to the prosecution's table. "Your witness."

Wetherbee was on his feet immediately. "Mr. Forney, you have told us that the defendant was wealthier than his late wife."

"That is so."

"How much wealthier will he be now that she is dead?"

"I beg your pardon?"

"The defendant will certainly profit from his wife's death, won't he?"

"No, Sir, he will not. There was an antenuptial agreement signed at the time they were married. What was hers remained hers, and what was his remained his."

"Well, since she died intestate, he'll still inherit her estate."

"She did not die intestate."

"We have found no will filed in Fulton County."

"Of course not. Her official residence for tax purposes was her ancestral home in Oglethorpe County, and her will was filed there within the required period of time following her death. In due course, a certified copy will be filed in Fulton County for the purpose of disposing of her property in this area."

"To whom did she leave her estate?"

"The house was left to her parents, although Mr. d'Autremont has the right to reside in it for life, should he choose to do so, and the rest of her estate goes to various charities."

"When was her will written?"

"Shortly after her marriage, although she updated it every couple of years. She was contemplating revising it again in light of her pregnancy."

"She had discussed her pregnancy with you?"

"Certainly. Both she and Mr. d'Autremont were quite pleased about it and were planning to revise their respective wills accordingly. In addition, he was planning to set up a substantial trust fund for the child."

"That was generous of him," Wetherbee said with a slight sneer, "considering that it could hardly have been his child."

"Oh, but it was."

"Are you saying that the defendant was responsible for his wife's pregnancy?"

"I am indeed."

"You cannot know that."

"Of course I can. I assisted them in arranging it."

Wetherbee, clearly shaken, asked, "How?"

"Mr. and Mrs. d'Autremont maintained a most unusual lifestyle. Theirs was a marriage of convenience, entered into for the sake of appearances. She had a life separate and apart from him, and he had a life separate and apart from her. They'd agreed to that in the beginning. They had consummated their marriage, but neither of them particularly enjoyed having sexual relations with the other. She was under considerable pressure from her family to produce an heir, so I arranged for them to go to a fertility clinic in another state, where she was artificially inseminated with his sperm. As I said, they were both quite pleased with her pregnancy."

Wetherbee evidently decided to quit before any more damage was done to his case.

I had a few more questions for Randolph to wrap up his testimony. "Mr. Forney, to sum up your testimony for the court, is it fair to say that Mr. and Mrs. d'Autremont were both happy with their somewhat unusual arrangement?"

"Oh my, yes. Very much so. We discussed it frequently over the years."

"And Mr. d'Autremont will neither profit from nor lose by his wife's death?"

"Well, he certainly won't profit from it. On the other hand, he lost his posterity, didn't he?"

"You are referring to his wife's pregnancy?"

"Yes, of course. The man has, by his own effort, built a sizeable estate. Now, of course, he lacks an heir to leave it to."

"Thank you, Mr. Forney, you have been most helpful."

Randolph's testimony had taken nearly two hours, and the judge decreed a lunch recess until one o'clock.

Mark had to run back to the office, and Philip and I went to lunch, joined by Richard along with William Lane, both of whom had been seated at the back of the courtroom. William was to testify next, Richard having picked him up at the airport.

When we were seated at a table, I asked William, "How much of Randolph's testimony did you hear?"

"We were there by nine thirty, so I heard the majority of it. You set the prosecutor up, didn't you?"

"Absolutely."

"What do you mean?" Philip said.

"Charles cleverly omitted any references to either your wife's will or her pregnancy, and the prosecutor was forced to make the same mistake twice."

"What mistake?" Richard said.

"The most serious mistake any trial lawyer can make. He asked not only one but, two questions, the answers to which he did not know and was clearly not expecting," William said. "Charles set him up, and he took the bait."

"I had no idea," Philip said.

"You have an extremely clever and devious defense lawyer," William said. "I certainly wouldn't want to go up against him."

This was getting out of hand, and I was becoming embarrassed. "Enough, already," I said. "Besides, we have a long way to go, and it isn't over until the fat lady sings."

Philip smiled at me and then said to William, "Will you be in town long enough for us to take you to dinner?"

"If we can be done in time for an eight thirty flight."

"Absolutely," I said. "We can run by the house after court adjourns for the day and then go down to Annie's Bistro. Richard can make it a foursome, if he likes."

We had a light lunch and were back in the courtroom with time to spare. William's testimony was probably superfluous and could have been eliminated, but I was stalling for time. The longer I dragged out my few witnesses, the more chance there was that Richard's people would be able to locate the elusive Ruby. I took pains to establish that the firm of Cabot Lodge Lane had acted as an intermediary between the publishing house and Philip for several years, and confirmed that the annual amounts of money flowing from royalties were as Randolph had indicated in his testimony. Wetherbee wasn't even interested enough in William to ask him more than a few perfunctory questions.

The rest of the afternoon was taken up by the testimony of several men who'd been involved with Philip in one or more real estate transactions over a period of several years, my intent being to establish, independently of Randolph's testimony, that Philip was now and had always been a man of substance. Court adjourned for the day a little after four, and William, who had waited patiently through the afternoon, walked back to the office with us.

I canceled our usual end-of-day conference, and William rode home with us, where Richard was waiting with the small bag that William had left in Richard's car. Richard had already changed, and I showed William up to the guest room, where he could freshen up and change clothes if he wished, and Philip and I retired to our room to do likewise.

When Philip and I arrived in the library, Richard was waiting for us, and when William appeared we went to dinner. We were at Annie's Bistro in a matter of minutes and, as it was early, didn't have to wait for a table. We spent an enjoyable hour, and William seemed pleased with our choice and the menu. During dinner, Philip remembered his promise to take Gran a dictation device that evening, and after dinner, we dropped him by the house so that he could take his car to Gran's. Richard decided to go along and visit Gran, so I drove William to the airport.

When I returned, Philip and Richard were back from their trip to Gran's and waiting for me in the library, so I said, "How did it go?"

Philip said, "All right, I think. I stayed long enough to show her how to use the machine and to get her to talking about the subject at hand. I think she'll do just fine, but I promised to stop by tomorrow evening and check on her progress."

"Great. I'm ready to call it a night, how about you?"

"Right behind you."

"Is that a promise?"

"What?"

"You'll be right behind me all the way to the bed?"

"If you like."

"If!" I spun him around, grabbed him, and stuck my tongue down his throat. He came up for air, and I repeated, "If!"

"Shut up and take your clothes off."

Which I did. In that order.

30

Philip

TUESDAY morning, Richard was the first witness called. Charles led him through a series of questions concerning his investigation of the murder scene without interruption from the prosecutor. Charles then asked him to describe the next phase of his investigation, which was the search of Lucinda's condo. Wetherbee attempted to stop this line of questioning but was eventually overruled by the judge. Under Charles's prompting, Richard described the process of finding the set of fingerprints as well as the clothing that didn't belong in the apartment. Charles managed to introduce both into evidence over Wetherbee's objections.

"Have you been able to identify the owner of the fingerprints?" Charles said.

"No, Sir, we have not. The police refuse to cooperate, and when we submit them through private channels, they keep getting lost in the shuffle."

"Is this normal?"

"No, Sir, it isn't. The police are usually cooperative with private investigations, and in ten years I've only known one other occasion when the crime lab lost such a request."

"What can you tell us about that occasion?"

"We discovered that someone in authority had pulled strings to have our request conveniently overlooked for a while."

Wetherbee was on his feet immediately and said, "Are you suggesting that the police department is obstructing an investigation?"

Charles gave him a cool look. "I don't know. Are they?"

Wetherbee began to object, but Charles gave him a pitying look and said, "Withdrawn."

Charles returned to his questions and said, "Mr. Greene, do you know why the police are refusing to cooperate with your investigation?"

"Yes, Sir, I do."

Wetherbee objected to that as well. "Does counsel have proof of these allegations?"

Charles gave him the same look, this time a little chillier. "In point of fact, I do. At the appropriate time, we will produce sworn affidavits from more than one Atlanta police detective to the effect that they have direct orders not to pursue any line of investigation in this case that leads them away from this defendant."

With that, Wetherbee shut up, and Charles continued with Richard, who began to describe his search for witnesses. After Richard described his first interview with Lily Sanders, Charles asked for leave to interrupt his questioning of Richard to call Lily Sanders.

Wetherbee, of course, objected, but Charles prevailed, and Lily Sanders was called.

Lily Sanders, whom I hadn't seen before, was fiftyish and very butch. Charles showed her a picture of Lucinda, who she said was a regular customer at the bar where she worked. Then he asked, "When was the last time you saw the deceased?"

"The Saturday before she died."

"How can you be certain of the date?"

"Because I went on vacation the next day, and I haven't seen her in the bar since."

"Was there anyone with her that Saturday?"

"Yes, Sir."

Charles produced the artist's sketch of the woman known only as Ruby. "This woman?"

"Yes, Sir."

"Do you know this woman's name?"

"Her first name is Ruby, but I never heard a last name. She's a regular in the bar."

"Can you tell the court anything else about her?"

"She was a very rough customer."

"Meaning?"

"Only that she's very butch, what might be called a 'diesel dyke', and is rumored to be somewhat mean."

"When was the last time you saw Ruby?"

"Same as the deceased, that Saturday night."

"Not since?"

"No, Sir. She usually comes in two or three times a week, but I haven't seen her since that Saturday."

Charles introduced the sketch into evidence, thanked the witness, and said, "No more questions."

Wetherbee, curiously, didn't have any questions for Lily. As soon as he'd declined to ask the witness any questions, the judge ordered a lunch recess.

Mark, Richard, and I followed Charles outside, presumably to go to lunch. Instead of suggesting a restaurant, Charles took his cell phone from his briefcase, punched a speed dial number, and said, "Rosemary, call downstairs for sandwiches and drinks for four, we're on the way for a conference. Thanks. Bye."

Mark spoke for the rest of us, asking, "What's up?"

"An idea. Tell you as soon as we get to the office."

As soon as we were in his office, Charles sat down, not at the conference table, but at his desk. He turned on the speakerphone and made a call.

"Good morning, Cabot Lodge Lane," said a female voice.

"William Lane, please, Charles Barnett calling from Atlanta."

"One moment, please."

William's voice came over the speaker. "Hello, Charles, what can I do for you?"

"A great deal, I hope. We're on a speaker, and present with me are Philip, Richard, and Mark, an associate of mine whom you've met. Court is in recess for lunch. We have a set of fingerprints that seems to get lost every time we try to run them through the usual channels. I have reason to believe that somebody in authority locally is pulling strings to keep us from having these prints identified. What I would like from you is a referral to somebody in your area who can submit the prints as though they originated there. Perhaps that will allow us to sneak in the back door with them."

"Just a minute. I'm going to put you on hold and make a call," William said.

"We'll wait."

Richard said, "Damn, why didn't I think of that?"

"I know," Charles said. "We both should have thought of that weeks ago."

William came back on the line. "You still there, Charles?"

"Yes."

"Good. A man named Edward Roberts, who's with a local agency, is expecting a call from you or Richard. He's ex-FBI and has more than enough contacts to get past any interference. He can be reached at this number." He gave a number and continued, "Got that?"

"Yes, I do, and thanks."

"My pleasure. Bye, and good luck to all of you." The line went dead.

Charles got a dial tone and punched in some more numbers. This time a man answered. "Morris Agency, Roberts speaking."

"Mr. Roberts, my name is Charles Barnett, and I'm calling from Atlanta. I believe William Lane just called you concerning our problem."

"Yes, Sir, he did."

"We have a set of prints lifted from an apartment maintained by the victim in a murder case. The police didn't investigate the apartment in question. We've sent the prints in a number of times for identification, but they seem to get lost in the paperwork every time."

"William mentioned the nature of your problem."

"Good, then I'm going to hand you over to my investigator, Richard Greene of Greene & Associates here in Atlanta. His crew obtained the prints, and he'll make the necessary arrangements with you, and thank you very much."

"No problem."

Charles turned off the speaker function, handed the handset to Richard, and said, "Go for it."

We went over to the conference table, where Rosemary was laying out sandwiches and soft drinks for us. In the background we could hear Richard arranging to send the prints to Boston by the fastest means available. Charles grinned and said, "Ain't technology wonderful?"

The rest of us were too busy eating to comment on his rhetorical question.

When court resumed after lunch, Richard returned to the witness stand and Charles led him step by step through a detailed account of his investigations. When he'd brought him up to the present, he said one final thing. "Mr. Greene, you've had a number of investigators working on this case now for three months." It was not a question.

"That is correct."

"Have you formed any professional opinions as to who might have murdered Mrs. d'Autremont?"

Wetherbee didn't like the question. "Objection, calls for speculation on the part of the witness."

Charles shot back, "I didn't ask him to speculate. I asked him for a professional opinion based upon his ten years of experience in the field."

"Overruled," the judge said.

Charles repeated his question. "Again, Mr. Greene, have you formed any professional opinions as to the killer?"

"Yes, Sir. I think we're looking for a woman, one who was driven by jealousy to kill Lucinda d'Autremont. There's every likelihood that the suspect for whom we're searching will turn out to be the killer."

"Thank you, Mr. Greene."

Charles, by virtue of asking about every painstaking detail of the investigation, had managed to drag Richard's testimony out for almost two hours. The prosecution cross-examined Richard perfunctorily for about half an hour and sat down. After Richard was excused, the judge declared court in recess for the day.

Charles was surprised, as it was only a little after three thirty, and said, "I wonder why she recessed so early?"

"I don't know, but I've been watching her a bit today and I don't think she feels well."

"You may be right," he said, and we went back to his office, where he gathered a mound of paperwork from his desk, stuffed it into his briefcase, and said, "Let's go home."

We were home by four thirty, followed shortly thereafter by Richard. We invited him, as usual, to go to the Y with us, and this time he accepted the invitation. Not, he said, because he wanted to swim, but because he wanted some time in the steam room.

Richard hadn't seen Charles and me naked since the last time he'd joined us at the Y, which was some time before we had become smoothies. The three of us stood in front of adjacent lockers and undressed. As Charles and I were just about to step into our respective Speedos, Richard happened to turn and look at us. He pointed at our pubic areas and said, "What brought this on?"

"Remember the trial with the pubic-hair defense?" Charles said.

"Yeah."

"Philip and I decided to try it and found that we liked being, as the nudists say, 'smoothies'."

"Whatever turns you on."

"Oh, I can assure you, it does... in spades. The first time we shaved each other was easily the sexiest thing I've ever done."

By that time, we were suited up and Richard had a towel wrapped around his waist, so we went our respective ways.

Later, after our swim and an early supper, we were in bed, reading, when Charles's telephone rang. I didn't pay any attention to his conversation, as I was concentrating on my book. When he hung up, he got my attention.

"You were absolutely on target," he said.

"About what?"

"The judge. That was her secretary calling to advise me that Her Honor is ill and the trial won't resume until Thursday morning."

"Is that good or bad for our case?"

"Probably good, in that it gives Richard's people more time to search for Ruby."

Charles went to his office on Wednesday, and I spent most of the day working on my new project and catching up on correspondence. When he returned from work, I was in the kitchen wearing an apron over my bare skin, laying the groundwork for our dinner. This time I heard him sneaking up on me but pretended not to be aware of his presence until his erection was pressing against my bare buns. This, of course, led to a pleasant twenty minutes or so upstairs, followed by our evening trip to the Y, where we swam our usual laps.

As soon as we were back home, I put the finishing touches on our dinner. It was the first time I'd cooked since the trial began, and I'd decided to be creative and try a couple of new dishes. Happily, they were successes.

We'd just cleaned up the dishes when the judge's secretary called to advise Charles that the judge had been ordered by her doctor to stay home in bed for one more day. The trial would definitely resume on Friday morning. We went up to the study and spent an hour or so working before retiring.

After Charles left for work Thursday morning, I spent a couple of hours at my desk, then called Gran to check on her progress. She invited me over for an impromptu lunch to discuss her project. I spent a delightful two hours with her and carried home three microcassettes full of dictation, which I placed in a briefcase to take to Rosemary the next morning.

I was working at my desk and lost track of time, so I was taken by surprise when Charles came home around five thirty. He expressed disappointment that I was wearing clothes, so I immediately took them off and sat back down at my desk. I suggested that he looked somewhat ridiculous standing there fully dressed, so he stripped too.

We wound up on the floor in the study—it would have taken too long to get to the bedroom. After our lust had been temporarily satisfied, Charles lay back on his back, and I sort of lay on my side with one leg thrown across his and my head on his chest. We were on the verge of drifting off to sleep when we were interrupted.

"Jesus! Don't you people know what beds are for?"

I looked up, saw Richard standing in the open doorway, and said, "Life is short, and sometimes you simply have to take your pleasures where you find them."

Charles picked up the theme. "Yeah, you may come home tomorrow and find us on the kitchen floor or the dining room table."

Richard frowned and said, "At your ages you should be more appreciative of comfort."

"At the expense of spontaneity?" I said.

"I give up. Have it your way."

We got up, gathered our clothing, and carried it to the bedroom.

Richard followed us and gave us an update on the investigation while we dressed.

Charles told him about the call from the judge's secretary, and we invited Richard to go to the Y with us, saying that we were planning a visit to Rick's afterward for supper. To my surprise, he accepted our invitation—it wasn't the first time we'd asked Richard to exercise with us, but in the past, he'd declined most of those invitations. To have him agree to go to the Y twice in a row was unusual, and Charles couldn't resist pointing this out.

"Richard, are you on an exercise kick all of a sudden?" he said.

"What?"

"You've accepted two invitations to exercise in a row, and I was wondering what prompted you to do so."

"If you must know, Bruce is wearing me out, and I need to build up my stamina."

"This sounds serious. Is it?"

"I don't know."

Charles wisely left it at that; we gathered our gym bags and left.

At the Y, Charles and I swam at our usual pace, which enabled us to complete thirty-six full laps (1800 yards) of the pool in about forty minutes. Richard wasn't a dedicated swimmer and dropped out after about a dozen laps, saying that he was going to go and do some routines in the weight room. He managed to catch up with us by the time we were in the steam room; then we went to Rick's and consumed a healthy meal, followed by an equally unhealthy dessert. After his workout, Richard was in rare form and kept us in stitches throughout the meal. The three of us arrived back at the house in the best of spirits, acting as though we hadn't a care in the world. It was too dark outside for us to see the black clouds gathering overhead.

31

Charles

THE trial resumed Friday morning on schedule, although I thought the judge looked pale and drawn. I really didn't have much more to offer in defense and was mostly interested in delaying things just a little longer, hoping that one of Richard's people would turn up with the elusive Ruby. In an attempt to strengthen our hypothesis, I spent the morning calling various witnesses that Richard had turned up in his investigations. Finally, Wetherbee grew tired of it, as I'd suspected he might, and objected mightily to what he referred to as a "parade of useless witnesses, producing drivel for testimony."

I objected to his characterization of my witnesses, although privately I was forced to agree with his assessment. We argued back and forth for a bit until the judge stepped in. As I had no more witnesses of this type anyway, I agreed to call no further witnesses on the same theme, admitting that I had a few character witnesses for after the lunch recess and I expected to rest my case by midafternoon. The judge decided to recess for lunch at that point, and Philip, Mark, and I went out for a bite. We were in our places promptly at one o'clock, and I called the first of six witnesses who, I hoped, would establish firmly in the minds of the jurors that Philip was a man of exemplary character.

Finally, at three thirty, having presented my last witness, I said to the judge, "The defense rests, Your Honor."

A few minutes later, the sky fell on us.

The judge looked at the prosecutor and said, "Anything further, Mr. Wetherbee?"

"Yes, Your Honor, we call Alice Treadwell."

I was on my feet in a flash, objecting to the introduction of a surprise witness. Wetherbee stated flatly that the witness in question had only just come forward that morning and he hadn't had an opportunity to notify the defense as required. I didn't believe him for one minute, but eventually the witness was allowed to take the stand.

Alice Treadwell was in her midsixties, slight, gray, and generally mousey in appearance. As she stated her name and address, I noticed that Mark was taking it down, so I didn't bother doing so.

Wetherbee asked his first question. "Mrs. Treadwell, what can you tell us about this murder case?"

"Well, Mr. Wetherbee, I live in the Ansley area, but my married daughter lives way out in Marietta. She and her husband have a hard time finding a babysitter for their two children, that is, my grandchildren, so I go out there every Sunday after church and stay with my grandchildren so that Mary, that's my daughter, and her husband can go for a drive or take in a movie." She paused.

"Please continue," Wetherbee said.

"Well, don't you see, in order to get to Marietta from my home, I drive up Piedmont to Paces Ferry Road, then straight out to the interstate."

I didn't see but had a sinking feeling that I was about to.

"What time do you return home?"

"I always get home in time to watch a religious program on the TV, which comes on at seven o'clock."

"Did anything special happen on your way home on the Sunday in question?"

"Oh, yes. I was running late. It was Mother's Day, don't you see, and the children—not the grandchildren, you understand, but my daughter and son-in-law—had taken me to a wonderful Sunday brunch instead of going out themselves. We'd lost track of the time, and I was hurrying to get home in time for my program. And that was when it happened."

"When what happened, Mrs. Treadwell?"

"I almost had a wreck."

"A wreck?"

"Yes. A little blue car came roaring out of the driveway of one of those big homes on West Paces Ferry Road. It barely slowed down for half a second, then pulled right out in front of me. I had to slam on my brakes to avoid hitting it."

"Did you notice what kind of car it was?"

"No, Sir, it was blue, small, and foreign. One of those kind that only seats two people."

He produced a picture and said, "Could this have been the car?"

"Yes, Sir, it surely looks like it."

"Let the record show that this photograph is a picture of the defendant's BMW coupe. Did you get a look at the driver of that car?"

"Oh my, yes. He turned and looked right at me as he pulled in front of me."

"Do you see that person in this courtroom?"

"Yes, Sir, I do. It was him." She pointed at Philip.

"You are indicating the defendant, Mr. d'Autremont?"

"Yes, Sir."

"Mrs. Treadwell, I have to ask you why you waited until now to come forward with your story? This trial has been well publicized in the papers and on television. Surely you must have seen the defendant's picture in them."

"Well, I only read the religion section in the paper, and I never watch the TV news, it's too depressing. All that horrible sex and violence coming right into your living room—it's enough to make a Christian woman blush. Yesterday evening, though, I was over at my friend Agnes's house, and she had the news on. Agnes is a dear friend, but she just doesn't know to shut off the TV when she has a visitor, so I sat and watched the news with her. That's when I saw his picture."

"You mean the defendant?"

"Yes, Sir. They were doing a story about this trial, and they showed his picture."

"And you recognized it?"

"Well, not right away. After I got home, I got to thinking about it, wondering where I'd seen that face before. Then I went down to the basement and looked through some old newspapers and found a story about the trial which had a picture. When I read where the poor dead woman was found, I realized where I'd seen that man before. It was too late to call the police last night, so I called this morning and was referred to one of your young men."

There was more in the same vein, but not much. Finally, Wetherbee thanked her and said, "Your witness." He managed to allow himself a little smirk for my benefit as he said it.

Before I got up to cross-examine Alice Treadwell, I wrote in bold letters *Find Richard* on a pad and passed it to Mark, who hurried from the courtroom.

I tried every way I knew how to shake her story, but she stuck doggedly to it. A little too doggedly, I thought, but since I already knew she was lying, my impression of doggedness might have been mere wishful thinking. By four fifteen, the judge was looking very tired, so she interrupted my questioning and asked Wetherbee and me to approach the bench. When we were in front of her, she said, "Mr. Barnett, do you have many more questions for this witness?"

"Your Honor, this is a surprise witness, and I would really like to have the weekend to check out her story. I can easily finish with my questions on Monday morning."

Wetherbee objected, but the judge seemed determined to quit for the day and declared court in recess until Monday morning.

Mark had come back from calling Richard, and he and I led Philip, who was clearly shaken, from the courtroom.

Mark said, "The reporters will be swarming out there. Shall we go out the back way?"

"No. We'll march right down the front steps with our heads held high."

As he predicted, the reporters were all over us the minute we were on the courthouse steps, shouting questions at the three of us. Finally, I held up my hands for silence and said, "I know you all have questions, but I just want to make a brief statement." A dozen microphones were immediately thrust in my face.

"The testimony you just heard in the courtroom came as a total surprise to us, and we will be checking out Mrs. Treadwell and her story over the weekend, but I can tell you this much right now. Mrs. Treadwell may have relatives in Marietta, and she may even travel back and forth on West Paces Ferry Road every Sunday, but she most emphatically did not see either my client or his automobile on that street on that date. As to that, she is lying."

They wanted more, but we wouldn't give it to them and managed to extricate ourselves from their midst so we could walk back to the office.

Richard was waiting for us in my office, and the four of us settled down somewhat gloomily at the conference table while I gave Richard a précis of what had just happened. "Richard," I concluded, "you have one weekend to take this woman apart, piece by piece, and put her back together again for us. I want to know everything there is to know about her, up to and including how many times a day she breaks wind. We all know that she's lying, but what we don't know is why. We've got to find out why she did it."

"Shall I drop the search for Ruby?"

"Absolutely not. Ruby is more vital to us now than ever. Call in more help if you have to—just do it."

He left to set the wheels in motion, and Mark went back to his own office. Philip looked as though he wanted to cry as I took his hand and pulled him to his feet. I gave him a hug and a kiss. "Please don't worry about this setback," I said. "We'll figure it out in time."

"Let's go home, now. Please."

We drove home as quickly as possible, went upstairs, and held each other for a very long time. Later, we decided on a run through the park to let off steam, rather than going for our usual swim. Neither of us felt like cooking, nor did we feel like being around people, so we ordered pizza. When the pizza arrived, we carried it out on the deck with our drinks and sat there in silence for a long time until the January chill drove us back inside, neither of us wanting to talk about the events of the afternoon. Finally, we cleared away the remains of our impromptu supper and went up to read and/or watch television in the bedroom. We'd consumed just enough alcohol to make us drowsy, and drifted off to sleep with the television still turned on—something I almost never do.

Saturday morning, we slept in and didn't go for a run until well after nine. Afterward, when we came downstairs from our shower, Richard was at the breakfast table, waiting for us. Without preamble, I said, "Anything to tell us this morning?"

"Not much. So far, the old girl comes up squeaky clean. To all intents and purposes, she appears to be prim, proper, and very religious."

"Well, keep on it. Somebody must have gotten to her. We just need to know who and how. We all know that she couldn't have seen Philip on that street on that date—he was in another city—so there's got to be an explanation for her perjury."

"I've got three guys on it as we speak, and I'll be doing some snooping myself later this morning."

"Good. Call me if you turn up anything remotely significant."

"Where will you be?"

"On the road, most likely. I think we'll drive over to Social Circle and then down through some of those little towns that have all the old houses and antique shops. Anything to get our minds off the situation at hand."

"Roger that. But don't get your hopes up, there may be no rabbits to pull out of this hat."

Richard departed, and I said, "How does my idea for the day strike you?"

"Right on target. It's been quite a while since I made the rounds of those little towns, and they're always so interesting."

We finished up our breakfast, dressed, and were on the way out of town shortly thereafter. Philip insisted on driving, and as there would be no mountain curves on our itinerary, I made no attempt to dissuade him. *Focusing on the road will take his mind off things even more,* I thought.

We spent the rest of the day rambling through the heart of Georgia, starting first at Social Circle, a small town about fifty miles east of Atlanta, then to Madison and on to Monticello. We did an enormous amount of sightseeing and had lunch in a little café in one of the towns. We were back home in time for a nap, followed by a run, after which we dressed and went to dinner at Annie's Bistro. The happy atmosphere of the place enhanced the mood that had come over us during the afternoon, and we returned home and went to bed with the events of Friday very much out of sight and temporarily, at least, out of mind.

Sunday we kept to our usual routine with one exception. We again decided to go to church somewhere where we weren't known and hopefully wouldn't be recognized. We had a light lunch at home and spent a couple of hours in the study trying to get some work done.

Later that afternoon, while Philip was upstairs taking a nap, the doorbell rang. I was in the library working on ideas for impugning Mrs. Treadwell's testimony on Monday, and ran quickly downstairs before the bell could ring a second time and wake up Philip. The caller was in his late thirties and dressed in casual clothes. He introduced himself as Special Agent Tolar of the FBI and produced the credentials to prove it.

"What can I do for you, Agent Tolar?" I said.

He said, "The appropriate question, Mr. Barnett, is what can I do for you?"

"Why don't we go upstairs to the library?" I said. "We can talk up there." Then I led him upstairs, but before we sat down, I offered him a drink, which he politely declined.

He was clearly uncomfortable and made small talk for a time before he came to the point and said, "Mr. Barnett, does the name Armando Bergonzi mean anything to you?"

"Of course, he's reputed to be a kingpin in organized crime here in Atlanta. I've been involved in a major trial and not paying much attention to the news, but isn't there a federal grand jury at work on him?"

"Just so. The federal grand jury returned a series of indictments late Friday afternoon."

"Don't remind me of Friday afternoon; it may have been a good day for you guys, but it was dreadful for my trial."

"I know, I saw the news. That's why I'm here."

"I don't understand."

"I've led the team investigating the Bergonzi case for the past ten months. For the last four of those months, we've had a legal wiretap on all of the telephone lines in the various Bergonzi residences and offices."

"Go on."

He reached into the breast pocket of his jacket, pulled out a standard audiocassette, and said, "On this tape is a recording of a telephone call that was placed from the Bergonzi residence. I think you'll find it interesting." He handed it to me.

"Shall I play it now?"

"Yes, please. It isn't very long."

I carried the cassette over to the stereo system, inserted it in the tape deck, and turned the system on. We listened in silence to a five-minute telephone conversation between two men. When the tape had ended, I retrieved it from the machine, returned to the sofa, and said, "Jesus H. Christ."

"Just so. Understand this, Mr. Barnett, the bureau was reluctant to release this tape. You can use it, and you can even leak it to the media if you like, although we would ask that you not divulge the location from which the call was made. Our indictments are secure and won't be affected. What you cannot do, however, is put any of our people on the stand. As an attorney, you surely understand that we can't risk being asked the wrong questions under oath. We don't want any of the wrong testimony to become a matter of record until the Bergonzi trial begins."

"I see your point and your dilemma, and I think we can handle it to your satisfaction." A plan of action had formed in my head while he was talking, and I outlined it for him. He agreed to my ideas, and I showed him to the door, thanking him profusely.

I went back up to the library and quickly rounded up some blank tapes. My system had dual cassette decks, and it took me a half hour or so to make a number of copies of the tape that Agent Tolar had left with me.

Then I went upstairs and woke Philip up. "Splash some water on your face and come down to the library. Have I got something to show you!"

He went groggily to the bathroom, and I went back to the library, where I set up the stereo and settled down on the sofa. When he came in, I was grinning, and I said, "Walk over and press the play button on the tape deck and then come sit down."

He gave me a puzzled look but complied. When the tape had finished, he had a stunned look on his face as he said, "Where did this come from?"

"I'll tell you all about it in the car. Right now, we're going to drive downtown and lock the original and two copies of this tape in my office safe. This house could burn down tonight, and I don't want anything to happen to that tape."

On the way downtown, I told him about my visitor and how I intended to handle the present Agent Tolar had brought me. "Wow!" was all he could say.

"That, my love, is the understatement of the decade."

Having secured both the original and two copies of the tape in my office safe, we returned home. On the way, I telephoned Mark and asked him to come by around eight o'clock for an evening strategy session, saying only that I had some news of interest. When we got home, I tracked Richard down and asked him to please try to make it home by eight as well. I also called Andrew and told him what had occurred and what I proposed to do about it, asking him to join us at eight if he could. He promised to be there.

Richard showed up while Philip was fixing a light supper, just in time to get his name in the pot, as they say. I played the tape for him while Philip was putting the finishing touches on our food. "Holy shit," he said when the tape ended. Then he surprised me, adding, "I've got some news too."

"What?"

"Your friend Sam the computer man came through, in spades. Look at these." He handed me three documents.

I glanced through them quickly, then more carefully, and said one word: "Dynamite."

"Aren't they?"

Philip stuck his head in the door and told us to come eat. I was almost too excited to eat but managed to do justice to the meal that Philip had prepared. Richard and I helped clean up the kitchen; then we carried a couple of the chairs from the breakfast table into the library. By eight o'clock, the group was comfortably assembled in a semicircle of chairs, with drinks at hand, and Mark and Andrew had legal pads in their laps. I recounted the story of my afternoon visitor and then played the tape.

Even on the third and fourth hearing, the tape was amazing, even astounding. For Andrew and Mark, who were hearing it for the first time, the impact was tremendous. When everyone had settled down again, I shared with them the news that Richard had brought me before supper. Again, I had to wait for the conversation to die down.

When I finally had their attention, I told them precisely what I wanted each of them to do the next morning, ending by asking if there were any questions or suggestions. Both Mark and Andrew offered viable suggestions, and I worked these into the game plan.

Shortly after we finished, Andrew left to return to Decatur and Miss Emily. Mark lingered a bit to go over the details before he, too, went home. As I let him out the front door, he grinned and said, "We're going to have some kind of fun tomorrow, aren't we?"

"You bet," I said.

32

Charles

MONDAY morning, as soon as the judge had taken her seat, I was on my feet and said, "May we approach the bench, Your Honor?"

"You may."

Mark and I walked up to stand in front of her, and Craig Wetherbee and Tom Shields followed us.

"Yes, Mr. Barnett?" she said.

"Your Honor, I acquired a rather special piece of evidence over the weekend. I think we need to talk about it in chambers, if we may."

"What kind of evidence?"

"It is an excerpt from a legal wiretap, provided me by an FBI agent."

"What has the FBI got to do with this case?" Wetherbee said.

"It's not from this case but from an unrelated matter. However, the tape itself bears directly on this case."

Wetherbee started to object, but the judge cut him off, saying, "All right, Mr. Barnett, I will hear your evidence in chambers. You may step back."

We went back to our respective tables, and the judge declared a short recess. We followed her to her chambers, Mark carrying a small battery-operated tape player. When we were seated, the judge looked expectantly at me. I took the tape player from Mark and placed it on the edge of the judge's desk. Then I took a tape out of my breast pocket and placed it in the machine.

"Your Honor will perhaps be familiar with the name Armando Bergonzi?" I said.

"Yes, Mr. Barnett, I am. I understand that a federal grand jury issued several indictments of Mr. Bergonzi on Friday afternoon."

"Just so," I said. "Yesterday afternoon, the lead FBI agent on the case came to see me. They've had a legal wiretap on all of the Bergonzi telephone lines for many months. The conversation on this tape was obtained from one of those wiretaps, and the call was placed from the Bergonzi residence."

Mark and I were sitting in a pair of chairs at an angle to the judge's desk, facing Wetherbee and Shields in a similar pair of chairs across a low table. I watched Wetherbee's face carefully as I continued, "The tape speaks for itself, and with Your Honor's permission, I'd like to play it now."

"Go ahead, Mr. Barnett."

I turned the machine on. The first sounds from the speaker were the unmistakable sounds made by dialing on a touch-tone telephone. We heard the ring of a telephone at the other end of the line, and finally a man's voice answered.

"Hello." It was a voice familiar to millions of television viewers, that of the Rev. Isaiah M. Foible, who presided over a large Southern Baptist congregation in central Virginia and a vast television congregation over cable and broadcast television. I frequently thought of him as the most smugly self-righteous bigot in America. Others, less charitable, played on his name and referred him as the Rev. Infallible, or even the Rev. I'm Full of Bull.

"Isaiah, how are you? Craig Wetherbee here."

"What the hell are you doing calling me, boy? You know you're not supposed to call me direct unless it's an emergency."

"Calm down, will you? It's definitely an emergency."

"All right, then, you'd best tell me about it."

"The trial isn't going well at all. That rat fuck of a tax attorney and accountant was on the stand this morning, and he blew our case right out of the water."

"Did he?"

"You bet your sweet sanctified ass he did. It turns out that the little faggot is a multimillionaire. Compared to him, his late wife was practically a pauper. He did not, as we suspected, gain from his wife's death. So as it stands now, we're dead in the water."

"What do you want me to do about it?"

"You said before that you might be able to help in some way."

"So I did, so I did, and as it happens, I did make a few inquiries."

"Inquiries?"

"Yes, inquiries into potential witnesses among my followers down there, don't you know."

"Did you find one?"

"I might have done. I just might have done."

"Might have done won't cut it, Rev. That faggot is going to go free unless somebody pulls a rabbit out of the hat."

"Well, Sir, you just leave it to me, you just leave it to me. I think I can safely say that a reliable witness might just come forward. Might just, indeed."

"Make it soon."

"Oh, I will, I will. And then I expect you to nail that cocksucker. I've got a national campaign lined up to smear the so-called 'gay' community from head to toe with this one, but I can't do it unless you serve me up a french-fried sodomite."

"You find me a witness, and I'll do just that."

"Oh, I'll find you a witness. I'll find you a witness, no problem. The rubes that watch my program will do just about anything I tell them to, especially if I convince them that it's God's will."

"Even contribute to my campaign for governor?"

"Of course, my boy, of course. I can guarantee that after one mass mailing from me, you'll have more fifty- and one-hundred-dollar checks than you can fucking say grace over."

"Thank you, Rev."

"Don't thank me yet. You've got to nail that cocksucker first. You've got to nail him."

The conversation continued in that vein for a few minutes more before it ended, and when it did, there was a stunned silence in the room.

I said, "Your Honor, I won't even begin to speculate as to why the district attorney was a guest in the home of a reputed crime figure, let alone why he felt comfortable enough being there to make a long-distance call. That tape, however, places a huge cloud of doubt over the testimony we heard last Friday from Mrs. Treadwell."

The judge said, "What do you propose doing with this tape, Mr. Barnett?"

"With the court's permission, I would like to play it for Alice Treadwell. Perhaps it will prompt her to reveal just who put her up to telling her ridiculous story."

Wetherbee, who'd been strangely quiet throughout the playing of the tape, became almost incoherent in his objections. I almost felt sorry for him, but I said, "Mr. Wetherbee, the judge may or may not allow me to play that tape in open court. In the end, it won't matter, because it will be in the afternoon papers and on the six o'clock news this evening—you can count on that. In addition, the senior partner of my law firm is, as we speak, petitioning a federal judge for warrants to impound all of the records from your office and from the police department that pertain in any way to the d'Autremont case."

He jumped up at that and stormed out, but not without a parting shot. "You fucking faggot!" he yelled. "I'll get you for that, and your client too." His face was contorted with hatred and anger as he said the words.

I looked at the judge and said, "I think Mr. Wetherbee just recused himself, Your Honor."

"Indeed!" she said. "Mr. Shields, I expect you to take over."

"Yes, Your Honor," he replied, adding, "please understand that I knew nothing about Mr. Wetherbee's actions."

"I'll accept your word for that, Mr. Shields," she said.

"Your Honor," I said.

"Yes, Mr. Barnett?"

"The FBI has requested that if this tape is admitted into evidence, it be with the stipulation that none of their people will be called upon to testify. They fear having to answer questions that might accidentally bear on the Bergonzi case. Earlier today, Special Agent Tolar gave a sworn deposition in my office as to the provenance of the recording. It is our hope that his deposition will suffice."

"Yes, I can understand their problem and concur with the solution. Any objections, Mr. Shields?"

"None, Your Honor."

"Anything else, Mr. Barnett?"

"I'm afraid so, Your Honor."

"Continue."

"Last night, I also came into possession of clear evidence that the police have known all along the identity of a woman who is in all probability the real murderer and have been covering it up."

"Counselor, you must have had a very busy weekend," she said. "Can you share your information with us now?"

"Basically, I have copies of two earlier versions of Sergeant Kellerman's report, which indicate that another set of fingerprints was found at the scene of the crime, which fingerprints belong to one Ruby Lee Johnston, who has a record of sexual battery on women. This Ruby Lee Johnston is, no doubt, the mysterious Ruby that was identified by one of my witnesses. We've had investigators searching for her for months but without success."

"How do you propose handling this evidence?"

"After I've finished with Mrs. Treadwell, I'd like to recall Sergeant Kellerman. I believe that my new evidence will convince the sergeant to tell the court why he falsified his report."

"Anything else?" she said.

"No, Your Honor, I think that's quite enough, don't you?"

"Indeed it is," she said, "although you might try to look a little happier about things."

"Oh, I'm happy for my client. He's been put through a nightmare, especially this last week, purely to satisfy the egos of two demagogues. On the other hand, I've spent my working life believing in the essential fairness of the criminal justice system, and it pains me to be party to exposing such a serious flaw, which can only damage people's faith in the system."

The judge gave me an odd look and said, "I don't think you need to go about wearing a hair shirt, Mr. Barnett. The system will heal itself, survive, and be strengthened in the process."

"Thank you, Your Honor."

Mark and I returned to our places, and Tom Shields took his place at the prosecution's table. The judge returned to the bench, court resumed, and I recalled Mrs. Treadwell to the witness stand.

Without getting up from my position at the defense table, I said, "Mrs. Treadwell, you have positively identified the defendant in this case as the man you observed on West Paces Ferry Road the day of the murder."

"Yes, Sir, that is correct."

"For the record, I ask you one more time to point out the man you saw."

"It was him," she said, pointing to my left.

"Are you referring to the gentleman seated on my left?"

"Yes, Sir."

I turned to my left and said, "Would you stand up, Sir, so that Mrs. Treadwell can see you more clearly?" Turning back to the witness, I said, "One more time, Mrs. Treadwell, is this the man?"

"Yes, Sir, it is."

I got up, walked over to stand in front of her, and said, "I'm sorry to have to tell you, Mrs. Treadwell, that the man you just identified is not the defendant in this case. You have just identified one of the attorneys from my office. The defendant, Mr. d'Autremont, is currently sitting in the second row of spectators, some two rows behind the man you just identified."

When I said that, it was Philip's cue to return to his normal seat, and my associate, having served his purpose, returned to the office. The witness was disturbed at my trick and said, "Well, it looked like him."

"True, but it was not he. But we'll let that pass for the moment. Mrs. Treadwell, you testified that you were hurrying home to watch your favorite Sunday evening television program."

"Yes, Sir."

"What program might that be?"

"The Rev. Foible's Sunday evening broadcast. I never miss it."

"You are a devoted follower of Mr. Foible, are you?"

"Oh yes. He is such a good, saintly man," she said, her face assuming an expression of almost rapture.

"Have you ever met Mr. Foible?"

"No, I haven't."

"Have you ever spoken to him?"

"Oh, yes. He has telephoned a couple of times to tell me that he is praying for me."

"Has he, indeed!"

"Oh, yes, he is such a good man."

"When did these telephone calls take place?"

"Last week, or perhaps the week before, I really don't remember on which days. He also sent one of his associates around to my house to pray with me. Such a nice young man, he wouldn't even accept a contribution."

"Mrs. Treadwell, as a devoted follower of Mr. Foible, is it safe to say that you would honor any request he made of you?"

"Oh, yes."

"If Mr. Foible or one of his associates asked you to come into this courtroom and perjure yourself, would you do it for him?"

"I'm afraid I don't understand," she said somewhat nervously.

"Let me rephrase the question. Mrs. Treadwell, if Mr. Foible or one of his associates asked you to come to this courtroom and lie about the defendant, you would do it without hesitation, would you not?"

"Of course not," she said. "It's a sin to tell lies. It would be unthinkable for the Rev. Foible to suggest anything improper."

"Mrs. Treadwell, a very wise man once wrote that 'only an unthinking mind finds anything unthinkable.'"

She didn't respond, so I continued, "Mrs. Treadwell, I'm going to play a tape recording for you. You may recognize one of the voices on this tape." To the court, I said, "Let the record show that this tape recording is a portion of a recording obtained by the FBI in a legal wiretap. The defense enters the recording as an exhibit for the defense, along with a sworn deposition from the FBI agent responsible for turning it over to us, as stipulated earlier, in chambers." I handed the deposition to the bailiff and then placed the cassette in the tape player, which Mark had brought up and placed in front of the witness.

I turned the machine on and said, "Please listen carefully, Mrs. Treadwell. I think you will find this enlightening."

There was a faint buzz of whispering in the courtroom as the tape began, but when the identities of the two voices became clear, things got very quiet. In fact, during the time it took for the rest of the tape to play, you could have heard the proverbial pin drop. As soon as it became clear that the end of the tape had been reached, the buzz among the spectators changed to an uproar, and I turned around in time to see several members of the press heading for the door, presumably to telephone in what they hoped would be a scoop.

Mrs. Treadwell, on the other hand, was sobbing and fumbling in her purse. She produced a handkerchief and dabbed at her eyes before she blew her nose noisily.

When she'd regained her composure, I started my questioning again and said, "Now, Mrs. Treadwell, I think you recognized one of the voices on that tape."

"Yes, Sir," she said, this time with a tremble in her voice.

"For the record, the two men we just heard were the district attorney, Craig Wetherbee, and the Rev. Isaiah M. Foible. Mr. Wetherbee has absented himself from these proceedings for the time being, possibly even the duration. Now, Mrs. Treadwell, I ask you again. When Mr. Foible's associate came to pray with you, he also asked you to lie to this court, didn't he?"

"Yes, Sir. He somehow knew that I regularly go back and forth on West Paces Ferry Road. He told me that I should come forward and say that I had seen the man in his car. He told me that it would be all right to tell this story, as I would be doing the Lord's work. That the defendant in this case was a sodomite and that he was going to burn in hell anyway."

"He told you that?"

"Yes, Sir."

"Let us go back over your testimony now. It is true, is it not, that you drive back and forth along West Paces Ferry Road every Sunday."

"Yes, Sir."

"But you have never seen the defendant, Mr. d'Autremont, on that road."

"No, Sir."

"Not on Mother's Day or any other day, isn't that correct?"

"No, Sir, I mean, yes, Sir, you are correct."

"Thank you, Mrs. Treadwell," I said. "Oh, by the way, you are familiar with the Ten Commandments, are you not?"

"Yes, Sir."

"Including, I presume, the one pertaining to the subject of bearing false witness against your neighbors?"

"Yes, Sir."

"I just wanted to be sure. That will be all, Mrs. Treadwell."

Tom Shields had no questions for the witness.

As she was replacing her handkerchief in her purse in preparation for leaving the stand, Mrs. Treadwell looked at me and said, "What will happen to me now?"

"I honestly can't say. I expect you will be charged with perjury. Perhaps the prosecutor will go easy on you if you cooperate with the authorities, who will doubtless be charging Mr. Foible and his associate with suborning your perjury, but I really can't speak for them."

33

Philip

WHEN she had stepped down, Charles recalled Sergeant Kellerman, who appeared to be a trifle nervous. Charles had arranged to have Kellerman kept sequestered so that he wouldn't know what had taken place in court that morning.

Charles began by saying, "Sergeant Kellerman, I just have a couple of questions concerning your report, and you'll be free to go."

"Sure, ask away."

"When you read your report in court earlier, you stated that no fingerprints were found at the murder scene other than those of the deceased, the defendant, and the servants."

"That is correct."

"Are you absolutely certain?"

"I said, that is correct." Kellerman was getting annoyed and allowing it to show.

Charles walked over to the table and picked up a piece of paper. Then he turned back to the sergeant and said, "Then, Sergeant Kellerman, how do you explain the fact that this early draft of your report clearly states that another, unidentified set of fingerprints was found at the scene?"

"Where did you get that?" Kellerman asked angrily.

Charles continued, saying, "I'm the one asking the questions,

Sergeant, but to answer your question, it was shoved through my mail slot last night in a plain brown envelope, perhaps by the good fairy. Now, answer the question, please. This document, which is clearly a first draft and is dated one week earlier than the report originally submitted, indicates that another set of prints was found. How do you explain that?"

"It wasn't important."

"Not important! A stray set of fingerprints at a murder scene not important! Really, Sergeant, you amaze me."

"They couldn't be identified, and we didn't think it significant."

"Not significant, you say. I'll let that pass for the moment. Are you certain the prints weren't identified, Sergeant Kellerman?"

"Of course. If they were, that would be in the final report."

Charles returned to the defense table and picked up another piece of paper before continuing, "How very interesting. Then perhaps you can explain this later version of your report, dated two days before the one filed in evidence last week? I think you know what it says."

"Where did you get that?" Kellerman was repeating himself.

"As I said, some Good Samaritan passed it anonymously through my mail slot—the source is really not relevant. The report, however, makes for very interesting reading. So much so, in fact, that I would like for you to read the highlighted portion to the court."

Charles handed the document to Kellerman, who looked at it in silence until Charles prompted him, "The court is waiting, Sergeant Kellerman."

"It says that 'a set of prints found at the murder scene have now been positively identified as belonging to a woman named Ruby Lee Johnston', and that said Ruby Lee Johnston 'has a record of several arrests and one conviction for sexual battery on women'."

"Thank you, Sergeant Kellerman," Charles said, and he took the document from the sergeant's hands. "The defense enters both of these documents as exhibits for the defense." He handed the two pieces of paper to the bailiff.

Some slight noise in the courtroom must have caught Charles's attention, because he looked around before he continued. I turned to see what he was looking at and saw Richard standing at the barrier separating the spectators from the participants. Charles walked over to him and was handed a note, and he glanced at it. He looked in my direction and flashed a brief smile before he turned back to his witness.

"Now, Sergeant Kellerman, I want you to reflect carefully before you answer my next question. At this point, I suspect only your rank has been at stake. If you compound perjury upon perjury, you may well jeopardize not only your job, but your pension rights as well." He paused a moment to let that sink in. Then he continued, "Sergeant Kellerman, did the police make an attempt to locate Ruby Lee Johnston?"

"We looked for her for a while but couldn't locate her."

"Is that so? How hard did you look?"

"What kind of a question is that? We searched for her like we would for any other potential witness."

"If you were so interested in her whereabouts, why were all references to both her and her fingerprints omitted from the report that you produced in this court?"

"Mr. Wetherbee ordered me to change my report."

"Sergeant, I must remind you that you do not work for Mr. Wetherbee and are therefore not subject to his orders."

"Yeah, that's what I told him, so he went over my head, and the word came down through the ranks to cooperate with Wetherbee, or else."

"Sergeant, is it your final testimony on the matter that you A, did not locate Ruby Lee Johnston, and B, do not now know her whereabouts?"

"Yeah. I mean, yes, Sir."

"Sergeant, I wish, for your sake, that you hadn't said that," Charles said with a sad tone in his voice. "I was just handed a note which indicates that my investigators located Ruby Lee Johnston about an hour ago, and she has a very interesting tale to tell. Would it surprise you to learn that she claims that you and two other detectives have been keeping her in another city, in a so-called safe house, ever since you picked her up for questioning, which was a few days after the second version of your report was written, that is to say, almost seven months ago?"

Between Charles's last question and the time it took the judge to restore order in the courtroom—an uproar having once again broken out among the spectators after Charles's revelations—Kellerman began to assume the look of a man who clearly wished himself elsewhere. He didn't answer the question and said only, "I'm not saying anything else until I talk to a lawyer."

"Very wise of you, Sergeant. Too bad you didn't possess such wisdom earlier."

Charles came back to the table and sat down before he said, "Your Honor, the defense rests."

The judge looked at Mr. Shields and said, "Does the prosecution have anything else?"

"No, Your Honor."

She called both sides up to the bench, where there was a whispered conference, after which Charles and Mark came and sat down and Mr. Shields returned to his seat. The judge banged her gavel one time to get everyone's attention; then she looked at the jury and said, "Ladies and gentlemen of the jury, normally at this time, you would hear closing arguments first by the prosecution and then by the defense. This has not, however, been a normal case. In point of fact, it is abundantly clear that this case should never have come to trial. I could, at this point, dismiss the entire proceedings, but the defense would like a verdict. Therefore, the jury will retire immediately to deliberate, but be advised that I am directing you to find the defendant not guilty."

We sat in silence as the jury left the room. I whispered to Charles, "What now?"

"They'll be back in a jiff. Just wait and see."

He was right. In less than ten minutes, the jury was back and returned the directed verdict of not guilty. After the judge restored the courtroom to order, she had a few things to say.

She thanked the jury for their time and patience and apologized for their time having been wasted in a proceeding that should never have taken place. She also apologized to me on behalf of the criminal justice system. Then she said the magic words: "Case dismissed."

I walked out of the courthouse "free" for the first time in months, free of the cloud that had hung over me like an invisible pall. We emerged onto the courthouse steps, where at least a couple of dozen reporters and cameramen were waiting for us. Charles was on my right, Mark on my left, and questions were being shouted at us so rapidly that it was impossible to follow them. Finally, Charles made a gesture for silence.

When they were quiet, he said, "I know that you folks have hundreds of questions. Right now, all I can say, speaking for my client, my associate, and myself, is that we are pleased with this morning's outcome. We're also tired and hungry. If you will be in the conference room of my law firm at one thirty, we'll have a little press conference, where we will make a prepared statement and then entertain questions for thirty or forty minutes. This should give all of you ample time to meet your respective deadlines."

They grumbled a bit but gave way, and we were driven away by Richard, who'd been waiting for us in what I later learned was Andrew's Lincoln Town Car.

Lunch was a catered affair at the conference table in Charles's office, where we were joined by Andrew. Various others of the law firm came in and out over the course of the thirty minutes it took us to eat.

Charles and Andrew worked briefly over the prepared statement that Charles would read at the press conference, and we discussed what we should and should not say in response to the inevitable questions. Before we walked to the main conference room, Rosemary handed Charles a corrected draft of his statement. He quickly scanned it and told her to make enough copies so that any reporter who wanted one after the conference could have it; then he looked at me and said, "Ready to face the horde?"

"I guess" was all I could say in reply.

The conference room was a very large room dominated by a table that could have seated twenty in comfort. When Charles, Andrew, and I came in through a side entrance, the table was vainly trying to accommodate twice that number. There were three chairs at the end of the table reserved for us. We took our seats, and Charles addressed the group.

"Thank you for coming. I do apologize for the cramped quarters, but we're not accustomed to handling crowds in here. You all recognize Mr. d'Autremont on my left. The distinguished-looking gentleman on my right is Andrew Chandler, senior partner and head litigator of this firm. Before we answer specific questions, I have a statement to read, and Mr. Chandler has something to say. Afterward, my secretary will provide each of you with a copy of my statement, should you wish it."

He paused, reached for a glass and took a sip of water, then started to read:

"What you have witnessed over the past two weeks, and what my client has been living over these many months, is an example of the worst that our criminal justice system has to offer. An example of a demagogue who allowed his private phobias and personal ambitions to rule his actions with a total disregard for the rights of others. Fortunately for the citizens of this great country, that is the antithesis of what our justice system is all about. It may even constitute the proverbial exception that proves the rule. This sort of thing must not be allowed to happen again, or if it seems to be about to happen, it must be stopped before it can flourish.

"Fortunately, the defendant in this instance possessed the resources to A, obtain adequate legal counsel, and B, conduct his own private investigation. I don't know what the total cost of his defense will be, but the bills from the one local and two national investigative organizations involved have already exceeded $250,000. The total cost of this trial for the defendant may well exceed a million dollars. All of which leaves one wondering what would have happened had the defendant been of modest means or, worse, indigent.

"You may have heard testimony during the trial that the late Mrs. d'Autremont left the bulk of her estate to charity. She did not, however, specify what charity or charities she wished to benefit from her bequest. Mr. d'Autremont, as executor of his late wife's estate, is empowered by her will to name the charity or charities to which the estate will ultimately be distributed. In honor of that request, he has decided to establish a foundation to be formally known as The Integrity Foundation. It will be the recipient of that portion of his late wife's estate which was not specifically bequeathed to her relatives, which is to say, the bulk of the estate. In addition, he will be donating an even $1 million of his own funds to the foundation.

"The Integrity Foundation will have one primary function, and that will be to assist anyone whose individual rights are being trampled upon because of his or her sexual orientation. It will be looking into several of the more virulently homophobic organizations in our society, and most particularly will be investigating closely the affairs of some of the television evangelists. The foundation will make an effort to ensure that funds collected by these organizations are both accounted for and used for charitable purposes. Any organization which refuses to cooperate with such investigations will find its tax-exempt status challenged in the appropriate state and federal jurisdictions. I should add, parenthetically, that funds spent by these organizations to spread their messages of hate and intolerance will not be deemed to have been spent for charitable purposes.

"The foundation will perhaps be involved in one or two other activities, all falling within the general scope of preserving the Bill of Rights."

Charles took another sip of water. "Now, I believe the senior partner of this firm has a couple of things to say, although he hasn't discussed his thoughts with me."

Andrew stood up and smiled first at the group, then at Charles, who had resumed his seat. "Thank you, Charles. Indeed, you do not know what I am going to say, but I think you will find it interesting."

He directed his attention to the reporters gathered around the room. "I won't waste your time talking about the recent travesty which has brought us all together in this room, as Charles has done that most adequately. What I have for you is more in the nature of a press release, copies of which will be available from my secretary after we adjourn. As some of you may know, this firm was founded many years ago by my grandfather, and I have been the senior partner since my late father retired some forty years ago. I have also been the head litigator of the firm since that time. I had expected that my son might one day continue in my place, but his life was cut tragically short some years ago in Southeast Asia.

"Fortunately for me, another young man came along to take his place. For some time now, Charles Barnett has been performing more and more of the duties of senior partner, and has been chief litigator in all but name for most of the last seven years. Charles has long since earned the right to have the titles bestowed him that more nearly describe his duties, and it occurs to me that the eve of his triumph in this perplexing case is an appropriate time for that to happen. With that in mind, I am announcing my retirement, effective next month, by which time I expect to have turned over all of my duties to Charles Barnett. Charles is one of the most able young lawyers with whom I have ever had the pleasure to be associated, and I cannot imagine the firm's affairs being in more capable hands."

Andrew sat down. I got the impression that he had planned to say more, but he seemed to be more than a bit choked up.

Charles looked stunned, almost as though he had been hit over the head with a baseball bat. He recovered, stood, and said, "Andrew, I don't know what to say except, thank you."

"That will do nicely, my boy. You have more than earned it."

Charles focused on the press. "Ladies and gentlemen, there is one thing that was omitted from my prepared statement. I neglected to mention that Mr. d'Autremont will be bringing a civil suit against Mr. Wetherbee, individually, as well as the Fulton County District Attorney's Office, and the police authorities collectively for false arrest. He will be seeking damages for the expenses of this trial and punitive damages, as well. He will also be bringing a similar suit against the Rev. Mr. Foible and his organization. Now, are there any questions?"

The first question focused on Charles's last statement. "If your client wins those cases, he will be a very rich man, won't he?"

Charles said, "Mr. d'Autremont is already a very rich man. After he recovers the actual costs of this trial, any other proceeds of such suits will be donated to The Integrity Foundation."

Another reporter asked, "Mr. Barnett, how does it feel to be responsible for the downfall and disgrace of a famous television evangelist and a prominent local official at the same time?"

"They are responsible for their own fates. In the case of Mr. Foible, I can only say that I have no sympathy for people like him, who prey upon the weakness of others. As for Mr. Wetherbee, I'll tell you the same thing I told the judge this morning in chambers. I'm happy for my client, but as one who has always had faith in the system, I regret in some ways being part of a process that brings it into disrepute."

"What did Her Honor say to that?"

"That the system would heal itself and be strengthened in the process, or words to that effect."

Someone from a television station wanted to know, "What are your plans for the immediate future?"

"Well, as I have nearly a month of unused vacation time, I will probably use up a week or two of it immediately." He looked at Andrew before continuing, "It seems that I won't have much time for vacations after the first of next month."

The questions continued to fly at Charles, and he answered them all in turn carefully and thoughtfully. Finally, the reporters turned to me, and I tried to be as graceful in my responses as Charles had been. Eventually, one of them asked what my immediate plans were.

"Oh, I expect a long vacation is in order. After that, I can't say."

I probably should have kept my mouth shut, because when I mentioned an immediate vacation, an aging sob sister made an obvious connection between what I'd said and what Charles had said earlier, and asked point-blank, "Mr. d'Autremont, are you and Mr. Barnett an item?"

I looked at Charles and said, "I don't know. Counselor, are we?"

He smiled and sidestepped by saying, "Sorry, I never talk about the personal affairs of my clients." He changed the subject adroitly, adding, "There are a number of people whose collective efforts have made this case so successful, not least of these are my associates and my secretary. Also, a tremendous amount of credit goes to the investigation team headed by Richard Greene of Greene & Associates. And now, if you folks will excuse us, it has been a very long morning."

Charles and I, preceded by Andrew, slipped out via the side door through which we'd entered the room. Charles followed Andrew to the latter's office, and I tagged along. When we were inside and the door had closed, Charles said, "Andrew, are you sure you want to step down?"

"Yes, my boy, I am. Miss Emily has been after me to do so for nearly ten years because she wants to do some traveling while the two of us are still able to enjoy it. I'd always resisted even the thought of retirement because there was never anyone around whom I deemed capable of taking over. Then you came along, and I recognized something in you that told me to start grooming you early on for this job."

"There are six other partners in this firm. What about them?"

"You know very well that none of them are capable of handling the job, and in fact, at least three of them want no part of being senior partner. I called a meeting this morning, and the vote was unanimous."

"Jesus, Andrew, it won't be the same around here without you."

"It had to happen sooner or later, my boy. Now, enough about me. What are you going to do?"

"Well, as I told the press, I was thinking of taking a vacation. You know that before all this began, I'd penciled in some time in late spring. There isn't anything on my plate at the moment that Mark and the others can't handle."

"Where will you go, and when?"

"I need to discuss the where with Philip. As to the when, probably by Wednesday or Thursday at the latest. It'll take me most of tomorrow to clean up some odds and ends."

"Well, then, you two run along and get this business out of your minds. I'll look after things around here."

"Great. Would you and Emily care to join us for a little victory celebration tonight? I plan to ask Gran as well."

"We'd be pleased to join you."

"Wonderful. Come by the house about seven for drinks. We can all go out to eat from there. Now, I need to go talk to my client for a minute."

We left Andrew in his office and went back into Charles's office, where he closed the door behind us and stood with his back against it. "Alone at last," he said.

"Not as alone as I'd like for us to be right now," I said as I put my arms around him. "You put on an impressive performance in court this morning. Thank you for saving me from God only knows what sort of fate."

"I only did it because I'm selfish. I want you around for a good long while yet. Now, about our vacation—any ideas?"

"Not really, but I bet you already do."

"Sort of. Ever been to San Francisco?"

"Yes."

"So have I. But have you ever been there with somebody special?"

"No."

"For some reason, neither have I. What I'd like to do is spend at least ten days out there. We can ride the cable cars, sit at that wonderful bar in Ghirardelli Square and watch the bay, and most importantly, we can walk hand in hand down Castro Street in broad daylight."

"Is that all?"

"Well, it's a start. We could visit the Napa Valley and tour some wineries, or whatever else comes to mind. What do you say?"

"I say let's call a travel agent and set it in motion."

"I've got a better idea. Let's have Rosemary call the travel agent and set it up. That way you and I can go home and be truly alone for a while."

"Deal," I said, and we sealed it in the customary manner.

He sat down at his desk and picked up the telephone to summon Rosemary, who came in, pad in hand, and took a seat.

"Call the travel agent we use and make some reservations for two. First-class tickets to San Francisco and back. Book a room for two at the Francis Drake and reserve a car for us at the airport. Departure should be early Wednesday, return flight two weeks later. Call me at home as soon as you have confirmation. And Rosie?"

"Yes, Sir?"

"Thanks for everything you've done during this trial."

"Just doing my job, boss," she said, but she looked pleased.

"Your job, as you put it, is going to get a little harder in the near future, as you may have guessed from Andrew's announcement."

"Oh, yes, I heard it on the grapevine before the press conference. By the way, congratulations."

"Thanks, and we'll discuss appropriate adjustments to your salary when I get back from this trip. Is Richard lurking about the premises somewhere?"

"I believe he's in Mark's office."

"When you get back to your desk, find him, and ask him to stop by for a minute before we leave."

"Yes, Sir. Anything else?"

"Not at the moment."

Before she could leave, I spoke up, saying, "There is one thing?"

"Yes, Sir?"

"First, make a record of this American Express number," I said, and I read her the number and expiration information from my card. "Then use it for one of the plane tickets. It'll make things less complicated to settle up later. You might as well make a permanent record of it for any future traveling that Charles and I may do."

"I'll take care of it," she said.

Rosemary went back to her desk, and Charles picked up the telephone and punched a few numbers. There was a pause, followed by, "Hi, Gran. ... Yes, it's all over, and you can see it on the early news at five o'clock. ... Listen, we're having drinks at my place to celebrate, then we're going to dinner. Probably Sean & Gabe's. Andrew and Emily are coming, and I'd like to send Richard around to pick you up about seven, okay? ... Great, we will see you then."

He'd just hung up the telephone when there was a knock at the door, following which Richard came in and said, "What's up, doc?"

"Not much. I want to hear all about the locating of Ruby, but not now. Can you pick up Gran at seven and bring her to the house?"

"Sure."

"Good. Andrew and Emily are coming over, then we can all go out to have a little victory dinner. You can be Gran's date, if you like. When you get back to Mark's office, ask him if he'd like to join us this evening. He can bring his current lady friend, if he wishes."

"I'll be there, and I'll tell Mark. Got to run now, boyo. Loose ends to tie up and all that."

Richard hurried out, and Charles gathered his briefcase in preparation for departure. Instead of departing, however, he walked over to the door and very carefully and quietly locked it. He then came back and stood in front of me. "We have some unfinished business that's been more or less on hold for these past months."

"What do you mean?"

"I'm referring to the bargain we made the night we met. You agreed to be in my bed until your legal problems were over or we got tired of each other, whichever took the longest."

"I remember."

"Well," he said, taking both of my hands in his, "your legal problems are over, but I'm certainly not tired of you. Are you tired of me?"

"Hardly."

"Well, then, I need to tell you something and ask you something."

"Yes?"

"I'll start by saying that I love you and have done so from that first evening, and I know that it's mutual, because you've said so."

I started to speak, but he put his finger to my lips and got down on his knees.

"Let me finish. I'm head over heels in love with you, and I would like to spend the rest of my life with you, if you'll have me. I'm asking you on bended knees, just like a character in one of your books."

I pulled him back to his feet and said, "I love you too, babe, and I can't imagine spending my life with anyone else. You're stuck with me, it would seem, forever."

He grabbed me, kissed me deeply, and said, "Good, let's go home and celebrate."

I followed him out to Rosemary's desk, where he stopped and instructed her to deposit my bail money—which Mark would shortly be retrieving—in the firm's trust account, pending my instructions. A few minutes later, we were on the way home.

34

Philip

ARRIVING back at the townhouse, we stopped in the kitchen long enough for Charles to quickly survey the liquor inventory and express satisfaction that everyone's wishes could be accommodated this evening. He also called Sean & Gabe's and reserved a table for eight o'clock. He also made one other call and then went into the library and set the recorders to record both the five and the six o'clock news. Having taken care of mundane matters, we went upstairs and celebrated our victory in a time-honored manner, after which we slept for an hour or so.

We woke up from our nap with just enough time for a run before we had to get ready for the arrival of our guests. Our return from the park coincided with Richard's arrival home to clean up before he picked up his "date" for the evening. We decided to let Richard have dibs on the hot water and spent some time carrying bottles, mixes, and ice buckets down to the living room, where there was a small sideboard that served as a bar.

There was nothing else for us to do but go upstairs, clean up, and dress. The house was already clean, as the Merry Pop-Ins had long since been given a key and now came every Monday to clean the house thoroughly from top to bottom. We were dressed and relaxing in the library by the time Richard left to pick up Gran.

Shortly before seven, the doorbell rang for the first time, and we went down to greet our guests. Andrew and his wife, whom I hadn't met, were at the door. Miss Emily, as he called her, was a younger version of Gran, though she lacked anything approaching the presence that Gran brought with her into any room she entered. Miss Emily was Aunt Pittypat with brains and common sense, where Gran was Melanie infused with Scarlett's steel and determination. The introductions had been made and we were all settled down with drinks when Richard arrived with his "date" for the evening.

As soon as the six of us were settled down again, talk turned inevitably to the trial. We were interrupted by the telephone, which turned out to be Mark calling to say that he was running late, so Charles told him to meet us at the restaurant.

Gran and the Chandlers had seen the evening news broadcasts, and they all expressed surprise on learning that we hadn't done so.

Charles said, "We went for a run in the park at about that time, but I recorded channel five from five 'til seven, so we can watch it later. You know how I like to use my toys."

We spent a pleasant twenty minutes in conversation before Andrew looked at the clock and suggested that we might need two cars for the trip to the restaurant. This prompted a chuckle from Charles, who said, "I had a brain wave earlier, and we'll all go to the restaurant in the same vehicle. It should be arriving any minute now."

Almost on cue, the doorbell rang. I went to answer it and found a liveried chauffeur at the door, and I could see a Lincoln stretch limousine in the driveway, its motor running. Returning to the living room, I announced that the chauffeur was waiting. We let the three old folks ride in the comfortable rear seat, and Charles and I sat on the seat facing them, while Richard rode up front with the driver.

When we arrived at Sean & Gabe's, Mark was waiting for us in the bar, sans girlfriend. She hadn't been feeling well, it seemed, and had finally persuaded him to come along without her.

The two hours we spent over dinner were full of lively, spirited, and intelligent conversation. The Chandlers possessed Mrs. Barnett's ability to talk at length on almost any subject, all three of them evidently being well-read and very much informed concerning what was happening in the world.

We also had a surprise encounter with Lydia, who was seated in one of the booths. If her gentleman companion was typical of the men she dated, I understood why Charles had quickly pegged the hapless Harry as not having been her type—even without the vibes his antennae had registered. Lydia had spotted us as we were being shown to our table, and came over and kibitzed for a while. She knew everyone present, including Mrs. Chandler, but politely declined Charles's invitation that she and her escort join us. She, too, had seen the news broadcasts, and she congratulated Charles on his victory before she returned to her companion.

The occasion ended, as all such occasions must, and we returned to the limo. Charles directed the driver to Gran's house, and after we pulled up in her driveway, he walked her to the door and saw her safely inside.

Back at the townhouse, Andrew and his wife declined our offer of a nightcap and were quickly on their way home to Decatur. Charles settled with the driver, and we went in and cleaned up the living room before we went upstairs to bed.

When we were snuggled together in bed, he looked at me.

"Now, Sir," he said, "I think it's time you told me where you were and what you were doing the weekend of the murder."

"Is it important?"

"Not particularly, but I admit to being consumed with curiosity."

"Well, it's really not very complicated. I spent the weekend in a suite at the Desoto Hilton in Savannah."

"And?"

"I was with a married man. Not only is he married, but he's about three years short of his thirtieth birthday."

"And?"

"On that date, he'll gain control of the principal of a trust fund created by his grandfather's will. We're talking millions and millions of dollars. His family is very conservative, very strict, and very religious. Any hint of scandal at this time would bring a flock of greedy relatives out of the woodwork to challenge his inheritance—it seems that there are some strings attached to it concerning character and morals, etcetera."

"And you were willing to risk your freedom and your life for that?"

"I thought it was the right thing to do. Think of it as a calculated risk—at best, I would get acquitted. At worst, I would be convicted, in which case the appeals could take years. By that time, he would have control of his trust fund and could come forward with an alibi."

"And what if he died in the interim?"

"There's a notarized deposition from him in my safe deposit box. In addition, there is also a notarized deposition in Andrew's possession. Also, it wouldn't be difficult to obtain statements from various hotel staff and room service personnel."

"You seem to have thought of everything."

"Not at all, Andrew's the one who put it all together. That was the course he laid out at the meeting the week before you and I met."

"I don't know what to say."

"Then don't say anything," I said, making sure that he couldn't.

Tuesday began like all of our weekdays, with the exception that a great weight had been lifted. The day, however, began with a surprise. Charles dressed for work, but instead of leaving right away, he asked me to come get in the car with him.

"Why?" I asked.

"Just wait," he said. "You'll understand in a few minutes." He drove for several minutes without speaking and finally turned into the entrance of Westview Cemetery, a venerable old cemetery that had served Atlanta since shortly after the Civil War. Driving through what was obviously a more recent portion of the cemetery, he finally pulled up and slowed the car in what appeared to be one of the oldest sections, if the dates on the monuments were any indication. He pulled up to a plot surrounded by an iron fence, and I noted that the plot contained numerous "Barnett" headstones, many dating back to the late nineteenth century. He stopped the car, got out, and opened my door for me. Taking me by the hand, he led me to one corner of the plot.

It was, of course, Robert's grave, which was marked by a small marble stone of much more recent vintage than the other headstones in the plot. Charles put his arm around me, and we both looked at the marker. After a lengthy silence, he said, "Robert, I want you to meet Philip. You know that some part of me will always love you, but now I love Philip also, in exactly the way that I loved you, and he brings me the same joy that you did." He stood with his head bowed for a few minutes, then led me back to the car.

"That was very sweet," I said. "Thank you."

"It was time. A year ago I couldn't have come out here for any reason, but now I can face anything."

He dropped me off at the townhouse and went on to work to spend the day clearing the decks for our trip. Our reservations had been confirmed, and we were scheduled to leave on an eight o'clock flight Wednesday morning.

I spent the morning at my computer and the afternoon mostly on the phone to Boston, speaking first to the architect and then the contractor, both of whom promised to have preliminary plans and proposals waiting for us when we returned from our trip. By four thirty, however, I was in the kitchen dressed in my customary apron-only costume, laying the groundwork for our dinner. I hadn't turned the stereo on and wasn't expecting Charles before five thirty or later, so I was taken off guard when I heard the stairway door open and footsteps in the kitchen.

I was even more startled when I heard Richard's voice saying, "So this is what keeps Charley hurrying home every day. Very nice, very nice, indeed."

Then another voice answered, "Nice, yes, but it's not covered with all that lovely fur, like yours."

I turned to face Richard and Bruce and said, "Look all you like, but touching is off-limits."

They visited for a while and politely declined my offer to expand dinner to include the two of them, saying that they had plans to go out later. Then they excused themselves, presumably to go up to Richard's room.

About thirty minutes later, I heard the door open again. I turned to catch Charles's attention before he could slip upstairs. "Before you start running around bare-assed, be advised that Richard has a guest upstairs."

"I saw the car but thought he was alone."

"No, he's up in his room, entertaining or being entertained by Bruce."

"Speaking of entertaining, why don't you come up and entertain or be entertained by me?"

"I'll be at a stopping place in about five minutes."

"I'll be waiting," he said. Then he disappeared up the stairs.

A few minutes later, when I went up to the bedroom, he was in bed waiting for me.

Later that evening, after dinner had been consumed and the remains cleared away, we took care of packing for the trip and then loafed for an hour or so before bedtime.

Charles had brought home a number of out-of-town newspapers, and we spent some time comparing their coverage of the trial with that of the Atlanta papers. The front pages of all of them were covered with news of the trial, generally under headlines such as (in the Atlanta papers) "Local Prosecutor All Washed Up." The out-of-town papers focused more on the Rev. Foible, with captions such as "Another TV Evangelist Bites the Dust." Somewhat less attention had been focused on the press conference, most of the papers having made some mention of the proposed foundation without going into particulars.

When I'd finished perusing the various newspaper articles, I said, "I think we picked a perfect time to ride off into the sunset together."

"Yeah. Maybe by the time we come back, the furor will have died down a bit."

"You think?"

"I can hope."

"Right now, I hope you'll show me how much you love me."

"I thought you'd never ask."

"Do I have to ask?"

"Are you going to talk all evening or kiss me?"

Coming Soon

Tribulation

Appearances: Book 2—Sequel to Trial

Two weeks after Philip d'Autremont is acquitted of his wife's murder, it's time for him and his partner and lawyer, Charles Barnett, to start building their life together. But it turns out that not everyone in Atlanta is as ready to leave the trial in the past as Charles and Philip, and a surprise attack leaves Charles in the hospital and Philip's arm in a sling.

With thoughts of their own mortality fresh in their minds, Charles and Philip make a decision that will change their lives forever. Future plans and home renovations take their minds off the attacks, but the danger isn't over yet: the people behind the attacks are still at large, and they weren't acting alone.

Triumph

Appearances: Book 3—Sequel to Tribulation

Charles Barnett and Philip d'Autremont have settled down to raise their children, but their domesticity is disrupted when Philip's nephew Steve is delivered to their doorstep early one morning after being beaten senseless by his homophobic father.

So the family grows, but of course, that's the easy part. A rabidly fundamentalist sheriff and a gay-bashing incident leave Steve and his new boyfriend in legal hot water and at the mercy of the deputies' harrassment, and Charles must once again take up the fight for justice for his loved ones.

http://www.dreamspinnerpress.com

Etienne lives in central Florida, very near the hamlet in which he grew up. He always wanted to write but didn't find his muse until a few years ago, when he started posting stories online. These days he spends most of his time battling with her, as she is a capricious bitch who, when she isn't hiding from him, often rides him mercilessly, digging her spurs into his sides and forcing the flow of words from a trickle to a flood.

Visit Etienne at http://www.etiennestories.blogspot.com. You can contact him at Etienne.Reynard@comcast.net.

The Avondale Stories

http://www.dreamspinnerpress.com

More Avondale Stories

http://www.dreamspinnerpress.com

Also by Etienne

 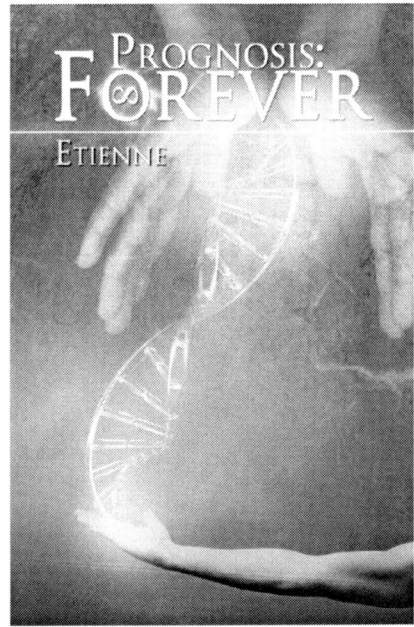

http://www.dreamspinnerpress.com

CPSIA information can be obtained at www.ICGtesting.com
Printed in the USA
BVOW080853071212

307476BV00007BA/203/P